The Desires of the Heart

Other books by Kathy Hawkins

The Heart of a Stranger
The Heart of a Lion

The Desires of the Heart

Kathy Hawkins

kregel
PUBLICATIONS

Grand Rapids, MI 49501

The Desires of the Heart

Published by Kregel Publications, a division of Kregel, Inc., P. O. Box 2607, Grand Rapids, MI 49501. Kregel Publications provides trusted, biblical publications for Christian growth and service. Your comments and suggestions are valued.

For more information about Kregel Publications, visit our web site at http://www.kregel.com.

Cover Illustration: Ron Mazellan
Cover Design: Alan G. Hartman
Book Design: Nicholas G. Richardson

Library of Congress Cataloging-in-Publication Data
Hawkins, Kathy.
The desires of the heart / by Kathy Hawkins.
p. cm.
1. Bible. O.T. Samuel—History of Biblical events—Fiction. I. Title.
PS3558.A823165D47 1998 813'.54—dc21 98-38003
CIP

ISBN 0-8254-2871-8

Printed in the United States of America

1 2 3 / 04 03 02 01 00 99 98

To Don Hawkins,
my greatest encourager
and my soul support
for the last three decades

My deepest thanks to the following people, who helped make this book possible: Betty Norton, who went through the manuscript many times, eliminating errors; Allen Bean, for research on chronology and the priesthood; Kris Beckenbach, for encouragement and input; and Diana Gordon and Brent Hawkins, for computer help. I also appreciate the assistance of Rachel Derowitsch, Barbara Williams, and the editorial staff at Kregel.

Historical Notes

Writing a book about people and events from 3,000 years ago presents many challenges. One of these is deciding what kind of language to use. The ancient Hebrews certainly did not speak English, nor even modern Hebrew, but spoke an ancient tongue even Hebrew scholars do not completely understand.

The ancient Hebrews were essentially just like us, with the same spiritual needs, foibles and sins, hopes and aspirations that we have. The passage of so many years, however, sometimes becomes a barrier between us and the people of Bible times.

How, then, should we portray the way they spoke? In order to breach that barrier of time, *The Desires of the Heart* is written in the contemporary vernacular.

King David was a man extraordinarily blessed and gifted of God as a musician, warrior, statesman, and prophet. He also sank to the most depraved depths of sin when he committed adultery with the wife of one of his most loyal warriors and then had the man murdered to cover up the truth. The ripple effect of this sin, not only in David's and Bathsheba's lives but also in the lives of many others, is examined in *The Desires of the Heart.*

Many commentators place equal responsibility for the affair on Bathsheba and David, or even more responsibility on her. However, David was nearing the age of fifty when the affair occurred, while Bathsheba may have been as young as twenty. With the wisdom that comes with age, David surely knew better than to succumb to the temptation.

The strongest argument that David did the seducing, if not outright taking, comes from the testimony of Scripture. God gave the prophet Nathan a parable with which to confront David. In the parable, David is a rich man with many sheep (i.e., wives), while Uriah is a poor man (by comparison) with only one very young female sheep (i.e., Bathsheba).

One only has to read Proverbs to know that wanton seductresses are not characterized in Scripture as helpless little lambs. If David had been ensnared by such a female, surely God would have chosen a different metaphor for Nathan to use in his confrontation.

The fact that Bathsheba took a bath in the open courtyard of her house has led some to assume that she purposely enticed David. But it was not an uncommon practice in those days for people to bathe in their courtyards, and the text does not indicate that Bathsheba was aware she was being watched. Add to that the fact that David sent for her in his capacity as king—a summons she could hardly refuse—and the evidence is convincing that David was the instigator of the affair.

David's army was led by a group known as the *Gibborim,* or "mighty ones." They were also known as "The Thirty," because their number was kept roughly at thirty as members fell in battle or retired and were replaced. You will find them listed in 2 Samuel 23 and 1 Chronicles 11. Included on the list are Jonathan, the son of Shageh, Ahiam, and Benaiah.

In its account of the repairs made to the city of Jerusalem, Jeremiah 3:16 refers to a place called the "House of the Mighty" *(Bet Gibborim).* It is the only reference in Scripture to this place, which evidently was part of the city in the time of David. I have assumed that this was special housing, probably located very near the palace, for David's "mighty men of valor."

In his book *The Antiquities of the Jews,* the historian Josephus records that Uriah served Joab as his armor bearer *(Ant. 7:7).* Though the Bible does not confirm this, we do find in 2 Samuel 18:15 that the general had ten armor bearers, or more precisely, bodyguards.

Joab had made many enemies and thus needed this cadre of men around him. These would have been men who had proved themselves fearless in battle and unstintingly loyal to Joab. If Josephus is correct, Joab betrayed a loyal friend and servant, Uriah, when he unhesitatingly obeyed David's order to set Uriah up to be murdered.

Second Samuel 18:15 does not give us the names of the ten armor bearers. The author has chosen to call one of them "Talmon" in this book. It isn't too much of a stretch to assume that one or more of these young men would have had such a nature as the fictional Talmon, especially in light of their actions as recorded in that verse.

The words *Ahmi* and *Ahbi* are phonetically transliterated terms for "Mama" and "Papa" in Hebrew. *Keziah* means "cassia, a fragrant flower." *Talmon* means "violent oppressor." A *Rab* was a chief, or great leader or teacher.

The battle scenes in the Heart of Zion series are brutal and graphic because that was the nature of warfare in Old Testament times. Most of the descriptions of the battle in *The Desires of the Heart* are taken from archaeological discoveries such as bas-relief carvings. Some of the practices of warfare have been omitted out of consideration for the sensibilities of the reader.

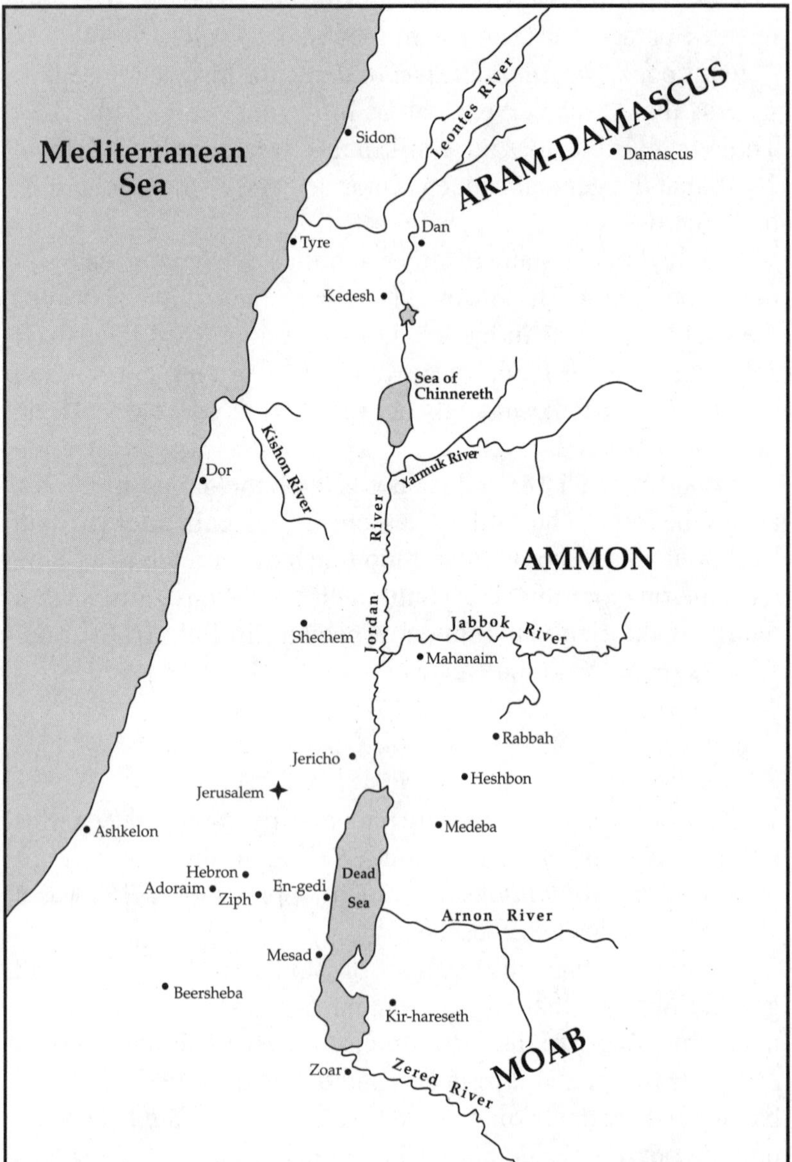
Mediterranean Sea
Sidon
Leontes River
ARAM-DAMASCUS
Damascus
Tyre
Dan
Kedesh
Sea of Chinnereth
Kishon River
Yarmuk River
Dor
Jordan River
AMMON
Shechem
Jabbok River
Mahanaim
Rabbah
Jericho
Heshbon
Jerusalem
Ashkelon
Medeba
Hebron
Adoraim
Ziph
En-gedi
Dead Sea
Arnon River
Mesad
Beersheba
Kir-hareseth
MOAB
Zoar
Zered River

Characters

Fictional

Adah (AY duh), Issac's sister
Ailea (eye LEE uh), an Aramean; wife of Jonathan
Benjamin, army veteran; friend of Isaac and his father
Darkon (DAHR kahn), servant of Isaac
Issac, aide-de-camp to Jonathan, one of the *Gibborim*
Judith, wife of Ahiam; Isaac's mother
Keziah (kih ZIGH uh), only child of Aaron, the priest
Milcah (MIL kuh), Keziah's aunt
Rachel, friend and servant of Isaac's family
Talmon (TAL mahn), one of Joab's armor bearers

Historical

Absalom (AB suh luhm), David's son by Maacah, princess of Geshur (2 Samuel 3:3; 13–19)
Ahiam (uh HIGH am), Isaac's father; one of the *Gibborim* (2 Samuel 23:32–33; 1 Chronicles 11:34)
Ahithophel (uh HITH oh fel), Bathsheba's grandfather; counselor of David (2 Samuel 15–17)
Bathsheba (bath SHEE buh), Uriah's wife; later, David's (2 Samuel 11:3; 12:24; 1 Kings 1:2–2:19)

Benaiah (bee NIGH uh), one of the *Gibborim* (2 Samuel 23:30; 1 Chronicles 11:31)

David, king of Israel (1 Samuel 16–1 Kings 1)

Joab (JOH ab), David's nephew and general of Israel's army (2 Samuel 2:13–1 Kings 2)

Jonathan, son of Shageh; one of David's *Gibborim* (2 Samuel 23:32; 1 Chronicles 11:34)

Maacah (MAY uh kuh), one of King David's wives (2 Samuel 3:3; 1 Chronicles 3:2)

Shageh (SHAY geh), the wise Rab of Ziph; father of Jonathan (1 Chronicles 11:34)

Uriah the Hittite (yoo RIGH uh), one of the *Gibborim;* husband of Bathsheba (2 Samuel 11:1–27; 23:39)

Pronunciations are from the book *Pronouncing Bible Names* by W. Murray Serverance, Broadman and Holman Publishers, © 1994.

“Delight yourself also in the LORD,
And He shall give you the desires of your heart.”
—Psalm 37:4

Prologue

The streets of Jerusalem were thronged with celebrants making their annual pilgrimage for the Feast of Passover. The dun-colored walls of the city provided a backdrop against which the brightly colored turbans and clothing of the caravaners and startlingly white robes of the Levites stood out in contrast. From atop the walls, military lookouts searched the throngs below, looking for signs of trouble.

A prosperous couple with their little girl made their way through the Watergate into the city-proper. The mother had her arm linked through her husband's in order to keep from being separated in the crowded streets. Even the most cursory glance revealed that the woman was expecting a child and was near the time of her travail. Yet her serene smile told anyone who took notice that her condition did not alter her placid nature.

From her perch on her father's shoulders, the little girl laughed and waved at the other pilgrims. People made way for the family when they saw that the father was dressed in the white robes of a priest. They smiled at the little girl, whose auburn ringlets were striking in a sea of dark-haired people.

Keziah was thrilled. It was her first visit to the City of David, and she could hardly take in all the exciting new sights and sounds and smells. But most exciting of all was to be held by her father. Usually Aaron had too many important things to do than to pay attention to a five-year-old girl. But today, away from his duties in their hometown of Hebron, Father was more relaxed. He had been happy recently, boasting that he would soon have a son.

Keziah felt a pang of jealousy when she thought of the baby. If it turned out to be a brother, he would be favored over her. Every Hebrew parent, mother or father, wanted boys. This seemed unfair to Keziah, although her *Ahmi* had tried to explain to her that the family line was carried on through the sons. She knew it was naughty to wish it, but she secretly hoped for a sister. Surely if she had a sister, Father would favor Keziah, his firstborn daughter. *Ahmi* she didn't worry about. She would always be her mother's favorite, of that she was certain. But for at least a while longer, she would have her father to herself. The thought made her grip her father's thinning hair more firmly.

"Stop that, Keziah!" Aaron yelped and slapped her hand. "I am tired of carrying her, Miriam. I can take her hand if we let her walk."

"Oh, Aaron, I would be so concerned that she would get lost. She will be very still now. Won't you, baby?"

Her lower lip still quivering from the slap her father had given, Keziah quickly agreed.

~ ~ ~

Keziah was frightened. *Ahmi* had been closed up in her chamber now for two days, trying to get their new baby born. Only the midwife was allowed to see her. Father had been gone most of the time since the birthing began. Before he left the house, he had warned her sternly not to go into the birthing chamber. But about an hour ago, Keziah had heard terrible cries coming from her mother. She had rushed to the door and asked in a loud voice if she could come in and help. But the midwife had angrily told her to go away.

She had been sitting in the same spot right outside the door ever since. She hadn't heard a thing for a long time now, and she wondered what was happening. It sure took a long time to get a baby, Keziah reflected.

A few minutes later, she heard a weak cry, almost like the tiny new foxes that she had found at the edge of *Ahmi's* flower garden behind the house. As quietly as possible, she lifted the latch and peered into the room. She stifled a gasp when she saw a knife in the midwife's hand. But in another moment, she turned around with a red, squirming baby in her hand.

"Look, my lady. You have a son. Won't your husband be proud? You have to rest now, so you can take care of him. I will send your daughter to fetch her father."

Abruptly the woman turned around and spied Keziah, eyes huge with wonder and fear. The big woman stood blocking her view of her mother, and Keziah wished she would move, but she didn't.

"Go and get your father, child, and be quick about it! Tell him he has a son. Go on now."

And so Keziah lost an opportunity to see her mother one last time. She ran to get Father, who was saying a prayer of dedication over a vineyard on the hillside above their house.

"Father," she whispered as she pushed her way through the little crowd gathered around him. He ignored her and continued praying. With tears in her eyes, she waited for the lengthy prayer to end. When Aaron was finished, he looked at his daughter with such intense anger she was unable to speak. Finally she was able to tell her father he had a son.

When he heard the word *son,* his frown turned to laughter. He laughed and picked her up, swinging her to ride atop his shoulder for the first time since their trip to Jerusalem a month before. Keziah thought that if her new brother put their father in this kind of mood all the time, she might not mind having him around after all.

But when they arrived home, they were greeted with shocking news. *Ahmi* was dead, the midwife told them right away.

"What of my son?" her father asked as Keziah skirted around him and ran to her mother, who lay so still and white against the bed linens.

Keziah traced her mother's features with a small finger. She felt cool, but otherwise, she looked as she always had. She appeared to be asleep.

Yes, that was it. Her mother was only sleeping. Keziah leaned over and whispered in her ear. "*Ahmi,* wake up. The new baby is here. It's a boy, just like you wanted. You have to wake up." When there was no response, Keziah shook Miriam's shoulder. Her head flopped over in a strange way that frightened Keziah. She started to yell. "Please, *Ahmi,* talk to me."

Keziah looked around for help and saw her father holding the baby. In her anguish, she forgot to be properly respectful. "Father, put the baby down. You have to help *Ahmi*. She won't wake up."

Her father scowled at her and turned again to the midwife, who had been talking to him in a low voice.

Keziah ran over to him and pulled on his arm. He shook her off. "There is nothing I can do for your mother, Keziah. She's dead—in Sheol with Abraham. It is your brother we must think of now. He is very weak. He might die. My son might die!"

Keziah felt a fury such as she had never experienced in her five years. "I don't care about that baby. It's his fault she is dead! I hate him! I hate him! I want her back!"

Her father struck her such a hard blow that she fell to the floor, her ears ringing. The room dimmed. Keziah wasn't surprised. The light had gone out of her life.

Chapter One

Keziah made her way upward through the winding streets of Hebron past the simple whitewashed mud houses that were burnished gold by the afternoon sun. Her father would be angry if she was late, so she picked up her pace. Her home was in the upper city, where the more prosperous citizens of Hebron lived, not far from Machpelah, the grove and cave where Father Abraham and Jacob were buried at the northwest edge of the city.

She was returning from an errand at the fuller's, who had his business located at the edge of town, at the foot of the long, sloping incline on which her town was built. The odors caused by the substances he used to whiten or dye the fabrics that were brought to him—lye, putrid urine, and certain noxious desert plants—required that his business not be located in close proximity to the homes of Hebron.

Keziah spotted two familiar people coming down the path toward her, and she broke into a broad smile. It completely transformed her face from its usual somber aspect and brought an answering smile from her two friends, who were now drawing close to her.

"Ira, Haggadah. I'm so glad to see you. I wish I could stop

and visit, but I have been on an errand for my father, and I have to get this back to him." She indicated the bundle she carried.

The brother and sister were the only friends Keziah had of her own age. Although they lived near her, she seldom had a chance to visit with them. That Haggadah was younger than Keziah was evident by her shorter stature and plumper face. Her carefree nature evolved from being the youngest child and the darling of her parents. Now Haggadah poked out her bottom lip slightly in a hint of a pout.

"But you are always on some errand for your father. Sometimes I wonder if Aaron thinks you are his slave instead of his daughter."

Even as Keziah reddened in embarrassment and tried to think of something to say in defense of her father, Ira rebuked his sister.

"Haggadah, if you don't learn to be more moderate in your speech, you will never find a husband, and no one will be left in Hebron who will speak to you. You will have offended all of them! Please excuse my sister, Keziah," Ira smiled at her and her embarrassment vanished. He was older than Keziah by a year, tall and gangly, as young men are wont to be at his age, and quite self-conscious.

"I looked for you at the New Moon feast last week. Almost everyone in Hebron was there."

Ira wasn't just trying to make conversation, Keziah knew. He had a genuine interest in her, and Keziah suspected that if her father were not such a stern and imposing figure, he would have asked for her in marriage already. After all, she was already past the age when most girls were betrothed.

Perhaps he would soon muster the courage to do so, or, more likely have his father do it. Keziah wished for Ira to be her brother more than she desired him as a suitor. Her father inspired respect but not friendship, and Keziah guessed that even Ira's father might hesitate to approach him. She retained flashes of memory of her father as a friendlier, happier man, but not since her mother's death.

But Keziah doubted that her father would entertain any offers for her as long as he remained unmarried himself. His second wife had died several years earlier, leaving him without a male heir, so it was essential that he find another wife—a young wife. The requirements for the wife of a priest were more stringent than for the rest of the population. Besides, Aaron was very particular. Keziah doubted there was a family in Hebron he would consider worthy of being united with his.

"I suppose your father has still not changed his mind about letting you attend." Haggadah's statement, which brought her a nudge from her brother's elbow, brought Keziah's wandering thoughts back to the conversation.

"No, Haggadah. He is sending me to Adoraim to stay with my aunt. I won't even be in Hebron for the New Moon. Besides, Father never changes his mind about such things. He believes that the New Moon feasts should not be observed because it is not written in the Torah."

"But it is not forbidden in the Torah, either. And sacrifices are always made to Adonai, and that is commanded in the Torah."

Keziah just shrugged. She knew that most people did not understand her father's strictness in matters of the Law of Moses. She didn't understand it herself. She only knew there were dozens of things practiced in Aaron's household that other families in Hebron never observed. Her thoughts about her father's strictness reminded her that she was late, and he would not be happy about that.

"I have to go now. Perhaps I will bring you back some almonds from Adoraim when I return. I will be gone a month while Father is in Jerusalem, but I will try to come to your home for a visit when I get back."

She addressed her words to the sister, but they were meant for Ira as well, and as she parted from the pair, she entertained the thought that someday it might be pleasant to be married to Ira. That would mean she would have Haggadah for a sister.

But so far Keziah's father had discouraged all suitors. He did not allow her to go to the New Moon feasts, where young people mingled and often chose their mates. Most people looked forward to these social occasions and even observed a spiritual rededication with a special offering.

Keziah knew her father would never change his opinion of these events. For one thing, he did not approve of young people mingling and forming their own opinions about who they wed. He believed that only fathers should decide who their children should marry—especially daughters. Keziah knew that when her father finally chose a husband for her, he would not ask her opinion of the match at all. So Keziah had very little social interaction and very few friends of her own age in Hebron, even though it was the city of her birth.

As she had tried to explain to Ira and Haggadah, Keziah's father also rejected the New Moon feasts because the Law of Moses had not specifically prescribed them. The only New Moon feast that Aaron observed was in the month of Tishri, the seventh month. This feast, commonly called the Feast of Trumpets, had been commanded by Moses, and Aaron had proudly declared that he would celebrate no other. Keziah looked forward to the festival each year.

One reason Keziah wanted to accompany her father on his journey to Jerusalem was so that she might see new things and meet new people. But she also wished to spend time with him, to demonstrate that she was worthy of his love and would bring him honor.

Her shoulders lifted as she heaved a sigh. So far, she had not been very successful. No matter how hard she tried, it seemed she always fell short of winning her father's approval.

Keziah possessed a pleasant nature and a wide smile that often prompted a smile in return from those who saw it, but since she had very little chance to interact with others, she did not realize this about herself. She only knew that her smile brought no answering smile to her father's face.

Her pleasant nature seemed to leave no impression on him either; in fact, it appeared to make his own more sour than ever. She still had vague memories of a mother's smiles and kisses, but her mother had been dead since Keziah was five years old, and those memories grew less clear as time passed.

Keziah had never thought to question her father's treatment of her. She had always known he rejected her, at least since her mother died, and had always assumed it was her fault that he did. But with a natural optimism and the resilience of youth, she continued to try to win her father over. So she quickened her pace as she neared her home, hopeful that Aaron would not be too angry that she was late and that this time he would take her with him.

Keziah's father stood in the doorway of his house with a scowl on his face. "I told you to go to the fuller's early today so that I might have my things ready early and be able to get enough rest. I leave at dawn tomorrow, Keziah. Can you never consider the welfare of your only parent? What have I done to have such an ungrateful daughter?"

Another daughter might have broken down into tears over such a scathing rebuke for such a small trespass. But Keziah was used to hearing such lectures from her father.

She knew that if she explained that she had stopped to talk to friends it would only make matters worse and possibly lead to his forbidding her to see them again. So she offered a simple apology. "I'm sorry, Father." She handed him the bundle and followed him into the house.

Aaron immediately went to his chamber, where a woven bag stood open on a chair. He carefully folded his freshly laundered ephod, the sleeveless vest that marked his position as a priest and a son of the tribe of Levi. He always looked forward to wearing it during his stay in Jerusalem.

As he placed the ephod with his other belongings for his trip to Jerusalem, he smiled in anticipation. Always impressed with himself —after all, he had been named for Israel's first high priest, the brother of Moses—he was never more proud than when his priestly duties called him to Jerusalem to take part in the rotation of priests that King David had set up for the worship in the tabernacle he had erected there.

Since the King had returned the ark of the covenant to Jerusalem after its hundred-year exile with the Philistines, worship in Israel no longer centered in Shiloh or Gibeon, where the brazen altar was housed, but in the capital itself. David had organized the worship, appointing musicians and bringing in priests from all over Israel to participate. Aaron would surely see the King on this trip, for David often came to the tabernacle.

"Father, won't you take me with you this time? You promised me that one day I could go to Jerusalem with you."

Aaron broke off his pleasant musings at the sound of his daughter's voice. Keziah stood in the door of his chamber, holding a small cloth bag filled with bread and cheese that she had prepared for his journey. Her dark auburn hair curled riotously about her face, framing rich brown eyes that complemented her hair and a wide mouth that curved in a pleading smile.

Aaron suppressed a momentary pang of guilt. Since the death of her mother, he had never taken the girl, his only child, with him to Jerusalem, not even to the Passover Feast, which had become an annual pilgrimage since David had centered his people's worship in Jerusalem. Most families made the trip together, enjoying the time away from mundane daily life.

But Aaron did not enjoy spending time with Keziah. To take her with him would remind him of her mother and the time they had taken Keziah with them to the feast. He did not want to be reminded of his first wife and those happy days before his life had turned to bitterness.

Such a disappointment Keziah was to Aaron. If only she had been a son; he gladly would have taken a son with him to Jerusalem. But Adonai had not smiled on him. He had lost two wives trying to get sons. The first, Keziah's mother, had actually presented him with one before she died, but he was a weak thing who had survived his mother by only a few hours.

Why had his only son been too frail to live when Keziah had been born fat and healthy, with a lusty cry and that ridiculous red hair? Aaron knew that most Hebrews considered auburn hair to be beautiful, a rarity among a swarthy people who nearly always had black hair. And now that they had a king with hair the shade of a golden sunset, they admired it even more.

But Aaron did not want his daughter to be admired for her beauty. He wanted her to be known for her virtue, her piety, so that someday he might be able to arrange a marriage for her to one of the sons of the high priest. But that could wait. He had no wife to see to his household, and it was convenient to keep his daughter with him until he found another wife. Finally, he turned to Keziah to answer her question. "No, daughter. There is no one to look to your safety while I go to serve in the tabernacle. Jerusalem is a large city, and there are many dangers. I would have you go to your aunt and uncle in Adoraim. You'll be safe there. But I do intend to begin making inquiries to find you a suitable husband."

Aaron had repeated this promise often over the past few years. Most young women were betrothed by the time they reached puberty or soon after. But, of course, since the death of Keziah's mother and then her stepmother, she was the only one to keep house for her father. He had been in no hurry to see her married.

Besides, in his opinion no other Levite families living in Hebron had produced a son he would choose for his daughter. No, Aaron had dreams of giving his daughter in marriage to one of the offspring of Zadok or Abiathar, men appointed by David to share the office of high priest.

Perhaps on this trip to Jerusalem he would approach one of his friends in the priesthood to be an intermediary with one of them. If his daughter married into one of the high priestly families, Aaron might be able to move to Jerusalem and become one of the inner circle of priests who served perpetually at the tabernacle. He could picture himself with bodyguards, living in a fine house with marble floors, and maybe even becoming a confidant of the court.

Aaron didn't think this was at all beyond his reach because he was of the tribe of Levi, which was accorded special honor in Israel. Having received no land in the division that was enacted under Joshua, they were to be given land by whichever tribe among whom they lived. And they were to receive a tithe in payment for their spiritual services to their brethren, services such as presiding over feasts, teaching the Law, offering blessings, and the rotation of service in the tabernacle of David.

As a priest, Aaron was actually more prosperous than many of his neighbors. The roomy home that he shared with Keziah was better than most. Its foundation had been laid with native quarried stone, and its ceiling was supported by heavy oak beams. He had no servants, not because he couldn't afford them, but because he was most ungenerous and preferred to allow Keziah to perform all the duties to which a servant would normally attend. He would never have admitted that he did so because of a vindictive anger toward a daughter who had failed to be born a son.

The next morning at dawn, Aaron and his daughter gathered up their things in preparation to depart, the priest to Jerusalem and Keziah to Adoraim some nine miles to the west of Hebron. As they prepared to leave, Aaron eyed his daughter critically. "Depart for Adoraim right away, Keziah. You want to arrive well before dark. And don't forget to cover your hair."

The young woman tossed her head as she felt a surge of resentment. Uncovered hair was a sign of availability. Until a girl married, she was allowed to go with her head uncovered. After all, a young woman's uncovered head served to attract the attention of would-be suitors.

But Keziah knew that her father was ashamed of her hair. He believed it drew attention to his daughter and made her appear immodest. He also felt a deep distrust of human nature. He was constantly on the lookout for improper behavior either on her part or by others.

Her father was a difficult man to love, Keziah admitted to herself. But he was all she had. She kissed him good-bye, and they headed their separate ways, he to the north, she to the west.

Chapter Two

Talmon of Gibeah impatiently made his way along the road that led to Hebron, calculating that it would take at least one more full day of travel before he reached Jerusalem, especially since his manservant, Ishobeam, puffed, panted, and constantly complained about the pace Talmon set for them.

Joab, commander of all Israel's armies, had sent him on this mission to Philistia, a trip that had proved futile as well as exhausting. Talmon had been slowly ingratiating himself with the general. He had finally been appointed one of several bodyguards, honorary armor bearers who did the general's bidding. Up to this time, Talmon had never failed to fulfill an assignment, but the futile trip to Philistia had left him in a nasty frame of mind. He couldn't wait to be back in Jerusalem, indulging in the vices that entertained him.

Of course, he would not have long to enjoy himself. He would soon have to report back to Joab at Rabbah. Talmon had detested waiting outside the city gates to starve the rebellious Ammonites into submission. Violent by nature, he always looked forward to the cruelty and slaughter of the battle.

But this was a siege, not a battle, so Talmon had volunteered to take a message to Ziklag. The general had thought to pressure the Philistines into sending a contingent of soldiers to assist in the siege, but the wily king of Ziklag had been well aware that Joab was too busy subduing the Ammonites to retaliate for a lack of cooperation. Not only had he not been cooperative but also he had provided Talmon with the poorest of accommodations and had granted him only a brief audience. Talmon had expected to be feasted and entertained but had been rudely ignored. There had been nothing he could do but return, his mission unaccomplished.

Still, Joab did not like to be denied, and Talmon knew that the general would not forget his failure to gain the Philistines' cooperation. Just as Talmon's father had always publicly humiliated him as a child for any infraction, Joab would almost certainly ridicule him in the presence of the other aides.

Talmon's mind replayed an incident that had happened in his fourteenth summer, when his father had sent him to deliver two donkeys that he had sold to a neighbor. Bandits had accosted him and beaten him on the road, taking the animals. When Talmon reached home, he received no sympathy. Instead he had been beaten again by his father and humiliated in front of the entire household. He imagined Joab doing the same thing to him in front of the troops.

As his mood grew darker with these thoughts, he felt a need to vent his ire on someone. Talmon's appearance utterly belied what was inside. His finely chiseled, handsome features, and ready smile served him well in deceiving those he met. But his true nature was anything but pleasant. From childhood he had despised most other people, convinced no one could match his superior intelligence and cunning. For the most part, that opinion had turned out to be accurate. Talmon lived for self-gratification and ambition, and he felt not a moment of empathy for any other human being.

Attaining what he wanted was Talmon's only goal in life. Most of the time that could be accomplished best with charm and manipulation. For that reason, most people never saw his baser, cruel nature. Those who did see it never forgot the experience.

Ishobeam was one of the few who knew the true extent of Talmon's evil, but since he was a man equally as wicked, for the most part he enjoyed his association with the young man he had served these past ten years. At this moment, though, Ishobeam was the only person near enough to serve as the focus of Talmon's anger. He drew his sword from its sheath and whacked the flat of it against the older man's backside.

"Move your lazy carcass, old man, or we will be another week getting to Jerusalem." The older man grunted his protest but picked up the pace, and they moved quickly along the deserted road.

They were some two miles from Hebron when they spotted the child. She was singing as she moved among the trees that lined the road, picking some of the plants and placing them in a basket.

Talmon paused for a moment to watch her. Here was a diversion, someone he could dominate in order to lessen the shame of his failed mission. And Ishobeam would forget to sulk over his recent harsh treatment if his thoughts were diverted by the little girl. The old man always found satisfaction in tormenting any creature smaller and weaker than he. Ishobeam was used to his master's frequent changes of mood and action, so he wasn't surprised when Talmon put his finger to his lips and motioned him to silently approach the girl. Evidently his master was now willing to pause in the journey long enough to make sport of the child.

~ ~ ~

Keziah sauntered along the road that led to Adoraim. It was the month of Iyar, and she was enjoying the pleasant spring day. The day was cloudless and beautiful, and Keziah turned her face up to the sun as the breeze feathered her hair back from her face.

The road was a winding one, with rocky outcroppings and an occasional stand of oak or cedar trees. It transversed an area of undulating hills that sometimes dropped off into deep ravines. There were still many hours of daylight left in which to reach Adoraim.

Keziah was in no hurry to arrive at the home of her aunt and uncle. They were not expecting her at any particular time, though she usually stayed with them when her father went to Jerusalem. Her father's sister, Milcah, was just as dour as Aaron. Although Uncle Benjamin was more pleasant, he was too cowed by his wife to offer any assistance in persuading her to give Keziah freedom to mingle with the other young people in the village. Instead, she would spend her time doing chores for her aunt.

Keziah doubted her father would keep his promise to look for a husband for her, but he might look for a wife for himself. At his age, if he were ever to have sons, it must happen soon. By law he was not allowed to wed a divorced woman, nor one whose virtue had been questioned. Not that her father would consider such a woman for his wife anyway.

Keziah hoped that Aaron wouldn't choose a woman like Aunt Milcah, or like Hannah, her deceased stepmother. Keziah remembered the conflicting feelings of guilt and relief she had when Hannah had died. It was a pity that a woman so young had to die, but Hannah had been so cruel toward twelve-year-old Keziah that she could not grieve her loss.

Perhaps Father would find a woman with a better disposition this time. Besides, once he remarried, Aaron might seriously seek a husband for Keziah. Then she would have a home of her own, a family, and a child to hold and love.

What would it be like, she wondered, *to have another human being love and trust her completely?* She couldn't imagine, but it was a goal she looked forward to reaching, as did every Hebrew girl.

Her hopes did not include having a husband's love. From what she had seen in her own home, Keziah believed that duty was the primary bond between husband and wife. The husband provided shelter and protection, and the wife gave him sons.

Her musings were interrupted by a sound coming from a grove that stood some distance from the road. It was a high-pitched sound such as might be made by a small, frightened animal. Keziah stopped and listened. It came again. A child's treble tones—clearly upset, though Keziah could not distinguish the words. And the answering deep voice of a man. *Probably just a small child unwilling to do his father's bidding,* she thought as she started to walk again. But then the high voice raised to a plaintive wail once again.

Alarmed, Keziah crept through the rugged boulders between the road and the trees toward the sound. If nothing was amiss, then whoever was in the woods would not need to know she was there. But if the child needed help. . . .

"Please don't take my basket. It holds only herbs for a salve my mother makes."

Keziah saw that the plea came from a little girl who appeared to be about eight years of age. A large, rather ugly man in his middle years held the basket over the child's head, just out of reach. A younger man, dressed in military uniform with leather mail covering his upper body, and a large broadsword strapped to his left side for easy access, leaned against a large oak a short distance away. His hair was thick and black, his features patrician.

"See whether she's telling the truth, Ishobeam."

"Good idea, my lord," the older man replied, and opened the lid, tilting it so that his master could see, and in the process dumping some of the contents on the ground. With a cry of outrage, the child kicked the older man in the shin. He dropped the basket and hopped on one foot, swearing. The child grabbed the basket and started to run, but the young man reached out his arm and snared her around the waist.

"You shouldn't have done that, brat. Ishobeam doesn't like it when people kick him. You'll have to be punished. What shall we do to her, Ishobeam?"

The older man grinned, showing a couple of missing teeth, one on either side of his two front ones. As he started toward his master and the child, the little girl screamed in terror and squirmed helplessly in the young man's strong grasp. Keziah was so incensed that she forgot her own fear and stepped from her hiding place.

"Leave her alone!" she commanded indignantly.

Three heads swung in unison toward the sound of her voice. The servant's eyes narrowed suspiciously. The little girl's face lit with hope. The younger man looked her over with a hungry expression that made Keziah's heart clinch in fear. But she held her ground, determined to stare him down.

The soldier, whose countenance had seemed so comely from a distance, now made chills run down Keziah's spine. The look in his eyes was cruel and predatory, and Keziah sensed that she had now become the prey.

"Do as she says, Ishobeam," he said without taking his eyes from Keziah.

"But, Master . . ."

"Let the child go," Talmon ordered. "What need do we have of a little lamb when this sleek gazelle has appeared?"

As he continued to stare at her, his gaze came to rest on her hair. Keziah instantly regretted having disobeyed her father's instruction to keep her head covered.

The servant released the child, who stood for a moment, looking questioningly at Keziah.

"Go along now. Run home, little one," she told the child, who raced away. While the men's attention was on the child, Keziah seized her chance to escape as well. She ran faster than she ever imagined she could, back to the road, then in the direction of Adoraim.

At first, Keziah thought she might outdistance them, for when she glanced back, she did not see the men. Where were they? They must be somewhere among the boulders. Her side had a terrible catch in it, but she did not slow down, nor did she dare to look back again.

She came to a curve in the road that skirted a huge boulder.

As she rounded it, she was suddenly knocked to the ground. Her breath left her body in a whoosh. She was stunned for what seemed an eternity, then she heard the mocking laughter of her two tormentors. They had stationed themselves on a boulder and waited for the opportunity to pounce. They had merely been making sport of her!

Keziah became so angry at the thought that again she forgot to be afraid. She struggled against her captor's hold and screamed at the top of her voice until he silenced her with a stunning blow to her face. With the help of the older man, he dragged her off the road into another stand of trees. Keziah, though dazed by the blow, still fought valiantly. She managed to scratch the young soldier's face.

"Ishobeam, hold her arms. No, over her head."

Keziah wanted to scream again, but found she could not. The warrior kept one hand over her mouth, and she felt she was suffocating. She tried to kick, to dislodge him with her legs, but his weight held her immobile. She attempted to jerk her arms from the servant's hold and almost succeeded, until he knelt on them.

As the brutal attack continued, the only sounds were the warrior's strident breathing, an occasional lewd laugh or comment from the servant, and the stifled moans coming from the helpless girl.

Keziah was mercifully near unconsciousness some time later when she felt herself being roughly dragged some distance. When the motion stopped, she managed to partially open one of her swollen eyes and saw that she was lying near the edge of a deep, rocky ravine dotted with scrub brush. She heard her attackers—they were talking about pushing her over the ravine. Keziah knew that she would soon die. At that moment she almost felt relief; perhaps her father would think only that she had fallen to her death, if she were ever found, and would never know of her shame.

The next instant Keziah felt the push of a foot, then sensed herself falling through space, until a bone-jarring impact brought blessed blackness.

~ ~ ~

Adah was in sight of Hebron when she made up her mind to go back. At first she had only thought of escape, but she soon became worried about the stranger who had helped her. The kind lady who had helped her was in trouble. Those were mean men. They had laughed in a funny way and frightened her. The lady would be no match for the two men. Adah decided she would sneak back.

As she retraced her steps, she stopped several times to pick up rocks that were just the right size and weight to fit her hand nicely. She intended to be ready if those hateful men were still about. She would hide in the trees and throw rocks. Maybe the men would think travelers were nearby and leave the older girl alone.

She rounded a bend in the road where a huge rock jutted out. There were drops of red sprinkled across the road. Adah stooped down for a closer look and realized it was blood. Frightened, she was tempted to run away, but she remembered the young woman who had helped her and started to search the area. Then she saw the two men who had accosted her leave the cover of the trees that bordered the nearby ravine.

Quickly, Adah ducked behind the rock. When she could no longer hear their voices, she crept from her hiding place and ran toward the area from which the men had come. She had walked along the edge of the ravine for several moments when she heard a low moan.

She paused to listen, and in a moment another moan, this one louder than the first, alerted her that her rescuer was somewhere below her. Adah knelt and peered over the edge of the ravine. Her heart sank when she saw the distance to the bottom. Then something moved a few feet below and captured her attention.

Adah scrambled down the incline. Halfway down, on a ledge

that had broken her fall, lay the pretty lady. Only she wasn't pretty anymore. Her eyes were nearly swollen shut and her clothing was torn.

The little girl knelt down beside the battered, bleeding young woman and spoke soothingly. "My lady, did the bad men hurt you? Don't worry. They are gone now. I will help you." Adah untied the small skin of water she had tied at her waist. It wasn't much, but it would have to do. "Here is some water. Can you raise your head?"

Keziah moaned but lifted her head slightly when the little girl's hand slipped under her neck to help her. The water stung her bloodied lip. The little girl dampened the bottom of her tunic and tried to wash the bruises and cuts on Keziah's face.

Long moments passed before she regained the strength to sit up. She gasped and winced in pain, but for the sake of the child she bit back the groans that tried to escape her. Adah found Keziah's discarded cloak and brought it to her.

"Please, lady, can you walk? I will take you to my mother. She will know what to do. Come. Come. Those men might come back at any time."

That admonition registered with Keziah, even in her dazed state, and she stumbled painfully to her feet. It took a long time to climb back up to the road, and Keziah sprawled, panting and exhausted, when they reached it. The little girl wiped the beads of perspiration off Keziah's brow and once more gave her water to drink.

"Come now, lady, please get up again. We have to leave this place as soon as possible. My mother will help you as soon as we reach Hebron. That's the way, just lean on me."

Keziah wanted nothing more than just to lie there and die, but the child was so insistent and so persistent that, eventually, it was simply easier to allow herself to be helped to her feet and guided along.

They made their way very slowly back to Hebron. Keziah fell to her knees more than once before they reached the city.

When they were almost to Hebron, she covered her head with her cloak and insisted they not enter by the main road that led into the marketplace but by a small path that was not heavily traveled. Unlike any other town of its size, Hebron had no city walls, so it was approachable by numerous paths.

She allowed herself to be led to the little girl's house because she was afraid that if she returned to her own, a neighbor might see her and send word to Aaron. Although the thought of anyone learning of the humiliating attack horrified Keziah, the idea of her father knowing caused her limbs to tremble and her stomach to churn. Her father could never find out about this! Never! That was the foremost thought echoing through Keziah's mind.

Chapter Three

Judith hummed a tune as she kneaded the dough for the last time. Her mind was not really on the mundane chore of baking bread—after all, she had done it thousands of times. As she worked the dough in the long, rectangular wooden bowl, her thoughts were on Isaac and Ahiam, her son and husband, who were gone away with Israel's army to lay siege to Rabbah, the capital city of the Ammonites.

Pinching off a piece of the fermented dough, she placed it in a small covered bowl to be used as a "starter" for tomorrow's bread. Then she shaped the bread into round loaves to be baked in the oven that stood in the courtyard. On impulse, she reached for her precious jar of cinnamon, working it into a third and final loaf. Finally, she added a small amount of honey for sweetness.

Perhaps Ahiam and Isaac would return home today, and she could serve them the special treat for their evening meal. Judith sighed as she wiped the sweat off her brow with the cloth she kept in the girdle of her tunic when she cooked. Her husband and son had been away for two months now, and there was no reason to believe they would return any time soon. Still, she hoped. If they did not come, well, then Adah and old Rachel down the street would both enjoy the cinnamon treat.

Where was Adah, anyway? The sun was well past its zenith, and still she hadn't returned with the herbs Judith needed to make the salve for old Rachel's sensitive skin. Judith left the main room of the house and went to place the loaves in the clay oven that had been heated earlier. Then she walked to the gate that led out to the street and looked both ways. Adah was nowhere to be seen.

Judith went back to her chamber to get her hooded cloak. After all, no married woman would leave home with her head uncovered. But she must go in search of her daughter, who, in the way of most eight-year-olds, often became distracted when given a chore. Likely Adah was dangling her feet in some brook or had stopped at a friend's house to play. That is where she would look first, Judith decided.

As she passed once more through the gate, she saw Adah drawing near, moving very slowly. She was supporting a woman who leaned heavily on the much smaller child for support. By the way the woman moved, Judith assumed she must be elderly, though she could not make out her face. It was concealed by her cloak, which she had pulled low over her face.

Judith wondered who it could be. It wasn't Rachel, who lived in the opposite direction and, though frail, would never allow Adah to support her in such a way. It must be a stranger.

As Judith opened the gate wide for them to enter, her daughter looked up. "Oh, Ahmi, please help her. They hurt her badly."

At that moment, the woman's legs buckled. Judith reached out and grabbed her, pulling the stranger's arm around her neck and wrapping her own arm around the woman's waist. At that moment, the concealing cloak fell back, and Judith got a good look at her face.

Why, this was no elderly person at all. It was a young woman, and she had been beaten—badly! Judith took a deep breath. She must remain calm for Adah's sake. "Just keep your arm around her waist as you have been doing, dear. Let's get her to my chamber."

It was not until they had reached Judith's bed and eased the girl back on it that Judith spoke again. The young woman had fainted. She looked carefully at the swollen face and the fiery hair.

"I believe I recognize her, Adah. She is the daughter of the priest, Aaron. I don't recall her name, but I have seen her at the market before. And at the sacrifices, as well. What happened to her?"

As Adah started to answer, Judith looked her daughter over to see if she also had been harmed. In the shock of seeing the pathetic young woman, she had not thought to be concerned for her daughter. Now her face paled with concern for what her own child might have witnessed.

"Ahmi, she saved me from the bad men. They found me as I was picking herbs in the woods. They poured some out, but I have brought the rest." The child thrust the basket at her mother. Chin quivering, she turned away.

Judith set the basket aside, striving for patience to get the story out of Adah. "That doesn't matter, Adah. Go on, child. Tell me about the men. What happened?"

"They were being mean to me, and this lady told them to stop. She got them to let me go, but they came after her instead. At first I was so afraid that I ran and ran. Then I thought about what the lady had done for me, and I went back to help her. But the men had hurt her badly. She was lying on a ledge where they had thrown her and not moving when I found her, and there was lots of blood. Will she be all right, Ahmi?"

"I'm certain she will, darling," she said, drawing Adah into her arms. "I am so proud of you. What you did was very brave."

After a moment, she released her daughter and stepped back to look her over carefully, just to reassure herself that her daughter was unharmed.

Judith's mouth compressed into a thin line as she thought about the possibilities of what could have happened to her baby. And what had in all probability been done to the unconscious girl who was lying so still in her bed. *I can't allow Adah to see the ugly reality of this girl's injuries,* Judith thought desperately. *She has seen too much already.*

"Adah, be a good girl and go to the courtyard." She handed the child the basket of herbs. "Wash these and put them in the jar where I usually keep them. Then wait for me to call you. When I have finished helping your friend, you may come back and see her. She will be fine."

Judith forced a smile, then waited until Adah was gone before turning to help their visitor. She quickly undressed the girl, who moaned in pain when she was moved but did not awaken.

Judith prayed that she would not, as she took in the great purpling bruise that covered the girl's right side and also saw the evidence she had feared she would find. The young woman had been brutally raped. Oh dear God, that such a thing could happen in Israel. Was there no fear of God in the men who had done this horrible act? And it might have happened to her Adah but for the intervention of this guardian angel.

Tears ran down Judith's cheeks as she bathed the woman's wounds, rubbing aloe on them and dressing her in Judith's own softest linen tunic. Still she did not speak, for she did not want her charge to awaken any sooner than was necessary. It was God's mercy that she slept, His way of protecting the mind against the unthinkable horror of what had so recently happened.

When Judith had done all that was possible for her guest, she went to find Adah. She must learn all she could about the incident, then send word to the young woman's father. Surely Aaron would come quickly to comfort his daughter and to see that justice was administered to her attackers.

She found her usually lively daughter sitting atop the courtyard wall, her chin resting on her drawn-up knees, looking pensive and frightened. Judith put her arm around Adah and kissed the top of her head.

"You did very well today, Adah. You helped that young woman. You saved her. She will be all better soon."

Judith felt a bit guilty as she made that assertion. The girl's body would certainly heal. She was young and otherwise healthy. But her mind, her spirit, were a different matter. Judith doubted those would be better for a very long time.

"Really, Ahmi? She will be all right? May I go and see her?"

"Later, my darling. She is sleeping now. But you can go for her father. Now you must listen carefully to what I tell you. Go to the home of Aaron the priest. Speak to him and him alone. Tell him only that his daughter is ill at our house and that he must come at once. You are not to tell him what happened in the forest. And you are not to bring anyone but him, nor tell anyone else that the priest's daughter is here. Do you understand?

Adah's eyes were wide and serious. "Yes, Ahmi, I am to go and bring Aaron the priest here, and no one else, and don't talk to anyone, even the priest, about what happened today in the woods."

Judith made her way back to her chamber, her heart breaking for the young woman and for her daughter, who was witness to such an ugly thing. She began to pray for the Lord's mercy on behalf of the still-sleeping girl, and for the punishment of her attackers. She prayed aloud, hoping the girl would be comforted if she heard the petitions.

"O Adonai, you are our refuge. Put your everlasting arms around this helpless one. Destroy the wicked men who harmed her, even as you promised your people in the days of Moses. May their names be blotted out from among your people."

Judith paused in her prayer as it struck her she had never been so filled with anger. She hoped God's vengeance would soon fall on those evil men.

A few minutes later, she heard Adah's piping voice. "Ahmi! Ahmi! He was not at home. A neighbor says that Aaron the priest is gone to Jerusalem."

Adah appeared at the door just as the young woman stirred and made a sound of panic. She shook her head violently. "No! No! Please, no!"

Judith motioned Adah out of the room and gently pushed her

charge back onto the bed. "Be calm, my dear. We will send for your father." She recalled that Aaron's wife had died some years ago. Such a pity. The girl really needed her now.

The injured girl grabbed Judith's arm as she forced the words between her swollen lips. "Please," she croaked, "you must not tell my father. He can never know what has happened. By God's mercy, promise me you won't tell him."

"But, my dear, you especially need his comfort and protection now. He will see that the harm done you is avenged."

"No, you must promise me. Don't tell my father. Don't tell anyone!" The young woman was quickly becoming hysterical.

"Very well, if that is your wish, Adah and I will not tell your secret. Rest easy now."

The injured girl sank back on the bed cushions in relief. Judith fussed a little with the bed covers. "By the way, I am Judith, and my daughter's name is Adah. What is your name?"

"Keziah. O God, what will become of me? It would have been better if they had killed me." The girl turned her face aside, but not before Judith saw the tears sliding beneath the swollen eyelids.

"Nonsense! You will recover. Life will seem good again after some time has passed. You will stay here with Adah and me. It is the least I can do when you have saved my daughter from the fate you just suffered. I'm right, aren't I? They intended her as their victim until you came along."

When Keziah closed her eyes and nodded her head, Judith put her arms around Keziah's shoulders. "Then I can never repay the debt I owe you. Please allow me the privilege of taking care of you—at least until you regain your strength."

Keziah, too weak to offer any real resistance, agreed.

Over the next three weeks, Judith and Adah did their best to help the broken girl. Keziah gradually regained her physical strength, but her emotions remained raw, especially at night, when she would dream either of being smothered or of falling and falling, knowing she was going to die when she landed.

Many nights, Judith would be awakened by her cries and come and sit with her until she fell asleep again. Adah, thrilled to have a new companion, made the days bearable by involving Keziah in games or answering questions.

~ ~ ~

There was only one incident during her stay that frightened Keziah. When she had been at Judith's home for two weeks, Judith's son returned from Rabbah. Keziah was sitting under the part of the courtyard covered by a canopy. She was teaching Adah how to spin thread by using a distaff rod to hold the wool in place while using a spindle to twist the fibers into thread. Adah's fingers were clumsy as she practiced the skill that every woman needed to master, so Keziah's full attention was centered on helping her little friend. She did not notice Isaac come into the courtyard.

"So, my little sister, you are learning to be a woman," a teasing voice said. "You must not grow up too fast, or I'll have no one to play with."

"Isaac! You're home! Did you kill all the wicked Ammonites? Where is Father?"

Keziah's hands paused over the yarn. She still did not look up.

"He will be here in a week or two. Jonathan came with me, and we will be traveling on to Ziph. I had to stop to see how you and mother were doing."

"I have been helping mother and Keziah. Keziah, wait . . ." Adah called as the young woman started to enter the house. "You have to meet Isaac."

Keziah stopped and turned around. No use trying to avoid meeting Judith's son now. She had hoped to slip quietly away. The fewer people who knew her whereabouts the better. Besides, her face was still discolored from the bruises she had received.

She felt embarrassed by the way the tall, wiry young man

was studying her. The expression in his warm brown eyes was pleasantly curious, and she studied him for a moment as well. He wore his beard short—only the stubble of a few days growth. She wondered why. He also wore his hair quite short, not even shoulder length. The locks at his temples were braided and tied with strips of leather.

"Welcome to our home, Keziah. I am the son of the house, and my name, as you heard from my sister, is Isaac. Forgive my dirt. We've just come from the field of battle."

"Oh, I'm sorry. I'll get you some water to bathe your hands and feet."

She hurried to the large jar of water near the doorway and dipped some into a small basin that sat on a bench beside it. She brought him the basin with a clean cloth but kept her head down and her eyes averted as she held it for him to wash his hands. When he took the cloth to dry his hands, she knelt with the basin and washed his feet. Isaac noticed that she jumped as though startled when he shifted his weight.

"I . . . I will get your mother," Keziah stuttered, then quickly gathering up the basin and cloth, she turned and left the presence of the stranger.

Isaac stood staring after her. She was pale, except for a yellowing bruise around one eye and a purple one on her neck. How had she gotten them? And those doe-like eyes had also been wary, perhaps even frightened. Of him, he wondered? She wore her heavy auburn hair unbound and tumbling about her shoulders. It was somewhat mussed. Maybe that was what had made her bolt like that. He shrugged and bent to answer one of Adah's many questions.

After telling Judith of her son's arrival, Keziah hid in her room for the rest of the day, praying that Isaac would not seek to rest in his chamber and find it occupied. He had said he wouldn't be staying, but did he mean he would not spend the night? She would just have to return to her own home if he did. Then her thoughts turned to another, more troubling question, one that caused her heart to sink like a stone in a pond. Would Adah and Judith tell him what had happened? Of course not, she tried to reassure herself. They had promised not to. There was nothing to worry about. But Keziah was very uncomfortable that Judith's son had seen her.

After a few hours, Keziah heard a light tapping at her door. Was it Isaac, come to claim his room? Timidly she opened the door. It was Judith.

"You needn't hide anymore, Keziah. My son and his friend Jonathan are gone now. They continued on to Ziph. They go there to train more soldiers for the king's campaign. Were you afraid Adah and I would betray your secret? I merely told them you were a friend visiting us."

Keziah was relieved. She would be able to stay here a little longer. The prospect of being alone in her own house had been frightening. The two men who attacked her might come back and find her. Adah, too, was bothered by this fear. The child would sit for hours each day atop the gateway to her home, watching everyone who passed by. When Judith asked her what she was doing, Adah merely told her she was making sure Judith and Keziah were safe. For the child's sake, Keziah tried to hide her own fear and depression.

Chapter Four

ZIPH

Isaac squeezed his eyes tightly shut against the beam of sunlight that fell across his bed. He didn't want to rise, but he knew that the rest of the household was probably already about their business; so he threw his long legs over the side of the bed and stood, stretching his long, sinewy frame to its full length. His fingers brushed the ceiling, his muscles rippling as he rolled his shoulders to get the blood flowing. Then he bent over the basin of water in the small guest room and splashed a generous amount of water over his face.

He had not slept well the night before. He never did when he stayed at the home of Jonathan. *I should have remained in Hebron,* he thought, disgusted with himself for accepting the invitation to continue to Ziph.

Jonathan was his best friend and mentor, so it was not a lack of welcome that brought the unease. And it wasn't that the accommodations were uncomfortable. No, the guest room, though small, was well furnished, including a bed on a raised platform with a comfortable mattress made of goat's hair, sewn with leather and covered with soft linen.

As Isaac dried his face with the square of cloth placed beside the basin, he admitted to himself that the home of his best friend and commander was most comfortable. Jonathan and Ailea always made him feel more than welcome, and he loved being here. That was the problem. Isaac loved being here too much. It wasn't his home. And it wasn't his wife. But he often wished they were.

Angry with himself, the young man tossed the towel aside. Such thoughts were bad enough in the daytime, when he could push them away. But at night, in his dreams, they returned. And in that vulnerable state, he couldn't fight them. *She* came to him then, her long, black hair billowing like a cloud around her, reaching out to him. Isaac shook his head to clear it of the sinful image. He squeezed his eyes shut.

He knew that Ailea thought of him only as a friend, or perhaps a brother. But his feelings for her were definitely not brotherly. She was the wife of the man Isaac served, his best friend. *O Adonai, show mercy. I do not want to covet my friend's wife. She is his life! Please, cleanse my thoughts.* With this prayer, he opened the door and stepped out into the open inner courtyard of Jonathan's home.

"I hope you slept well, Isaac. After weeks camped on the hard ground, did the soft bed keep you awake?" The subject of his thoughts smiled at him as she asked the question.

"I, uh, it was fine, Ailea. I . . . I slept very well, thank you. Where is Jonathan?"

Inwardly, Isaac berated himself. As usual, he stuttered like a tongue-tied adolescent whenever he spoke to Ailea.

It wasn't only her surpassing beauty that affected him. Ailea had spirit, courage, and kindness. She was everything any man could wish in a wife—but she could never be his wife.

I cannot stay here another day, another moment, Isaac told himself as he looked at the wall just above Ailea's right shoulder, trying not to lose himself in the hypnotic lure of her deep green eyes as she answered his question.

"He is just getting dressed now. Come with me. I'll feed you both before you have to meet the recruits."

As he followed Ailea, he looked around admiringly. In the past two years the formerly modest dwelling of Jonathan and his father, Shageh, the Rab, had been transformed into a richly appointed villa. Rooms had been added in anticipation of the large family Ailea and Jonathan wanted. At present they had only one son, Micah, about two-and-a-half years old. As if Isaac's thoughts had summoned him, the little one came running to greet them.

Isaac's mind went back to the time he had first seen the boy—at his circumcision feast. Jonathan had just reconciled with Ailea, whom he had suspected of being a spy, and had brought her and the newborn back from En Gedi, where Ailea had given birth all alone. He had been amazed at her strength and perseverance.

Isaac scooped up the little boy, who held up his arms, and the young child turned his cherubic smile full force on Isaac. Micah was not only tall and sturdy but also very striking. He had inherited the catlike shape of his eyes from Ailea.

But whereas Ailea's eyes were green, Micah's were an unusual amber—the same color as his grandfather's, the highly respected Rab of Ziph. They had a luminosity that made you feel as though those eyes could see right through you. Isaac wondered if the lad would grow up to be a Rab like Shageh.

"What a fine young man you have become! You have grown much since I last saw you, Micah," the young soldier said, groaning a little for emphasis as he swung the boy up above his head.

Behind him, Ailea chuckled. "Yes, he has. It is all I can do to lift him anymore." She affectionately pushed the child's hair back from his forehead.

Isaac's mind flashed back to the time, three years ago, when he had first seen her. She had pushed his own hair back from his fevered brow as he recuperated from his first battle wounds at her home in Damascus. He had been captivated by her from the very moment he looked into her eyes, and that attraction had grown day by day as Ailea helped nurse him back to health. But from the first Isaac had known she could never be his. Ailea and Jonathan belonged together, bound by a love that had overcome many obstacles. Isaac shook his head, as if to shake Ailea from his mind. But he knew he could not. The knowledge was agony.

That was why, as they hunted deer in the Judean hills that afternoon, Isaac asked Jonathan if he might return to Hebron to help Ahiam recruit there. "You saw the disappointed look on my mother's face when I told her I would be staying at Ziph," he reminded his friend, knowing Jonathan's fondness for Judith would make his heart soften.

"Ailea will be disappointed," Jonathan remarked. "She enjoys playing chess with you. Claims it's no challenge anymore to defeat me."

The two friends made their way quietly through the thick forest for several more minutes before Jonathan continued. "If you insist on leaving, then go back to Hebron in the morning. Busy yourself recruiting warriors until your father comes, then help him with the training. When I have my unit ready, I will join you, and we can all return to the field together. We shouldn't tarry long, or Joab will accuse us of trying to shirk our duty."

Isaac was relieved at Jonathan's capitulation. He was not only Isaac's friend but also his captain. "I will go to Hebron immediately," he replied quickly.

"You will go in the morning," Jonathan corrected. "Today you will help me hunt."

Isaac couldn't insist without seeming ungracious, so he reluctantly agreed to stay the night. He stayed away from the house and Ailea as much as possible, hunting the rest of the day, even after helping Jonathan dress the doe that both had shot. When he brought back a brace of quail at sunset, Ailea insisted that half be taken to Judith.

After the evening meal, Isaac joined Shageh and the men of the village at evening circle by the village gate. Jonathan, of course, did not join them. He wanted to take advantage of every moment he could spend with his wife and son.

As the Rab of the village, Shageh taught from the Law of Moses. It pricked Isaac's conscience that he wasn't learning the Law out of piety but out of a desire to avoid the temptation he felt whenever he was near Ailea. He felt certain that no one was aware of his feelings for her, but sometimes when the Rab looked at him, he wondered if the old man could see right through him.

Then there was Benjamin, the old veteran who had been Jonathan's right-hand man in many battles and who had adopted Isaac, so to speak, because he was Jonathan's armor bearer. Isaac would sometimes catch Benjamin looking at him through narrowed eyes whenever they were both guests in Jonathan's home. But he got the distinct impression that Benjamin believed his feelings for Ailea were just a youthful infatuation and not worth worrying about. If only that were the case!

As exhausted as he felt, Isaac still did not fall asleep for hours. He set his mind to solving the problem of his attraction to Ailea. After mulling over several possibilities, he decided to begin the process of seeking a bride. Perhaps if he had a woman of his own, he wouldn't covet his friend's.

He would speak to his parents about it tomorrow, when he returned home. They would be more than glad to be of help. The thought brought a smile. Judith would be thrilled and undoubtedly have a list of at least ten eligible girls at her fingertips. Finally, his mind made up, Isaac fell asleep.

~ ~ ~

JERUSALEM

The King paced the length of his rooftop garden as he waited for her to come to him. He was filled with the same restlessness that had plagued him of late. *Maybe I should have gone to Rabbah after all,* he mused. But it was just one more battle, and he had had his fill of battles. It seemed that life had held one battle after another since he was seventeen years old and had defeated the Philistine champion, the giant Goliath. Now, as he was approaching his fiftieth year, the prospect of battle no longer excited him.

In fact, nothing much seemed to excite him anymore, except for his long-held plans to build a glorious temple to honor Adonai. But recently the prophet Nathan had informed him that because of his bloody history as a warrior, he was not to be the one who would actually build the temple but one of his sons after him. Still, David had continued to move the project forward, planning and acquiring the raw materials that would someday be needed in the temple's construction.

Yet, at times, even that great undertaking was not enough to satisfy him. He had been in the grip of that dissatisfaction on the evening he had first seen her. And since then, she had filled his thoughts as nothing else had in long months.

He had been here on the rooftop in the early evening some two months before, after rising from his nap. Now his mind replayed the events that had begun to unfold that night, events that had changed his life.

As he had looked out over the western parapet of the palace, the one that rendered a full view of the city below, washed by the deepening lavender shadows of the gathering twilight, David happened to glance down into the courtyard of a house that backed up to the palace. There he had seen a young woman, who, with the aid of an elderly female servant, let down her long black hair and removed her clothing. Then, stepping into a bathing tub shaped like a large, shallow bowl, she stood still while the old woman poured pitcher after pitcher of water over her supple young body.

David had recognized this as the *mikvah,* the ritual bath that purified a woman at the end of her monthly cycle. Feeling his body respond to the beautiful young woman, he at first had turned away. But after walking a few steps, he turned back to look more closely.

He continued to stand there for long moments after the bath

was completed and the two women had disappeared into the house, his mind still filled with the image of the lovely form of the stranger in the courtyard. He wondered what it was about the woman that so enthralled him. It wasn't as if he had no access to beautiful women. He had seven wives and at least a hundred concubines in his harem. He wasn't even sure of the exact count.

His wife Maacah, a princess from Geshur, was acknowledged to be the most beautiful woman in the kingdom. She had given him Absalom and Tamar, his two most attractive children. But Maacah was jealous and possessive. She was also nearing middle age, and no longer at the peak of her beauty.

Still, there were certainly lovely young women in his harem who adored him, and would welcome his attentions at any time. Why then did he feel no desire for any of them? Perhaps because there was no challenge involved in being with them. And the King was bored. Calling Amoz, his personal servant, he inquired about the occupants of the house behind the palace.

"Uriah the Hittite has lived there for several months, my lord, with his young wife. He purchased the home after his marriage so as to be more readily available to do the King's bidding—and the general's, of course."

Uriah was one of Joab's armor bearers. David's nephew Joab had made enemies over the years and needed a number of bodyguards. David respected Uriah, whom he knew to earnestly follow the Lord God even though he was a Hittite by birth. He paused for a long moment before asking Amoz, "Who is Uriah's wife?"

"She is Bathsheba, the daughter of Eliam, my lord."

David nodded in recognition. Eliam had been one of the *Gibborim,* or mighty men, David's elite circle of warriors. Eliam had been killed in battle some years earlier, and David couldn't recall ever having met any of his children, though it seemed that Eliam's wife had been a lovely woman, if David remembered correctly.

"She is also the granddaughter of Ahithophel, my lord," Amoz continued, referring to one of David's foremost counselors.

"Ah, yes. But I don't believe Ahithophel has brought her or her mother with him to court. Hmm. Amoz, I would have you send for her."

Amoz's eyes widened in surprise. "Tonight, my lord?"

"Yes. As quickly as possible."

And so she had come to him, trembling in fear, wondering why the King, whom she had never met before, would send for her. And he had seduced her. True, the attraction had been mutual from the first moment they laid eyes on each other, but Bathsheba was nearly thirty years younger than he and had come before him with no idea of the King's intentions.

Yes, David admitted to himself, the responsibility for the affair rested on his shoulders. He had called for her several times since but had been concerned for her reputation. He also felt guilty for taking the wife of a man who was risking his life to expand David's kingdom.

So he had not called for her now for a month, and he had felt very proud of himself for resisting temptation. But today she had sent a message by the method they had agreed upon—from the mouth of Bathsheba to her elderly servant woman, then from her servant to Amoz, who passed it along to the King. She wanted to see him.

It had given him a thrill of exhilaration not unlike what he sensed preceding a battle. He felt more alive, younger. It had also soothed his conscience that it was Bathsheba who sought the meeting this time.

"David."

The soft voice called him back to the present. He turned, and she was standing there, her shoulders slumping, her eyes downcast. He knew immediately that something was wrong and went to her, taking both her hands in his.

"I have missed you, my lovely one. Has it been well with you?"

The question and concern reflected in his tone brought tears to Bathsheba's eyes. "I . . . had to come. I don't know what to do. Please do not be angry, my lord, with what I have to tell you." She was trembling now, and she bit down on her lower lip to stop the tears that had formed in her eyes.

He drew her down to sit beside him on one of the ornate couches scattered throughout the rooftop garden. "I could never be angry with you, my dear. Tell me what troubles you."

She lowered her eyes to her lap and answered in a quavering voice. "I am with child, David."

The King sucked in his breath. He felt as though he had been struck in the stomach with the blunt end of Goliath's massive spear. He wondered why he had not considered this possibility before. But whenever he had thought of problems that could occur from his affair with Bathsheba, he had been concerned about the damage to her reputation should they be found out. And he had worried about the reaction of young Uriah if he were to find out. He, who had fathered nearly threescore children, honestly had not thought of pregnancy.

Stupid of him, he realized now. Uriah had been in the field for months. There was no chance he could have fathered the child. But perhaps it was not too late.

"Don't worry, my lovely one. I will take care of everything. You are to go home and await your husband's return. I will send to Rabbah for him. He will spend time with you and think the child is his. But in order to avoid gossip, we shouldn't see each other again."

But David could not bear to send her away this night, not upset and afraid as she was. So it was the next morning before Bathsheba returned to her house to await Uriah's return.

~ ~ ~

Not far from the palace, Aaron sat next to Zadok, the high priest, and enjoyed a sumptuous meal. Yesterday he had contrived to be invited to this social gathering of Jerusalem's priestly elite.

"This bread is delicious. Almost as good as my little girl makes. She is a most excellent cook. I could well afford to hire a cook, of course, but the child has always insisted in doing everything for me herself. Totally devoted. She has kept my household immaculate since the death of her mother years ago."

Aaron put his hand in front of his mouth. "Oh, my, I am doing it again. I speak of her too often, but she is everything to me. I will hate to see her leave me, but I know I must see her safely wed soon. It is difficult though, to find a young man worthy of her."

Zadok grunted noncommittally. He did not want to encourage Aaron in any way, though he realized that it mattered little what he did. The man would approach him or Abiathar, the co-high priest, about the possibility of a marriage with one of their sons. He would try as graciously as possible to put him off.

He was not interested in having Aaron's daughter become a member of his family. She was probably just as pushy and pretentious as Aaron, and even if she were the paragon he made her out to be, he refused to be burdened with such a man as a father-in-law to one of his sons. The old priest bit back a smile as he contemplated warning his sons that if they displeased him, he could see to it that they had Aaron and his daughter to deal with the rest of their lives.

As he had expected, Aaron sought out Zadok after the meal, and somehow before the meeting was over he found himself telling Aaron to bring his daughter to Jerusalem on his next visit, so that she could meet the offspring of Jerusalem's priestly families. His eldest son had been surly and somewhat disrespectful lately, and Zadok decided that when Aaron of Hebron returned with his daughter, he would give his firstborn the responsibility of entertaining them while they were in Jerusalem.

The next day, Aaron started home in a very good mood. Keziah would be thrilled that she would finally get to go to Jerusalem. Next month was Nisan, the month of Passover. He would take his daughter with him to Jerusalem to celebrate the feast.

HEBRON

Slowly, Keziah had improved under Judith's care. At first, she had been withdrawn and deeply depressed. But Adah had befriended Keziah and, in her childlike way, had comforted her as no one else could have. She thanked Keziah again and again for saving her from those "wicked men." Each time Adah said this, Keziah would remind her that she had returned to look for her, so they had actually saved each other.

Judith also continued to befriend the young woman, whose eyes seemed so sad and haunted. Against Judith's protests, Keziah remained adamant about not telling her father what had happened to her. "He will cast me out if he learns that I have been defiled," she explained.

"But it is not your fault!" Judith insisted. "Surely if I tell him what you did for Adah and . . ."

Keziah had shaken her head firmly. "It will not matter. He will feel I have disgraced him and blame me anyway. He is very harsh."

Reluctantly, Judith had agreed to keep the secret, and Adah, bless her, seemed to understand that this was something she should never mention to anyone else. Judith had insisted that Keziah stay with them until it was near the time for Aaron's return from Jerusalem. Keziah stayed inside the house, so that she would not be seen by anyone she knew, and aside from the unexpected appearance of Isaac, no one else had, not even old Rachel, who was a friend of the family. Judith and Adah had gone instead to visit the widow in her own home.

They also went to visit Judith's best friend in Ziph. "It has been weeks since we've seen each other, and I know that if I don't go to her, she will come here soon to see me," Judith explained apologetically. "I could leave Adah here with you if you don't want to be alone."

"No, take Adah with you. I will be fine here. I need to get used to being alone, truly."

"We will leave at first light, then, and be back by dusk." Keziah smiled and waved as they left, but she spent a very uneasy day, jumping at every sound and constantly peering out the window to make certain no one was coming—Judith's friends or neighbors, or the two attackers. She knew it was irrational, but without Judith and Adah to distract her, her fears multiplied. But when the two returned, she assured them she had fared well. And as she said it, she realized she had. She had made it through a day on her own. She felt stronger.

She stayed for a week after Isaac's departure. By then she felt well enough to return to her own home. Both Judith and Adah begged her to stay a little longer, and she felt her heart warm at the sincerity of their pleas. She promised her two new friends she would visit often, and that they could visit her. But she must be home when her father returned so that he would believe she had simply returned a little early from Adoraim.

As Judith watched Keziah disappear down the winding streets of Hebron, she hoped that the future would bring some happiness to the young woman. To this point, life had not been very kind to the girl. According to what Judith had learned from her, Keziah had endured the loss of her mother; the abuse of a father who was cold, rejecting, and violent; and an unprovoked attack by two vicious criminals.

Surely the Lord would have mercy on Keziah, perhaps even bring her a husband who would understand that her loss of innocence had not been her fault. Keziah had told Judith she planned to remain unwed in her father's house. The girl could think of no other option, for surely no man would want a woman who had been defiled.

But Judith knew there were men, such as her own husband, who would not be so unkind. With that thought, her longing for Ahiam's return came back in full force. When would this dreadful siege be over? It was well past time, in her opinion.

Chapter Five

RABBAH-AMMON

To the east of Israel, in Transjordan, lay the Semitic state of Ammon. David had already defeated the other Transjordan states of Damascus, Zobah, and Moab. But Hanun, the King of the Ammonites, had been unwilling to submit Ammon as a vassal state of Israel. Instead, he had insulted David's ambassadors by shaving off half the beard of each and cutting the hems of their tunics to make them immodestly short. Hanun had by this degrading act sealed the fate of his people.

The army of Israel completely surrounded the city of Rabbah. No one had gone in or out of the citadel walls of Rabbah for weeks. No military terms had been discussed since the refusal of the Ammonites to surrender the city. There was no point in negotiations as the fate of these people had already become clear. Eventually, the city would fall. Starvation would break the will of these ancient enemies of Israel.

That was the plan Joab had in mind as he stood on a rise that overlooked Rabbah. The general, though a man of middle age, could easily carry the armor that weighed heavily on lesser men. Instead, he chose a simple short tunic, a leather girdle that carried his sword, and heavy, hobnailed, leather sandals that held up under months of strenuous desert duty.

Joab liked to come here to look down on his army in their camp. His dark, piercing eyes missed nothing as he observed. His face was etched with the marks of time, sun, and relentless desert wind. As was his habit, he reviewed his battle plan in his mind.

He could attack the city, of course, bringing this whole campaign to a rapid conclusion. But that would likely result in many casualties, and Joab was unwilling to risk the loss of his men, unless entirely necessary.

He was unconcerned about the number of losses to the Ammonites. In fact, a battle would probably mean fewer deaths among the city's inhabitants, and certainly less suffering. But the general of Israel's armies had little compassion for anyone and none at all for his enemies. Joab was unstintingly loyal to his uncle, King David, but he believed the King had a weakness—showing mercy to his enemies. The differences of opinion between David and Joab had almost always concerned this; otherwise, they had worked hand-in-glove to make Israel a dominant power.

At this point in his career, David no longer thought it necessary to lead the army personally. He had never used the siege as a tactic of war and saw no reason to leave the comforts of Jerusalem to play a waiting game with the enemy. This provided a great stroke to Joab's ego.

David had shown his complete confidence in his general by staying in Jerusalem for this campaign. Instead, he had sent the ark of the covenant with them to Ammon. The holy relic now occupied a prominent place in the center of the camp. Its presence had the desired result of bolstering the confidence of the men, though David had reminded them before they set out that the mere presence of the ark did not guarantee victory.

In the days of Eli the priest, the ark had been taken into battle against the Philistines and been captured. A rectangular box about two feet wide by three feet long and two feet deep, the ark was made of acacia wood and covered with gold. It contained the tablets of the Law, Aaron's rod that had miraculously budded, and a golden pot filled with manna that had been collected during Israel's journey from Egypt to the land the Lord God had promised. These relics were meant as an object lesson of God's provision and power and were not to be worshiped. This was something entirely different from the idolatrous nations around Israel, where idols of wood and stone were worshiped as a matter of course.

Joab was glad enough to have the ark in the camp. But the wily general depended more on his own military expertise than he did on the Lord. Joab's keen ebony eyes swept the horizon like those of a raptor looking for prey. He spotted a rider approaching from the west, the direction of Jerusalem. It might be a dispatch from the King. Joab hurriedly returned to the camp and was already in his tent, washing the dust from his hands and feet, by the time the messenger arrived.

Ordinarily, the King simply issued verbal communiqués, but this time the message arrived on parchment, sealed in a leather pouch. It must be confidential and very important.

Joab dismissed the messenger and stepped behind the curtain that divided his personal quarters from the receiving room of the tent. He sat down on a camp stool and unrolled the parchment, taking note that the message had been written in the King's own hand, and not in the professional script of Sheva, the scribe.

By the time he had finished reading the communiqué, his heavy brows were joined together in a deep, furrowed frown. Something was strange here. He had been instructed to send Uriah the Hittite back to Jerusalem with a report on the campaign. What would induce David to call Uriah back to Jerusalem in the middle of the siege? Besides being one of the *Gibborim,* Uriah served as one of Joab's armor bearers and was a very important aide. David knew this well. So why not let someone of less importance bring the King a battle report?

Something of which Joab was unaware must be going on in Jerusalem. And the general did not like to be in the dark. He gave a mental shrug. There was nothing he could do about it now. He certainly couldn't leave Rabbah. And he had no choice but to obey the King's command.

Joab left the large command tent, looking for Uriah. He would also seek out several other men to accompany Uriah. But he remained puzzled. What in the world was David up to?

Chapter Six

As Keziah looked around the deserted house she had left only three weeks before, she felt a strange combination of dread and relief. She was relieved to be back in advance of her father's return and, in a way, relieved to be alone.

With Judith and Adah she always had to put on a good face. She didn't want to upset them. Then there were the son and the husband who could return any day. Even her one short encounter with Isaac ben Ahiam had shaken her.

But she dreaded being alone, especially at night. She had a constant feeling of being unsafe and found it very hard to sleep. The events of her attack still haunted her, but as the time for her father's arrival neared her fear of his reaction if he learned what had happened was greater than her fear of the men who had ruined her.

Aaron arrived four days after Keziah had returned home. As she had expected, he did not question her about her supposed sojourn in Adoraim. He hardly ever displayed enough interest in his daughter to question her about such things. Only at times when he thought she might have done something to reflect badly on his status as a spiritual leader did he pay attention to Keziah. This time he merely asked after the health of her aunt and uncle, and when she answered, "They are well," he grunted in acknowledgment and went to the city market to see the elders and find out what had happened in Hebron while he was absent.

Keziah had one problem that threatened to betray her secret. She had begun to have nightmares since the assault and would sometimes wake up screaming. The feeling she had experienced when the warrior had covered her mouth with his hand, the sense of suffocation, kept returning with frightening realism. How she had wanted to scream that day—scream and scream—but she could not. So, in her dream, that was always what she was doing when she wakened.

Fortunately, Aaron's chamber was not next to hers, and he was a heavy sleeper, so only once—the second night after his return—did she waken him with her dreams. He shook her awake roughly, and for a moment she had fought him before she realized where she was. She apologized, saying merely that she had had a bad dream. Aaron, in his typical way, did not question her about it. Nor did he offer comfort. He simply went back to bed, grumbling about having his sleep disturbed.

But some two weeks after her father's return, Keziah woke one morning feeling ill and weak. As she prepared the morning meal, the odors of the cooking food nauseated her. By later in the day she felt well. After this pattern had repeated itself over several days, Keziah was forced to admit to herself that there was something out of the ordinary going on with her body.

A horrible thought occurred to her—perhaps she might have conceived a child as a result of the attack. Surely not, she hoped. From just that one encounter? She needed to talk to someone. As she reflected on all the people she knew, she realized there was only one choice. Judith was her only friend, the only person, aside from little Adah, whom she trusted.

That afternoon Aaron was away to say a prayer of blessing on a new house. She knew his duties would take a while, so Keziah paid Judith a visit. Before reciting the blessing, her father would place the *mezuzah* box near the top of the right doorpost of the dwelling.

This practice had become popular since David had appointed Sheva the Tyrnian as his scribe. Sheva instructed the priests in the art of writing whenever they came to serve in Jerusalem. In turn, the priests and Levites often taught the young boys in their cities to write. The skill was becoming more common.

Aaron loved the mezuzah ceremony, since it gave him an opportunity to demonstrate what a learned man he was. Inside the small wooden box he would place a parchment he had inscribed with the words of Moses:

> Hear O Israel: Adonai is our God, Adonai alone. You shall love the LORD your God with all your heart, with all your soul, and with all your strength.
>
> And these words which I command you today shall be in your heart. You shall teach them diligently to your children, and shall talk of them when you sit in your house, when you walk by the way, when you lie down, and when you rise up.
>
> You shall bind them as a sign on your hand, and they shall be as frontlets between your eyes. You shall write them on the doorposts of your house and on your gates.

The dedication ceremony always took several hours because the family would ask the priest to stay for a meal of celebration.

As soon as Keziah arrived at her friend's house, Judith greeted her warmly.

"Sit," she ordered after taking in Keziah's strained features, "and tell me what is troubling you. Bad dreams again?"

Keziah sighed with relief and amazement at how well her friend discerned her mood. She didn't want to have to pretend to Judith.

"I wish it were only the nightmares that troubled me. At least I eventually wake up from them. I am afraid this won't go away so easily. But maybe I worry for nothing."

"What is it, Keziah? What troubles you?"

"It's just that I . . . I haven't been feeling well. My stomach is upset all the time and . . ." Keziah blushed and dropped her gaze from Judith's as she placed a hand over her breast. "I have been very tender here."

If she had secretly hoped her friend would allay her fears, Keziah was to be disappointed, for Judith paled and placed a hand over her mouth. Her soft brown eyes brimmed with tears of compassion. Shaking her head, Judith said nothing.

Finally, Keziah spoke. "It is true then. I carry a child from my shame. Oh, Judith, what am I to do? My father will find out. The disgrace! It will kill him."

Judith still said nothing; she merely rose from her seat and went to Keziah, enfolding her in a fierce hug. They remained that way for many moments, locked in an embrace, each feeling a sense of overwhelming anxiety. Judith finally managed to speak calmly and with assurance.

"Keziah, don't be afraid. You are a strong person. If you could save my daughter and live through what was done to you all those weeks ago, you will also survive this."

"How, Judith? How will I ever get through this? There seems to be no hope." There was desperation in Keziah's voice.

Judith hugged her friend again. "Shh . . . there is *always* hope. I will remain your friend, no matter what happens. We will cry out to God. He will answer our prayers."

Keziah tried hard to trust Judith's words. But right now God seemed very far away. And where had He been when those two vicious men had attacked?

It was quite late by the time Keziah finally left Judith's house. And she wouldn't have thought about the time even then had not Judith's huge, jovial husband interrupted them. Keziah jumped up in alarm. "Oh, I'm sorry! I didn't realize your husband was here."

The man appeared quite intimidating. His deep, resonant voice seemed to shake the beams of the house. Keziah supposed that all thirty of David's greatest warriors must be just as physically imposing.

Judith sensed her friend's unease and laid a reassuring hand on her shoulder. "It's all right, Keziah. Ahiam returned a few days ago. I forgot to mention it."

Again the booming voice sounded, but this time it was accompanied by a smile that radiated warmth toward her. Keziah knew she would never have anything to fear from this man. She liked him.

"Please, sit down and stay. I must wash off. I've been teaching goatherds and vineyard keepers to wield a sword today. It is hot and dusty work," Ahiam chuckled at his own jest but noticed that neither of the women seemed to be in a humor to appreciate it, so he made a hasty exit.

"Yes, do stay, Keziah. I don't want you to be alone at a time like this," Judith remarked kindly when her husband was gone.

"Oh, no. I simply must hurry home. My father will be wondering what has happened to me."

Keziah made a hasty retreat, feeling some resentment that she wouldn't have her friend to herself now that the husband and son had returned.

Where was the son, she wondered? With two men around, Keziah would feel most uncomfortable visiting Judith and Adah now. Perhaps she would send them word to visit her instead. Of course, her father discouraged her from having guests, but maybe she could arrange it when he was not at home.

As she hurried down the path that led to her house, Keziah hoped that she would arrive home before her father. But Aaron was awaiting her.

"Where have you been for so long, daughter? The sun is nearly set. It is almost Sabbath, and you haven't made preparation."

Keziah felt a moment of panic. She had completely forgotten that the Sabbath was upon them. She would not be able to light a fire, nor cook, nor do any housework until sunset tomorrow. She looked around rather desperately. The courtyard was swept clean, and there was no straightening to do.

She breathed a secret sigh of relief as she remembered that

the clay oven that stood in the courtyard was still hot with coals. Of course, it would have to be extinguished before the last rays of the sun disappeared. But there was a whole leg of lamb left from yesterday, and she had prepared two loaves of bread just this morning. She had been so distracted that she had hardly been aware of what she was doing. Thankfully, she had constantly cleaned and cooked in the last few weeks in order to keep from losing her mind.

"Well, girl, what is wrong with you? Give me an answer!" Keziah looked at her father's stern face for a long moment before it came to her what his question had been.

"I went to see my friend, Father. She is Judith, the wife of Ahiam. She and her daughter asked me to visit. Her husband, Ahiam, is one of the *Gibborim,* you know."

Keziah knew that the fact that Ahiam was a man of importance would cause her father to approve the friendship between her and Judith. She was not mistaken.

"Oh, very well then. But you have neglected your duties here, Keziah."

"No, Father. I prepared before I went out. I need only to warm the lamb in the oven before we eat. It will take only a few moments."

"A few moments is all you have before it is time to extinguish the fire."

"Oh, you can pour water over the coals now, Father, and I will put the lamb in afterward. The steam in the oven will finish heating it."

"How can you even suggest such a thing, Keziah? Adonai has commanded you not to cook on the Sabbath day. The steam from the oven is the same as a flame.

"But our neighbors. . . ."

"Our neighbors try to think of ways to avoid the strictures of the Law. We keep the Law in all points. Do you understand, girl?"

Keziah took in her father's face, mottled with anger, and tried to placate him.

"I'm sorry, Father. You are right. Forgive me." She slid the lamb into the oven even as she said this.

Within a couple of minutes, after standing there and watching, Aaron said testily, "It's time to take it out, daughter. It will be cold, of course. That is what happens when you go running about from house to house. You are not to do such in the future."

Aaron mumbled and complained all through the Sabbath meal. It left Keziah feeling quite nauseated. She prayed that her father would not notice, but he eyed her closely. "What is the matter with you, Keziah? Are you becoming ill?"

"No, no, Father. I am fine."

All the next day, her mind was in a turmoil. What would become of her? What would her father do when he found out? She couldn't tell her father the truth of what had happened, though that had been Judith's advice to her.

Judith just did not know Aaron. Ordinarily, if a young girl found herself pregnant without being married, her father or older brother would force the offending man to marry her immediately. He would also pay her father a fine and the union could never be dissolved.

But this was a case of rape, and to marry a man who would do such a thing was unthinkable. The man who had done this to her was a monster!

Besides, she didn't even know who he was. Even if that could be determined, it was likely that Aaron would seek the death penalty for the man. And Keziah knew that her father was no match for the sheer, cold evil of her molester. If Aaron brought a charge against him, he might even kill her father. Keziah couldn't allow that to happen.

Her father's most likely reaction would be to blame Keziah totally for the incident and have her stoned. Judith's eyes had widened in alarm when Keziah had told her as much.

"It is true," Keziah had insisted, "he would have me put to death, for that is the fate a daughter of a priest faces if she has been wanton."

But Judith had remained adamant. "You are mistaken, my dear. No father would treat a virtuous daughter in such a way. Oh, I can see Aaron banishing you if you were a complete wanton, for I have heard that he is a stern man. But the sentence of stoning is almost never carried out, even though the Law allows for it. Surely your father honors the principle of mercy, Keziah. Even Moses called the Almighty a God of mercy."

Keziah had realized then that Judith had no idea what her father was like. Her friend's own husband and grown son must be men of compassion and mercy. How different she might have felt if her father were like them. What would it be like if she could have called for him, even at the beginning, and had him come and offer her comfort and guidance as to what to do? The idea was beyond her imagination.

Judith had been sweeping the smooth dirt surface of the courtyard when she heard laughter from the street. Ahiam was talking to someone, and they were headed for the house. She set her broom aside. Who would he be bringing home at this early hour? If it was an important guest, she must not be seen until she made herself presentable. Then she heard Ahiam's distinctive laugh, followed by another familiar voice. It was Isaac! She reached the gate just as the men entered. Judith embraced her tall, handsome son as Ahiam stood by for a moment, grinning at the reunion.

"You changed your mind," Judith said happily, kissing Isaac's cheeks for the third time. "I knew you couldn't bear to spend your entire leave with Jonathan in Ziph. Come in. Come in. Adah will be so happy. She's playing on the rooftop."

As Judith led the way through the gate and into the courtyard, Adah came hurtling down the stairs, flying into her brother's arms. She squealed as he swung her up over his head and held her there.

"I knew you would come! I knew it! Jonathan gets to see you all the time. It wouldn't be fair for you to stay in Ziph the whole time and not see us. I told Ahmi, didn't I?"

"Yes, you did, dear. Now run out and play. Allow your brother to catch his breath."

At Judith's words, Adah motioned for her mother to bend down and whispered in her ear. Judith nodded permission and Adah skipped off to visit her secret friend, Keziah.

The morning after Sabbath, Keziah served her father his meal, then forced herself to nibble a small piece of bread. She was relieved that her father left home before the usual nausea overcame her.

A half-hour later, Keziah was in the flower garden her mother had planted behind the house, being wretchedly ill, when Aaron returned unexpectedly.

"What is wrong with you, girl?" he asked sharply. "You have been behaving strangely ever since I returned from Jerusalem."

Keziah turned to face her father, blotting her mouth with the edge of her tunic. "It is nothing, father. Just something I ate."

Aaron's eyes narrowed. "How could that be when you have had the same ailment several times recently?" Aaron stepped toward her, his hands closing around Keziah's shoulders. "What is wrong, Keziah? Tell me now!"

"Father . . . I . . ."

"What is it you have done? Do not lie to me!"

"Father, please don't be angry. I have done nothing wrong!"

"But you are pale and ill each day. What is the reason?"

Keziah could not bring a lie to her lips, so she bowed her head and said nothing. Her father shook her forcefully, so hard that her head snapped back.

"Have you done wickedly? Has a daughter of mine played the harlot and lain with one of the young men of Hebron, or perhaps, Adoraim?"

"No, Father, no!"

"Are you with child, girl? Tell me now!"

"Oh, Father." Keziah started to cry as she realized she would have to tell her father the entire story. She almost felt relief that the fear and suspense were over.

Maybe she would find out she had been wrong. Perhaps her father would enfold her in his arms and tell her everything would be all right, that he would avenge her honor, that he would take care of her and the child.

A sharp slap to her right cheek interrupted her thoughts.

"Confess now, Keziah. I would know of your filthiness in your own words." The priest slapped her again.

"I am so sorry, Father. Two men . . . they attacked me on the road to Adoraim. I tried to fight them, but they were too strong for me. They threw me over a cliff, thinking they had killed me. They. . . ."

"I wish they had!" Aaron yelled. His face turned almost purple in his fury. "Now I'll have to do it myself. It isn't right that I suffer because of your wickedness." He slapped Keziah again and then left the room briefly, returning with a long, thin rod. He lashed out with it. Keziah lifted her arm to protect her face, but the blow raised an ugly welt.

"Father, no! They forced me. I tell you the truth!"

"You lie. And even if it were true, you will still bear a bastard. People will not believe you, and they will cut me off, turn me out of the priesthood. No man whose daughter commits harlotry can be a priest."

Aaron's voice was growing louder and more strident with each word. As he raised the rod again, Keziah stepped back and tripped over a stool. She sprawled on the floor. Her father kicked her in the side, then continued to kick and hit her as he called out epithets concerning her lack of virtue. Keziah could only try to curl herself in a tight ball for protection.

Aaron gave full vent to his rage, unaware that a pair of frightened little eyes were watching. He heard the sound of a pot being knocked over on the patio outside the window, but the noise didn't really register. Aaron was held in the grip of his anger, not really consciously trying to kill Keziah or her baby, but wishing the problem would go away.

Chapter Seven

As she hurried to Keziah's house, Adah tried to think of some way to persuade her friend to return with her to her home. She wanted Keziah to get to know her brother Isaac; she had slipped away the last time he was home. But Adah didn't really hold out any hope that Keziah would come willingly. Why, just three days ago she had left quickly when she found out Ahbi was there. She just didn't seem to want to be around people. Adah felt certain it was because of those wicked men. Her young heart ached for her friend, and she longed to make it up to Keziah that she had run away like a coward after Keziah had protected her and been hurt by those awful men.

Having been lost in her thoughts, Adah was surprised to find herself so quickly at the gate of Keziah's house. She opened it quietly. Adah knew that grown-ups sometimes disliked noisy children, and she hoped to make a good impression of Keziah's father. She stood just inside the gate and listened.

Thwack. Thwack.

It sounded like something was being beaten. Was Keziah knocking the dust out of a rug with her broom?

Thwack.

This time the sound was followed by a low moan. Then Adah heard a man's voice, raised in anger.

"Name the man! Name him, Keziah, or I'll flay every inch of skin from your back!"

Adah crept close to the window from which the sound came and peeked in. An older man gripped a long, slender rod in his hand. This must be Keziah's father, the priest. Keziah crouched on the floor, whimpering. When the rod came down viciously on Keziah's back, Adah almost jumped through the window to intervene. Her friend was being hurt again! Then she thought of Ahmi and Ahbi and Isaac. They could deal with the priest much better than she. So Adah turned to run for home as fast as her feet would carry her. She scarcely noticed the flower pot she overturned in her haste.

"Ahbi, Ahmi, he's hurting her! Come help me make him stop, Ahbi!"

Adah burst into the house, interrupting a funny story Ahiam and Isaac had been telling Judith about a warrior who had awakened to find a small mouse tangled in his hair.

"What are you shouting about, Adah? Calm down so that Ahmi and I can hear you," Ahiam admonished. A shocked look came over his face when his daughter burst into tears.

"It's just like when the bad men hurt her, Ahmi. Please help Keziah, quickly," she pleaded.

Judith knelt down and took Adah's small face in her hands. "Who is hurting her, Adah?" Then an awful thought crossed her mind. "The bad men haven't come back, have they? to Hebron?"

"What bad men?" Isaac questioned impatiently. Adah and Judith both ignored him. "No, Ahmi, the priest, her father. He is beating her with a rod."

"Come!" Judith called over her shoulder as she ran from the house. Since they didn't know whom she had addressed, the entire family followed—Ahiam, then Isaac, and finally Adah.

When they reached the house of Aaron, Judith paused for a moment. "Keziah! Keziah, are you here?"

She heard the distinct sound of a moan, and a few moments later Keziah, her clothes disheveled and her hair in tangled disarray around her face, appeared at the door. There was a red mark in the shape of a hand upon her cheek.

Clearly taken aback at the sight of a group of people accompanying her friend, Keziah straightened and winced at the pain in her side. "Oh, Judith, I am fine, truly I am." But the desperate look in her eyes gave away the lie to her reassurance.

Isaac found himself strangely moved by her eyes. They were an unusual color of reddish brown that almost exactly matched the color of her hair and they were filled with hopeless sorrow.

Why was the daughter of a respected priest in such despair? Isaac had seen the man many times but could not remember having ever noticed his daughter. Judith had mentioned that the girl was an only child and that her mother had died years ago.

One would assume her father would cherish her. But something must be very wrong here. Isaac remembered the day of their brief meeting. He had noticed a fading bruise on her cheek. Had Aaron the priest been responsible for it or the other "bad men" Adah had mentioned?

Judith must have had the same reaction as her son, for she went to gather the girl in her arms. Keziah gave a sharp gasp and flinched away, but Isaac took her by the arm and turned her around. He uttered a gasp of his own when he saw that the back of her tunic was shredded in several places. Blood stains seeped through the torn cloth.

"Who would do such a thing?" Isaac growled in anger. When the girl flinched at the sound of his voice, he felt guilty for frightening her. "Don't be afraid," he continued. "We just want to help you."

"Yes, Keziah," Adah piped up, "we won't let your father hurt you any more. You can come home with us like you did before. . . ."

"Before?" Isaac roared. "He has done this before?" As Keziah flinched, he again chastised himself for scaring her. He carefully moderated his voice and continued. "Your father has beaten you before?"

Isaac knew that parents had every right to beat their children, but Judith and Ahiam had used the rod with love and compassion; they never would have drawn blood! Isaac thought it disgraceful for a man to treat either his wife or children in such a cruel way.

He noticed that his sister had covered her mouth with her hand as if to stop any more uncensored words from coming out. What was going on here? Judith, Adah, and Keziah all looked as if they had kicked over the bucket and spilled the cream. "Your father has beaten you before?" he asked again.

"No," Keziah answered. "I mean, yes, but not about this. Oh, please, just leave before my father gets back." She looked at Judith when she said it. *Why won't she look at me?* Isaac wondered.

"You need your back tended to," Judith observed. "I will stay, Keziah, but the others will go home."

But Ahiam shook his head. "Judith, I won't leave you alone here to face an angry man."

Hearing the determination in his voice, Judith nodded. "Very well, but wait outside in the courtyard. Try to calm the priest if he returns before I finish. But Keziah and I must be alone."

"I'll take Adah back home," Isaac offered. He wanted to get his little sister alone so he could question her. Like Ahiam, Adah balked at being asked to leave, but Judith assured her that she would take care of Keziah. Reluctantly, the girl agreed to go, but before doing so, she wrapped her arms around Keziah's legs and promised, "If your Ahbi is mean, you can come stay with me in my room this time."

This time? Isaac stroked his beard, wondering.

"Adah," Isaac asked as they walked home, "when did Keziah get beaten before, and who did it?"

Adah looked up guiltily. "I'm not supposed to tell. Keziah said."

"Oh. Then tell me about when Keziah stayed with you."

Adah thought for a moment as if to consider whether this information were also confidential. Deciding that it wasn't, she told her brother, "It was . . . in the month of Ayar—three moons ago— Ahmi let Keziah use your room since you were gone. Do you think Keziah will be all right?"

He really shouldn't trick a child, he knew, but Isaac needed to know what happened. "I think she will be safe enough from her father. But I'm not sure we can help protect her from the bad men unless you tell me what they look like so Ahbi and I will know to recognize them in case they come back."

Adah again took time to consider before answering. "One was old and very ugly. He had two teeth missing, but not like when I lost mine. He had one tooth missing on either side of his front ones. It made him look frightful when he smiled. He was older than Ahbi. The younger one called him Ishobeam. I think Ishobeam was his servant."

"And the other man was younger?"

Adah nodded solemnly. "He was somewhat older than you. Not much. He didn't look as frightening as his servant, but he was much worse. He let the other man tease me. And when Keziah came to help me, I think he was the one who hurt her so much. But I'm not sure, because they were gone by the time I came back and found her. I shouldn't have run away like she said. I should have stayed."

"I see," said Isaac, though he really didn't see at all.

"She saved me, Isaac," Adah blurted, rubbing her eyes very hard as if to keep from crying.

"Don't worry, she will be all right, little one. Mother will help her."

Judith and Ahiam waited for more than two hours and Aaron still had not returned to his house. Keziah finally persuaded them to go home.

"I know my father will not harm me further," she assured them with a confidence she did not really feel. "He gave me the beating he thought I deserved. He may decide to throw me out, but I'm sure he won't actually harm me."

"If he does, will you come to us?" Ahiam asked, and Keziah felt a wave of gratitude for the man's generosity. He had just come back from Rabbah and found his family embroiled in this unpleasant situation. She knew Ahiam and Judith would not leave until she agreed, so she nodded her head in assent. But she would do all she could to avoid dragging them further into her problem.

~ ~ ~

By the time his parents had returned, Isaac was waiting with questions. "Quite a lot happened while Father and I were gone, I gather. I coaxed Adah into telling me some of it. Now I would like to hear the rest, Mother. Have you already confided in Father?"

Judith sighed. "Not yet, but I promised him I would. I hate to break my promise to Keziah, but you have been brought into it now. Let me put Adah to bed and I'll tell you everything."

"I already put Adah to bed. She was worried about her friend but very tired. She's already asleep."

"Then I might as well tell you now."

Soon, Ahiam and Isaac knew the full story of Keziah's rescue of Adah at the risk of her own life.

"We owe her much," Ahiam said, his voice gruff with emotion.

"And her father beat her when he found out?" said Isaac, his voice rising. "Didn't he think she had suffered enough?"

"He didn't believe her," Judith answered as she placed a finger over her lips to remind him not to wake his sleeping sister.

"Why would any woman make up such a story? Besides, there is Adah to corroborate what happened."

"Keziah told her father that," Judith replied, but he thinks the testimony of a child is not trustworthy enough for him, especially as it concerns the people of Hebron."

"The people of Hebron? Why would anyone have to know

about this but those of us who know already? Unless the molesters come back. Then I'll gladly kill them."

"Everyone will have to know, son," Isaac's mother replied softly. Ahiam squeezed his eyes tightly shut and shook his head in dismay as he comprehended what Judith was saying. Isaac did not.

"How so?" he asked.

Judith's large eyes filled with tears. "She carries a child, Isaac. From the attack. She came to me to confirm it just three days ago. When we were with her, she told me—her father guessed the truth when he found her being sick this morning. I have tried to think of a solution but could come up with none. Oh, how I wish I had reported this attack immediately. Now, after so much time has passed, Aaron may be right. Keziah might not be believed, even with Adah's testimony."

Isaac felt his stomach turn over at his mother's words. Oh, Lord, how could anyone suffer such things without going mad? And then to be beaten when the truth of what she had suffered came to light? As for the reaction of the good people of Hebron, Isaac knew well that they would make the girl and her child outcasts. A self-righteous lot, no doubt about it. His father seemed to agree.

"People are likely to think that the girl is making up an excuse for being with child," Ahiam said. "Maybe if her father threw all his influence into protecting her, it would be different, but he has already demonstrated his position."

"Ahiam," Judith turned to her husband. "Keziah told me that Aaron threatened her with stoning. You don't think he would seriously consider such a thing, do you? I mean, she is his own flesh and blood, after all, his only child."

"Maybe he was overcome with shock. It would be a terrible thing for any father to learn."

"But, Ahiam, you would never act in such a way. It could have been our own daughter to suffer so, but for Keziah." The tears now began to spill down Judith's cheeks.

“Come now. You have done all you could. We will see to Keziah tomorrow. But tonight we all need rest.”

“Would you stay for a moment, Father? Adah described the men to me in some detail, and I think you should know what they look like. We may be able to identify them, especially if they’re bold enough to show themselves in Hebron.”

When Isaac had finished relating Adah’s account of the attackers, Ahiam sought his rest. Isaac retired also, but sleep eluded him. He kept seeing a pair of beautiful, suffering eyes and blood oozing from soft flesh that had been torn by a chastening rod. And when sleep finally came, he dreamed of a girl being dragged outside the city to be stoned.

~ ~ ~

Aaron did not return home that night. He did not think he could bear the sight of his daughter. Years ago, his father had been given a vineyard a short distance outside the city as a payment of tithe that each tribe owed the Levites. Aaron’s father had built a watchtower there. During harvest time, vineyard owners manned these watchtowers to make sure thieves did not steal the grapes. The tower had not been used for several years, but it provided a decent temporary shelter. There was even an old leather pallet left inside, but Aaron did not use it.

Instead, the priest paced back and forth atop the tower as he tried to deal with this tremendous blow to his pride. Filled with self-pity, he cried and raged to God. How could this kind of disgrace have happened to him? Hadn’t he always been meticulous in his service to Adonai? Always kept the Law? Hadn’t he guarded his daughter’s purity, refusing to allow her to mix with other youth of Hebron? Had he not just spent days in Jerusalem trying to arrange a suitable marriage for her?

His anger, at first directed toward God, gradually shifted to Keziah. Her flaming hair and full wide mouth had always proclaimed that she would go astray. And she was useless, utterly useless, nothing but a burden to him. No man would pay a bride price for her now. As soon as he found another wife to take over the household duties, he would be better off without her.

As the hours passed, Aaron continued to pace in his agitated state, trying to decide what to do. Find her a husband? Not likely any respectable man would accept her. He could hide Keziah's condition. No, that wasn't possible. At the point of the consummation of the marriage, all would come to light and he would bear more public shame than ever.

He seriously considered beating the girl until she lost the baby, but he was afraid it wouldn't work. Worse yet, he might have to answer questions if Keziah died of the beating. He began to mull over the instructions in the Law concerning this kind of situation.

When the idea to have his daughter stoned and burned first occurred to him, he had dismissed it with a shudder, but the words of the Law of Moses continued to echo through his mind. A daughter of a priest or Levite who prostituted herself was to be stoned, then burned with fire. By the time the sky over Hebron began to pinken with the dawn, the priest had decided to have his daughter, his only child, executed and burned.

~ ~ ~

The next morning, Isaac was up early, talking to the merchants in the city market, listening to Hebron's elders discuss city business and exchange gossip. He wanted to be there in the event anything was said about punishing Keziah.

He did not see Aaron the priest. But about noon, Asher, one of the elders and a stone mason by trade, approached a group of the city leaders.

"I bring a message from Aaron the priest. An hour from now all the elders and the leaders of the city will convene under the big oaks."

One of the merchants, disgruntled at the prospect of having to close his business down for a meeting spoke up.

"What is the purpose of this meeting?"

"I am unsure, but I believe it is a serious offense that may carry the penalty of stoning."

The stir that rippled through the marketplace assured that no one would miss this event even despite any inconvenience it caused.

City business was often conducted under the big oaks where, according to the Torah, Abraham had rested, since Hebron had no walls, and therefore no city gate.

"Does no one know what this is about?" Simon the vinedresser asked.

"He said it concerned a matter of iniquity. It must be an abomination if Aaron thinks it may call for a death penalty," another elder speculated.

"Aaron is certainly one for rooting out iniquity," old Eliazer observed. "I wonder who he's after this time. Hope it isn't me."

The entire crowd chuckled nervously, everyone, that is, except Isaac. As soon as he heard the word *stoning,* the bile had risen in his throat.

Isaac quickly left the group in the marketplace and went in search of his father. Surely Aaron would not do such a thing. Surely not. Still, Isaac would be there, along with Ahiam. Just in case.

~ ~ ~

Keziah had not seen her father since he had beaten her and stormed out of the house the night before. She had gone about in a daze, doing everyday duties without really thinking about them. She prepared a meal for Aaron, not knowing when or if he would be back. Each time she stooped or turned, her smarting back reminded her of their last encounter.

She thought of Judith and her family. They had come to her aid. Judith and Ahiam had stayed with her until she had insisted they leave. She needed her friend with her, but her fear of her father's reaction surpassed her need for comfort.

Still, Keziah couldn't help but hope they would appear again. When they did not, she tried to tell herself that it didn't matter. Judith was simply obeying Keziah's request that they stay away.

When the sun was straight up in the sky, Aaron came into the courtyard. She pushed back a lock of hair that had fallen in her face. "Father, I have the meal ready for you. Are you hungry now?"

Aaron was not placated by her offering. "There is no time for eating. Get your cloak and your head covering and come with me." He showed no expression, but his eyes were as cold as ice. Keziah shivered at the look but slowly complied.

Without a word, Aaron led her down the lanes of Hebron to the oak grove of Mamre outside the city. As usual when they were out in public, she followed several strides behind her father with her head covered. A growing crowd of men and a few women stood under the ancient oaks.

Keziah's mouth went dry. Her heart started to pound. "Father, what are we doing here?" she asked, trying unsuccessfully to keep the fear out of her voice.

"You will see," was all he answered, as he drew her toward the center of the gathering. People began gaping at her with open curiosity. Keziah recognized most of the men as the elders of the city. *Oh, no. surely Father isn't going to speak of my shame. Surely he isn't going to demand that they help him find the man who attacked me. I can't look at them. I can't.* She dropped her gaze, then, without thought, pulled her head covering closer about her face. She didn't see the compassionate looks on the faces of three people in the gathering.

Isaac stood next to Ahiam and Judith at the back of the crowd. He felt glad they had left Adah at home with Rachel. It was possible that this would turn into something a child shouldn't see. He saw Keziah stop once and ask her father something. Aaron paused, then motioned her forward.

"He's really going to go through with this," Ahiam said in a low voice. "If he does condemn her, don't let him say too much before you interrupt."

"Are you certain you want to do this?" Judith whispered.

"She saved Adah's life. We have to do something."

"Why did you call us here in the heat of the day?" old Eliazer asked.

"It concerns my daughter. You all know what the Law requires concerning the daughter of the priest?"

"She has to be virtuous," a gray-haired woman answered.

"She can't bring shame on her father," another voice piped up.

"That is right," Aaron agreed. "And I have brought my daughter before you today because I would not fail in my responsibility as a priest to keep sin outside the camp, even if it concerns my own daughter."

Time seemed to stand still for Keziah. There was a ringing in her ears as she realized that her father was talking about punishing her. The Law of Moses called for an unchaste daughter of a priest to be stoned and her body burned, and she realized that Aaron would be the first to light the pyre. He would not hesitate to burn her in the sight of all Hebron. A voice in her head screamed for her to run, but her feet seemed to be nailed to the spot. Then she felt someone brush by her as he made his way to Aaron's side.

"We all know that the Law demands—"

"Don't tell them, my friend. Let me have the honor," a voice boomed from the back of the crowd, interrupting Aaron's solemn monologue.

"What?" Aaron asked.

"I said, let me make the announcement."

"About Keziah?" Aaron asked, confused.

Throwing an arm loosely around Aaron's shoulders, Ahiam said, "About Keziah, of course, and my son Isaac."

"Your son?"

Ahiam nodded affably, then addressed the crowd. "Aaron and I would like you to witness the marriage contract between our two children. Due to the war, my son and I must leave in only three more days. Therefore, we call you to witness the clasping of our hands in agreement and invite you all to the marriage supper tomorrow evening. The feasting will continue the next day. I regret that we cannot celebrate our joy for an entire week, but perhaps we will be able to continue it as soon as we have defeated the Ammonites."

Fishlike, Aaron's mouth opened and shut several times. He had clearly been rendered speechless by the turn of events, and Ahiam took full advantage. "You are all invited to the wedding feast," he shouted good naturedly. "Come early and join the procession to Aaron's house to fetch the bride."

People clapped and shouted congratulations to Keziah and Isaac as well as to Aaron and Ahiam. Of course, most of them believed that this talk of punishment and the Law had been a ploy by a worried father to bring a young man to the point of commitment to his daughter. They assumed that, like so many young people in Israel, Keziah and Isaac had impetuously followed their youthful passions, and now the two fathers were trying to rectify the matter.

Judith stepped forward and gently took Keziah's arm. "Do not worry, all will be well," she whispered as she led the young woman away.

The small group, consisting of Aaron, Keziah, Ahiam, Judith, and Isaac, made their way to the priest's house. Keziah's mind was reeling from all that had happened, and she supposed the others must feel much as she did because no one spoke.

Aaron waited until they were at last inside the courtyard before loosing his anger. He shouted at Ahiam as if unaware the powerful warrior could snap him like a twig if he chose.

"What is the meaning of this? Why would you announce that Keziah and your son are to be married? Are you insane? The wedding must go forward now. Did you think to stop her just punishment and then somehow not honor a public contract? That must be what you had planned. Why else would you want a girl such as this one completely dishonored and ruined?"

Aaron did not wait for a reply before turning on Isaac. "Unless you are the one who is responsible! Is it your child she is to bear? It must be. Why else would you want her? Our families have never spoken of an alliance. The child must be yours!"

Isaac's eyes flashed angrily, but he answered calmly. "Yes, the baby will be mine and Keziah will be mine. You will be careful which words you choose when you speak of them in the future. Now, with your permission I would like to take Keziah for a walk in the rear courtyard. You have a lovely flower garden there, do you not?"

Seeing the surprised look on Aaron's face, he explained, "It can be seen from the road above it. I always admired it when I passed by. Now, since Keziah and I have many things to discuss, you will excuse us." He nodded to Keziah to join him.

She seemed to be engrossed with the mosaic pattern on the floor, so he gently took her arm and led her outside. He stopped under the spreading branches of a large oak tree. "Keziah, is there anything you wish to say, anything you want to know?"

"Why are you doing this?"

"You saved my sister's life."

"Perhaps, but marrying me is taking gratitude too far, don't you think?"

"Not if it is also very convenient to do so."

"Convenient?"

"Yes. It is time my parents found a wife for me anyway. This way I am saving myself and them the bother of traveling to other towns, haggling over the marriage settlement, and having to make a choice. It is time for me to marry, and you need a husband, so, here we are. It should be beneficial for us both."

"But, you could have any girl you want. Your father is one of the *Gibborim.* You will probably have that honor yourself some day. It is foolish to choose a ruined girl, one who is going to have another man's child. I thank you for rescuing me, I truly do. But you should reconsider. You must! We can tell our fathers that a marriage between us would be disastrous, beg them to mutually agree to break the contract." She stopped when Isaac laid two fingers across her lips.

"Please, don't say anymore. I am telling the truth when I say it would suit me very well to marry you. If you would have the complete truth, then I will give it to you. I love a woman who can never be mine. Since I cannot have her, it is best that I choose someone else, because I will never love another. So if I am not too repugnant in your sight, I would be pleased to be your husband."

Keziah opened her mouth to respond, but he silenced her again in the same way. *His hands are warm and gentle,* she thought to herself.

"I would have you know you need not fear me, Keziah. I will never hurt you in any way. Sometime in the future you will become my wife in truth, but not until you are ready. And as for using a rod on you, I would never strike a woman. Do you believe me?" He felt a great sense of relief when she silently nodded her assent.

"But, what of the child?" she asked fearfully.

"I will not lie to you, Keziah. I will fervently pray that the child is a girl. And if the Lord wills, I will have an heir of my own seed. But if your child is a boy, I will accept him as my firstborn and he will be my heir. This I vow to you. Now, will you have me . . . willingly?"

Tears glistened in Keziah's eyes. The man was offering her salvation; she should be happy. She should simply accept and vow her eternal gratitude. But the overriding sense of fear and dread that had come over her since she had discovered her pregnancy still hung like a dark cloud over her mind. It made her heart pound and clogged her throat. This wasn't right. Nothing would ever be right again.

"Keziah?" It was a demand that she answer. What choice did she have? Well, whatever her fate as Isaac's wife, it could certainly be no worse than what had already befallen her, or what would happen if she refused the safety and respectability of marriage to him.

The word did not want to leave her throat, but she forced it out. "Yes."

"Then it will be done tomorrow night. My father and I will have to report back to Jerusalem in three days. You will live with my mother. If anything happens to me in battle . . . well, you know my mother. And my father is the same. You will always be their daughter. You and your child will be loved and protected. Is this enough to bring you contentment?"

When Keziah only stared at him with a bewildered look, it occurred to Isaac that she might love someone, might still be hoping that the man would have her as his wife despite the circumstances. But it was highly unlikely. Most men would not even consider taking a woman who carried another man's child.

Still, he had to ask. "There was no other man whom you wished to be your husband? No other marriage contract negotiations?"

"No, my father wished to wed me to a son of one of the priestly families in Jerusalem. But he hadn't started formal negotiations yet. I believe he wished to find another wife for himself before he let me marry. There is no other choice for me than what you have offered. I am so thankful, and I will do my best to make you glad you did this."

Her almost worshipful look made Isaac feel guilty, and he looked away. As he had lain awake through the hours of the previous night, he had concluded marrying Keziah would offer him an escape from his guilt over the way he felt about Ailea. It would help him avoid either of two scenarios he had envisioned for choosing a wife.

The first scenario would be to marry for bloodlines or wealth with no emotion involved. Such an arrangement would be like the purchase of any commodity. That kind of marriage seemed cold and barren to Isaac, since he had grown up in the presence of deep love and respect such as his parents shared, and seen the same commitment in Jonathan and Ailea.

He realized that he had very strong, protective feelings toward Keziah. He wanted to heal the hurt he saw deep in her eyes. As for her feelings toward him, she obviously needed him and felt gratitude. Surely their marriage would not be cold and heartless if based on protectiveness and gratitude.

The other marriage option was the one he had really shied away from—marriage to a girl who gave him her whole heart when he could not give his. Three years of trying unsuccessfully to get over her had taught him that it would always belong to Ailea.

Knowing how it felt to love and not have that love returned, he didn't want a wife who would suffer the same pangs he had. It wasn't a matter of love between Keziah and him; it was simple necessity for her and convenience for him. Such an arrangement would do very well.

Isaac felt almost lighthearted by the time he and his family were ready to take their leave of Keziah and her father.

Isaac searched his mind for something respectful to say to Aaron that wouldn't be a lie. He settled on, "We are your family now. I will care for your daughter and do my duty to you as a son would."

"I have no son," Aaron responded.

Having seen Aaron's treatment of his daughter, Isaac knew he shouldn't be shocked by the venom in the older man's voice. But coming from the loving family of his birth, the words still felt like a cold slap. Isaac bristled.

"You do have a daughter, and I will see that no one ever hurts her again." With that veiled threat hanging in the dusty air, Isaac, Judith, and Ahiam departed.

The meal Isaac shared with his family that evening was subdued, quite unlike their usual lively dinners. Even Adah seemed overawed, though she had been thrilled to learn that Keziah was to become her sister.

"She will make a good wife," she solemnly announced to her brother. "Keziah is very brave—as brave as Deborah when she led our people against Jabin's army."

Isaac could not suppress a smile at the precociousness his sister displayed in her speech.

"Come with me now, little one," Ahiam said to his daughter. You promised to tell me once again what you saw on the road to Adoraim that day."

"So you can look out for those bad men and protect me and Keziah," Adah proclaimed with unflagging confidence. She placed her small hand in her father's large one, and they left the room. Isaac excused himself a short time later.

His mother sought him out in his room before he slept. "Isaac, my heart is burdened, even though I am so proud of you because you saved Keziah. I'm afraid that later you might regret having done this."

Judith paused for a moment, touched her son's hand, then continued.

"When Keziah stayed with Adah and me, I came to love her. She is a very fine person. But you can't know that. You have scarcely even spoken to her. I had wished you the kind of marriage your father and I have, but . . ."

Isaac reached out and stroked his mother's hair. "I know you want the best for me, Mother. Believe me when I say I want this woman to be my wife."

Chapter Eight

The only people who truly seem to be in the spirit of celebration at this wedding, aside from Adah, are Jonathan and Ailea, Isaac mused as he sat beside his bride in the place of honor at the feast. He was relieved and a little surprised that neither Jonathan nor Ailea seemed to think anything was amiss in this hasty union. Or they were concealing their concern very well.

A runner had been sent to Adoraim to invite Keziah's aunt and uncle. Likewise, a messenger had been dispatched to Ziph to invite Jonathan's family to the marriage. The two families were so close that it would have been very awkward to explain later why they hadn't been invited.

They had arrived in Hebron this morning accompanied by Jonathan's father, Shageh. The entire family had congratulated him and had expressed their interest in befriending Keziah. Ailea, especially, had declared that she would soon be as close to Keziah as she was to Judith, her best friend.

Isaac briefly wondered if this might not be awkward, given his feelings for Ailea. Then he remembered that his mother had told him that Aaron had kept Keziah so isolated that she had very few friends, and he decided that it would be a good thing for Ailea to befriend her. He would just remove himself from their proximity when they were together.

Aaron stood with a frown on his face during much of the celebration. Isaac was surprised that he wasn't rejoicing that his daughter had been saved from disgrace. It even crossed his mind that Aaron might be out of sorts that he had been thwarted in his attempt to have Keziah executed. Surely not. Even a father as mean-spirited as Aaron would not wish such a thing. Isaac supposed he still felt that his daughter had betrayed him.

When he and his friends had retrieved Keziah from Aaron's house, Isaac had seen the shame she felt. She had no fine new bridal clothes; she wore no jewelry other than a headband of a few small silver coins, which Isaac found out later had belonged to her mother. She wore no chaplet of gold coins as most brides did to display their dowry. Aaron had shown his disdain for his daughter by sending her to her husband without a dowry. The man was certainly coldhearted, Isaac thought.

As he greeted the guests, he noticed that most of them were filled with avid curiosity over just what had happened with that hastily convened meeting with the city elders. He could almost see their minds churning with questions over this union. It made Isaac feel naked and exposed before them. The worst, though, was Shageh.

The Rab kissed Isaac and Keziah, then placed his gnarled hands on each of their heads, giving them his blessing. His eyes were filled with compassion and far too much awareness. It made Isaac uncomfortable. How did the old man always seem to know what was in people's hearts?

Isaac found Shageh's uncanny gift comforting but also somewhat disturbing. His feelings for Ailea remained hidden from everyone, Isaac was sure; especially from Jonathan and Ailea. But occasionally the Rab had cast him a probing look that made Isaac wonder if the wise man of Ziph knew the depths of feeling Isaac felt for his daughter-in-law.

For that reason Isaac had recently avoided Shageh, afraid that somehow he would look right into Isaac's soul and see the covetous thoughts toward his friend's wife that he fought so hard to banish. When Shageh finished his blessing on the marriage and moved away, Isaac breathed a sigh of relief.

He knew that his bride had sensed his discomfort, because she had stiffened up after the Rab had passed by. He tried to smile at her, but his feelings were so confused that he could barely force himself to pay attention to the conversations his guests tried to hold with him.

The feast, such as it was, did not last long into the night as was customary. The guests, made uncomfortable by the scene of the day before and the obvious constraint between the bride and groom, drifted away throughout the evening.

When it was time to go to his bride, there was scarcely anyone left except for Jonathan and his family, who were to spend the night. It was an awkward moment when Ailea offered to go with Judith to assist Keziah in readying herself for the groom.

Keziah's face flamed. "No, I don't want anyone to—I mean, it will be enough if Judith comes with me." The bride looked pleadingly at Judith, who seemed to sense what was bothering her new daughter-in-law. Hoping to comfort the young bride, Ailea began to relate her own experience.

"I seriously considered running away on my wedding day. Here I was a captive bride in a foreign country. All the village women hated me; I was convinced my groom did also!"

Keziah's eyes widened, and her face broke into the first genuine smile anyone had seen all day. With a puzzled look, she turned to Judith, "Is she speaking the truth?"

"I'm afraid she is, Keziah," she laughingly replied as she gently placed her arm around the shoulders of her new daughter-in-law. "Perhaps Ailea should come with us and finish telling the story. It's really quite amazing."

As Judith and Ailea prepared Keziah for her groom, they kept up a steady stream of amusing chatter to divert her mind from any fear.

“It’s time for Ailea and me to leave now,” Judith told her some time later. “None of this nonsense of a great number of people escorting the couple to the bridal chamber. Everyone realizes things are being much more simply done in this case due to the fact that Isaac and Ahiam must rejoin the army immediately. You and Isaac will be left alone.”

The look of relief on Keziah’s face was obvious. Often at a large wedding feast great ceremony was made over the consummation of the marriage, which was embarrassing to any bride, but especially to Keziah, under the circumstances. Judith’s heart went out to her. And to Isaac as well. Would her son come to regret his gallant decision to rescue Keziah by marrying her?

When Isaac entered his small chamber a short time later, Keziah was waiting under the covers of the bed. He lifted the small oil lamp he carried to better see her. She was shaking like a leaf in a stiff wind. *Of course she is terrified. What did you expect after what has happened to her? And we do not even know each other.*

He spoke softly in what he hoped was a soothing voice. “Keziah, I know this is very strange. Our marriage has happened very suddenly—not in the ordinary way of things at all, where our fathers might have betrothed us years ago, giving us an opportunity to know each other well, or at least to get used to the idea of marriage.

“I do not want you to be afraid of me ever, Keziah. Please look at me.” When she complied he continued. “I would never hurt you. I am your lord and protector now, and I will care for you as I would myself. I would give my life to keep you safe.”

“Oh, I know that, Isaac. And I am grateful. But . . .”

“Are you afraid that your attackers might come back? I promise you they will not be allowed to hurt you again. If you will try to remember exactly what they look like, I will hunt them down for you and, well, I will certainly punish them."

"No, I'm not really afraid they might come back, at least I'm not afraid in the daytime. I dream of them sometimes at night, and then I wake up frightened."

"From now on I will be with you through the nights, Keziah, except when I am deployed with the army." Isaac saw Keziah's eyes widen. *I shouldn't have said that; she is as skittish as a young colt and I have just reminded her of the fact that she must accept me into her bed.*

She seemed flustered for a moment, but then she changed the subject with a slight shake of her head. "I am most afraid that you will soon regret taking me as a wife. I will try to be a good one, but I don't know if I can be what you want. Since you only chose me out of gratitude and, perhaps, pity, I don't see how you could be content."

Isaac sat the small lamp on a table near the bed and blew it out. He would have preferred to have left it burning so he could see her expressions, but he doused it, thinking she would rather have the privacy the darkness accorded. He was glad it was a moonlit night, so the room was not in complete darkness.

"Keziah, never doubt that I wanted to wed you. It was time and past time for me to take a wife. Knowing how you risked your own life for my sister is only one reason I spoke up for you outside the city yesterday."

"As I said, you pitied me," she spoke in barely a whisper.

"Perhaps, but that is still not the only reason."

"You said you cared for someone who could never be yours. In this life things are always changing. Maybe someday you might have wed this person; maybe some day you *will* marry this woman."

"No. That will never happen. Nor will there ever be any other wife for me, if you are concerned about that. I don't think it is wise for a man to have more than one wife; the lessons of

Abraham and Jacob have taught me that. So it is you who must ask yourself if you will regret this day, because I won't . . . not ever."

Isaac had been disrobing as he spoke, and now he slid under the covers. He reached out and pulled her close. "Tonight you will sleep in my arms, Keziah. You will become accustomed to me, your husband, and maybe soon you will learn to trust me, for I vow I would never do anything to hurt you."

He made her comfortable in the crook of his arm. He rubbed his hand down her back in a soothing gesture and she flinched. His hand froze in mid motion.

"It was not . . . I was not moving away from you," Keziah said. "My father . . . I mean, my back is still tender."

He stifled an exclamation and started to get up. "I will put some healing lotion on it."

But Keziah stopped him. "No, Isaac. Your mother has already tended to it."

So he lay down again, this time on his back, clasping her hand in his. At first she was stiff as a board, but soon enough she realized that Isaac did not intend to make any demands on her, and she slept, for indeed, she was exhausted. There were no nightmares that night.

"Isaac, Keziah, are you awake? The guests are already in the courtyard, on the rooftop—everywhere. This is the final day of the feast, and you are the guests of honor. Ahmi said I could wake you. May I come in?"

Isaac groaned and raised himself up on his elbows. "No, Adah, you may not come in. Go and tell Mother we will greet our guests soon."

Keziah had been awakened by the conversation, and when Isaac glanced her way, she cast her eyes down. Before he could greet his wife, the little voice piped out once more.

"Keziah, did you rest well? I have some of mother's salve, and she says I'm to apply some to your back before you dress. May I come in?"

Isaac snorted in disgust—the sort older siblings feel when their orders are ignored by younger offspring. His scowl turned into a grin when he heard Keziah chuckle. His younger sister was responsible for relieving the tension of the moment.

"You might as well come in," he called out as he belted his best tunic and slid his feet into his sandals. Adah scampered in with only a glance at her brother. She bounded onto the bed and kissed Keziah on the cheek.

"Now turn around, Keziah, so I can apply the salve. Your hair is all tangled. I will help you comb it out. What are you going to wear today?"

His sister strung out her questions and comments so rapidly that Keziah could not have answered even if she wanted to. Isaac saw that his wife was smiling. His sister had set her at ease. With only the reminder that they should join the guests as soon as possible, he slipped from the room.

There was more feasting that day as relatives and friends from other nearby towns and villages came to wish the couple well, although the haste in the proceedings precluded anything like the celebration there normally would have been.

Jonathan's family had stayed and had greeted Isaac and Keziah warmly when they emerged. Isaac stayed near them all morning. He tried to include Keziah in his conversation with Jonathan and Ailea, but the three started sharing old memories, and soon forgot she was there. She didn't mind. She wanted the opportunity to study her new husband.

After some time, Keziah noticed a certain glance that Isaac gave Ailea. It was somehow different. His earlier words, that he could never have the woman he desired, came back to her, as did the earlier statement that she belonged to another man. Intuitively, Keziah knew then that Ailea was the woman Isaac loved.

She felt a sense of hopelessness. Ailea was so beautiful, just the opposite of Keziah—tiny and feminine, with shiny black hair, and the most incredible green eyes. Surely Isaac would never get over her. She felt sorry for him, knowing how high his regard was for Jonathan. Certainly he must feel very guilty to have these feelings for his best friend's wife. She found it very difficult to watch Isaac and Ailea together, so she left the group and went to greet other guests.

Aaron was again in attendance, this time without a scowl on his face. Her aunt and uncle had come up from Adoraim, and the woman lost no time in conveying her opinion of the hasty nuptials.

"Hummmph, I knew something was amiss when you failed to come to us as usual," Milcah said, without concern as to who might overhear. "And lying to your father too! You are indeed fortunate that the young man has been willing to save you from disgrace. Such things were not countenanced in my day, I tell you."

Keziah made no response but looked around to see who might have heard. No one had heard but Isaac, who had come seeking Keziah, and now introduced himself. He told Aunt Milcah what a happy fellow he was to obtain such a bride, and from such a prestigious family too. In no time at all he had sour Milcah eating from his hand. Then he gave a secret wink to Keziah and went to speak with his father.

Though Isaac was kind, there was no one who made her feel more at ease than Ahiam. The burly man was as sweet-tempered and charming as a carefree child. He hugged his new daughter-in-law unabashedly and often, frequently kissing her on each cheek as if greeting her after a long absence.

Once he whispered in her ear, "My son will make you happy. Have no fear, girl, this family has accepted you fully. Judith and Adah are overjoyed, for you meant a lot to them before you ever set eyes on my son. They have told me so much about you, and I am sure I will soon come to share their opinion fully." He squeezed her hand lightly before going off to attend his guests.

Keziah watched her father-in-law interact with all the members of his family and was amazed. Several times Adah made mistakes, once stepping on a lady's toes as she rushed to play with the other children. Another time, she spilt her milk, sloshing some of it on Ahiam. Both times, he admonished the little girl gently, then patted her on the head to soften his scold.

Keziah thought back to the time when she was Adah's age and had made the same kind of childish mistakes. Aaron had rebuked her loudly and harshly, and sent her to her room, where she waited in dread, knowing that most infractions brought a beating with the rod. This household was so different from anything she had ever known. An incident with her father made that clear to Isaac as well as Keziah.

Before he left the celebration, Aaron sought her out as she stood with her new family. "I will be leaving now, Keziah, but I will expect to see you tomorrow after your husband departs. I don't know how I will get by now that you have left me all alone, but I suppose if you come over at least once a day to cook and clean, I will."

"Keziah will be too busy in her new life to come every day, Aaron, but you are welcome to come here and take your meals." Isaac's voice was soft and pleasant when he interrupted her father, but Keziah sensed that he was irritated at his father-in-law. And she could tell that Aaron was angered by Isaac's impertinence.

She hastened to smooth things over. "Oh, it will be no trouble to go home each day after I have finished my chores here."

"Your home *is* here, my dear, though that thought is such a new one that I won't blame you for forgetting. Your father understands that you are now my wife, and he will find someone else to be his washerwoman and cook."

Aaron's face grew red as he blustered a moment, trying to come up with a response. "Very well," he sputtered. "I will survive somehow."

Judith, every bit as much a peacemaker as Keziah, hastened to offer a suggestion. "The widow of Akim the tanner is destitute. I am sure she would cook and clean for you at a very reasonable price."

But Aaron's feelings were hurt, and he only mumbled that he would look into it before he stalked off in a huff.

Isaac felt ashamed of himself when he saw Keziah's dismay as she watched her father leave, but he could not like the man at all. It was obvious that the only use he had for his daughter was as a drudge. He was glad Keziah would now be a part of his family and would have a caring mother and father.

Isaac was determined that after the pain his bride had been through over the past months, the next ones would be free of worry for her. Even though he couldn't be present for a while, he knew he could trust his sister and mother to take good care of Keziah. He would remind his mother before he left not to let Aaron take advantage of Keziah.

Keziah was surprised to find that the second night of married life was as peaceful as the first. She knew by his manner that her husband did not intend to make their relationship intimate yet. Again she wondered why she trusted him so instinctively. She quickly fell off to sleep as Isaac was relating another amusing tale from his sister's many misadventures. She woke the next morning surprised that her sleep had been so deep and restful. No terror had dared interfere with the newfound serenity Isaac's presence brought.

When it came time for the men to depart the next day, Keziah was both relieved and anxious. On the one hand, she needed time alone to absorb all that had happened in such a short period of time. On the other hand, the two nights he had lain beside her and drawn her into his arms, she had felt something else besides uneasiness. She had felt sheltered, safe. And now he was going away to fight, perhaps to die. She was afraid for him.

Isaac seemed remarkably unconcerned, even jovial, as he and Ahiam prepared to leave Hebron. He clasped Keziah's shoulders and leaned over to say in a low voice, "You will let no thoughts trouble you while I am away, wife."

Keziah's heart gave a happy lurch as she heard her husband use her new title.

"You will help Mother with the duties of the household, and you will sleep deeply at night while you dream only good dreams. And when I return, we will continue to acquaint ourselves as husband and wife." Then he gave her a swift kiss on the cheek and turned away to help his men form up a straight column for the march to Jerusalem.

Ahiam kissed Judith, Adah, and finally Keziah good-bye and headed out the gate behind Isaac and the men. Then suddenly he turned back. He cupped Keziah's chin in his big, rough hand.

"Take care of Judith and Adah for me," he instructed. There was an intensity in his voice that tugged at Keziah's heart. She whispered a prayer as she watched them depart.

"O Lord of Israel, keep them safe and deliver the Ammonites into their hands so that they might return home soon."

Home—it was her home now as well.

JERUSALEM

It hadn't worked.

David paced the rooftop garden that was his personal retreat, the place where his servants and family knew not to disturb him unless they were called for. He couldn't believe his carefully laid plan to protect Bathsheba had come to naught. Uriah was infuriatingly committed to his military honor. He had refused to go to his house last night, choosing instead to stay at the *House of the Gibborim*.

What to do now? David paused to pick up half a pomegranate from a tray of fruit before continuing his pacing. He would just keep Uriah here until he succumbed to a man's natural desires. But that could take more time than David had if he were to pass off Bathsheba's child as Uriah's.

Uriah's attention was focused on his military duties, but he was no fool, and he could count to nine. So could others around the court. No, something had to be done immediately.

David placed the half-eaten pomegranate back on the tray and threw the seeds into a potted plant. He went in search of Sheva, his court secretary. Hiram of Tyre had sent him to David some years ago, and the learned man had made himself indispensable at court, not only teaching the skill of writing to the scribes who copied the sacred writings but also keeping records of the court and a history of David's reign.

The portly secretary appeared promptly, as usual. His keen intelligence was reflected in his dark eyes. He made a dignified bow, then waited for his instructions.

"Send word to Uriah the Hittite that the King requests his presence tonight at a dinner in his honor. Also invite the men of rank in the palace guard," David commanded.

"Are the wives to be included?" Sheva queried.

David hesitated. If Bathsheba were to spend the evening in her husband's company, Uriah would be much more likely to return home with her. On the other hand, David would be uncomfortable entertaining his lover and the husband he had cuckolded at the same time. And he seriously doubted that Bathsheba in her present emotional state could carry on as if everything were normal.

"No, Sheva, no ladies are invited. This is to be a feast for the men only. But do call for those dancing girls we had perform last month." No harm in turning Uriah's thoughts toward feminine beauty.

Ahiam and Isaac were relaxing with Jonathan in the comfortable section of the military barracks known as the *House of the Gibborim*. A few years earlier, David had built these special accommodations for the Mighty Men—his elite officers. There were rope beds for the men to lay their pallets on, warm blankets to keep them warm on the outside, and wine provided to keep them warm on the inside.

They had arrived in Jerusalem just at sunset and would spend the night here before continuing to Rabbah. Their raw recruits were housed in the more austere quarters next door.

"I guess we will be leaving at dawn," Ahiam said as he spread his pallet out on the wood-and-rope beds that lined the walls of the sleeping chamber.

Jonathan paused in unpacking the leather bag that contained his belongings. "I don't know. I think Uriah is to travel with us and carry a dispatch back to the general from David. At least that is what I was told when I reported to the palace. But we will depart as soon as we can get these green troops in line to march and as soon as Uriah joins us. After all, we wouldn't want to keep Joab waiting. I'm sure the general has missed us."

Ahiam laughed gruffly. "Like a sore on his backside. Well, it will be awhile before we sleep in a bed again. Let's take advantage of it."

Ahiam settled himself in his bunk, and Jonathan and Isaac soon followed.

They had not yet fallen asleep when Uriah entered the room. He stumbled over a stool and grumbled under his breath.

Isaac sat up. "What are you doing here, Uriah? This is the last night of your leave. You're supposed to be at home in your own bed."

The tall soldier whispered his response, believing Ahiam and Jonathan were asleep. "I went as far as my gate on my first night back, but realized I could not in good conscience enjoy my own bed when the armies of Israel are sleeping in tents outside Rabbah."

"What about your wife? Was Bathsheba not angry that you did not spend every extra moment with her?" Isaac had caught a glimpse of Uriah's beautiful young wife as she bid her husband farewell some four months ago when the army had marched out of Jerusalem to begin the siege of Rabbah. She had stood out from the crowds that thronged the streets of Jerusalem like an exotic flower in a field of weeds. Isaac was impressed with the commitment Uriah showed in choosing the army over such a wife.

"My wife understood. I explained it to her the night before last. She was disappointed, to be sure, and begged me at least to come to her tonight, but I just can't. Last night, the King honored me by inviting me to dine with him. I'm afraid I had too much wine and ended up outside my own house again, before I came to myself. The King seemed to be angry when I told him I slept here instead of my own house. I told him I would cut off my own arm before I took my ease in my own bed. The rest of the army is enduring hardship. Why should I not, also?"

"Quiet, man, people are trying to sleep here." Ahiam sounded sleepy and disgruntled. Uriah grunted and quietly continued to disrobe. Isaac shrugged and turned over to go back to sleep.

Who am I to question Uriah's decision not to sleep with his wife? he thought. *I have only spent two nights with my own, and even then, perhaps I didn't do the right thing in leaving the marriage unconsummated. But Keziah is so . . . wounded. Surely it is best to give her time to adjust.*

Isaac didn't question his decision to marry her, but he wondered if Keziah regretted it. Time. That was what they both needed to adjust. Isaac fell asleep, and for the first time in months, he did not dream of tiny Ailea and her raven hair but of his wife and her auburn tresses.

Their departure for Rabbah was delayed while Uriah went to the palace to receive a dispatch from the King. Jonathan, Isaac, and Ahiam had the new recruits lined up and waiting at the city gate when Uriah joined them. He carried a leather pouch under one arm.

"Must be important. David usually sends verbal reports. The King looked very solemn as he handed me this," Uriah said.

Chapter Nine

They arrived at Rabbah at midday the following day. Uriah stopped at the general's tent to give him the dispatch from the King, while Isaac continued to the other side of the encampment to rejoin Jonathan and the new troops as they set up their tents.

"Benjamin, what has happened in our absence?" Isaac asked the brawny veteran, who was sharpening the tip of a javelin with a flintstone. Benjamin gingerly tested the weapon for sharpness with the edge of his thumb before answering.

"Nothing has happened, Isaac, exactly nothing. Joab is still planning to starve the poor devils out." Benjamin unfolded his large frame and stood with a grunt, spitting into the campfire. "It's enough to drive a good fighting man to madness. Give me a good, honest battle anytime."

Isaac chuckled. "Knowing your bloodthirsty nature, I'm not surprised to hear your opinion, my friend, but I would just as soon spend a few idle weeks as to have to worry about one of these Ammonites separating my head from my body." Benjamin shrugged his disagreement and began to poke at the fire.

Joab read the missive quickly, showing no reaction to the words. When he was finished, he replaced the small parchment in the leather bag and turned his attention to Uriah.

"You may seek your own tent now," was all he said. As he left the general, Uriah wondered about the message. As one of Joab's bodyguards, he was often privy to military information as soon as it was received. *Perhaps this was a personal matter,* he thought as he made his way through the camp.

~ ~ ~

The next morning, Isaac was shaken awake by Jonathan. "Orders have changed. We are to make an assault on the walls of Rabbah today."

Isaac pushed his sleep-tousled hair out of his eyes. "Why the sudden change in strategy? You were convinced that Joab was committed to a siege."

"I don't know. The general was adamant about not risking our troops in an assault on the walls. And I'm certain he hasn't suddenly found compassion in his heart for the innocent citizens of Rabbah."

"What heart?" Isaac asked with the lift of a brow, and both men laughed.

"I've been considering this, and I've come to the conclusion that this maneuver is not Joab's idea at all. I think he received orders from Jerusalem in that packet Uriah carried."

Isaac was thoughtful as he braided the side locks of his hair and tucked the braids behind his ears. He was of the opinion that long hair or a long beard could be a liability to a warrior in battle.

"You think the King ordered this? It's not like him to order such an operation without personally leading the troops."

Jonathan frowned. "It's not like David to absent himself from battle anyway. But Joab has been urging him more and more not to go out with the army. He says David should be more 'kingly' and attend to matters of state; let his warriors take care of the fighting for him."

"But there is no greater warrior in Israel than David."

"Exactly."

~ ~ ~

Less than an hour later, Israel's army was assembled in full battle array before the gate of Rabbah, archers, slingers, and battering ram ready to unleash their fury on the Ammonites.

The troops were stationed far enough from the city's walls to avoid deadly arrows or boiling pitch or oil from the ramparts. Isaac passed among his new recruits, speaking to them with quiet confidence, calming their fears. He remembered his first battle more than three years earlier when Jonathan had done the same for him. Now Jonathan frequently left such matters to Isaac, who served as his aide-de-camp/armor bearer.

While Isaac was reviewing the troops, briefing them on the attack, Jonathan was conferring with Ahiam, Uriah, and the other *Gibborim.* Joab was drawing the battle plan with a stick in the sand. Jonathan's, Ahiam's, and Uriah's units were to be the leading vanguard of the attack.

Ordinarily, Uriah would not have led a separate unit since he was Joab's head armor bearer. But Joab said he wished to personally supervise the men using the giant battering ram, with the larger part of his own battalion arrayed behind him, protected by an umbrella of shields constructed specifically to deflect the arrows, or whatever else the enemy chose to rain down on them.

Ahiam happened to look up during this strategy session. At the back of the circle of warriors, he saw a middle-aged man, someone's servant, he supposed. He had not seen the man before. When Joab made some jest about the Ammonites, the man opened his mouth wide in laughter. There was a tooth missing on either side of his front two teeth. He turned his attention back to Joab's instructions; a moment later, it struck him. *No, Ahbi, it's not like my missing front teeth. The teeth on either side of his front ones are missing. . . . He was a servant of the younger one. I think his master was a warrior, because he had a very good sword, but I am not sure.* Could this man be one of the men who had accosted Adah and Keziah? Was the man's young master here, perhaps in his own battalion? Ahiam oversaw more than 2,000 troops and did not know even half of them well.

As soon as Joab dismissed the meeting, Ahiam followed the man as he made his way through the camp. He stopped in front of a tent. It was not occupied. Ahiam grabbed the man's shoulder and turned him around. "Who are you, and who is your master?" he asked sharply.

"Why do you ask?" the man replied insolently.

Ahiam's hand shot out and grabbed the front of the man's tunic. With that one arm, he lifted the man off the ground. "I ask because I want to know. And you will tell me."

"I . . . I am Ishobeam," the man answered in a choked voice, his face turning red because Ahiam's grip was cutting off his wind. Ahiam's kind nature asserted itself, and he loosened his grip.

"And who is your master?"

"I serve Talmon of Gibeah, my lord, one of Joab's bodyguards."

Ahiam's eyes narrowed. This Talmon fellow had not been in Joab's service for long, maybe two or three years, and Ahiam was not really acquainted with him. Joab's cortege tended to keep to themselves. But he did remember one particular incident that had sickened him. They had gone into Philistine territory to retaliate for some raids a Philistine band had made on southwestern Judah. They had found the raiders in their village and had slain them all, but left their women and children unmolested.

Sometime later, when Ahiam had been gathering the troops together to return to Jerusalem, he had come upon this Talmon of Gibeah and a few of his men in a stand of trees not far from the village. They were tormenting and ravishing four young Philistine girls. Talmon had been standing there, just looking somewhat bored until his men started to torture the youngest, a girl about twelve years of age.

There had been a look of almost unholy satisfaction on the man's face as his men caused the child's pitiful pleas, her screams. Talmon had taken two steps in the direction of the group, doubtless to join them in the travesty, when Ahiam put a heavy hand on his shoulder.

"This is more than enough. Call them off. Now!" he had said, fighting the urge to plant his fist in Talmon's sullen face. The younger man had backed down and called off his men, leaving Ahiam alone to try to help his bleeding victims.

Ahiam felt his bile rise at the memory of that day and at his realization that Talmon of Gibeah would indeed be capable of such a deed as had been done against his daughter and Keziah.

He forced his thoughts back to the man he was questioning. "Some three months past, you and your master came upon a helpless child on the road to Adoraim. When a brave young woman intervened, you raped her and threw her into a ravine, did you not? You left her for dead!"

Ishobeam's eyes widened in alarm as he realized he had been found out. Ahiam, who still had the man by his tunic, could feel his skinny body tremble.

"No, my lord, it was not me or my master. You are mistaken." The servant whined the denial while directing his gaze to the ground. Ahiam knew that the man was lying and started to shake the truth from him. He was interrupted.

"Ahiam of Hebron, your troops await you. Would you hold up this battle while you chastise a servant?" Joab's voice was full of anger. Ahiam turned to look at the general and realized by his countenance that this was not the time to bring the sins of Ishobeam and Talmon to his attention. The matter would have to wait until after the battle.

Ahiam shook Ishobeam like a lion shakes its prey. "You have

been given a reprieve this day, Ishobeam. I hope you enjoy it, because, as the Lord lives, neither you nor your master will see another." Ahiam released the man, who scurried away, no doubt to warn his master of his threat.

Ahiam went to join his troops, passing Joab's men, who were positioning the battering ram for the attack. Because of the phalanx of large metal shields that would cover them, these men would be in less danger than Ahiam, Jonathan, Uriah, and their troops, who would have to scale ladders that would take them over Rabbah's walls.

Isaac, who stood on a rise near the forefront of the army, faced the peril calmly, ordering his men to bring up the long ladders. He called for volunteers to station themselves at the bottom rungs to help steady them when the Ammonites tried to push the ladders away from their walls. He picked the strongest men for this job and the fastest men in his battalion to be the first to scale the ladders.

As usual, he had more than enough volunteers. These men had seen the unprecedented success of Israel's armies over the past two decades, with battle after battle being won against superior forces. They all acknowledged that it was Adonai who in truth won the battles, and they went in full confidence that he would offer his protection. If an individual warrior fell, then that was the will of the Lord.

After assisting Jonathan in forming the ranks, Isaac positioned himself near his father's regiment, hoping to see him before the charge was called. In a few moments Ahiam appeared, deep in discussion with one of his lieutenants. As soon as the young man left Ahiam's side, Isaac went to his father.

"I'm glad we have a chance to talk before the battle," he stated calmly. Both men knew that this could be their last time together on earth, but neither spoke of the fact. "What do you make of this sudden change in strategy?" the young man continued.

Ahiam stroked his beard for a moment. "The general gave no reason, but I assume it has something to do with the communiqué

Uriah brought him from the King. Perhaps David grows tired of this waiting game and wants matters quickly concluded."

"I'm amazed that the King chose not to come himself to lead us in such a dangerous move." Isaac reiterated the doubt that had been niggling the back of his mind since Joab had given the new orders.

Ahiam shrugged. "After thirty years as a warrior, David deserves to leave the fighting to others, and as head of state, his hide is much more valuable than ours."

"Still, it's uncharacteristic of him," Isaac responded.

"Well, no matter the reason, we are ready to defeat Ammon this day." Ahiam paused, wondering whether to tell his son about finding the men who in all probability had been the ones to attack Keziah. He decided not to distract Isaac from the business of fighting. He would let him know after the battle. He grasped his son's shoulder. "Look well to yourself, son, and trust in Adonai."

"You as well, Father," Isaac responded, and started to turn away, but something compelled him to reach out one last time to his father. He took the weathered face in his hands and kissed Ahiam on each cheek, then whacked him soundly on one shoulder before returning to his men.

Within minutes the signal came from Abishai, Joab's brother, who climbed atop a cart and raised his arms high in a time-honored battle cry—

> Do not be afraid
> Do not be dismayed
> by their numbers!
> For the Lord our God
> goes before you this day.
> The battle is not yours, but the Lord's!

A great roar reverberated along the walls of Rabbah as Israel's armies began the assault on Rabbah. At first it seemed that the Ammonites were concentrating all their men on the warriors who were using the battering ram on their gates. Soon fiery arrows were flying, and Isaac could see a giant cauldron being moved into position. He could smell the burning pitch, and he prayed that the large metal shields would deflect most of it. His own men had placed their forty-foot ladders and had started to ascend. At first nothing happened.

Each long ladder now held several men, and they were scaling the wall very rapidly. Then several Ammonite soldiers appeared at each ladder position. One from each group drew an arrow from his quiver and lighted the ball of pitch and straw at the tip before notching it into the bowstring. But before they could let loose their arrows, the Israelite archers shot two of the Ammonites. Two more immediately took their place.

But three of the Ammonites' burning arrows took flight, all of them aimed at the burly warriors stationed to secure the ladders. All hit their intended targets. The clothing of each burst into flame, and they all dropped to the ground. Two of them managed to extinguish the flames and with the assistance of others were able to retreat. The third warrior never moved. He just continued to burn, the arrow having pierced his eye. Isaac prayed fervently that the man had died instantly. Then he watched others take the places of his fallen men.

In the meantime, several Israelites had topped the wall and were now in hand-to-hand combat with the Ammonites. Isaac saw one of his men wielding a mace, taking down at least three of the enemy. One of the ladders was being pushed away from the wall by Ammonites who used a very large two-pronged instrument, rather like a threshing fork.

The first warrior hurried to reach the top before it was too late. He climbed one-handed, holding his sword in the other. He managed to wound the Ammonite closest to him, but the two still holding the forked instrument threw all their weight against him, and the ladder was slowly pushed away, despite the efforts of the men on the ground.

The warrior fell more than twenty feet, but fortunately, two of his comrades managed to break his fall. As soon as the ladder was back in place, he immediately mounted it again. At this point, however, the Ammonites were hoisting several pots of burning pitch, and Jonathan shouted a command to pull back. Isaac shouted for his men to come down and withdraw, then went to Jonathan.

"Joab has just issued the order to pull back. Finally showing some sense," he shouted to be heard above the din of battle. The troops retreated to a nearby rise. "Where is father?" Isaac asked, looking around him.

Jonathan pointed to a figure approaching a group of men near the wall. "There, speaking to Joab's aide. I'm sure that Talmon is even now telling your father and Uriah to have their units fall back and join us."

Isaac watched as Joab's assistant, a man he hardly knew but didn't care for at all, spoke to Uriah and his father. He was pointing to the city gate, not the rise where Isaac stood, directing them toward the only site of fighting now.

The Ammonites had opened their gate enough to let their finest warriors out to engage the Israelites, in an obvious effort to keep the battering ram from being used. Talmon was directing the two units to aid those warriors who were trying to drive the Ammonites back inside. Benjamin stood in the forefront of this group. In the confusion of the fighting, he found himself surrounded by enemy soldiers as the huge gates once more were being closed. He was taken alive by the Ammonites. "O God, no!" Isaac yelled, then turned to look for his father.

When he saw what was happening on the ramparts above the fighting, he gasped in dismay. A score of archers was preparing flaming arrows as two huge cauldrons of pitch were being hoisted directly above the fray. Just then he saw the general, who was also gazing at the scene from some distance away. He shouted and beckoned to the men who were fighting to pull back.

Thanks be to the Almighty, Isaac thought. Then he saw that Talmon was still directing his father and Uriah to take their troops to the gates. Courageous leaders that they were, neither Uriah nor Ahiam hesitated, both at the forefront of their men as they engaged the enemy. But now all the other troops were retreating, leaving the remaining Israelites seriously outnumbered.

"What does he think he's doing?" Jonathan shouted above the din. "He'll get them all killed."

At that moment, though David's warriors were more than holding their own in hand-to-hand combat, the archers from above unleashed their arrows. Several of the archers aimed their flaming arrows at Uriah, realizing his importance as a leader. Numerous arrows pierced him, and he fell to the ground. At that moment, both cauldrons were tipped, and Ahiam, along with three of his men, was covered in burning pitch. Isaac shuddered as he heard their screams, even at this distance. He ran toward his father, who was still on his feet but screaming in agony. The other men lay motionless on the ground.

Benaiah was also headed toward the scene, yelling and threatening the Ammonites, diverting their attention to himself, as he deflected arrows with his shield, which was as tall as an average man.

Benaiah was anything but average. The captain of the elite guard of non-Hebrew mercenaries known as the Pelethites and Cherethites, Benaiah was from the hills of southern Judah, just as Ahiam and Jonathan were. There were only three men in Israel's army of higher rank.

His tactic seemed to work. A barrage of flaming arrows came his way. He deflected them all with his shield, while helping two other warriors escape.

But it was much too late for his father, Isaac saw as he drew closer. He heard Talmon, who was just standing there watching, call back several young soldiers who were going to the aid of their fallen comrades. "Leave them," he said coolly.

Isaac was running full-out, still several yards away when he saw the flaming arrow sink into his father's shoulder. Immediately the pitch that covered much of his torso ignited, and Ahiam became a living torch. Isaac heard Talmon shout at him to stop, that the general had ordered a retreat. Isaac ignored him. The Ammonite who had been fighting Ahiam turned away to seek another opponent, fully aware that Ahiam was a dead man.

Isaac was immediately aware of that as well. Still, when he reached his father, who had fallen to the ground, he rolled him in the sand to extinguish the flames, heedless of the sticky hot pitch that burned his own hands. "Father, Father, hold on. I'm here. I'm here."

Finally, when it was too late, Joab himself appeared, calling for a full retreat from the gates. The Ammonites had taken the distraction as an opportunity to slip back inside the city.

Isaac lifted his father over his shoulder, carrying the much larger man back to Jonathan's large field tent. He was filled with rage at Joab and Talmon. Why? Why had they ordered such a foolish advance? But there was no time to ask about that now. He had to help his father. He repeated a prayer like a litany: "Adonai, have mercy. Adonai, have mercy."

He kept repeating the prayer even as he saw that all the hair was burned from his father's head, that charred flesh mingled with hardened pitch, creating a nauseating stench, that his father's features were so blackened and grotesque that he was unrecognizable. The sight was bad enough, but Ahiam's pitiful moans were torture to Isaac, who could do no more than try to get poppy juice past the burned lips in an attempt to ease the agony. But the brave warrior continued to cry out in pain.

Jonathan came into the tent once and knelt beside his old friend. He had to lean close to hear Ahiam's question. "What happened?" he asked in a raspy whisper.

"Uriah and Benjamin are lost, and four others. You must live, my friend. I have already lost Benjamin this day," Jonathan said, his voice choked with emotion. One tear appeared at the corner of Ahiam's swollen eyes and he shook his head slightly.

Jonathan started to back away when Ahiam asked one more question, his eyes moving from Jonathan to Isaac. "Why?" Then he slipped into unconsciousness. Why indeed. Ahiam woke only once more. He moved his charred limbs restlessly.

When Isaac came near to try to quiet him, Ahiam grew even more agitated. His mouth opened and closed several times, and Isaac realized that his father had something to say to him. He leaned over with his ear very close to his father's mouth.

"Easy, Father. Don't try to speak loudly. I will hear you." Ahiam could only manage a whisper of sound. "He did it. . . . Tal . . ."

Isaac thought of that moment when Talmon had so callously turned away from his father. Evidently Ahiam had been all too aware that he was being betrayed by his fellow warrior. "Yes, Father, I know Talmon did it. I won't rest until he pays for what he did."

This statement seemed to upset Ahiam. He tried to shake his head, which caused him such awful pain that he cried out. "No! . . . He . . . Adah . . ." The effort had exhausted him. Ahiam closed his eyes and seemed to be unconscious.

Isaac sat beside his father, hoping he would say something more. If he was going to die, Isaac wanted an opportunity to say good-bye. At least he had mentioned Adah. Surely he would have mentioned Mother, too, if he had not lost consciousness.

Benaiah also paid a visit to the tent. He stood beside his fallen comrade for a moment before motioning Jonathan and Isaac to follow him outside the tent.

"Two questions," the burly man said in his usual terse manner. "First, what in the name of heaven is wrong with Joab? I have never known him to act so foolishly."

When Jonathan shrugged and Isaac shook his head, Benaiah motioned them to follow him around the other side of the tent. This was the side that faced Rabbah's walls. He pointed upward.

A horrifying sight met their eyes. The Ammonites had impaled Benjamin on a pike atop the city gate. He was still alive. Even from this distance they could hear the jeers and taunts as their enemies gloated over their capture of an Israelite officer.

They would keep Benjamin alive as long as possible, so that he would experience maximum suffering, and the morale of Israel's army would be affected.

"Who's going to do it?" Benaiah asked, knowing full well they would understand what he was asking.

Isaac's eyes watered. He didn't look at Jonathan. Benjamin was one of Jonathan's best friends. Knowing Jonathan was incapable of speaking, Isaac answered for them both. "We can't," was all he said.

Benaiah nodded, spat on the ground, then pulled an arrow out of his quiver. His bow and arrows were twice the average size. He sighted carefully but quickly, and the arrow left the bow with a whistling sound. It went straight to Benjamin's heart. His tortured, quivering body immediately slumped in death. Benaiah said something harsh and indecipherable as he swung his bow onto his back. "This is a day I will never forget," he said before stalking off.

Mercifully, Ahiam never regained consciousness, even though he lived throughout the night. Isaac kept vigil at his side, talking constantly, reliving good times and family memories for hours on end, sometimes not even making sense, just talking so that his father would know he was not alone as he died.

Ahiam's breathing grew more and more labored as time went on, and his body continued to swell from the burns. He finally drew his last shuddering breath just as the sun appeared on the horizon. Isaac stayed by the body for a long time, unable to believe that his strong, happy, bighearted father was no longer with him. He thought of his mother and Adah. How could he face them with this terrible news?

A short time later, Jonathan appeared again and led him away. It was only after his friends had forced him to take food and wine that Isaac's lethargy was replaced by fury. Joab had ordered his father into a death trap, and Talmon, who had been the general's messenger and closer to the skirmish, had allowed neither a retreat by the doomed men nor other units to go to their aid. *Why? Why?* He finished the wine and stood up.

"Where are you going?" Jonathan asked warily.

"To get some answers," Isaac flung back over his shoulder. Jonathan rose to follow him, well aware that his younger friend was in a dangerous mood. Isaac went in search of Talmon's tent first. Talmon observed him approaching. He had a cold, almost gloating look in his eyes, though his expression remained impassive.

The arrogance of the man struck Isaac so forcefully that he ran the rest of the way, going straight for Talmon's throat, knocking him to the ground and choking him until Talmon's face became nearly as swollen and discolored as Ahiam's had been. In his murderous rage, Isaac found immense satisfaction in the pain he was inflicting.

Jonathan had followed his friend and was trying to pull him off Talmon before he committed murder, but Isaac's grief and fury gave him extra strength. Not until a club, wielded by Joab, stunned him into near unconsciousness did he release his death-hold on Talmon.

Isaac came to when a bucket of cold water was sluiced over his head. He squinted up into the sun and saw the general frowning over him.

"Explain why you would try to kill your fellow Hebrew when we have already lost too many of our own this day," Joab commanded.

Isaac's pain was too great for caution and he blurted out: "Because he sent my father to his death, then stood there and did nothing while the Ammonites roasted him alive!"

"I was merely following orders," Talmon's voice was low and rough as he continued to rub his neck.

"That is correct, soldier. Talmon was obeying my orders to call the men back."

"You lie! I saw you order my father's and Uriah's units to fight right under the wall while you pulled back all support. You let them be killed!" Isaac jumped up and lunged for the general, but Jonathan and another warrior held him back. A deathly quiet descended on the soldiers at the insubordination. Joab took a long moment to respond, his face revealing no emotion.

"I am willing to make certain concessions due to your loss, son of Ahiam, and in deference to your father's great courage and sacrifice in battle, but when you call me a murderer and a liar and would try to harm me, you show disrespect for your king and country, for I represent both." He turned to two of his armor-bearers. "Give him twenty lashes."

When the general turned to go, Jonathan, who was afraid to release Isaac for fear of what he might attempt, called to him. "Joab. Wait. Please reconsider. He is unhinged by his loss. You cannot hold him responsible."

"I *am* making allowance, son of Shageh, or else I would have ordered thirty-nine stripes as the Law allows, or I could have ordered him executed for treason. And if he makes any further attempts to harm anyone, I will do just that." Joab turned and strode away. Jonathan knew that there was no use trying to persuade him, so he stayed by his friend as he was stripped of his tunic and tied to a post.

Talmon also stayed, making no pretense of doing anything besides gloating. Just before the first lash fell, Isaac met his gaze and promised, "You will regret your deeds of this day. I am not finished with you, Talmon." And he held the other man's stare until the whip rang out and the pain caused him to shut his eyes tightly.

~ ~ ~

An hour later, Jonathan was applying soothing salve to Isaac's bleeding back as they talked about the events of the last twenty-four hours.

"I cannot believe the order to launch that attack came from David," Isaac said. "This was Joab's work. He wanted those men to die. I know he did not particularly like my father nor my father him, but I don't think my father had done anything to make the general hate him so much he would deliberately try to get rid of him, do you?"

Jonathan shook his head. "No. Joab would much rather see me dead than Ahiam, I am sure. We have been enemies for a very long time. But perhaps your father was not the target, just included to cover up the real motive. Maybe Uriah had done something to anger him."

"Surely it was not anyone of lesser rank," Isaac offered thoughtfully, "or he would not plan anything so elaborate. The only men he need fear to touch are the royal family or the *Gibborim.* Anyone else, he would simply kill outright."

Jonathan stood up and wiped the salve off his hands with a rag. "You stay put, my young friend. You must rest and prepare to take your father's body back to Hebron for burial. I think I will seek out the general and volunteer to take the news to David. I will be able to tell by his reaction if he had any part in this. If he did not, I will ask that he punish Joab and Talmon as well. But don't hold your breath. David is lenient to a fault when it comes to his family and close friends."

"You will come to Hebron as soon as your mission is finished and you will tell me the truth, no matter how ugly. Vow to me before you leave, Jonathan."

The older man placed his hand on Isaac's shoulder. "I vow it, my friend, but don't let your passions over this matter rule your head. Your mother and sister need you now, and you have a new bride. Your father would not wish you to forfeit your own life avenging his death. He was my best friend. Let me undertake this mission to Jerusalem. It is the last thing I will be able to do for him."

Isaac's emotions nearly overcame him when he saw tears on Jonathan's face, but he brought himself under control with a shudder. He nodded once to Jonathan who left the tent to seek out Joab.

~ ~ ~

Joab refused to see him, but Jonathan ignored the armor bearer who tried to bar his way, and went through the curtains that divided the living quarters of the tent. He found Joab seated on a camp stool before a low table. He held a rush pen in his hand.

He looked very irritated at being disturbed. "What do you want, son of Shageh? I am busy writing a report of the battle."

"I have come about the report. I am requesting permission to take it to Jerusalem myself."

Joab quirked an eyebrow. "Why? So that you can bear tales to the King undermining my leadership?"

"I would give David nothing but the truth, which, I am sure, is also contained in the document you are now preparing."

A sly smile passed over the general's face. "I know you would never seek to discredit me, Jonathan. Very well. I will allow you to deliver the report. Feel free also to give the King your version of the battle. See how much good it does. My dear uncle is ever loyal to me and I to him. When are you going to learn that you cannot create strife between us?"

"I seek justice, not strife."

"Your highblown sense of honor sickens me, Jonathan. It is soft, like a woman, and will one day be the death of you. Now get out of my sight. I will send the report to you when it is ready, and you may take it to Jerusalem."

In less than an hour, Jonathan was on his way to Jerusalem.

~ ~ ~

As the sun dipped low in the sky, Talmon and Ishobeam stood just outside the Israelite camp, where they could converse without being overheard. "Tell me again the exact words Ahiam used when he spoke to you," Talmon commanded.

When Ishobeam complied, Talmon asked, "You are certain he used the words, 'left her for dead'?"

"Those were his exact words."

"Then we must assume that the young woman lived at least long enough to talk. I want you to go to Hebron, Ishobeam. Find out if Ahiam has a daughter the age of either of the girls. He must be related to one of them to know enough to have recognized you. You will make your journey tomorrow. It will be best if we are not seen together for a while. And don't tell anyone in Hebron that you serve me."

"What am I to do if I find either of the girls, master? Should I get rid of them?"

Talmon considered for a moment, then shook his head. "I don't think that is necessary at this point. The risk is too great. Ahiam is dead. I will try to find out if he talked before he died. He may have. Perhaps that is why his son came after me, but I really doubt it. Isaac has no self-control; surely he would have blurted out the whole story if he knew it. He certainly would have pleaded his case with Joab to avoid the whipping he received. I think it will be more prudent if we find out what is going on in Hebron and make our plans accordingly."

JERUSALEM

When Jonathan was summoned into the King's audience chamber, he noticed that David looked drawn, as if he had not slept. His hair was in disarray, as if he had been running his hand through it.

"How did the battle go?" he asked.

Jonathan thought by the look on his face that the King expected bad news. Odd, since the siege of Rabbah had been going so well. Had David ordered the attack, then realized his folly after it was too late to recant his instructions?

"Joab ordered us to scale the walls and attack the gate of the city. We were not successful, though we did drive them back inside their walls."

David swallowed audibly. He did not meet Jonathan's gaze when he asked, "What were our losses?"

"Several of the men died at the gate, two of the *Gibborim* at the wall. Benjamin, the son of Ishri, was taken alive and impaled atop the city wall. My friend, Ahiam of Hebron, and Uriah the Hittite were also killed."

David's eyes squeezed shut and a pained look passed over his face. Now, Jonathan thought. Now he will ask me what on earth the general could have been thinking to make such a foolish assault. Perhaps he will send me back with a message to Joab to present himself in Jerusalem to answer for his folly.

But for a long while David said nothing. He walked over to the window and looked out. At last, he turned to Jonathan, but kept his gaze on the floor.

"Take a message to Joab," he said in a flat voice. "Don't be discouraged by the setback. The loss of men is inevitable in battle. Continue and intensify the campaign against Rabbah."

Jonathan was shocked that David did not seem to be angered by the news of the needless deaths of some of his best men. He decided to inform the King in more detail what had happened.

"The siege was going well, my lord, until the general sent us right into range of their weapons. Of course, they had the advantage of shooting down upon us. Then the general sent his armor bearer, Talmon of Gibeah, to pull the troops back. But Talmon left two units to face the Ammonites alone. My friend, Ahiam, was covered with pitch, then struck with a flaming arrow. Talmon did nothing to help him, just stood there watching."

"Are you saying that Talmon acted against the general's orders?"

"No. I don't know. But it was not right. They were left to die."

David put an arm on Jonathan's shoulder. "In your grief you speak hastily, my friend. We have fought together many years, and I know you are loyal, so I will overlook your momentary lapse in discipline. You temporarily forgot that you are under the authority of Joab, and you and your men are to follow orders without question.

"It may be that Joab makes mistakes, but we can only have one leader, or the entire army would fall into chaos. When I am not there, Joab acts in my stead. I will be very displeased if I hear any murmurings in the ranks concerning Joab's leadership.

"Now, I will let you return to Rabbah with your message." The King turned his back on Jonathan and once again went to stare out the window. He was clearly dismissed.

But Jonathan could not go back to Hebron and face Isaac without accomplishing something in the way of recompense for Ahiam's death. He decided to have a talk with Benaiah when he returned to Rabbah. He would ask him to join in making a complaint against Talmon. He was certain he would have the powerful warrior's backing.

~ ~ ~

David was alone in his chamber—a vast room larger than many of the homes owned by the common people of Jerusalem. The high arched windows bathed the lavishly furnished room in light. From the curtains to the rugs on the floor, to the cushions on the bed, the room was decorated in blue of all hues, the pale blue of a morning sky to the rich deep blue of lapis lazuli. It was a restful room, a room to lift the spirits.

But the King couldn't rest, and nothing seemed to lift his spirits. He had ordered everyone out and instructed his servants that he was not to be disturbed under any circumstances—not by his wives, or children, or any of the court counselors.

He turned away from the large tray of fruit and bread and cheese that had been left for him. The very sight of the food made him ill. He went to the large bed that had been set on a raised platform, and sank facedown among the many pillows. It had worked! Uriah had been killed honorably in battle, and would be remembered as a hero in Israel. And David could have Bathsheba without any word of censure. In fact, people would probably praise him for taking care of the widow of one of his cherished officers.

When he had come to his room an hour ago, right after his encounter with Jonathan, David had overheard his servants whispering as they obeyed his order to leave him. "He is grieving that he was not at the battle site. Our king cares about each one of his men, and now he feels guilty because some of his best were killed," one said to the other as they left the room.

They thought him a kind man, a great warrior who would die for his men. Instead, he was a murderer. David bit on his knuckles to keep from crying out at the thought. Then he forced the truth to the back of his mind, and tried to convince himself that there was a war with the Ammonites, and that it wasn't murder if Uriah died in a skirmish.

After all, Joab had only ordered an advance on the enemy. Even he could not be certain that Uriah would be struck down in the battle. David was almost certain that Bathsheba herself would not suspect he had ordered the death of her husband. If she did, he would do all he could to disabuse her of the notion. She did not deserve to bear the guilt of her lover's actions. He would pay his respects to her tomorrow and try to find an opportunity to tell her that very soon after the seven day period of mourning he would marry her.

He would never let her find out that Uriah's death was his doing. He told himself that it would serve no purpose, only upset her and cause her to blame herself. But, as he lay there, prostrate on his bed, he knew that the real reason he would keep the secret was shame.

He had done a shameful thing, and Bathsheba would hate him for it if she ever found out. That possibility terrified him, because he was bound to this woman until the day he died. He had never felt like this about another person. The only relationship that came close had been his friendship with Saul's son, Jonathan, whose loss he still mourned deep in his heart.

He tried to pray then, to ask God never to allow Bathsheba to be taken from him, but he could not pray. He knew that God would not answer his prayer, because God knew he did not deserve to have Bathsheba. That thought brought anger against the Lord, a sullen resentment that would last for months.

Later, David rose from his bed. He ate most of the food on his tray. Then he dressed in his most resplendent robes and went to call his servants. He wouldn't allow himself to think about anything but preparing the rooms adjacent to his for Bathsheba. She was all he desired. He would be happy once he had her with him, he assured himself.

~ ~ ~

Isaac allowed himself only one day to recuperate from his stripes before returning his father's body to Hebron. Only under the most dire circumstances did the Hebrews postpone a burial for more than twenty-four hours. But Isaac would not bury his father in the land of the Ammonites. Strong spices—aloe and myrrh, cloves and cinnamon—were placed in the shroud and the body carried on a litter by two of Ahiam's lieutenants.

In all, more than a dozen soldiers were given leave to take the body back to Hebron. This was permitted only because of Ahiam's stature as a member of the *Gibborim,* the thirty greatest warriors in Israel. A message had been dispatched to the King, who would send an emissary to Hebron, another indication of the high regard Ahiam was given in Israel.

Chapter Ten

HEBRON

In her new role as a family member in Isaac's household, Keziah found herself more at ease than at any time since her ill-fated journey to Adoraim. The days of nausea were over, and she felt as healthy and strong as she had been before. Judith had more than accepted her as a daughter-in-law. She treated Keziah as a favored daughter, showering her with as many hugs and words of encouragement as she gave Adah. To Keziah, who had not had the companionship of another woman since the death of her mother, it was a balm to the spirit.

And the division of household work among three, for Judith allowed Adah to contribute her efforts, made Keziah feel almost sinfully idle when she found herself with so much leisure time.

Instead of finding fault each time she did something for them like her father did, both Adah and Judith would thank her. They often praised her cooking, or her weaving or sewing, and gradually Keziah came to accept their praise as sincere. She stopped living under the cloud of believing she could do nothing right. Her new life was so much better than the life she had lived in her father's house.

She often went to visit her father, still compelled by duty to try to please him. Deep down, she felt it was somehow disloyal to Aaron to be so happy away from him. So she would take him food, and stay to help keep his household clean and organized. He always acted pathetically glad to see her. That was strange, since he had seldom paid her any attention before her marriage.

"Thank you, Keziah," he said one afternoon after she had spent the day directing his new housekeeper, Agba, a large, slothful woman, in her duties and prepared a large meal for her father. Aaron had ignored Judith's suggestion that he hire Akim's widow, reasoning that Agba's extra flesh must mean she was a good cook, a premise he had to admit was false.

"The house is falling into disarray since you left, and I don't have much to eat, just what little of Agba's swill I can force down. I am afraid my final years are upon me, and I will die unhappy and alone."

Keziah couldn't help feeling a surge of guilt. "But Father, what about your plans to marry again? You are not too old, surely, to have a wife and sons yet to bring you comfort."

Aaron shook his head in self-pity. "No, Keziah, I think not. I'm afraid the house of Aaron will not continue; there will be no son to carry on my name. Only you will inherit what little I have accumulated in this life. You can at least look forward to that."

"Father, don't be foolish. I don't look forward to any such thing." And she set about trying to lift his spirits, only partially succeeding. All her life Keziah sensed that she had somehow failed her father, that she wasn't a good enough daughter, and that she should not have been born a woman.

That view of herself was etched too deeply within her to ever be completely erased. Even now those feelings returned whenever she visited her father. Her heart still ached with the desire for his love. But it remained as distant and unattainable as ever.

But that ache had in large part been diminished by the joy she found in having a mother now, for Judith insisted that as Isaac's wife, she was as much a daughter as Adah. And Adah was a delight, such a bright, cheerful little thing, her huge, round eyes exactly like her mother's.

Despite her naturally ebullient nature, Adah did show some signs of having been traumatized by that dreadful encounter on a lonely road. She was extremely solicitous of Keziah, and protective of her new sister as well as her mother. She often sat atop the post of the courtyard gate, a little sentinel ever vigilant against danger.

One day as they took their rest from the noonday sun, Adah asked in a carefully casual voice, "Do you think they will come back for us?"

Keziah, who had been gazing off into space, now gave her full attention to the child she had come to love as a sister. She did not pretend she didn't understand Adah's meaning. "Those men are not interested in coming after us, Adah. They have long since forgotten you, and they believe me to be dead, so why should they come back?"

"But maybe they will come back to Hebron for some other reason and see us," Adah responded, still in that unnaturally calm voice.

Keziah shook her head. "No, Adah, they were not from Hebron, nor anywhere near here. I am sure of it. I believe that's the reason they were not afraid to attack us. They were just passing through and believed they would be gone long before anyone accused them." After that, Adah seemed to relax her vigilance a little. Keziah hoped that in time she would no longer suffer from that terrible encounter on the road to Adoraim.

But in the days that followed, as if Adah's fears had given birth to her own, Keziah could not shake that feeling that she was being watched. It wasn't a constant feeling, but each time she went into the city market she felt as if eyes were following her movement. Repeatedly, she would turn around and scan the crowd of vendors and buyers, but invariably she saw no one who appeared to have sinister motives. Keziah told herself it was just the aftereffects of the trauma she had suffered and the suggestion Adah had placed in her mind.

~ ~ ~

Keziah wondered each day if this would be the day that Isaac returned. Though the men had told them that the siege could last many more months, they all hoped it would end sooner than anyone expected.

Keziah found herself looking forward to her husband's return with both longing and dread. She wanted him back home and safe. She wanted to see him again—just feast her eyes on the man who had changed her life completely, who had saved her, really.

But with the recent insult done to her honor and years and years of her father's subtle rejection, Keziah also dreaded Isaac's return, certain in her heart of hearts that if he came to really know her, he would not love her, but pity her, perhaps despise her.

One day, some two weeks after the men had departed, Keziah looked up to see Isaac coming through the gate into the courtyard. Behind him was a group of soldiers carrying a litter, which she scarcely noticed. With a cry of joy, she jumped up from her spindle and rushed over to her husband.

When she saw the pained, haggard look on his face, she knew that something must be terribly wrong. Then her eyes went again to the soldiers and the litter, and she realized that Ahiam was not standing there with his son. Her hands went to her mouth and she took in the meaning of the shrouded form on the litter. "Oh, Isaac," she whispered.

Isaac did not look at her. His attention was focused somewhere behind her. When she turned, she saw that Judith stood on the stairs that led to the roof. She must have heard something and come down to investigate. Now she stood frozen in place, her eyes riveted on the burden the soldiers carried.

Isaac swallowed hard. "Mother . . . I am so sorry." The sound of his voice released Judith from her paralysis. She ran to her son and threw herself into his arms. They both wept. Keziah felt the tears flow down her face. She wanted so much to comfort both of them, but in their grief they were unaware of her.

"Where is my father?"

Keziah turned at the sound of the belligerent little voice, and saw Adah, her hands fisted at her side, questioning one of the soldiers. Keziah reached out a hand and laid it gently on the child's shoulder. Adah shook it off and stepped closer to the guard, who looked as if he would like to be swallowed up by the earth he stood on.

"Where is my father?" she asked again in a louder voice.

The warrior studied the brave little girl and decided she deserved a forthright answer. "Your father has fallen in battle, little one."

Adah staggered back several paces—as if she had been struck. She stared in horror at the litter and shook her head vehemently. "No!" she screamed before turning around and running up the outside stairs to the roof. Keziah started to follow her, as Isaac and Judith, engrossed in comforting each other, had not noticed her departure. But after considering a moment, Keziah decided to leave her to grieve privately for a while. She remembered that at her own mother's death, she had wanted privacy for her sorrow.

The next hours were a nightmare for all of them. They hurried to prepare Ahiam for burial before sundown, now that they were in Hebron, as Hebrew Law prescribed.

Once the body had been prepared, all who had touched it made their way to the small stream that ran near the house. They were required to wash in running water before they could be considered ceremonially clean. Isaac was unable to spare the women all the horrors of Ahiam's death, for even the spices were unable to mask the burnt odor from his body. But Isaac didn't want to further distress his mother by telling her that Ahiam had died needlessly, and perhaps even deliberately.

He also kept from Judith and Keziah his own punishment for insubordination, even when his mother wrapped her arms around him, causing him to grimace at the pain from his lacerated back. Eventually she would know everything, but not now. Ahiam had been the sun in her sky, and Isaac knew that she could bear nothing more.

He had already asked the men who accompanied him not to mention the fiasco at Rabbah. They did not seem inclined to talk about it anyway, and he guarded his tongue around them, even though they had been particular friends of his father. If they were secret spies for Joab, they would gather no evidence from him, and if, as he believed, they were in sympathy with him and held the same opinion of the campaign as he did, he would not implicate them by bringing them into his plans.

The soldiers tried to make themselves useful building the cooking fire, preparing their own food, and going to the homes of Ahiam's friends and neighbors to inform them of the death. It was a large group of mourners who buried the honored citizen of Hebron, one of the King's "Mighty Men."

As the mourners made their way to the burial cave, an envoy arrived from the King. It was no less an important personage than Jehoshaphat, David's chief of protocol. He was accompanied by professional mourners, who immediately joined the procession and filled the air with their high-pitched wailing and the rattle of their sistrums. It was an honor indeed for the King to have sent them.

Keziah did not try to hold back the tears as they buried her father-in-law. She had barely known him, really. But in the few hours she had spent in his presence, she had felt the love and acceptance that flowed from him, and he had begun to fill the deep chasm in her spirit that needed a father's love. Now that chasm was back again.

She joined the family members, who wore torn tunics and sat on the bare earth of the courtyard when they returned from the burial. Friends came by, as they would continue to do for each of the seven days of their mourning, bringing food, taking care of everyday chores, and offering their condolences.

Before Jehoshaphat returned to Jerusalem, he gave Judith a gift of gold from the King and conveyed David's personal assurance that if she needed anything in the future, she was to appeal directly to him. Judith seemed comforted by the King's actions, but Keziah noticed that Isaac sat brooding as he listened to the King's man and bid him a curt good-bye.

Keziah left Isaac alone with his grief. He hardly spoke, except to comfort his mother or sister. Keziah felt a mixture of relief and dismay that Isaac seemed to have forgotten he had taken a bride. On the eighth day after Ahiam's burial, he had eaten little, then gone into the small room where all his father's things were kept—his armor, his weapons, even mementos of great battles he had fought in. She had gone by the room several times, and once she thought he must be crying, because his shoulders were shaking as he bent over his father's shield with a polishing cloth. Keziah had tried to talk to him, to sit with him, but her husband had made it apparent to her that he preferred to be alone.

She sat with Judith and Adah until it was time to seek her bed. Adah had been sleeping next to her mother since Ahiam's burial, probably as much because she sensed her mother needed her nearness as her own need to be comforted, Keziah suspected. Adah's astuteness sometimes amazed her.

In her own room she washed her face and hands and feet and lay down, but sleep would not come. She wanted so badly to comfort her husband, but what could she do? Isaac was almost a stranger to her. And now this great tragedy had befallen the family. Tears blurred her eyes as she remembered her kind father-in-law and his last words to her. She would take care of Judith and Adah, but she also wanted to take care of Isaac.

How could she help him? Isaac had saved her in her time of need, and she loved him. He had done everything for her and she had done nothing in return. Oh, he had thanked her for her ministrations to Judith and Adah, but that was something apart from Isaac and their marriage. After all, she had known and loved Judith and Adah before she ever met Isaac.

They had acted like polite strangers since Isaac's return, but they were not strangers. She was his wife, and Isaac needed a wife now. But Keziah was afraid she did not know how to be a wife.

Her cheeks flushed then, as she thought of their wedding night and how she had never been a wife in even the most elemental way. Of course, Isaac had been grieving since his return home, so she had assumed he wished to be alone in his room. She had continued to sleep in the small room she had become accustomed to during her convalescence. But now . . . maybe Isaac waited for her to be the one to begin their life together as man and wife. Had he not promised to give her time to get used to the marriage?

A short time later, she entered Isaac's room, relieved that he still was not there. Perhaps he would not come to his bed tonight, but would keep vigil in his father's room. But if he did come, she would be there, as a wife should be.

She slipped into bed, shivering even though the night was warm, but she had made up her mind, and she would not change it. She touched the slight rounding of her abdomen. Perhaps her husband would reject her. She would die of humiliation if he did, but she resisted the impulse to slip back to her own small room. Keziah settled in to wait. In a matter of minutes, her very busy and draining day had caught up with her and she fell into a deep sleep.

Isaac almost cried out in alarm when he sought his bed an hour later and realized he wasn't alone in his room. His room was in darkness, and he had to pull the curtain back before he realized it was a sleeping Keziah who had startled him. In the bright moonlight he could see that she slept deeply. His wife. He had not thought of her much since the battle. Other things had intruded on his mind. He did not know her, not really. Yet here she was, asleep in his bed, and he supposed she would be there each night for the rest of his life. It seemed strange, yet comforting.

When he got into bed beside her, she gave an indistinct mumble and turned onto her side away from him. He placed an arm around her waist and drew her to him so that they rested like spoons together. His wife was here. He wasn't alone. It felt right.

~ ~ ~

Later, Isaac thought that perhaps his original decision to sleep with his wife had not been so wise. He had known from the beginning that a girl who had suffered abuse as Keziah had would need to be wooed gently over time to overcome her fears. He had thought himself resigned to wait, and at first he had no trouble falling asleep, as exhausted as he was.

But at some point during the night, the combination of her silky hair brushing his arm, her soft sighs as she slept, the scent of almond oil on her skin, had wakened him and made him aware that patience was gone begging, replaced by urgent desire.

He argued with himself. If he woke her now with his demands, she would surely be frightened. Then it might take a very long time for her to trust him again. Still, it couldn't hurt to place a single kiss on that sweet spot on her neck where her hair fell away. Surely that would do no harm.

But after the kiss, he found that he could not resist running his fingers over the smooth length of her outstretched arm. And so it went. Soon his ardor became, like a leak in a dam, impossible to hold back. He knew then the wisdom of the Rab's teaching, which Jonathan had shared with him as he matured, that passion was as powerful as fire, and that a man should not think he could resist it once it was unleashed. That is why the Rab and Jonathan had taught him not to touch a woman until he was wed, and she was his by God's will.

But Keziah *was* his, he argued with himself. They were wed and it was his right. But he couldn't hurt or frighten her. Not ever. He made a vow to himself that he would stop his lovemaking if she became upset or frightened.

~ ~ ~

Keziah woke slowly. She was warm and comfortable. Her back was being stroked, and she stretched like a cat. Soft kisses fell on her forehead, her ear, her chin. She turned her head and the next kiss fell on her parted lips. She woke, suddenly aware that she was in Isaac's arms. Momentarily she stiffened in his embrace.

"Keziah?" She opened her eyes and saw uncertainty mingled with desire in his. He was her husband and he needed her. Miraculously, he wanted her. She kissed him back wholeheartedly.

He was exceedingly gentle. He banished all her fears and wooed her until all her pent-up love for him burst forth in a joyous cry. Amazed, Keziah wept with relief that this act, this joining with her husband, bore no resemblance to what had happened to her months ago. It had been so utterly different that not one moment of fear had marred the wonder of it. Together they formed one flesh, one spirit, as God had meant it to be from the beginning.

He caught a tear with his thumb. "You're crying. Did I hurt you, frighten you?"

"No! No, far from it. It was . . . something happened to me. I did not know it would be like this. I was afraid that . . . just afraid that I could never be a true wife, that maybe you would be repulsed."

He chuckled. "I wasn't repulsed."

"Neither was I." Her face lit with a wonderful smile. He had seen her smile at Adah, but this was her first smile for him.

When Isaac rose from the bed and went to wash his face and hands in the basin of water that sat on a tall chest, Keziah's contented smile changed to alarm.

"What happened to your back? Isaac, it looks as if you've been beaten! Was it the Ammonites?"

Isaac's laugh was tinged with bitterness when he answered. "No, it wasn't the enemy. Our own general thought I deserved a lashing for questioning his leadership."

"You questioned Joab's authority?" Keziah shivered with fear for her husband. "Isaac, you mustn't make an enemy of the general. Judith told me what happened with Jonathan and . . ." She broke off abruptly. Ailea was the last person she wanted to discuss with her husband.

But Isaac apparently knew what she would have said, because he finished for her, "and Ailea. Yes, Joab was convinced she was a spy for the Aramean alliance, and would have had her killed. Jonathan protected her, even though at the time, he believed she was guilty. Joab has been his enemy ever since."

"Did you?" Keziah asked, not knowing if she really wanted to hear the answer.

"Did I what?"

"Did you believe her to be guilty?"

Isaac didn't answer for a long time. Keziah felt certain his head was filled with thoughts of the raven-haired beauty. How foolish she had been to bring up her rival at a time when she had her husband to herself.

Finally, he spoke. "No. I knew she could never betray her husband in such a way, but I was only a green lad then, so neither Jonathan or Joab was interested in my opinion. But by virtue of my being Jonathan's man, I became Joab's enemy from that time on. I have mostly avoided the general since then, but I couldn't keep silent this time. He was at least partially responsible for my father's death, Keziah, he and one of his henchmen. I would be less than a man if I kept quiet about it."

He noticed his wife's pale face and tried to moderate his words. "Don't worry, I won't be so rash from now on. I intend to proceed very methodically to avenge my father and the others who died needlessly."

Keziah wanted to beg him to let it be, to tell him that she couldn't bear it if the same fate befell him as it did his father. After all, he did not care deeply for her, and besides, men never gave any credence to a woman's opinion. Had her father ever listened to her?

So she expressed her concern in the only way she thought possible, by briskly telling him to sit down on the room's three-legged stool so she could rub aloe into his still inflamed back and encouraging him to tell her what had happened at Rabbah.

Isaac was somewhat surprised to find himself telling his wife what had happened. He asked her to promise not to tell Judith yet. He was afraid it was still too soon for her to take in even more horror and grief. Keziah hated to keep anything from Judith but could see the logic in what Isaac asked, so she agreed.

The next day, Jonathan visited them, and Keziah was relieved that she wouldn't have to keep the truth from Judith after all, for he spoke of it in front of both Judith and Keziah. After an anxious glance at his mother, Isaac evidently decided she was strong enough to hear the entire story, because he didn't try to stop Jonathan from talking.

"I told the King how Joab had ordered everyone but a handful of men to pull back," he said, "and I pointed out that the general had to have known it would mean certain death for those men. David became very angry with me, Isaac. He doesn't want to hear any ill spoken of his sister's son."

"And Talmon's actions . . . did you tell him about that?"

Jonathan nodded gravely. "He seemed a little more willing to listen to that, but still, he did not say if he would punish Talmon."

Isaac slammed his fist down on the table between them, causing Keziah to jump. "I leave for Jerusalem tomorrow, Jonathan. I will demand that Talmon be tried!"

"I was afraid you would insist on going. Well, I'll go with

you," Jonathan said. "There are other men who witnessed the incident. But we have to plan our strategy, Isaac. You cannot go before the King making demands, or you're likely to lose your life."

Judith burst into tears. "Please, son, listen to your friend. If I lost you too I . . ." she broke off, unable to continue. Keziah wanted to add her pleas to Judith's but was not sure she had the right.

In a few moments, Judith composed herself and spoke to her son. "Isaac, there is a God in heaven who watches over all men. If this man has done evil, he will not go unpunished. Don't risk everything to punish him yourself." Then she left them and went to her room.

Jonathan watched his wife's best friend depart and determined to bring Ailea to Hebron to comfort her. "Isaac, you must see that your mother needs you now. Please wait awhile and consider carefully what you want to do. You are too distraught at this time to think clearly."

Isaac nodded grudgingly. "You're right. I am needed in Hebron right now. But as soon as possible, I intend to go to Jerusalem and get to the bottom of this. One thing I do know, my friend, and I owe it to you to inform you first. I can never again serve under Joab. I intend to apply to the King to be relieved of my duties. I will offer to do some other service for Israel, but even the thought of taking another order from Joab sickens me."

Jonathan could not hide his sorrow and disappointment. Isaac had served him for more than three years now, long since becoming more than just an armor bearer, but earning his position as Jonathan's right-hand man, an indispensable aid and assistant. More important, he had become, along with Ahiam, Jonathan's best friend. The older man's eyes misted over as he pleaded with Isaac to reconsider.

"I have lost two good friends already, Isaac. Your father was as close to me as a brother. He trained me as a warrior and fought with me in countless campaigns. And then there is Benjamin.

Though he knew he had no chance of rising in the ranks to the glory of the *Gibborim,* he helped Ahiam and me attain the position. He snatched our brands from the fire many a time. Now he is gone from me as well. Can you not have pity, and at least tell me you will ponder this a while before you make up your mind?"

Isaac looked into the eyes of his battle-hardened friend and saw that they were brimming with tears. The sight brought a lump to his own throat. He had never seen his friend so shaken except when Ailea had been missing and he had been frantic with worry over her. At the thought of Ailea, guilt stabbed through Isaac, and he reluctantly agreed not to tender his resignation from the military until he had had more time to think it over. And he agreed to put off the confrontation in Jerusalem until he had become more rational.

Chapter Eleven

Isaac found himself distracted much of the time, fuming over the King's reaction to the report of the battle, and planning ways to make Talmon pay. He would often mumble agreement to a conversation his mother, or sister, or wife was having with him, only to interrupt with—"Maybe I should forget appealing to the King, and go to Gibeah, find Talmon, and challenge him." Or, "If you go with me to Jerusalem, Mother, and petition the King for justice, he might be more willing to listen to the charges."

Both Keziah and Judith were alarmed that Isaac was so obsessed, but nothing they did seemed to have any effect. Well, that was not entirely true. Keziah knew that her husband was becoming more and more interested in her.

The intimate, physical side of their marriage was new and exciting to both of them; not just the physical, but the intimacy of thought that they shared in the dark, just before falling asleep. They were coming to know and trust each other more as they shared this most vulnerable time of day.

One night, Keziah cried out in her sleep, and Isaac shook her awake. "Keziah, wake up. It's only a dream." She wrapped both arms around him to still her trembling.

"Maybe you should tell me about the dream," he suggested,

stroking her hair. "If you speak it aloud, it might not come back as a dream again."

Keziah thought about this. Until tonight the dream had not reoccurred since her marriage to Isaac. What if the dream came back each night now? Isaac might lose patience with her. He might even refuse to spend the night with a wife who disturbed his sleep by crying out in the middle of the night. She didn't want that to happen.

"I . . . I'll try. But the dream is about . . . what happened."

His arm tightened around her. "I know. But I want to hear it. I think you need to tell it."

So she took a deep breath and told him everything from the time she had seen the two men accost Adah in the woods. And it had helped, somehow, to take some of the terror out of the event. She was ashamed to tell her husband such things, but, rather than drive him away, it seemed to bring them closer together.

The very next night, the night sky was obscured with clouds, and their room was in total darkness. "Tell me about the battle at Rabbah, Isaac," Keziah said, then held her breath waiting for his refusal.

Isaac expelled an explosive breath. "It is only fair, I guess, after I insisted you tell me everything. Very well. But stop me if the story is too much for your ears."

"It won't be. Go ahead."

"As I've already told you, Joab ordered every unit to withdraw from around the wall, except for Uriah's and Father's men. There was no way for them to survive the Ammonites overwhelming numbers. Joab didn't make a mistake with that order. It would have been obvious to the greenest recruit that those men would be doomed.

"Still, a few of the men did survive. My father was among them. Then he was down, and one of his men started to go to help him. That is when Talmon, as Joab's liaison in the field, ordered the man to leave Father to die. I was watching it all from a rise some distance away. By the time I got to my father, he was. . . ." Isaac had to stop for a moment but continued in a firm voice. "He had been hit by flaming arrows. There was no hope for him, but he lingered for hours in pain."

"Oh, Isaac, I am so sorry. Your father was such a good man." She wanted to hold him but remained still, knowing he had more to tell.

"It wasn't only Uriah and Father, Keziah. There were a score of others killed outright. And then there were those poor souls who were even less fortunate."

"What do you mean?"

"Men like Benjamin. He was a veteran, one of our best men, outside of the *Gibborim,* and the Ammonites knew it. He had battled them before. They captured him, unwounded. They . . . I won't tell you exactly what they did, but they tortured him. Atop the wall, for all of us to see. They were killing him slowly and very, very painfully.

"Once Benaiah called me outside the tent. Father was in such pain, I welcomed the chance to step away for just a moment. Then Benaiah pointed to the wall of Rabbah, and as soon as he did, I saw Benjamin. Jonathan and I just stood there, helpless. Then Benaiah decided to end it."

"How?"

"He's a very good shot. Put an arrow right into Benjamin's heart. I wouldn't have had the courage to do it, but I'm glad Benaiah did. Was it murder, Keziah? I can't believe it was. Benjamin was already a dead man. Benaiah just cut short his suffering. Will the Lord punish him for that, do you think?"

"Adonai tries the heart, Isaac. He knows that Benaiah did not have murder in his heart."

She continued to offer what comfort she could, but realized that the violent, wicked things that had happened to each of them had taken their toll, and that it would be a long time before either she or Isaac was free of haunting memories. Probably they would never be entirely free. In her prayers each day, she thanked God that they had each other.

~ ~ ~

Keziah had wondered what would happen to their budding relationship if Isaac were to find himself in Ailea's path again. She was to find out the next week, when Jonathan came to visit, in another attempt to persuade Isaac not to leave his service, not to leave the army, and not to embark alone on a mission to punish Talmon.

He also had come to invite the entire family to a feast, he informed them the first evening at table. "You are all to come to Ziph for my son's weaning feast. Please do not refuse, or Ailea will postpone the event again. She wishes to keep our son a baby. The trouble is, he is already half the size of his mother."

Judith laughed as she passed Jonathan the bread. "Micah is certainly a strong, healthy boy, but you must remember, Jonathan, that he *is* still a baby, still months away from his third birthday."

"Spoken like a mother," Jonathan chuckled.

"The boy seems older than he is." Isaac turned to Keziah, "He prattles on all the time, and sometimes manages to say a discernible word. Oh, and he can also count to four."

Jonathan laughed and beamed at the praise given his son. Keziah felt a pang of sorrow on behalf of her own child. Would he ever receive such love from his father, or rather, the man he would know as his father?

Keziah realized that she always thought of the baby as a boy; yet she prayed it would be a girl, so that Isaac would not have to taste the bitter gall of raising another man's son, conceived in shame, to be his heir. Maybe it would be a girl, and therefore easier for Isaac to love. She brought her attention back to the table to hear her husband assure Jonathan that they would attend the feast two days hence.

~ ~ ~

From the moment they stepped into Jonathan and Ailea's house, Keziah sensed that all her fears that Isaac still loved his friend's wife were well founded. Ailea greeted them all with the customary kiss, but it seemed to Keziah that her lips lingered on his cheeks just a second longer than the others, and that the look she gave him was distinctly warmer. Keziah chastised herself for such thoughts. Neither Ailea nor Isaac had behaved in any way unseemly. Still, she could not keep a knot of jealousy from clenching her stomach.

At the feast, little Micah, proud of himself in his new blue tunic and well aware that he had the undivided attention of the adults in attendance, performed every trick he could think of to ensure that he kept it. He spun around in circles until he fell down; tossed the ball given him as a gift by Isaac to each of the adults; played hide-and-seek behind the folds of his mother's tunic; and finally, tried to climb on the rim of the cistern that was in the center of the courtyard. He teetered on the edge until Isaac swooped him up and returned him to his mother.

As the child was passed to Ailea, Keziah saw the look of deep affection that Isaac's expression held as he watched Ailea with her son, and it shot straight to her soul like an arrow. He loved her still. And who could blame him? Ailea was everything that was feminine, everything that she, Keziah, was not. How could she bear to stay here and watch this for two days? The man she loved with the woman he loved.

That evening Keziah was very quiet. She tried to avoid Ailea. Once she noticed Isaac watching Ailea intently, and she turned away. She went and found Adah and played a game with her. When she had settled Adah down to sleep on a pallet in Micah's room, she went in search of the adults once more, and found them on the rooftop, enjoying the cooling evening breeze.

"I don't feel too well," she whispered to Judith while Jonathan related a story to the Rab of how he and Isaac had tricked a Philistine raider into surrendering his spear. Judith patted her sympathetically and tapped Ailea, motioning her to follow them.

The tiny woman seemed to glide across the floor as she went with them. Keziah felt the misery of envy when she compared her own thickening figure to the lithe form of Ailea.

"Keziah doesn't feel well, and would like to be shown to her room," Judith explained.

Ailea's perfectly arched brows came together in a frown of concern. "By all means. I remember when I carried Micah, I also tired easily."

Keziah's eyes widened and she looked at the other woman sharply. She knew! How could she know? Her face flamed with mortification. Ailea must think her the loosest kind of woman. Isaac must have told her. Why couldn't he have waited at least a respectable length of time? Was it because he had kept no secrets from the woman he loved? *Stop it!* She told herself silently. Her husband more likely confided in Jonathan, who had probably told his wife, or perhaps Judith had told her. Besides, everyone would know soon enough. There was no reason to feel betrayed. Isaac had done nothing wrong.

Ailea led them to a room on the first floor of the large home. "This room belonged to Jonathan's sister, Ruth. She was a widow for many years; but some months ago a merchant came to our market day here in Ziph and saw her with me. I could see that he was interested in Ruth, so I had the Rab invite the man to stay with us. Within a week's time, he had asked her to wed with him. They live in Maon now, not too many miles away.

"Ruth was very simple in her tastes, but I have attempted to make the room more comfortable with rugs and cushions." Ailea continued to point out the features of the room. The sleeping pallet looked soft and inviting with furs and pillows. There was a basin and a pitcher filled with fresh water.

Ailea continued to carry the conversation for a few minutes longer until she realized that Keziah was not responding with the same warmth. She stopped in mid-sentence. "Oh, just listen to me, going on and on, when you are tired and would like to be left in peace. Judith and I will leave you to rest now."

With that, Ailea kissed her on the cheek. Keziah knew that she should deny wanting to be left alone, insist that she was anxious to hear what Ailea had to say, but she could not bring herself to do it. She could hardly look at her beautiful rival without bursting into tears. So she bade the other two women good night.

When they were gone, she put out both the oil lamps that illumined the room, and lay on the pallet, fighting tears. Isaac thought she was asleep when he sought his rest an hour later. He made to draw her into his arms, but she mumbled as if in sleep and turned away from him. In a few moments, he was sleeping peacefully while his wife wiped at the tears that wet her cheeks.

~ ~ ~

The next day the weaning feast continued. Little Micah was given his first bit of meat. He promptly spit it out. All the guests roared with laughter, except for Keziah. Isaac had slipped closer to Jonathan's family. He was laughing. Now he was bending down to whisper something in Ailea's ear as she tried to coax her son into tasting the food. She looked up at him with a brilliant smile.

Overwhelmed, Keziah slipped through the courtyard gate and walked up a hill to an old sycamore tree. There was a stone underneath that resembled a seat. It had evidently been used as one for generations, because its contours were worn smooth as marble. Keziah sat down there and looked down at the village and beyond to the wilderness of Ziph, where the foliage became sparse, and the hills more rocky and craggy.

Soon she could see nothing at all, as tears ran down her face and her inner torment blurred her view. And the din of her agonized thoughts drowned out all other sounds, so that she did not hear him approach. A gentle pat on the shoulder intruded on her painful reverie, and she looked around to see Jonathan's father, the Rab Shageh, sitting by her. Somehow she wasn't startled by his presence. He smiled at her, and that simple gesture poured balm over her wounded spirit.

"I am so sorry, child. So sorry. May I sit with you?"

Keziah nodded her assent, and Shageh sat down beside her.

Surprisingly, the old teacher said nothing. For long moments they sat side by side looking toward the west as the sun sank lower in the sky.

"Isaac does not love me." *Why am I telling him this? I certainly can't tell him about Isaac's feelings for Ailea.* Keziah was shocked at her own outburst.

"But you have been married for only a short time, and during that time he has been away to battle and then has grieved for his father. You must wait. In time he will love you."

"No. I don't think he will. I don't think he'll ever love me."

"Because you don't believe anyone ever has loved you, nor could."

"My mother loved me."

"But she has been gone now for many years."

His quiet understanding opened a floodgate, and the next moment Keziah found herself sobbing out the entire story of her life, including the rape and her father's reaction to her pregnancy. All the love, all the acceptance that she had wished and dreamed of from her father, she found in the gentle goodness of the Rab.

Keziah did not try to hide her despair from him. "Sometimes I wish that small ledge had not been there to catch me when they threw me over the cliff," she admitted.

"Child, why do you wish such a thing?" His hand rested gently upon her bent head, and she heard no condemnation in his voice, only deep sorrow.

"Because my father hates me and would have had me stoned. He believed it was my fault."

"But we know it was not your fault, don't we, Keziah." Keziah did not answer, though the Rab waited for her to do so.

He continued. "Then if we don't know, we must seek wisdom

from the precepts of the Lord. It tells us very plainly that when a young woman is accosted and raped, she is no more guilty of a crime than is a victim of assault and robbery. All the blame is on the man who did so wickedly. This is what Adonai has said through Moses."

"Still, I am defiled. No man would ever willingly marry one such as I. And my husband only wed me to save my life. He also felt an obligation because I protected his sister."

"Keziah, what if your father had not chosen to have you stoned, but instead had believed you? What would he have done then?"

"Done? Why, he would have done what the Law said. He always follows the Law."

"Child, do you know that the Law says that your father should find the man and demand he marry you, and pay your father fifty shekels of silver? So let us suppose your father, following the Law exactly, had the man who hurt you hunted down and forced him to marry you. Would that have made you happy?"

"Happy! I . . . I would die if that animal ever touched me again. I think I would go mad."

"But the Law stipulates that the man who has so harmed a maid must keep her as wife all the days of her life and never divorce her, because he has so humbled her."

Keziah could not suppress a shudder. "That would be unthinkable!"

"So can you not see the loving-kindness of the Lord in saving you from such a fate?"

"You mean the things that have happened have worked out for the better."

Shageh nodded. "The Law was given to draw us to God, to deliver us from our baser nature, and to protect the weak. But sometimes the Law as written on parchment does not serve the human condition, and Adonai intervenes through circumstances, though we may not know it at the time, to show His love and mercy. Do you see?"

"Yes," Keziah responded hesitantly.

The Rab wiped away the tears that streaked her cheeks using his two callused thumbs. "Now that you see, do you think you can live in gratitude to Adonai for what He has given you—a righteous and honorable man as a husband and even more a sister and mother you never thought to have?"

Keziah paused. "I hadn't thought of it that way. You are right, Rab Shageh. I have been full of self-pity. It's time I started to be thankful for what I have."

So when they returned to Jonathan's house and Isaac sought her out, she smiled at him. "Where were you?" he asked. "You seemed unhappy earlier, but when I looked for you, you were nowhere to be found."

"I was talking with the Rab up on the hill. We watched the sunset."

"Ah, at the teaching rock. You look more . . . at peace. The Rab helped you, I can tell. He has a way of binding up a hurting spirit."

"Yes, he certainly does."

Not only had her conversation with the Rab made her feel better, but Keziah felt herself drawn to Ailea. The lovely woman seemed sincerely interested in becoming friends, and Keziah, who had few, could not help but respond to some degree, but she held on to her reserve and saw that Ailea was a little hurt by her aloofness.

Keziah had a hard time falling asleep that night. Isaac did not come to their room, and Keziah assumed he and Jonathan were talking over matters. Surely it wasn't Ailea he was with. When such thoughts began to torture her, she reminded herself of the Rab's words, and finally, she slept.

By the time she woke up and dressed the next morning, Ailea and Judith were sitting in the courtyard, in low-slung cane chairs, talking quietly. Keziah saw Judith wipe her eyes and knew that she was talking to her friend about Ahiam.

She felt ashamed of herself at the pang of jealousy she felt over Ailea's relationship with Judith. Judith had kept her sadness under control at home out of consideration for Isaac and Adah. She had every right to pour out her heart to her friend. But Keziah couldn't help but feel left out. She started to turn away, but Ailea called out to her. "Keziah, stop him, please. Amal is about to go up the stairs!"

Keziah turned toward the stairs to the roof and saw a black goat on the third step. She reached out for him, but he scampered up. She followed. When she reached the top, she thought she had him cornered, but he dodged her. She stared in surprise as he ascended a ladder with wide steps that led to the roof of the second-floor apartment.

"Oh, don't go after him, Keziah; not in your condition."

Keziah looked at her mother-in-law.

"Judith didn't tell me. I am just observant. As for Amal, he has tricked himself, because he can go up that ladder, but not down it. He is no mountain goat, even though he seems to think he is."

"His name is 'Trouble'?"

"A perfect name for him, believe me. Jonathan thinks he is possessed of an evil spirit. He can't understand why I keep him as a pet. When he gets loose up here, he only eats Jonathan's things, not mine. Excuse me while I remove him."

After Ailea had tethered the goat in the courtyard, she returned, and for the next few minutes entertained Keziah with a story about how the goat had once embarrassed Jonathan in front of the whole village. It had happened when they were newly married and before Ailea had truly "settled in," she explained. Ailea admitted she had liked having the goat get the best of the warrior who had made her his captive bride.

Keziah was confused. When Ailea spoke of Jonathan, she did so with great affection. Could her feelings for Isaac be nothing but friendship? Or had she once loved Isaac but been forced to marry Jonathan? She longed to ask questions, but she couldn't, of course, without sounding jealous.

The men returned, and they headed back home. Keziah still felt threatened by Ailea, but all-in-all, the visit had been better than she had expected, at least after her conversation with the Rab. She kissed him on the cheek in farewell, and he patted her on the shoulder. They shared a long look, hers conveying heartfelt thanks and his deep understanding.

Chapter Twelve

Keziah worried when Isaac went to Jerusalem with Jonathan to bring charges against Talmon before the King and to see that he was dismissed from the army. She could see that Judith was worried too, but they both held their tongues as the men departed. Both Isaac and Jonathan were confident that with Benaiah's testimony they would be successful. Keziah hoped they were right.

On the way to the capital city, Jonathan and Isaac went over their plans to expose Talmon's guilt, and in doing so, at least garner a reprimand for Joab as well. The two friends disagreed about David's possible involvement in the disastrous incident at Rabbah, Jonathan arguing that surely David could not deliberately order his men to be killed.

"But why would he wish to send his own men into a losing battle?" he asked.

"You saw the dispatch that Uriah carried from David. Immediately after Joab received it, he ordered the assault on the wall and left those units at the Ammonites' mercy. How can you deny it?"

"I don't deny that David ordered the attack, but it must have been a mistake. Even the best military minds make them. Or maybe Joab acted entirely on his own."

"I think you know better than that. David is much too brilliant a strategist to make such a mistake. I don't know exactly *why* he did what he did, but I think it was deliberate. You are blind where the King is concerned, Jonathan," Isaac told him. "You see David as you wish he were, not as he is. My father often remarked that the King has changed over the years, become more selfish, less concerned for the welfare of his men."

Jonathan did not argue the point. He knew that where David was concerned he would always give the benefit of the doubt. He had loved and served the King from the age of fourteen, when he had joined David's outlaw band in the caves of Adullam. He was somewhat disillusioned, but still fiercely loyal. And he attended the next day's meeting with full confidence that they would find justice. Isaac was not as certain.

As they had half expected, Joab took Talmon's part. At first the general tried to block the audience with the King, but Benaiah thwarted that.

"I have been with David since his exile in Gath," Benaiah said. "I and all the Cherethites and Pelethites have pledged our lives to protect him and no one, *no* one will come between me and my King, General."

Joab was not at all intimidated by the fact that Benaiah was twice his size. "The King and I share the same blood. You would be wise to keep that in mind."

A mocking smile broke across Benaiah's face. "I am ever mindful of who you are, General, but I repeat, I will bring this matter before the King. We will see which of us he listens to."

The hearing was held the next day. Joab was to speak for Talmon. When they came into the audience chamber, Jonathan and Isaac were already there.

Talmon's gaze immediately fell on Isaac. That gloating look was back in his eyes. Isaac clenched his fists at his side to keep from wiping that look off his enemy's face. *He is convinced that he can't lose with Joab speaking on his behalf,* Isaac thought as he returned the stare.

Joab's gaze and his animosity were directed entirely toward Jonathan. Isaac felt a moment of alarm. The conflict that had begun more than three years ago over Ailea when Joab had been convinced that Jonathan's wife was a spy for the nations of Aram had not been forgotten by either man. Joab had wanted Ailea arrested and punished, but Jonathan had protected her.

Now Jonathan was risking the wrath of the general, the most powerful man in the kingdom after David, in order to seek justice for Isaac and his mother in the matter of Ahiam's death. Jonathan had insisted that he would have come before the King anyway. "Never doubt it, Isaac. Your father was like a brother to me," he had said.

The King entered the meeting room looking rather harried. He did not seem at all pleased at the dissension among some of his top officers. "Let's get this matter settled," he said with a frown. "After today, I wish to hear no more of this."

Everyone's attention was drawn to Benaiah when he entered the room. Isaac was gratified to see some of the self-confidence drain from Talmon's face as the trusted mercenary took his place beside him.

Isaac tried to keep his voice calm and well modulated as he presented the facts to the King. He described his father's death and how he had seen Talmon order his father closer to the walls, then pull nearly all support away from the few units left fighting. He told of seeing his father reach out to Talmon, even as he was being burned alive, and how Talmon had deliberately turned his back.

"You are lying, son of Ahiam," Talmon snarled.

"He is describing it exactly as it happened, Talmon, and well you know it," Benaiah snapped.

"I did not see him." Talmon's tone was no longer belligerent as he addressed Benaiah. Now it held a desperate, rather wheedling note.

"My lord," Joab said in his most conciliatory tone after giving Talmon a quelling look, "it was in the thick of battle. I ordered the men to pull back and sent the message by Talmon. In the confusion, some of the men must have misunderstood the order. My armor bearer has served me faithfully for several years. He says he did not see Ahiam of Hebron, and there is no reason to doubt him."

"He was looking right at him," Benaiah said emphatically. "One of his fellow warriors was in need of help and the coward turned his back. I refuse to serve alongside such a man!" The last part of the statement was directed to David.

"I also refuse to serve with such a man," Jonathan added.

"Nor will I," Isaac declared.

Talmon looked at Joab, obviously expecting him to defend his own aide. But Joab said no more in his favor, only held the King's gaze for a long moment. There was a pregnant silence while the King, turning away from all of them, pondered his judgment.

At last he turned around, and with a great sigh, addressed Talmon. "You will retire from military service with all due honor. You have served the general well, and through him, me. But with your fellow officers no longer able to have confidence in your loyalty during battle, I see no alternative than to relieve you of your duties." Isaac bristled at the King's conciliatory tone, but evidently, Talmon did not think David was being generous at all.

Talmon sputtered but could form no other arguments. He looked at Joab, who was staring at David. The King spoke again, this time to Joab. "See that he leaves the military with a generous stipend. He may also apply to me for help in any future endeavor he might undertake."

Isaac knew he should not interrupt the King but saw an opportunity he could not pass by. "My lord," he said, "I request that I be allowed to resign my army duties. I have served you now these four years, and with my father dead, my mother and young sister need me, as does my wife, who is soon to have a child. Since you mentioned in your gracious letter to my mother that you would like to help her, I make so bold as to beg this favor of the King."

David could certainly not go back on his oath to Judith, especially not so reasonable a request as this. He nodded his assent. "Your request is granted as of this day, son of Ahiam. This matter is now ended. I will hear no more of it. Is that understood by each of you?" His gaze swept everyone in the room, pausing until each nodded acquiescence. Then he swept from the room, his stiff bearing indicating his displeasure.

Talmon shot Isaac a hate-filled look and stormed out of the chamber. Jonathan and Isaac left the meeting vastly relieved that they had won this skirmish with their enemies. Knowing Talmon and Joab, neither believed the matter was truly ended, not even by the King's command.

Benaiah seemed to relish the prospect of going against Joab. He brushed by the general in an insulting manner as he went to exit the room. "Every lad of ten knows the lesson of Abimelech in the days of the judges," he tossed back over his shoulder. "He got too near a tower wall at Thebez and was killed by a stone thrown down by a woman. You are slipping badly, Joab. I doubt not that one day you too will die if you continue to be so foolish."

Isaac held his breath, and noticed that Jonathan had gone still also. There was a barely concealed threat in the insult. Joab was grinding his teeth together, so great was his fury, but for some reason he chose not to challenge Benaiah. "I do not fear death at the hands of a woman—or anyone. It would behoove you to remember that, Philistine." With that most insulting of Hebrew insults, referring to Benaiah's close association with the mercenaries, Joab pushed right by Benaiah and left the room.

When Isaac and Jonathan returned to Hebron, Keziah noticed that there was tension between them. "We got what we went after," Jonathan remarked as they rested on the comfortable couches arranged on the rooftop, where the cooling breezes of the late afternoon. "I don't see why you don't put it all to rest now."

Keziah paused in pouring wine into pottery cups for the men to see her husband's reaction to his friend's comment. As she expected, he didn't want to hear Jonathan's opinion.

"I can't just forget what was done to my father. At times I wish I could. I still want to see Joab and David pay for what happened. I am honestly surprised that you can so easily pass over the death of your best friend."

Jonathan stood abruptly, his face flushed. "If I didn't believe that grief has distorted your opinions as well as your words, I would have to challenge that insult. I loved Ahiam—knew him for years before you were ever born. I have done what I could to see justice done to the man responsible for his death.

"But you—you accuse me of being a traitor to my friend because I don't challenge the King right in his palace! You also remove yourself from my service, as if I and all the training I have invested in you are worth nothing."

He sat down the cup of wine Keziah had handed him and turned to walk away, but Isaac stopped him.

"Wait, Jonathan. Don't go away angry. Of course I am thankful for what you have done for me. For the training you gave me in the arts of war. But I just cannot serve under Joab anymore. Can't you understand that?"

Jonathan stopped and turned around to face his friend. "Yes. Yes, I can understand. We will always be friends, won't we?"

"How could I ever forsake the friend of my father. You are like a brother to me Jonathan."

The two men embraced fiercely, then broke apart self-consciously, clearing their throats loudly. Keziah bit back tears at the touching scene.

After Jonathan left, Isaac asked Judith and Keziah how they felt about the news that he was no longer going to be in the army. Judith was thrilled. "I won't have to spend half my life fearful of receiving word that you have fallen in battle," she had told him with a kiss on the evening he had returned.

Keziah was also glad he would not be called upon to fight

except in a time of national crisis. "But what will you do now?" she wanted to know. Whatever it was, she wanted to help him in his endeavors. She wanted to be a good wife.

"Jonathan and I made inquiries into Talmon's activities before we left Jerusalem. We learned that he is going to seek the King's commission as royal merchant as soon as he returns from Gibeah, where he has gone to lick his wounds. I intend to return to Jerusalem before he does and seek the commission for the Via Maris myself. It is a plum of a commission with all the entitlements of royal merchant attached to it. I would be guaranteed a most-favored status with Tyre and Lebanon. But most of all, I would deprive Talmon of what he desires."

Isaac's obsession with revenge alarmed Keziah. "But I thought it was all over. You had the man thrown out of the army. Surely you don't mean to continue this hatred."

"As long as I have breath, I will never forget what Talmon did to my father. Any opportunity I see to hurt him, I will take. I have to do something anyway, since I have left the army. I might as well become a caravaner and become rich. The more wealth I have, the more power I will have to protect what is mine from men like Joab and Talmon."

Keziah shuddered at the coldness in his voice, but ceased trying to convince him to change. Instead, she begged him to take her with him to Jerusalem. She pointed out that she had not returned to the city since she was a small child, while almost everyone in Israel had been to the capital numerous times for the feasts. Judith and Adah added their requests to go, and finally Isaac, feeling outnumbered by the women in his household, consented.

Keziah was relieved when he relented. She had a feeling that he would need her, that she could somehow protect him.

~ ~ ~

Just two days later they left Hebron at dawn so that they could arrive at Jerusalem by sunset. It was too strenuous a journey for either Adah or Keziah to make on foot, so Isaac had borrowed two mules for them to ride upon. Keziah was placed upon one, along with their bundle of clothes, while Judith and Adah rode the other. Isaac walked beside them. He did not talk much, seeming preoccupied with his impending audience with the King.

When they reached the Kidron Valley, they paused to look up at the City of David. Jerusalem lay on a narrow spur of rock which jutted from the main ridge line of central Canaan. It sat like a crown upon the highest elevation, the summit of which was Mt. Moriah, where Abraham had offered the sacrifice of his only son to Adonai. Jerusalem was a virtually impregnable fortress against attack, which was one reason David had chosen to make it his capital. It was also the reason Joab had been elevated years ago to the status of general, when he had found a way to breach the defenses of the Jebusite city.

Keziah's eyes were filled with wonder as she looked up at the beautiful sight. "I remember it. I was only five years old when I came with my father and mother to Passover. I thought it must have been exaggerated in my child's mind, but it wasn't. It is awesome."

Isaac laughed. "Wait until you see the palace and the tabernacle the King has set up. I know the elders of Hebron complained when David moved his capital here from their city, but my father always said it was one of the wisest decisions he ever made."

Keziah nodded. "My father still sometimes complains and speaks of the days when Hebron was the capital city. But even he loves Jerusalem. I remember him setting me atop his shoulders when we entered it. He was afraid I would be lost in the crowd." Keziah smiled at the fond memory—one of the only ones of her father.

"Well, you cannot expect me to carry you on my shoulders this time. You have grown a bit since you were five." Isaac looked down at her burgeoning waistline when he said it, and Keziah burst into laughter. He relished the delightful sound.

Adah, who had been listening avidly to their conversation said, "I am not too big, Isaac. Carry me on your shoulders. Please do." Isaac pretended to try to pick his sister up, and staggered as if her weight was too great for him to manage.

"Children, I would suggest, if we want to arrive before dark, that we finish playing and start up the road. It looks to be a steep climb." Though she chided, Judith's smile belied her words, and they made there way happily into Jerusalem.

When they arrived at the palace they found that David had secured a house nearby for them, complete with a pleasant-faced servant woman to see to their needs. It was small, with a tiny courtyard and four small rooms, but was furnished with chairs, a table, beautiful rugs on the floors, and sleeping couches in the bedchambers.

After Isaac had seen them comfortably situated, he went to the *House of the Gibborim* to try to gather information. He found it. As soon as he entered the officers' barracks he heard an armor bearer and a servant gossiping about what had been going on in Jerusalem.

"Seems very timely for the King that poor Uriah passed away," the servant observed. "It has been rumored for months that he has been carrying on an affair with Uriah's wife. I myself saw her leave Uriah's house one evening as I was passing by. She was being escorted by the King's servant, Amoz, and they were headed toward the palace."

"That proves nothing, and if you want your tongue to remain in your mouth, you had better be careful what you intimate about the King," the armor bearer responded with some heat.

"Oh, I'm saying nothing against David. He has every right to take the widow as his wife. I guess as the King he can do whatever he wishes. Bathsheba's her name, Uriah's wife. She's a beauty. Saw her the other day. David had her brought to the palace after she finished her mourning. I think he intends to keep her."

"But David has . . ." the armor bearer paused to count "seven wives, and a harem filled with the most beautiful women in Israel. It wouldn't be like him at all to . . . umm . . . get rid of Uriah and take his wife."

"True, but Joab, now he would do just about anything to see that the King has anything he wants. And he certainly doesn't have any scruples about killing. And he was the one who ordered Uriah and the others to their deaths. If he knew the King wanted Bathsheba for himself, he wouldn't think twice about getting rid of any number of men. Don't forget what he did to Abner. Pretended to want to parley with Saul's general, then gutted him like a fish."

The armor bearer, made nervous by the old servant's careless tongue, looked about him anxiously, and Isaac stepped into the shadows so he wouldn't be seen. "I warn you, don't speak of such things if you want your head to remain attached to your body!" he hissed.

The older servant shrugged. "It's being talked about all over Jerusalem, by too many people to be gotten rid of."

The armor bearer snorted in disbelief. "Joab gets rid of his enemies, no matter how great their number."

Isaac had heard enough, and slipped out into the street without being seen. Isaac didn't doubt the servant's assertion that David had indulged in an affair with Uriah's wife. The King had always been attractive to and attracted by many women, and recently he had withdrawn from military matters, with more time to cater to his whims and desires.

Still, Isaac was no closer to the answer to the crucial question. Had David ordered Uriah and his father abandoned, or had Joab done it on his own initiative when he learned that the King desired Bathsheba? One theory that he couldn't subscribe to was the one that Jonathan held—that the assault on Rabbah's gates had been no more than a military mistake. He felt his stomach turn at the thought that his father had died for such a sordid reason, and he was more determined than ever to see to it that someone paid.

~ ~ ~

In their comfortable quarters, Judith helped Keziah remove her heavy head covering and loosen her thick hair, combing it out gently. "Get some rest now, daughter," she said. "I can see the tiredness in your eyes. The baby grows heavier each day, and you must make allowance for it."

Keziah stretched and rubbed her back, pleased to hear Judith address her as daughter. Judith was right. She did tire more easily these days. "I will rest awhile, then," she agreed, and allowed Judith to help her into bed. While she still wondered how she would feel about this child when it arrived, her blossoming relationship with Isaac, and Judith's sweet acceptance had changed the prospect of her impending motherhood from something she dreaded to an event she was beginning to look forward to.

~ ~ ~

It was still not quite dark outside when Keziah fell deeply asleep. She did not waken when Isaac came to bed several hours later. He drew her into his arms and still she slept. He wanted to make love to his wife but knew it would be selfish to deprive her of sleep. Perhaps he should not make love to her at all until after the child came. Could it be harmful? It was not something he could ask either Keziah or his mother.

Again he thought of his father and how many ways he missed Ahiam every day. His father would not have made crude jests at such a question, nor would he have been shocked. He would have answered his son forthrightly and with good humor.

As he planted a kiss on Keziah's forehead and settled himself to sleep, Isaac wondered if David ever missed his old friend, or if the King had forgotten all about Ahiam and the others who had lost their lives at Rabbah.

~ ~ ~

"We are to dine with the King tonight," Isaac told Judith and Keziah the next morning.

Judith paused in pouring milk into cups for them to have with their morning bread. "But we can't go with you, Isaac. Keziah and I have no clothing fit for an audience in the palace."

Isaac took two large gold coins from the girdle at his waist and placed one beside each woman. "That is why you are going to the marketplace today and buy something—new tunics, perhaps jewelry or an ornamental girdle, a new pair of sandals—whatever you wish."

Keziah picked up her coin and held it out to Isaac. "Surely just one of these coins will suffice for both of us. It isn't seemly to spend so much on . . ."

A look of disapproval came across Isaac's face, and his dark eyes flashed. "It is more than seemly, woman. It is essential. Would you have me ashamed before the King that I can take no better care of those in my household. And besides, Talmon will be there also. I will not have him look down his long nose at us!"

Judith paled. "Talmon will be there? Then why must we go? I don't wish to be in the same room with the man responsible for my Ahiam's death!"

"I don't either, Mother, but I discovered just yesterday that this is to be the night Talmon applies for the King's commission to ply the Via Maris. I will not let him have it! I will ask David in the memory of my dead father to award the commission to me. The presence of my widowed mother might just tip the scales in my favor. You have to come, Mother, if you don't wish our enemy to prosper."

Judith hesitated for a moment, then went to her son and smoothed back his hair from his forehead as she had done when he was a boy. "You want to use me to further your plans against Talmon. I will go with you, son, because I love you. But it is not a good thing for you to give your life over to revenge. The Lord will see to Talmon, as well as any others who had part in the death of those brave men. The wicked may prosper for a season, but—"

Isaac interrupted her. "I wanted to leave the army, Mother, and I want to engage in trade. Do you think I could go into battle again with Joab after what has happened? The King I can do nothing about, even if he did order that attack; I would be petitioning the King tonight even if Talmon weren't. But I won't pretend it won't give me great joy to thwart him." With that, Isaac turned and left his wife and mother without a word of farewell.

They did not see Isaac again until nearly time to leave for the palace. He was in a much lighter mood, giving Keziah an affectionate kiss of greeting and complimenting both women on their attire. Both had bought new overtunics and girdles embellished with semiprecious stones: Judith's in deep red carnelian and Keziah's in blue-green malachite that drew attention to her eyes and hair.

In addition, each was wearing a new headcovering made of linen so fine, it was almost sheer; and even though only a small amount of hair at their foreheads was uncovered, the full luster of their long hair shone through. Isaac declared himself the most blessed of men to be escorting them. They left Adah with the servant after promising to bring her a sweet morsel from the King's table and walked the short distance to the palace.

Upon their arrival, they were taken, not to the palace banqueting hall, but to the King's garden for the meal, escorted by Jehoshaphat, chief of protocol. Tables with comfortable couches were set with beautiful bowls and goblets; there were places for about a hundred. Only the King's family and a few other people were to dine here. While it seemed a large gathering to the visitors from Hebron, in actuality, it was not much larger than an ordinary meal. The King had seven wives and nearly sixty children, many of whom dined with him daily. Keziah looked around in awe at the towering palms that circled the garden, and the three fountains that bubbled continuously.

The King was already there and greeted them immediately.

He offered Judith his condolences. "I am so sorry about the loss of Ahiam. He was a great warrior and a loyal one." The King's words sounded sincere, but Keziah noticed that he couldn't quite meet Judith's gaze. Isaac's jaw clenched, and Keziah knew that her husband was struggling with his suspicions about David.

They were not seated at the King's table but very near it. A crippled young man was brought in by a servant about his own age. "I am Mephibosheth," he told Isaac, "grandson of King Saul. This is my personal servant, Ziba. May I sit beside you?" His question was directed to both Isaac and Keziah, and they both assured him he would be most welcome.

"I had heard of the King's kindness toward you," Isaac remarked after Ziba had departed.

"Yes, the King is very kind. It is on behalf of my father, Jonathan, that he has brought me here. I was only five years old when my father died and I was crippled. For years I was hidden and told that David would kill me if I were ever found."

"How did it happen?" Keziah asked, meaning his crippled legs. Mephibosheth understood what she was asking.

"As I said, I was only five years old when news of my father's and grandfather's deaths reached us at Gilead. My nurse feared that either David or the Philistines would have me killed. In her haste to escape with me, she took a dangerous narrow path that wound down from my grandfather's stronghold. She tripped and I fell, breaking both my legs."

He related the story matter-of-factly and completely without self-pity, and Keziah was immediately drawn to him. He had a handsome, noble face and laugh lines at the corners of his eyes, she noticed as he continued. "Years passed as I lived in fear for my life every day. Finally one day, word came that David would have me come to him. Naturally, I was frightened. Imagine my surprise when he informed me that I was to come and live in the palace, to be treated as one of the royal children. He often tells me that I remind him very much of my father. I think that is why he keeps me here."

Isaac also found the young man compelling but wondered at the wisdom of David taking to his bosom someone who might be a contender for the throne. Many of the Benjamites were still resentful that the kingship had passed to David instead of someone from the house of Saul.

Or maybe the friendly young man was just what he appeared to be. And maybe the King thought it best to have Mephibosheth here at the palace under his watchful eye instead of living with his fellow Benjamites, who might use him as a rallying point for rebellion. Jonathan had always held up David's treatment of Mephibosheth as an example of David's kind heart. Now, after all that had happened, Isaac wondered if the King's motives might not be mixed.

Joab joined the dinner party late, which relieved Isaac and Judith of the responsibility of greeting him. Keziah leaned near Isaac and whispered, "Is Talmon not here yet?" She felt compelled to see and identify her husband's nemesis, perhaps out of her desire to protect Isaac.

Isaac patted her hand. "Don't worry, Keziah. It isn't good for the baby."

"I can't help but worry. Each time I see the scars on your back from your first dispute with Talmon, I worry. I wish that you would just forget him."

"My father's blood cries out for justice, Keziah. I could never forget that." Isaac speared a piece of the tender beef, a rare delicacy, and brought it to Keziah's mouth. "Have some more of this delicious meat." The message was clear. He wanted her to stop questioning him.

The dinner was almost over, and Keziah's worries had diminished with Isaac's attention and the pleasant conversation of Mephibosheth, when Joab stood and said something to the King. David rose and accompanied him to the corner of the garden near the entrance. Isaac watched with a wary expression, and Keziah saw that the general and the King were conversing earnestly with a third man, who stood outside the circle of light in deep shadow.

"Who is that man?" she asked her husband.

Isaac's right hand unconsciously clenched the small dagger that was strapped to his waist. "I can't see clearly, but I think that is Talmon. I should have known he would use Joab to get to the King first!"

Keziah patted his arm. She knew nothing else to do. They continued to watch the trio until the King turned to rejoin his guests. Then Joab said something to the visitor, and he stepped closer, out of the shadows.

When the man stepped into the light, Keziah could not suppress a gasp of horror. It was her molester! The face that had been in her nightmares for months! Had he come for her? Keziah's eyes darted to and fro, looking for a way of escape.

Isaac was staring at the three men, and was unaware of her distress. "It is Talmon. I knew it was him!" he hissed in a low voice. But Keziah could not respond. She could not draw a breath. Her attacker was here, and he was Talmon, the man Isaac hated. The father of her child. The horror of it all caused the blood to drain from her face. She felt as if her heart had stopped. Then she fainted and collapsed to the floor.

"Keziah?" She heard Issac's voice coming from a great distance, and she felt him gently slapping her face and asking her to open her eyes. But Keziah did not want to open her eyes. She did not want to think. She did not want to see the look that would come over her husband's face when he found out that the child he was claiming as his own was actually the offspring of his greatest enemy.

She felt herself being lifted, vaguely aware of concerned voices speaking softly. In a short while she felt herself being laid down upon a bed. The strong arms that had been holding her were withdrawn.

When Keziah woke, she was back in her bed in the borrowed house, and Isaac was bending over her with a very worried look on his face. "You frightened us all very badly, Keziah. What happened?"

Suddenly she remembered the face she had seen illumined by torchlight in David's garden. She couldn't tell her husband the truth. It was too horrible to contemplate. "I felt faint. That's all. Now I must sleep. Please, don't worry. Just let me sleep." She turned her back to Isaac and felt him rise from the bed. He did not return that night.

But she couldn't sleep. Her mind spun with the horror of it. Talmon. Her attacker's name was Talmon. And he was her husband's greatest enemy. If Keziah had a son, he would carry the blood of the man who had raped her and had been responsible for Ahiam's death. Keziah lay dry-eyed and shivering.

She couldn't tell Isaac, of that she was certain. But if they stayed in Jerusalem, Talmon might see her, might recognize her! Perhaps he had already, with the display she had made of herself by fainting. She only hoped he had not been close enough to get a good look at her as Isaac swept her up in his arms and carried her out of the King's garden.

She had to think of a way to get Isaac and Judith to agree to return to Hebron. Once there and safe, she would beg Isaac to forget his vow of revenge. She would get him to stay in Hebron and see that he was safe. And she would never let him find out the truth, for how could he help but hate her if he did?

The next day, Keziah feigned illness. It wasn't entirely a pretense. Her stomach churned, and she had a blinding headache. She refused food and pretended to sleep most of the day. That night, she begged Isaac to take her home.

He kissed her. "It is just the baby who has you upset, my dear, but if you wish, I will take you home tomorrow. Today the King gave me his commission. I am to represent him on the Via Maris. I go to Tyre next month, but don't worry; I will be back before the baby is born."

Keziah smiled at her husband and pretended to feel better. But that night a frightening dream invaded her sleep. A monster with Talmon's face stood atop a high mountain with something, or someone, held over his head. The dream changed, and it was

Keziah who was held aloft. Then she felt herself falling and falling. She woke with a scream. Isaac was there, gently shaking her. "Keziah, wake up! It was just a bad dream. Come here. I will hold you."

But even in the safety of Isaac's arms she felt the menace of Talmon's evil. Fear had her so in its grip that she did not really have to pretend. She was pale and ill enough that Isaac made no further effort to delay their departure for home. She prayed they might never lay eyes on Talmon again.

Chapter Thirteen

Keziah breathed a sigh of relief the next morning as they closed up the borrowed house and started for home. Perhaps no one need ever find out about Talmon.

O Lord God, she prayed, *please don't let Isaac ever find out. Please don't let Judith ever find out. And please grant that I never see Talmon again. Adonai, hear my plea and protect us all from his wickedness. And Lord, help me to love my child, who is innocent in all this.*

"You still look very pale, Keziah. Are you certain you can withstand the strain of travel?" Isaac was so solicitous that it made Keziah feel even worse. She wondered what he would do if even now she told him the whole truth. She shook her head at the terrible thought.

"Very well. We will go back to the guest house and stay for a few more days. I'm glad you know your own limitations."

"What are you talking about?" she asked, confused.

"I asked you if you thought you were well enough for the rigor of travel and you said no."

Keziah again shook her head. "No, I didn't. I did not say no."

Isaac looked at her with obvious alarm. She could tell he thought her mind was affected. "But you shook your head no."

"Oh, I'm sorry, Isaac. I wasn't paying attention. I want to go home very badly. Please, let's not delay any longer."

Isaac raised his eyes to the sky. He obviously thought her eccentric behavior was due to her advancing pregnancy.

They made slow progress through the winding, narrow streets of Jerusalem, heading for the Valley Gate, which would put them on the road to Hebron. They inched along past the merchant stalls with Keziah and Judith riding the donkeys while Isaac led them with one hand holding the reins of Keziah's mount and the other grasping Adah's hand. Suddenly Adah let out a terrified scream.

"It's them, Isaac. It's those bad men! Please don't let them hurt us. Call the city guards. Don't fight them by yourself."

Isaac, Judith, and Keziah all looked in the direction Adah was pointing. For a moment, a puzzled look crossed Isaac's face. He looked down at Adah, who was clutching his arm, then at the two men she pointed at, who stood some yards away. Her screams had caused the men to look toward them, and Isaac saw them clearly. They were staring at Isaac and Adah, and in that instant, he recognized who they were.

Isaac's head jerked around and his gaze locked with Keziah's. She looked away. Just then, a procession of pack animals passed between Isaac's party and the two men. When it passed, they had disappeared.

"Where did they go, Isaac? Those are the men who hurt Keziah. Why are you just standing there. Go after them!" Adah was yelling at the top of her voice.

Isaac saw the men, much farther up the street now. He looked back at Keziah, whose hand was clutched at her breast. She looked as if she would faint again, and Isaac stepped nearer, thinking to catch her if he needed to. When he looked at her expression closely, he read more guilt than fear on it.

It struck him all at once. The men whom Adah had pointed out were none other than Talmon and Ishobeam. That would account for the fear in his wife's eyes, but why the guilt? She had seen Talmon last night right before she fainted. Surely she had recognized him, but she had not told her husband and had blamed her collapse on her condition.

He continued to stare intently at his wife as his mind whirled. Keziah's child was Talmon's seed. The child he must claim as his own had sprung from his worst enemy! He couldn't comprehend it. *God, what have I done to deserve such a thing?* He cried out in silent torment. And Keziah—how long had she known that her attacker and his father's murderer were the same man? He had to ask.

"You knew?"

Keziah's face, which had been ashen, now flushed with shame, and she cast her gaze downward, making the answer to his question obvious. She had known the identity of her rapist and had kept it from him. How could she do such a thing, knowing how he felt about Talmon? Isaac was too upset to think rationally; it would not occur to him until later that Talmon did not send Ahiam to his death until months after the rape, that Keziah had no reason to protect Talmon.

At that moment, it seemed to him that she was almost as guilty as her attacker. She had ruined his life. And though he hated himself for such a cruel thought, he couldn't keep from feeling that she was defiled, unclean, not by the rape itself, but because she had been touched by Talmon.

The feeling must have transmitted itself to his face, because he saw her sway precariously, as if she had been struck. But he could not offer any comfort. His own life was tilting dangerously out of control. And while he stood here, his enemy was getting away.

Isaac turned his back on Keziah and started to stalk away, but she slid from her donkey's back and ran after him, grabbing his shoulder. "Where are you going?"

Isaac's look conveyed the message that she ought to know full well. "I'm going to kill a beast," he growled and jerked away from her.

Not knowing where else to go, the women returned to the house they had just vacated. "Keziah, what in the world happened out there? Isaac is furious with you. Why?" Keziah only shook her head.

"It was the men who hurt her, Ahmi. Don't you understand?" Judith stared for a long time. Then her horrified gaze swung back to Keziah, who saw no choice but to explain.

"My attacker and Ahiam's murderer are one and the same." She admitted she had recognized Talmon at the palace. "But I give you my word that I didn't know who he was before. Please believe me!" she begged.

"I do." But Judith could not hide her shock and revulsion. It showed in her face. "We should talk about this later," she said, and tilted her head toward her daughter.

They both had to keep their emotions under control because Adah was terrified that Talmon and Ishobeam were in Jerusalem for the express purpose of harming her and Keziah again, and now she was afraid they would hurt her brother as well.

Keziah's heart ached for Adah. The death of her father, added to all the other traumatic things that were happening, had left Adah in a very fragile state. Both women were able to subdue their own fears and distress for her sake.

An hour passed, and Isaac still did not return. Keziah announced that she was going to appeal to King David to stop the confrontation between Isaac and Talmon. "Oh, why did I waste even this much time?" she asked Judith. "Isaac may have already committed murder! I only hope he has not been able to find Talmon or his servant."

"I will go with you," Judith said. "Because of Ahiam's status as a Gibbor and his death being so recent, I am more likely to get an audience with the King."

"But Adah . . ."

"The people next door have a little girl just her age. I'm sure they will be glad to have her visit."

~ ~ ~

Within the hour they were shown, not into the large audience chamber, but a much smaller, yet beautifully furnished, room. David was dressed informally in a long purple tunic of Tyrian purple. He looked surprised to see them.

"My lord," Keziah said, "we are here to implore you to intervene between my husband and Talmon of Gibeah. The animosity between them has broken out again, and I fear that they will fight to the death this time."

A look of hot anger flashed in David's beautiful eyes. Keziah understood for the first time why David was feared as a warrior as well as admired as a poet and statesman. She would never want to be his enemy.

"What has happened that those two chose to ignore a direct order from me to cease their fighting?" he thundered, causing both women to jump.

"Please don't ask me to reveal it, my lord. It concerns family honor. I promise that my son has good reason to hate Talmon besides what happened to my husband." Judith had stepped between David and Keziah, as if to protect the younger woman from his wrath. "We only wish for you to restrain Isaac, admonish him. Please don't have him punished. I could not bear it so soon after losing his father." Judith let a tear fall from her eye. She was shamelessly playing on David's guilt as well as his gallantry, but she would do anything to help her son.

The King grunted an inaudible reply and rang a bell that sat on a small table nearby. Amoz appeared. "Amoz, send for six of the Pelethite guard. There is someone I need them to find."

~ ~ ~

When Isaac had left the women in the marketplace, he had spent several hours looking for Talmon. He had kept his hand curved around the handle of his dagger, determined to use it when he caught up with his enemy. But there was no sign of Talmon or his servant, and eventually, he heard his name called.

He stopped in the middle of the busy street and saw a contingent of six soldiers approach him.

"Are you Isaac of Hebron?" the oldest guard asked. Isaac knew instinctively that they would take him into custody, and considered running, but he thought better of it.

"I am he," he answered reluctantly.

"Then you are to come with us by order of the King," the man demanded. The cohort surrounded him and escorted him to the palace. He was taken to a small room and held for a time. He heard footsteps in the hall, hitting the marble floors with military precision; then he saw two guards walk by with Talmon between them. A few minutes later, Isaac was taken before the King, where Talmon already waited.

David turned the full force of his anger on Isaac. "I have granted you the status of royal merchant on the Via Maris. I have allowed you to retire from the army, ignoring flagrant breeches of discipline. All this I have done for the sake of your father's memory.

"Now heed well my words. You will forget this grudge you bear against Talmon. You will keep well away from him, and in return, he will by my order keep far from you."

"My lord," Talmon objected in an offended voice, "I have never sought to harm this man. I did not even know he sought me until your men found me."

David studied Talmon closely for a long moment, and the look on his face made it clear that he didn't trust the man's words. "If you truly have done nothing to the son of Ahiam, and wish him no harm, that is all the more reason to stay away from him." Having said this, the King turned his attention back to Isaac.

"I should have you put in my dungeon for the unprovoked attack on Talmon after the battle at Rabbah, and your efforts to harm him again, but your mother and wife have been here to beg my mercy. I told your mother that because of the recent death of her husband, I would not deprive her of her son. But be assured that my patience is not inexhaustible."

Isaac's fury made him speechless, which likely saved his life. He was nearly certain David had ordered his father killed along with Uriah the Hittite, and now he was pretending such great love and respect for Ahiam's memory.

Then the King turned his attention to Talmon. "I do not know what you have done to provoke such enmity on the part of Isaac of Hebron. But listen well. You will do nothing to harm Isaac nor any of his. Your request to have my commission as royal merchant on the Via Maris is denied, but I do give you the royal seal to use in trade along the King's Highway. That should keep you two apart. But should you encounter each other, I expect you to refrain from furthering your feud. Is that understood?"

Talmon nodded readily. He had seen the outrage on Isaac's face when David had awarded him the King's Highway. He would have preferred the commission for the Via Maris and trade with Tyre, but he knew better than to question the King's decision.

He had counted on the fact that Isaac would not reveal his attack on his sister and wife. It had been quite a shock in the street today, when the little girl had pointed him out and accused him in a loud voice. He was glad he had sent Ishobeam to Hebron last month and had learned that the woman he had raped still lived and was married to Isaac, or he would have been totally unprepared for the confrontation.

Talmon smiled slyly to himself as he remembered the horrified look on Isaac's face. Isaac had been unaware until that moment that Talmon had taken his wife. It gave him great comfort to know that Isaac would suffer from the knowledge. And if the impression gathered from his brief glance was correct, Keziah was carrying his child. What a bitter draught that must be to his enemy. Talmon decided he would think of many ways to use the circumstances against Isaac.

Too bad he couldn't brag about it and thus shame Isaac even more. But it involved too much risk. The family of Ahiam of Hebron was not inconsequential. If they chose to charge Talmon with the rape, their story might just be relieved. No, he would have to be satisfied with the private knowledge that Isaac knew. His thoughts broke off as the King addressed his adversary.

"Have I explained the situation sufficiently, Isaac?" the King asked after a long silence. Isaac gave a curt nod and stormed out of the palace.

~ ~ ~

By the time he reached the rented house, his rage was boiling over. He found Keziah and Judith sitting on opposite sides of the common room, waiting anxiously for his return. They didn't pretend not to know what the King had said. They knew full well.

"So, you have both run to the King with tales of my plans," he fumed. "I will know to guard my words and actions well from both of you in the future. Mother, you would humble yourself before the very man who most likely had your husband killed. And you, Keziah, would plead for the life of the man who defiled you? It is often said that women do not know the meaning of honor, but I had not thought it true of either of you until today."

Judith blanched, but her gaze was steady on her son. "You speak from anger, Isaac, and don't truly mean what you say. I will forgive you those hurtful words." That said, she left Isaac alone with his wife.

"Isaac, you can't think I went to the King for Talmon's sake," Keziah said when she had gone. "Be angry with me if you wish, but please tell me you know me better than that," Keziah pleaded.

"I don't know you at all, but since I know your illness was all a sham, I will finish up my business here before I escort you home. There will be a guard at the door whenever I am away. Neither you nor Mother nor Adah are to leave the house," Isaac said, then left the house. After he was gone, Keziah felt a great need to be comforted, but Judith had withdrawn from her, and shut herself up in the small sleeping chamber she shared with Adah.

Keziah was desolate. In the short time she had been married to Isaac, she had come to cherish each one of his family members. Now she was going to lose them. Judith and Isaac would never forgive her, and soon Adah would sense their withdrawal. Then she would also lose the admiration of Isaac's little sister. There was a painful knot in her throat all day as she fought successfully to keep the tears at bay.

Isaac spent the rest of that day and all of the next on preparations for his first caravan. He hired drivers for the dozen donkeys he was taking, and began to gather the goods he would use in trade for the materials the King desired for his project of building the temple. When he returned to the little house at dusk on the second day, he found Adah waiting for him.

"Isaac, you have to take us back to Hebron. Mother and Keziah are very upset. They haven't spoken to each other, and will hardly talk to me. I think maybe it is because they are so frightened of those men. Is the younger one named Talmon? Where are they now. Do you know?"

Isaac put his arm around his sister's shoulder and hugged her. "They won't hurt you, Adah. I won't let them. They have left Jerusalem," he assured her, although he wasn't certain they had done any such thing. He knew Adah was trying to be brave and grown up, but he saw how she trembled.

So he escorted Keziah and his mother and sister back to Hebron the next day, bringing along Darkon, the male servant he had hired to guard them in Jerusalem, and instructed him to guard the women and the child very carefully while he was gone on his expedition. He avoided Keziah and spoke little to Judith. He was still resentful that they had gone to the King.

~ ~ ~

Keziah sat on the rooftop staring at nothing. She jerked at the sound of Isaac's voice. "I have told Mother and Adah already, but you need to know that I am leaving now. Darkon will protect you, though I don't believe Talmon would dare try to harm you again." Keziah winced at the reference, but didn't look at her husband. He remained several feet from her as he continued.

"I need to travel to Ziph for pottery to trade," he told her. "They have been expanding the pottery works, and Jonathan thinks they will soon be famous for it. He wants me to trade it for silver on my journey and to obtain examples of fine Phoenician pottery for his artists to copy." After he finished giving her this information, he abruptly turned around and left her presence. He had said nothing personal, nothing about the terrible situation they were in. Keziah couldn't blame him. She couldn't bear to even think of it, much less talk about it.

Less than two hours later, Isaac bid his family a terse goodbye when he left for Ziph. He wouldn't stop at Hebron on the way to the Via Maris, even though it would be right on his way. He had still not forgiven either Keziah or Judith for what he perceived as disloyalty. And he still had not accepted the fact that his wife would bear a child of Talmon's seed.

Judith was angry with her son for his stubbornness. When he was gone, she turned to her daughter-in-law for the first time since the encounter in Jerusalem and held out her arms. Keziah came into them. "He is ever like his father when he gets an idea in his thick head," she complained. "It takes him forever to admit he is in the wrong. Don't let him make you feel guilty in this, Keziah. Nothing that has happened is your fault. And my son will eventually come to see that."

But Keziah did feel guilty. How would Isaac ever come to forgive her? How could she ever earn his love and respect now? It was hopeless. She had actually been relieved when Isaac and his line of camels and donkeys and people had left Hebron. He would go through Adoraim, then turn north and pass through Gezer, Lod, and Ono and Aphek, through the plain of Sharon, then on to Acco and Tyre. It would take several weeks to make such a journey. Maybe his anger and revulsion would lessen during this absence from home.

Keziah turned her thoughts back to her mother-in-law. "You don't blame me for what has happened, Judith?"

"How could I? How could anyone?"

"But surely you don't want to be reminded of Ahiam's killer every day when you look at me." Her hand went unconsciously to the swell of her abdomen where the child of Talmon grew. "I could go and stay with my father, if you wish it."

Judith placed her arms around her daughter-in-law. "I do not wish it. It took a few days for me to absorb the shock the truth brought, but now that I have thought about the situation, I believe I can love your child when it comes, Keziah. After all, it will be part of you, and you are very precious to me." Keziah fought back tears as she returned Judith's embrace. But she could not confide her worst fear, the fear that she would not be able to love Talmon's child herself.

Three weeks later, Isaac and his caravan entered the massive fortified city-state of Tyre. The city was actually in two parts; one half built on the shore of the Great Sea, and the other half built on a rocky island. It boasted two harbors connected by a canal. On the land side, the walls of the fortified city rose to a height just over a hundred feet.

To the first-time visitor, it was a breathtaking sight. Tyre's population was more than 40,000. Ships from all over the world put in at her harbor and traded in every conceivable kind of merchandise. Adventuresome traders and sailors, the Tyrian ships plied the Mediterranean and beyond, exchanging their goods—particularly the famous purple dye from the murex shell—for valuable items from other places.

Isaac's pulse quickened as he motioned the caravan forward. He relished the chance to do some shrewd trading, both at the docks and in the shops of Tyre's craftsmen and artisans, who were the most skilled in the world. At the moment, his business, not revenge on Talmon, was foremost in his mind.

It was not as easy as he had thought to get an appointment with Hiram, who was next in line for the throne of Tyre and a very busy, powerful man. But Hiram was a personal friend of David, and so within a few days time, he was ushered into the presence of the charismatic leader, who was a little younger than King David. Isaac estimated him to be in his early forties.

Hiram studied his letter of commission, which contained a personal note from David. He smiled. "How does it go with my friend, your king?" he asked after he had finished reading.

"The kingdom of David prospers, my lord. May he live forever, and may his good friend Hiram, also."

Hiram laughed. "We have heard he is about to finalize another victory at Rabbah. I am glad to call myself friend to the Shepherd King. What can I do for you on his behalf?"

"I seek commerce between our two people, my lord," Isaac answered.

He stayed at Hiram's palace for two weeks. He traded not only for cedar and cypress for David's building projects, both for his palace and the future temple, but also for Tyrian purple. He saw the construction project that was the pride of Hiram, the fabulous temple dedicated to the worship of Melqart, the patron god of Tyre. Isaac took notes on the logistics of construction that Hiram had undertaken. He was confident that David would be interested in ways to expedite his own plans for the temple of Adonai.

One night just after sunset, he made his way through the crowded streets of the city. He had been all day at the docks, purchasing textiles and pottery, dyes and jewelry, utensils of copper and bronze and silver, all manner of things to trade or sell in Jerusalem and other parts of Judah. He had fulfilled the King's commission and had also done well for himself that day. He was contemplating his newly acquired wealth and not much aware of his surroundings as he took a shortcut through an alley to Hiram's palace.

Three cloaked figures stepped out of the dark. Isaac saw a raised dagger flash in the moonlight just in time to block its descent with his forearm. He received a superficial cut but was able to knock the smaller man to the ground. The assailant's knife went skittering on the cobblestones. Sensing someone behind him, Isaac spun around and received a glancing blow to the head from a club. He reeled from the hit, but he knew that to lose consciousness meant certain death, so he threw his body into his attacker, knocking him into the third man. Both fell to the ground, and Isaac took the opportunity to run.

He heard the rough voice of one of his attackers. "Get up! We don't get the rest of the gold if we let him get away!"

Isaac was not that familiar with the streets of Tyre, but he knew he was close to Hiram's fortress. He made it safely back. But he was left to ponder who had hired the assassins. There was only one person he knew of with a motive to kill him. He could not let the matter of Talmon die, because Talmon would not let it die. It would only end, Isaac now believed, when one or the other of them was in the grave.

The next day Isaac arranged to have the timber shipped to Acco, the port closest to Jerusalem, where it would be met by the laborers, mostly Moabites and other defeated peoples, who would transport it to Jerusalem. The rest of his bounty was loaded on the pack animals, and the caravan again set off. This time the destination was Jerusalem.

During the long days en route, Isaac had ample time to think of the convoluted circumstances surrounding his marriage to Keziah. Was she right, that he should now consider Talmon an issue of the past, that he should put away his hatred? How could he, when each time he thought of Talmon he not only had to face the memory of his father's death, but the horror of what the man had done to Keziah?

Isaac was not ready, not able to forget that. He didn't know if he ever could.

Besides, the attack in Tyre raised his suspicions. He had no enemies that he knew of, other than Talmon. If Talmon was out to kill him, then he had every right to try to kill Talmon first. He had the Law of Moses to back up his position.

~ ~ ~

Back in Jerusalem, when he went to make his report to the King, Isaac saw with his own eyes that the gossip he had overheard was true. The widow of Uriah was now living in the palace as David's wife. When Isaac arrived for his audience, he found the King and Bathsheba in quiet conversation, apparently oblivious to the number of people who had gathered for business with the King. David's attention was entirely focused on her, and his hand rested possessively on her swollen belly. Her child's birth was now imminent, and Isaac had no doubt the father was David.

Around her neck, suspended from a gold chain, Bathsheba wore the King's signet ring. It was a testament to anyone who saw it of his regard. Any message that went out with the King's signet stamped on it was regarded as a command from the King and Bathsheba was given free rein to use it. *He must be thoroughly besotted with her,* Isaac thought. It made Isaac so physically ill that he was afraid he would not be able to hold a civil conversation with the King.

As he stood in the doorway, composing himself, he noticed the other occupants of the room. Having seen the King's fifth wife, Maacah, before, Isaac recognized her immediately. Her beauty was still breathtaking.

A princess of Geshur, where her father Talmai ruled over David's vassal kingdom in the Transjordan, Maacah was tall, with a long, lovely neck, large eyes, and regal bearing. At the moment she was staring at David and Bathsheba, and from the look on her face, Isaac could tell she did not like what she saw any better than he did.

Standing beside her was a tall, exceedingly handsome young

man, whom Isaac recognized as her son, Absalom. Isaac had seen him and his entourage around the streets of Jerusalem. Absalom enjoyed the attention he drew while either being carried on a litter, or riding a large white mule about the streets, with his bodyguards running before him to make way. Those who knew the prince admitted he was extremely vain but claimed he could charm the birds right out of the trees.

At the moment, though, Absalom was staring at his father with a smoldering, sullen look. Isaac concluded that the young prince did not appreciate his mother being shunted aside by David for Bathsheba. It struck Isaac that already the King was paying the price for taking Uriah's wife for his own. Curiously, it gave him no sense of satisfaction. He had made David his hero since boyhood, and some of those feelings remained—along with a sense of betrayal.

David had been holding court this day. In recent years, the King had increasingly left the disposition of justice to his advisers. People had begun to grumble that he no longer cared for them. He had forgotten his lowly roots as a shepherd, they complained. Evidently David was trying to counteract that sentiment by holding court. Isaac would just have to wait his turn to present the King with the riches he had obtained on his first expedition.

A man with iron-gray hair began pushing his way through the line of supplicants. Isaac saw that he was strong and robust and not as old as he appeared, maybe no more than fifty, despite his gray hair. He heard someone murmur beside him. "That is Nathan, the prophet, adviser to the King. Thinks he needn't wait his turn."

Some of the supplicants had mumbled their petitions to the King, but Nathan could be heard throughout the judgment hall. "I have a story of injustice to tell you, my lord. I would have you render judgment in the case."

"By all means, Nathan," David replied. "We are glad to hear your case. You have made yourself scarce at the palace in the past months. Please proceed."

"My lord King, this story concerns two men who were neighbors.

One man was very rich. He had large herds of both sheep and cattle. The other man, however, was poor. He owned only one little ewe lamb, which he made a pet of. It lived with him and his children. It shared their table and even slept with the man; why, he treated that lamb like it was his daughter!

"One day a traveler came to see the rich man. The rich man did not want to use one of his own sheep or cattle to prepare a meal for his guest. Instead, he seized his neighbor's one little lamb and had it prepared for his guest."

Isaac found himself shaking his head. It was yet another example of how the wealthy and powerful took advantage of the poor. The King's reaction, however, was dramatic. His face suffused with anger, he half rose from his chair. "As surely as the Lord lives, the man who would do such a thing deserves to die. I will see that he pays back four lambs for the one he took from his neighbor. Who is this man who showed no pity?"

Nathan did not raise his voice, but still his answer reverberated throughout the chamber. "You. You are the man!" A look of confusion came over the King's face. He sputtered for a moment, then sat back in his chair, as if his legs would no longer hold him up. He sat perfectly still for a long moment, his gaze locked with the prophet's.

"It is a parable you have spoken to me." David's voice sounded hoarse and strained.

"It is the word of the Lord I bring to you," Nathan answered.

Bathsheba looked frightened, and moved closer to David's side. Two of the Pelethites, David's palace guards, stepped forward with hands on their sword hilts, but David shook his head. "Clear the hall," he instructed them. And in a few short moments Isaac found himself outside the palace.

But there was no keeping the gossip from spreading throughout the city. People knew that Nathan had confronted David about taking Uriah's wife, and those who were present related the prediction of strife and death for David's household, as well as Nathan's pronouncement of the death of Bathsheba's son.

But it was the King's reaction to Nathan's prophecy that shocked the city the most. Amazingly, David had not had Nathan killed or punished for his harsh words. Instead, the King confessed the sins he had been accused of. Each day for the next week he went to the tabernacle he had had erected on the Ophel, the hill he had purchased for the building of the temple. He offered sacrifices. By the end of the week, he had written a psalm, which he had the levitical singers perform.

> Have mercy upon me, O God,
> According to your lovingkindness;
> According to the multitude of Your tender mercies,
> Blot out my transgressions.
> Wash me thoroughly from my iniquity,
> And cleanse me from my sin. For I acknowledge my transgressions,
> And my sin is ever before me.
> Against You, You only, have I sinned,
> And done this evil in Your sight. . . .
> Purge me with hyssop, and I shall be clean;
> Wash me, and I shall be whiter than snow.

Isaac stood with the other worshipers at the door of the tabernacle and heard the sincerity of repentance that rang out as the song was performed. He did not want to forgive the King—not yet. He had felt elated at first, when Nathan had confronted David in public. And he had felt a desire for vengeance. But somehow, Nathan's announcement that the King would suffer for his sins, and the King's humble response, had taken the hot anger and hatred away. But there was still plenty of hatred reserved for Talmon. He had delayed his return for several days, but finally made himself leave Jerusalem and face his wife and mother.

Chapter Fourteen

Isaac returned from his expedition just at the end of the season of the latter rains, in the month of Shebat. He had done much thinking in the ten weeks he had been gone. He felt no small amount of guilt over the things he had said to Keziah before his departure.

Isaac had to admit that his wife was as much a victim of this whole obscene situation as he was. No, more of a victim. She, after all, had suffered a brutal rape, found herself pregnant with her attacker's child, been forced to marry a man who couldn't love her as she deserved to be loved. Then he had added to her suffering by reacting as he had when he found out Talmon was the father of her child.

Isaac ran his hand through his thick locks. If the child was a boy, he would just have to accept it, raise him as his own. He would see that the boy grew up to be nothing like the man who begat him. But perhaps Adonai would be gracious, and Keziah would give birth to a girl child. He smiled at the thought of a little girl with auburn curls like her mother's. Yes, it would be quite easy to love such a one.

Adah and Judith greeted him with enthusiasm and Adah began immediately to open the many bundles he had brought back.

He saw no sign of Keziah, but since he had sent men ahead with most of his treasures the day before, he did not ask after her. She had had plenty of warning of his arrival, and it was her duty as a wife to be there to greet him, after all. She had chosen to insult him by not being present. Somehow, he did not want to examine the logic of who had insulted whom too closely, so he questioned his mother about his planned project to improve their home.

"And where are the servants I told you to hire?" he asked, looking around. He knew that he still owed her an apology for his display of anger in Jerusalem and his abrupt departure, but his pride wouldn't let him.

Judith shrugged at the question. "There is Darkon, whom you hired, and the men who are making the additions to the house, of course, but Keziah and I were not able to find any that we were comfortable with except for Rachel. We have given her one of the new rooms you had the workmen build."

Isaac shook his head. "Poor, old Rachel. You will find yourself serving her more than she serves you. Keep her if you wish, but find at least two other servants, or I will do so myself."

Adah interrupted then with a squeal of delight when she opened the package meant for her. "It's a game of hounds and jackals! Can we play now, Isaac?" Adah was already setting the pieces out on a small table.

"Not now, little one. We will play after the evening meal, though."

"Isaac."

He turned to see his mother's worried frown and knew the subject she would broach. He wished he could postpone dealing with it.

"Isaac, you haven't even asked about Keziah. She is your wife, after all."

"I could hardly forget that, Mother. Please don't worry about Keziah and me."

"Don't interfere, you mean?" Judith gave her son a crooked

smile. "You are right, son. It isn't wise for a mother to instruct her grown children, but Keziah has been so unhappy since . . . what happened in Jerusalem. In her condition, it would be harmful if you were to deal with her unkindly."

Isaac was offended that his mother thought him capable of hurting Keziah. "I'm not a tyrant, Mother," he told her before stalking off.

Isaac sought out his wife, and found her in the back garden, grinding wheat into flour. She looked up as he approached, halting the rhythmic circular motion of the pestle against the mortar. The look on her face was certainly not one of joy, he noticed. "I am back from Damascus," he stated inanely, unable to think of anything else to say.

Keziah nodded and went back to her work, slowly adding wheat kernels with one hand while grinding with the other. "I am glad you are home safely," she said in a soft voice. He couldn't see her expression now because she was bent over her work, her hair forming a curtain to protect her from his scrutiny.

Isaac walked over and handed her the bundle of purple cloth he had brought back as a present. "I thought this would look good with your hair."

Keziah slowly reached for the cloth, then smoothed it with one hand. She came clumsily to her feet, and he noticed that her child had grown very large in his absence. She looked very uncomfortable, and he wondered if it was physical discomfort due to her condition, or if she was angry with him.

She didn't sound angry when she spoke. "It is beautiful. Thank you, Isaac. But it is so valuable. Surely you can't mean for me to make it into a tunic."

"I am a wealthy man now, Keziah. You must get used to being a rich man's wife." His mouth turned up as he said it, but she did not return his smile. She looked deeply into his eyes, and in hers he saw a bottomless well of sorrow. He hated the fact that he was at least partially responsible for it.

Afraid of unleashing a tide of emotion in either himself or

her, he took the coward's way out. He cleared his throat. "I suppose I should go and clean up now. We will talk later."

But they didn't, because Keziah found excuses to avoid being alone with Isaac, and he did not force her to speak privately with him. He was honest with himself and admitted that he dreaded facing her. He knew that he had to seek her forgiveness for his harshness before.

He wanted to tell her that Talmon didn't matter anymore, but he had to admit that his hatred still seethed within him, and he had nightmares of having to raise a child who would grow up to be the image of Talmon.

But the opportunity to talk never came, because Keziah began her travail late the next afternoon. Judith and old Rachel attended her, and Isaac sat with Adah under a canopy in the courtyard, teaching her to play hounds and jackals, or trying to. He could not keep his mind on anything but Keziah's suffering.

After several hours, there came a heartbreaking cry of pain from the upstairs chamber, and Adah lifted stricken eyes to Isaac. "Is Keziah going to die?" she asked in a quivering voice.

"No, Adah, of course not." Isaac answered in a cheerful and confident tone that was totally false. Adah, with a child's honest wisdom, saw right through him. She came to him and put her small arms around his neck.

After returning her embrace, he ordered her to her room to sleep. She would not be able to hear Keziah's cries as well from her room. After complaining that she wanted to be awake when her new niece or nephew arrived, Adah complied readily enough after exacting Isaac's promise that he would awaken her as soon as anything happened.

He longed to go to Keziah just long enough to reassure her and tell her how sorry he was for adding to all she had to bear. But labor and childbirth were taboo to men. He would not be allowed anywhere near her until the baby was safely delivered.

At one point during her travail, Keziah had a horrible dream. She dreamed that her baby was born, and that he had the face of Talmon. She screamed when she saw it, and tried to get away, but someone held her down.

"Be still. Be easy, my dear. You will hurt yourself. Rest now, between the pains." Someone was washing her face with a cool cloth. She opened her eyes and saw that it was Judith, her plump face wreathed in concern. In the next minute, she knew that seeing her baby had been a dream, because another powerful contraction overtook her.

Keziah prayed, sometimes out loud, for a girl, and the midwife thought that the pain had unhinged her. Didn't every mother pray for a boy child?

"We will be happy to have a girl or a boy, as Adonai chooses," Judith assured both Keziah and the midwife.

At midday the next day, Adah ran to Isaac with the news that the baby had finally come. She had been sitting on the stairway all morning, waiting for word. Isaac, in an effort to keep busy, had seen to the storing of all the things he had brought back from Tyre. He had made himself a wealthy man with just one expedition, and he would immediately add on to this house to make it one of the finest in Hebron. Then he would set out again. He had to gain enough wealth and power to have the means to ruin Talmon.

After announcing the birth, Adah flew up the stairs to see Keziah and the baby. Isaac started to run up the stairs behind her and then stopped. He dreaded knowing the sex of the child. His feet dragged as if he were going to his own execution. He reached the doorway and saw that Adah had climbed up beside Keziah in the bed and was peering avidly at the bundle held in her arms.

His eyes met his wife's for a moment, and a look of fear passed over Keziah's face. She drew the bundle more tightly to her, and he knew. He knew even before Rachel spoke. "You have a son, my lord. He is a little small and early but a beautiful child. Praise be to the Almighty."

He knew that Keziah was waiting to see what his response would be, and that he should go to her, and lift the baby in his arms, and vow to care for her and the boy for as long as he lived. Yes, he knew what he should do, but he didn't have the courage, not yet, anyway. Isaac turned and fled the room.

"The baby is not well," Judith told him at the evening meal. Isaac still had not visited his wife and child again. "I am afraid he may not live."

Isaac knew that his mother was eyeing him closely when she made this announcement. *By all that is holy, does she think I wish the child dead?*

He rose. "I will go and offer Keziah my comfort then."

The baby was making little mewling sounds as Keziah tried to coax him to take the breast.

"Come now, my precious one, You must eat."

Her eyes were filled with worry when she looked up and saw Isaac standing nearby. "He won't eat, Isaac. And he can't seem to take a deep breath." She stroked the wizened little face.

"The child will improve, Keziah. Try not to worry."

His wife stared at him for a long moment, tears brimming her eyes. Again he told himself to come closer, touch the boy or hold him, or put his arms around Keziah. But he was frozen to the spot. What would the future be like, now that Talmon's child was here? He knew he had to come to grips with it, but it was just too soon.

"Try to get some rest," he added lamely before he turned and left.

The baby grew weaker and weaker over the next two days. But Keziah seemed unwilling to accept it. "See, Judith. His color is better. He is not so pale anymore."

It was all kindhearted Judith could do not to burst into tears. It was true the baby no longer looked pale. Since this morning his skin had taken on a bluish hue. The child was unable to take in enough air for some reason. Judith had seen other babies who were born before their time suffer the same malady. All of them had died. And her son, who should be here offering strength and comfort, stayed away, like a coward. She felt Ahiam's loss very keenly in that moment, as she did many times a day. Her husband would have known how to handle Isaac. He would have talked to his son as a man.

~ ~ ~

The baby died the next afternoon. It snowed that day, an unusual but not unheard of occurrence in the hills of Judah. It was, after all the month of Tebeth, the coldest winter month. The snow seemed to coincide with the coldness of Keziah's baby, who turned blue and would not be warmed despite all her efforts.

She felt the coldness too, deep in her soul as she tried futilely to coax him to suckle. His breathing became more and more shallow until it ceased. "Thanks to Adonai for His mercy, your child did not suffer, Keziah, he did not struggle," Judith told her as she took the dead child from her arms.

Though her arms were now empty, Keziah still held her arms folded as if they were not. She rocked back and forth and continued to sing as she had while the babe still lived, chanting, "What now my son, my precious one. O my beautiful one, son of my womb. Not the son of violence; not the son of the oppressor. Not the son of my sorrow as I once feared, but a gift from God."

Judith was concerned that the baby's death might have overset Keziah's mind. She came close, and placed the dead infant back in his mother's arms, thinking perhaps her daughter-in-law needed to hold him for a little while longer.

"Yes, Keziah, you are right. He was a gift from God. We will remember him as Nathaniel. It is fitting that we do so."

When Isaac was informed, he came to the room and hovered

at the foot of the bed with his head bowed. He did not look at the corner of the room where Judith was preparing the little body for burial. *Even now he cannot bring himself to look at my child,* Keziah thought. She did not realize that it wasn't repulsion but guilt that directed her husband's actions.

When Judith had taken the child away, he came near and touched her shoulder. When he felt her tense, he let his hand drop. "I am so sorry, Keziah." It was so little, but it was all he could think of to say.

The next day Keziah lay propped up on several of the pillows Isaac had brought from Tyre. Her pale skin was in stark contrast to their scarlet and purple hues. Rachel had just taken a tray from her lap. It still contained a full bowl of dried figs, a wedge of goat cheese, and a large piece of bread. Keziah hadn't touched any of it.

"Give the tray to me, Rachel. I will see that your mistress takes some nourishment," Isaac said.

The old woman smiled toothlessly as she moved to obey his instruction. "The girl will be fit soon, my lord, if you see to it that she eats as she should. I try, but she needs a firm hand, Isaac."

"It appears so, Rachel. You may go now. I will take care of Keziah." When the old woman had departed, Isaac took the tray and sat down with it beside his wife. She turned her head away. Why did she always withdraw? *Because you rejected her,* he accused himself ruthlessly. He wanted her to be angry with him, yell at him, do anything but give up.

"Keziah, you will eat now."

"I'm not hungry."

"I don't care if you're not hungry. You must eat to survive."

"Perhaps it would be better if I did not. It would be better for you."

Isaac clenched his jaw at the hopelessness in her voice. "No, my problems would only be multiplied, and you would not be here to help me as a wife is supposed to do. In fact, you have yet to begin being a real wife to me. It is time you set about recovering so you may do so."

He was goading her deliberately, and though he hated the hurt look in her eyes at his harsh words, he was gratified to see the momentary flash of anger. At least he had evoked a response from her. But she quickly turned her head away again.

"Keziah, if you wish me to leave you alone, you had better eat this food. I won't leave until it is all gone." His tone must have convinced her that he meant what he said, because she slowly finished the nourishing meal. But she refused to do more than answer his questions in monosyllables.

~ ~ ~

Two days later, Keziah was sitting on the rooftop couch when Ailea and Jonathan came to visit. Isaac had carried her there, convinced that the warm sun would speed her recovery. Typically, the snow had melted the day after it had fallen, and the temperatures had risen steadily. Keziah admitted to herself that it felt good. She had been so cold since the baby's death.

She tried for a polite smile as Ailea came forward and took both her hands. *She is so beautiful. How could I ever replace her in my husband's heart?*

"I wanted to come as soon as I heard about your loss. I am so sorry. Micah has had a slight fever, and only today have I felt secure in leaving him with Ruth."

She has everything. A strong, healthy son, the love of her husband. And the love of mine, Keziah thought bitterly.

Ailea broke off her words when she saw the expression on Keziah's face. "Oh, I shouldn't have mentioned Micah. It is thoughtless for me to prattle on about my son when . . . when . . ." Ailea's large green eyes filled with tears of sympathy.

Keziah felt guilty for causing her distress. None of this was Ailea's fault. It was possible she was not even aware of Isaac's feelings for her. "No, don't worry. I can't refuse to hear about Micah just because my own son is gone."

Just then the sound of masculine voices on the stairs caught their attention, and both women turned to see their husbands approaching. Ailea quickly went to Isaac, taking his hands as she had Keziah's. "Isaac, I am so sorry for your loss. And a son, too. How brokenhearted you must be."

Ailea was interrupted by the sound of harsh laughter as Keziah rose from the couch. "Brokenhearted?" She laughed again. "You are mistaken, Ailea. Isaac can scarcely contain his joy. He can hardly wait for you and Jonathan to depart before he shouts his relief that the baby is no more." Keziah paced restlessly, her voice rising with each word. Isaac went to her.

"Keziah, you are overwrought. You must rest now." He spoke in a soothing voice as he sought to calm her by placing a hand on her shoulder.

She shook it off violently, enraged that he would pretend to be a caring husband. What hypocrisy! Keziah whirled away from Isaac and stood before Jonathan and Ailea. "He would never shock you by admitting it, but he never wanted the baby. Never wanted either of us. No. Don't touch me! Don't, Isaac. You know I speak the truth."

Isaac ignored her protestations and lifted her in his arms, descending the stairs without a backward look. Let his friends think what they would. He had more important problems at the moment.

As soon as Isaac had disappeared with Keziah, Ailea turned to her husband. "Something was wrong with this marriage from the beginning—the suddenness of it when Isaac had never even mentioned that he was seeking a wife. Now this reaction to the death of their baby when they should be clinging together for comfort. They are both so unhappy, Jonathan. Do you know why? Couldn't you offer to help?"

Jonathan shook his head. "In spite of what you appear to think, my dear, I cannot read minds; nor can I work miracles. Isaac has not spoken to me about anything concerning his wife. It is easy to surmise that the child was on its way before the wedding, but that is none of our affair. We will wait to be asked, Ailea, before we offer our counsel."

He was right, much as she hated to admit it, so she nodded her head in agreement and took her husband's hand as they departed for Ziph. She prayed silently, all the way home, that Adonai would heal and comfort her friends.

~ ~ ~

Isaac said nothing as he entered their sleeping chamber and sat down with his wife in his arms. He said nothing as she made a feeble effort to push away from him. He tightened his grip and said nothing as she sobbed out her grief. He said nothing until her crying had ceased and nothing remained but the occasional shudder or hiccup. Then he spoke in a low voice.

"You are wrong, you know. I never wished the babe any ill, not even when . . . when I found out about Talmon. And I certainly never wished you any harm, nor wished to be rid of you. I know it must have seemed that way. I know I behaved poorly at the time. I am sorry for that. But now is the time to let the past go. We cannot change it, though I wish that I could undo all the hurtful things you have suffered. Let us start over. When we go to Damascus we can . . ."

He broke off as Keziah slid off his lap and under the covers, turning away from him, a pointed message that she did not want to talk. He sighed loudly. "Very well. But we must talk soon." He left the room quietly and went to seek out Ailea and Jonathan. He would make some excuse for his wife's behavior. But they had spared him the necessity. They had already left. He told himself that things would be better once their journey to Damascus began. Keziah had never traveled outside the hills of Judah, except for her two trips to Jerusalem. He would take her with him and show her so many wonderful things that she would forget her pain.

Chapter Fifteen

She refused to go with him. There were no more outbursts, but she avoided him whenever possible, or used Adah and Judith as a buffer between them. Two days after the incident with Jonathan and Ailea, he found her in the courtyard making cheese. She was filling linen bags with curds and suspending them over basins to catch the remainder of the moisture.

"Should you be back at your chores so soon?" There was genuine concern in his voice, but Keziah did not seem to notice.

She answered calmly. "It takes very little effort to fill these bags. Besides, my confinement is over and I feel perfectly well. Your mother needs my help. She still grieves the loss of your father and worries herself sick over your plans for revenge. I won't add to her burdens by lying in bed all day."

Guilt stung Isaac because he knew that Keziah was correct in her assessment that his enmity with Talmon and Joab caused his mother pain. That guilt, however, made him respond defensively. "But you need to use this time to prepare for our departure, wife."

"I wish to remain here." Her voice was polite and controlled.

"What?"

His wife raised her eyes reluctantly to his. "I don't want to go to Damascus. I would rather stay here with Judith and Adah. They need me."

And you believe I do not. But you are wrong. "But I . . ." He almost blurted out that he needed her too. It was a fact that he just now realized. Isaac was convinced she might reject such a declaration, so he chose to exercise his power instead. "But I am your husband and I say you will come with me. A woman's place is with her husband."

"Very well." The words were compliant, but the look that flashed in Keziah's eyes was not.

In the days that followed, Isaac did his best to woo his wife. He began to talk about his trip to Damascus, describing the beauty of the city that sat on the convergence of two rivers and two trade routes, and the beauty of Mount Hermon, which they would see on their journey. "It is snowcapped this time of year, Keziah, a most beautiful sight."

"It sounds lovely, but I would rather stay in Hebron, unless you command me to go." Isaac gritted his teeth at her submissive-sounding words. She was determined to make him the uncaring and domineering husband. Well, he refused to become that. He would persuade her to go, but he would not command her. There would be no satisfaction at all in that.

Isaac began to seek her out whenever he had a moment between directing the workers who were changing their modest home into a beautiful villa. He asked her opinion on the addition, but she always deferred to him. He brought her flowers. She thanked him in a polite voice that lacked warmth. He knew that he had hurt her badly, and it would take time for her to believe he cared. He had to remind himself of that fact repeatedly as Keziah politely rebuffed every overture he made.

One day he decided to directly approach the subject. He found Keziah making a soft, woolen doll for Adah. "She will love the toy, Keziah. You have been very good to her. I thank you for that, among other things."

Keziah did not stop sewing the doll or look up. "If any thanks are in order, it is I who should thank your family for taking me in. I will spend the rest of my life trying to repay all of you."

"No, Keziah. You don't have to repay anything. You are a member of our family."

"A fact you no doubt often regret," she muttered.

Isaac came forward and knelt in front of her, taking the doll out of her hands. "I have told you before that I am sorry for the things I said when I found out about Talmon. None of it is your fault. And I understand now why you didn't tell me at first. Instead of comforting you as I should have done, I blamed you. I wonder if you will ever forgive me. What can I do to make amends?"

You can love me. You can replace Ailea with me in your heart, Keziah wanted to tell him. Instead she said, "It is not a matter of forgiveness, Isaac. If that were so, then it is I who should beg yours. You have had nothing but misery in your life since I came into it."

"That is not true. There have been happy times, and there will be more. Won't you come with me to Ziph today, Keziah? I promised Jonathan to take some of the pottery wares from the village with me to trade, and I have to make a list of items to bring back for the village. I want you by my side."

"Why? To remind you not to covet your neighbor's wife?" Keziah regretted her bitter words as soon as they were out of her mouth, but she could not call them back. Isaac's eyes clouded with pain; then a crimson flush made its way up his face and he turned away. But he didn't deny what she had said. And so Keziah did not go with her husband to Ziph. Instead, she stayed at home and tortured herself with thoughts of Isaac and Ailea together.

Isaac did spend time with Ailea. Jonathan was on leave from his army duties and asked his friend to stay with them for a few days before his journey. Isaac wanted to tell Jonathan about the attack in Tyre and get his advice. During his stay, he thought of something he wanted to bring Ailea from Damascus, but he told neither her nor Jonathan about his plan in case it failed.

He had been concerned that his friends would ask questions

about Keziah's outburst, but they didn't. Isaac was relieved, and asked them if they would look in on Judith and Keziah while he was gone. He told Jonathan that Talmon might cause trouble, though he doubted it. Jonathan thought he only referred to Talmon's dismissal from the army, and Isaac didn't explain things further.

~ ~ ~

JERUSALEM

They sat with the child between them. He had just been fed, and he made little gurgling sounds of contentment and kicked his feet.

"He is beautiful," the King boasted as he studied the baby's curly hair and chubby arms. He was a month old now and a picture of health. *Surely he will be all right,* David reassured himself silently. They never spoke about Nathan's prophecy that their son would die, although it hung like a cloud over them. Everyone in Jerusalem knew of the prediction, and often people would glance aside quietly when David looked at them.

David had repented, and the Lord hadn't struck him down. In his mercy, surely he would relent in his judgment on their son. Fear clenched his heart, and he prayed silently for the child. He looked up to see the same fear in Bathsheba's eyes.

"Take your son to his nurse and come for a walk with me," he coaxed. She hesitated for a moment. He knew it was difficult for her to leave the child at all, and he was concerned for her. She started to shake her head, and he knew she was about to refuse. "No, my darling, I insist. The baby will do perfectly well while you are gone."

When they got back from the walk, it was just as David had said. The babe was awake and ready to be fed. That night, the King heard the sound of weeping coming from his wife's chamber next door. It was Bathsheba. The proscribed time of ceremonial uncleanness had kept them in separate sleeping chambers since the birth. Now he drew on a belted robe and rushed to her side.

The nurse was there, but Bathsheba held the baby. She looked disheveled and distraught, as did the nurse. His son was quiet. His face was very pale except for two bright spots of color on his cheeks. He fought back his own dread for his wife's sake and laid a hand on the baby's brow.

"He is only a little warm to the touch. Surely it is just a slight fever, and it will be gone tomorrow. Or maybe he is cutting a tooth already. I remember that Adonijah cut two before the age of four months, and was very ill with it."

"The King is right, my lady. I have nursed many a babe sicker than this one. I only awakened you because you instructed me to let you know of the least indisposition."

Both David and the nurse tried to persuade Bathsheba to go back to bed and let the baby return to the nursery. But she insisted that his little bed be brought into her room. The nurse's cot was also brought. After getting them settled, he returned to his room, but he lay for hours, staring at the canopy above his bed, a picture of Nathan's judgment replaying itself in his head.

When the child worsened the next day, David called for a half-dozen of the most respected healers in the land. They examined the child and reported their findings. It was a serious fever, indeed. There was not much hope. They hadn't told the lady Bathsheba, certain he would want to see to that, they said.

It was the hardest thing he had every done, facing her. He knew immediately that he didn't have to tell her. She knew. After sobbing for a few moments in his arms, she pushed away from him and went running to her room. She shut the door behind her.

He went to a small, windowless chamber, seldom used. There he prayed the prayer of confession over and over again. "I have sinned most grievously against you, O Lord. I bitterly repent, and fall upon your mercy. Let this sickness fall upon me instead."

The hours passed until finally David fell asleep, prostrate on the floor. He woke to hear someone knocking on the door of the little room. It was pitch black, the oil lamp long since having burned out.

They have come to tell me that the child is dead, he thought. Then Amoz entered, carrying a tray of food. "It is noonday, my lord. You will surely sicken if you do not eat."

"How is it with the child?"

"There is no change, my lord. Let the King take nourishment. Then you can go to your wife and son."

"No, Amoz, she doesn't want me near. It reminds her, you see. It reminds her that I am to blame for this calamity. No, I can only stay here and pray, and perhaps Adonai will hear. Don't bother to bring food again, Amoz. I will let nothing pass my lips until I have the Lord's answer in the matter."

Amoz looked as if he would like to argue, but he could tell that the King was determined on his course. "Then I will leave water, my lord. Don't forget to drink. It won't interfere with your prayers." David nodded distractedly and once again fell, arms outstretched, on the hard stone floor.

"I am worried, Sheva. He has eaten nothing for seven days. If we tell him that the child has died, he may throw himself off a parapet or fall on his sword."

Amoz, normally the soul of serenity, with his dignified stance and graying beard, was now wringing his hands in dismay. The child of David and Bathsheba had died more than an hour ago, and no one had had the courage to tell the King. Finally Amoz had sought the advice of Sheva, the trusted scribe.

Sheva hastened to calm him. "I will summon others to go with us. But we cannot put it off any longer. The child must be buried before sundown."

A half-hour later they stood in the hall outside the room where David was grieving. With them were two of the Pelethite guards who served as his personal bodyguards.

"Be ready to intervene if the King tries to do harm to himself," Amoz was telling the guards. "He was so distraught while the babe still lived, that we fear what he will do now."

Just then, the door to the darkened chamber was flung open. David, in the same tunic he had worn for a week, and his thick hair standing up in wild disarray, asked them pointedly, "Is the child dead?"

Amoz took a deep breath, and with his voice trembling answered, "Yes, he died earlier this morning, my lord."

David squeezed his eyes shut, took a deep breath and held it, then let it out in a long sigh. He nodded. "Thank you, Amoz, for telling me without evasion. Now, I would have a bath drawn, please. And lay out my formal tunic and robe. Also have food prepared and brought to my chamber. I will eat as soon as I have washed and dressed."

He turned to Sheva and the two guards. "Thank you for coming, but Amoz will attend me now. You may go about your duties."

The three men looked at each other uneasily. They had certainly not expected this. The King was not even weeping. Sheva, who had been the court scribe of over twenty years was bold enough to ask the question that was on all their minds.

"My lord, if I may be so bold, what is the reason for your reaction to this terrible news? While the little one still lived, you fasted and wept for days, but now that he is dead, you rise and ask for your bath and food. I don't understand."

"While the baby was alive and ill, I fasted and wept because I thought, who knows whether the Lord may be gracious to me and allow my son to live? But now he is dead, and there is no further reason to fast. It won't bring my son back to me. He cannot ever come back to me, but one day I will go to him. Do you understand my reasoning, Sheva?"

"Yes, my lord," Sheva responded, his eyes tearing. "It is clear to me now."

Jonathan leaned against the gatepost of his house as Isaac took his leave. His shoulders were slumped. Isaac put his hand on his friend's massive shoulder. "What's wrong, Jonathan?"

"I was just thinking about David, the way he used to be in the early days. Saul was hunting us, stalking us like a lion does the sheep. David would never even consider wresting the kingdom from him. By that time, many in Israel were convinced that Saul's strange moods had crossed the line into madness, and we often begged David to declare himself king, set up his capital at Hebron. Most of the people would have supported his claim. But he always refused, saying that Saul was the Lord's anointed.

"He showed no covetousness then. How could he have changed so much that now he would see a number of loyal men dead so that he could have another man's wife? It makes me heartsick. Now I have lost both you and Ahiam." He shook his head, unable to continue.

"You haven't lost me, Jonathan. Even though I no longer serve under you in the army, I still serve you as a friend. And don't feel you have to withdraw your loyalty from the King because of what happened to my father. Joab ordered Uriah's unit to fight under that wall, but it was Talmon who deployed my father and his men. I believe he acted on his own. I am not saying that Joab and David don't bear blame for our losses that day, but they had no personal malice against my father. Talmon did."

Jonathan nodded. "I just haven't decided if I can forgive David. I guess it will take more time. Just be very cautious in Jerusalem and on the expedition. I don't want to receive any more bad news for a while."

Isaac nodded. "I'll be careful. You do the same. You are returning to Rabbah tomorrow?"

"Yes, but my heart isn't in it."

"All the more reason for you to go cautiously. The Lord keep you, my friend."

"The Lord keep you."

~ ~ ~

As soon as Isaac had left for Ziph, Keziah regretted not going with him. She tortured herself with visions of her husband with Ailea. And she knew she had no one but herself to blame. She had pushed her husband away. Isaac had tried to reach out to her, and she had rejected his overtures. Now he was gone and she missed him.

Keziah imagined traveling with Isaac, seeing faraway people and places. Perhaps they would grow closer. She decided that when he returned she would tell him she had changed her mind.

But when Isaac returned from Ziph, he immediately prepared to set off on his mission. He was tight-lipped and distant, and Keziah didn't have the courage to risk being told he was no longer interested in taking her with him. So she saw him off in the early morning four days later. A pack train of twenty donkeys and five ox carts carried all sorts of goods from Judah as well as many items for the King.

A dozen drivers moved out under Isaac's direction, along with two families who wished to travel with the caravan for protection against bandits. They stopped in Jerusalem for only one day to secure the letter of commission from the King that would allow him to trade with the artisans and merchants of Damascus as a representative of David.

Because of David's restriction on his using the King's Highway, Isaac would travel the less popular Way of the Plain to Ashtaroth, where he would intersect the Road to Bashan and take it northward to Damascus. Fewer caravans took this route because it was not as easy to travel. But Isaac decided he would take advantage of the fact that there was less competition for goods and exact a higher price as he traded along the way.

However, he found it difficult to get an audience with the King to secure his commission. "The child of Bathsheba died a few days ago," one of the palace stewards explained, "and the King has gone to the tabernacle each day since to sacrifice and pray. The prophecy of Nathan has been fulfilled, you know. It was a terrible thing to behold. Terrible." The old servant was unaware that he was being immoderate in his speech. He seemed genuinely grieved.

Isaac decided to seek the King at the tabernacle. He found David just after the sacrifice, with Abiathar and the sixty-eight Levite gatekeepers. He was helping Asaph, the chief musician, lead the Levite worship singers in a psalm. According to one of the Levites who stood nearby, David had just written it. Asaph played the cymbals as the harps and lyres joined in. Then the magnificent sounds of the worship choir joined in with the instruments. The words were among the most beautiful Isaac had ever heard.

> Blessed is he whose transgression is forgiven,
> Whose sin is covered.
> Blessed is the man to whom the LORD does not impute iniquity,
> And in whose spirit there is no deceit.
> When I kept silent, my bones grew old
> Through my groaning all the day long.
> For day and night Your hand was heavy upon me;
> My vitality was turned into the drought of summer.
> I acknowledged my sin to You,
> And my iniquity I have not hidden.
> I said, "I will confess my transgressions to the LORD,"
> And you forgave the iniquity of my sin.

The musicians accompanying the King had reached a dramatic crescendo, then paused at the King's direction. Tears glistened on David's cheeks as he stood, hands raised in worship of Adonai raising the last strains of the song to the heavens.

> For this cause everyone who is godly shall pray to You
> In a time when you may be found;
> Surely in a flood of great waters
> They shall not come near him.

You are my hiding place;
You shall preserve me from trouble;
You shall surround me with songs of deliverance.

Isaac stood, engrossed in the scene as the King poured out his heart. He could see the sincerity in David's demeanor and wished he had not come here. He did not want to forgive the King his part in Ahiam's death. He wanted to hold on to his rage, his bitterness. He wanted to believe David was devoid of redeeming features. Yet Isaac had to admit that his attitude was hypocritical and self-righteous. Had he not coveted Jonathan's wife? If Ailea had not been so devoted to her husband, might he not have succumbed at some unguarded moment to his illicit desires?

But I would never plot murder, he thought. Then he remembered the time in battle when Jonathan had been surrounded by enemy warriors and about to be cut down. Even as he rushed to his captain's defense, the thought had crossed his mind that if Jonathan were killed, he, Isaac would comfort Ailea. He would take care of her.

In the next instant, deeply ashamed of the thought, Isaac had banished it and rushed at the men who had Jonathan surrounded, striking down three of them before they realized he was upon them. Afterward Jonathan had praised his courage and told the whole camp how fiercely his armor bearer had fought. Isaac had been most uncomfortable at the praise because he knew his motives had not been that noble.

David had been guilty of coveting his neighbor's wife. So had Isaac. David had acted on that sinful desire; and while Isaac had not, he had been tempted to, at least once. As for murder, besides that time in battle with Jonathan, Isaac had to admit that his hatred for Talmon would allow him to commit murder, at least the murder of Talmon. Jonathan had told him to allow God to see to it that David's sins were punished; probably some of the Rab's teaching had sunk in with his warrior son. Isaac knew now that he could let go of his bitterness toward the King. Talmon? That was a different matter.

Isaac waited until the worship service was over to ask permission to walk along with David. He told the King his plans for the expedition to trade in Damascus for ivory, which came there from the major trade routes from the east.

The King seemed in a very amenable mood. He granted Isaac the commission he desired without even mentioning Talmon or admonishing him that the King's Highway was off limits. Isaac wondered if the King had forgotten the dispute. After all, David had much more on his mind these days than a dispute between two of his subjects. Whatever the reason, Isaac was thankful when he left the palace with a parchment stating he could make purchases in the King's name. His caravan left for Damascus the next morning.

Chapter Sixteen

Isaac did find ivory in Damascus, but he found something else that was even more valuable. On his first day there, he sent out inquiries to find out if anyone had a servant, probably of the rank of household steward, in his later middle years, whose name was Malik. He had promised himself that when he returned to Damascus, he would find the man for Ailea, the only person left from her former life in that city.

A week went by and Isaac was nearly finished conducting his business. Because he had a royal commission, he had been given quarters at the military garrison David had set up when he had taken Damascus more than three years ago. The room was spacious, the bed comfortable. Isaac sat at a desk and added up his profits, using a pen made of rush to calculate the figures on a piece of parchment. He smiled as he worked, for the total would be a very large sum, possibly three hundred shekels of silver.

Someone cleared his throat, and Isaac looked up to see a man standing in the doorway. His face was in a shadow, and Isaac did not recognize him.

"I see you have changed from a lad into a fine man since I last saw you," the man remarked. "And you recovered completely from your wounds."

Isaac stood up so quickly that the stool he had been sitting on toppled over. "Malik, my old friend! I had begun to fear I wouldn't find you."

"The messengers you sent out were diligent. Two of them found me yesterday. Or did you think you'd receive word of my passing? It is true I am getting old, but I have some good years yet left in me, lad." The portly man laughed as Isaac gave him the kiss of greeting. "How fares my lady?" he asked.

"Ailea prospers and is very happy, Malik. She sent word to you when her son was born. Did you receive her message?"

"Yes, and I have heard from her several times since, but it is never enough. My Cricket. I think of her like a daughter, you know. I took care of her for so many years."

"Well, why don't you make the journey back to Judah with me and take care of her once more?"

"What? Is she ill? I thought you said Ailea was well."

"Calm yourself, Malik. She is well, but she misses you as much as you miss her, and there is the child to tend. I think you should go to her."

"Did she send you?"

"No, Malik. I want to surprise her. She would be thrilled. She and Jonathan are very prosperous and have a large household. They really could use your help."

"She did write to me once, soon after her son was born, to ask if I could come to her. But at that time my new master was very ill. He died last year, but his widow has plenty of servants to see to her needs. I would be free to come if you think—"

Isaac interrupted. "Pack your bags, Malik, you're going to Ziph!"

~ ~ ~

Ishobeam stood in the city market of Hebron watching Judith bargain with a merchant over his beans and cucumbers. He had watched Isaac's departure a week ago, taking note that he had hired armed men this time to protect the caravan. This told Ishobeam that Isaac knew the attack in Tyre had been more than a chance encounter with ordinary footpads.

Ishobeam seethed anew when he thought about the bumbling incompetence of the men he had paid to carry out Talmon's orders. Talmon had been furious with Ishobeam when the plan had failed. Now he was far to the north, arranging again for "robbers" to accost Isaac—this time in a raid on the entire caravan. Ishobeam's assignment had been to come here to Hebron and find some leverage he could use if the direct attack on Isaac failed.

He watched Judith fill her basket with her purchases and contemplated snatching the woman from the market the next time she was there. He had watched the mother and son say goodbye when Isaac's caravan had left, their devotion obvious to even a casual observer. Ishobeam's eyes gleamed at the thought of the power Talmon could exert over Isaac with his mother at his mercy. It would be an easy matter to snatch the woman from her home. With all the workers coming and going in Isaac's building project, no one would notice if he slipped inside their home as well.

Two days later, Ishobeam was across the street from Isaac's home, observing everything that was going on. The gate opened, and Judith came out with Adah at her side. His plans immediately changed. The child was the one Ishobeam wanted to get his hands on. He had resented the fact that she had gotten away that day on the road to Adoraim, and besides, a child would be easier to take than a grown woman.

But then Ishobeam got a good look at Keziah as she swept the area by the gate. Despite the fact that Talmon had assured him that Isaac and his wife would never disclose what had happened to her on the road to Adoraim, Ishobeam was afraid of someday being brought to trial for the attack. His hands itched to silence both witnesses—permanently. But Talmon had insisted on his merely taking a hostage.

What would the master have him do? That strong young servant who had been hired before Isaac left kept a watchful eye on all three female members of his family. He had to think this through. He decided it would be easiest to take the child.

~ ~ ~

She should have gone with her husband, Keziah realized as soon as Isaac disappeared from sight. She had been afraid, she admitted to herself. Why had she treated Isaac in such a way when he had saved her life, her honor? But she wanted more. She wanted his acceptance, his love. Her heart yearned for Isaac to return her love, yet she had sent him away without ever having revealed it. How could she win him if they weren't together?

That mocking voice inside her head, her father's voice, reminded Keziah that Isaac's heart belonged to Ailea. But surely he could get over Ailea in time. Surely when Isaac returned, if Keziah welcomed him wholeheartedly and devoted herself to him in every possible way, seeing to his comforts, keeping his house, and giving him children, he would return that devotion in time.

But you can never wash away the stain of defilement, she heard the inner voice say. No! Keziah shook her head to banish the thought. The Rab had said she was guiltless. The Rab had said it was Talmon who was defiled and evil. The Lord God had declared it in His Law. She would behave as if she believed it, even if she did not always feel it to be true.

So Keziah supervised the work on the addition to the house, hiring extra workers to do a beautiful mosaic in the part of the courtyard that was now covered with a thatched roof. She wove bright mats for the floors of all the rooms. She obeyed Isaac's demand and hired a young woman to take on the duties that Rachel could not perform. She longed for the days to pass quickly and for Isaac to be home.

Adah sought her out one morning when she felt particularly

harried. "I will take the bread and cheese to Aaron, Keziah. I know you need to make certain the workers do their job, so everything will be finished when Isaac comes home." Adah clapped her hands together in excitement. "He will be so pleased. Then he will laugh again like he used to."

Keziah hesitated a moment before giving permission. Judith had gone to Ziph to see Ailea yesterday at Keziah's suggestion. She had been grieving especially hard for Ahiam in the past week as she saw all the changes being made to the house. "What use is there in having a beautiful home when my Ahiam is not here to enjoy it with me?" she had asked one morning when Keziah had found her crying. So Keziah had sent her to her friend and to the Rab for comfort, assuring her that she and Adah would be fine here in Hebron.

Now she answered Adah. "I suppose you may go. But come back soon, Adah, or else I'll worry." As she watched Adah leave, she felt a small qualm, remembering Talmon and Ishobeam. But surely they would have no interest in accosting Adah again. It would be herself they would wish to harm, if indeed they had seen her in Jerusalem and realized she was alive. She had to overcome her irrational fear that her tormentors might return.

But Adah did not return from her errand. Near sunset Keziah went to her father's house. When she learned that Adah had never been there that day, Keziah was frantic, ready to ask her father to assemble every man he could from Hebron to search for the child. Then a dirty little urchin appeared with a message. "A man told me to give you this and tell you that if you wish to retrieve what goes with it you must meet him at the gates of Jericho in a week. Oh, and he said you must bring two hundred pieces of silver for payment."

Keziah stared at the small piece of blue fringe the boy had placed in her hand. It came from the bottom of the tunic Adah had worn that morning. She questioned the boy, but he had no information except that a man with missing teeth had paid him that morning to wait until sunset to deliver the message.

An hour later, Keziah sold several bolts of cloth and two ivory boxes to some of Hebron's wealthiest citizens. She had the ransom payment. She had Darkon accompany her and the new household servant, Miriam, to Jericho.

She considered starting out that very hour, even though it was night, but she decided that a few hours rest would give them the strength they needed to make the journey very quickly. Maybe they would even overtake Ishobeam and Adah. She spent most of the night petitioning Adonai that he keep Adah safe.

~ ~ ~

Adah told herself to remain calm. Though the dirty rag that was stuffed in her mouth made it difficult, she could still breathe through her nose. The large basket in which Ishobeam had hidden her was loosely woven, so that air could be exchanged. Now that the sun was at its zenith, it was as hot as an oven in her prison, but she could survive. She mustn't give up.

The pack mule that carried the basket jostled her unmercifully as it plodded along over the uneven road. Adah reminded herself that she had to stay alive, stay alert to help Isaac and Keziah. Ishobeam had been unable to keep his unholy glee to himself after he had captured her, and as he walked along beside the basket, leading the mule, he had revealed his plan to use her to get Keziah to come to Jericho.

He had informed Talmon that he had the little sister of Isaac. He had sent word that Keziah would soon follow him to Jericho, bringing a ransom with her. He awaited his master's pleasure as to when and how to kill them. Ishobeam could not keep from bragging to Adah.

"Talmon is even now raiding your brother's caravan. Your brother will, of course, not survive the attack. But if by chance he happens to escape being killed, then my master will be able to use you and Keziah as bait to get him to come to Jericho as well," Ishobeam had pointed out with obvious pride. He thought himself brilliant. "It is a perfect plan, yes indeed. Even my choice of Jericho, which is about halfway between Damascus and Hebron. Everyone should arrive at just the right time." Ishobeam chuckled to himself.

We have to stop sometime, Adah told herself, fighting to keep her panic at bay. When they stopped she would wait for her opportunity to escape. She wasn't a baby anymore, and she refused to give in to the temptation to cry like one. Her hands were tied behind her back, so she rubbed her face against the fabric of her tunic that stretched across her bent knees. She furiously wiped away the tears that insisted on escaping her tightly closed eyelids.

Her nightmare had come true many hours ago when she had gone to the house of Aaron to see if he needed her help today. Not finding him there, she set about sweeping the courtyard.

He could have hired such chores done, but was much too stingy to do so, but Adah didn't mind, not really. She did it more for Keziah than for Aaron, anyway. Whenever Keziah did something for her father, he found a way to say it was not enough or to make her feel guilty, so Adah had taken to volunteering for the tasks in order to spare her sister-in-law. Aaron was also testy with Adah, but Adah didn't care. She knew it was just his way.

As she was contemplating these things, she heard a twig snap behind her and whirled around. Her eyes widened in horror as she saw the man who had crept up on her. Before she could react, even to scream, Ishobeam had stuffed the filthy rag in her mouth and tied her arms and legs tightly. Then he had crammed her into the large basket that stood beside Aaron's front door. Soon the basket was secured to the mule and they were leaving the city of Hebron behind.

Now as they made their way northward, Adah admonished herself not to indulge in self-pity. She must stay alert; she must find a way to escape before Talmon got Keziah and Isaac in his clutches. She had to save them. Somehow, she had to save them.

~ ~ ~

The next morning, before first light, Keziah left Rachel with a message for Judith. "Get one of the village boys to take it to Judith immediately."

Rachel shook her head. "This is not seemly. You, a woman, going off to face your enemy alone."

"I am not alone, Rachel. I shall have Darkon and Miriam with me."

The old woman shook her head again. "You should send a message to your husband, and maybe Captain Jonathan."

"There is no time for that, Rachel. The message said to have the ransom in Jericho in a week. Even the fastest messenger could not reach Isaac in less than a week, and Jonathan is on military duty. Send messages to them tomorrow if it will make you feel better, but I have to leave now."

"I will pray the Lord to deliver you from your own foolishness, then. And I will try to convince Lady Judith to stay put when she gets home."

Rachel was unsuccessful. When Judith returned that day, she listened to Rachel's account of what had happened, her eyes widening with fear for her daughter. Then she sent for a certain citizen of Hebron, Simeon, by name, who, according to Ahiam, had been one of David's prime warriors in the early years. The man had retired from the army several years ago, and though well over sixty years old, was still as robust and wily as ever. He eagerly accepted the mission of escorting his deceased friend's widow on her quest to recover her kidnapped daughter.

"It will be my pleasure to defeat the evildoers for you," he said, rubbing his hands together as he savored the thought. Then he proceeded to ready his two donkeys for their departure.

At midday the next day, they overtook Keziah and her small entourage. Keziah embraced Judith warmly, not really surprised that her mother-in-law had followed her. She was also relieved that they would have Simeon's assistance.

They skirted Jerusalem, and then turned northeast toward Jericho, which was located ten miles north of the Salt Sea. The former stronghold of Joshua's time had been rebuilt to some extent, but was no longer a walled city. The tribe of Benjamin, to which it had been allotted, had heeded the curse that had been placed on it by the Lord when it fell to Joshua and had never rebuilt its walls. Still, it was a town of some size, its abundant springs and lush palm trees making it a favored stop for pilgrims journeying between Israel and lands to the north. When they came within sight of the city, Simeon called a halt to their small procession.

"We must split up from here," he counseled. "They may have set a watch for us. Only I will accompany Lady Keziah. They won't have expected her to come alone, but I wish them to believe that a feeble old man is her only companion. We will take lodging at my nephew's house. The rest of you make camp at the spring at the northern end of the city. I will bring you word each day of what has happened." Judith was loath to be separated from Keziah, but acquiesced to Simeon's logical strategy.

They all laughed when Simeon took his staff from his pack and transformed himself into a bent and unsteady old man right before their eyes. Bidding the rest of the group farewell, he and Keziah entered Jericho first. The fine hairs stood up on the back of Keziah's neck as they made their way through the city's busy market. Ishobeam and Talmon could be anywhere, watching. And they had the advantage of holding Adah. They knew from past experience that Keziah would do anything to protect the child.

"I wonder how soon they will contact us," she whispered as she pretended to help her "frail" companion navigate the busy streets.

"They will probably wait until the week is up, but will watch us in the meantime to see how much help we have. My nephew is a merchant with three young children. We will not bring him into this unless necessary. I don't think the kidnappers will consider him a threat anyway."

When they reached the nephew's house, Keziah understood Simeon's words. His nephew was a small and slender man, almost effeminate. He was certainly not a man who would intimidate Talmon or Ishobeam. But he and his wife were gracious, and his three children, all girls, were well behaved.

They had two days before the week was up. They were days of tension and anguish for Keziah, as she wondered what had become of Adah. On each of the two days, she sent Darkon and Simeon out to search the city. She also went out both days to the market, accompanied by the wife of Simeon's nephew and two male servants. Simeon was unhappy with her decision to do this. But she thought she should appear in public in case Ishobeam and Talmon were looking for her.

Chapter Seventeen

Isaac was lying in a small tent some twenty miles south of Damascus, not far from the city of Heshbon. He had been more successful in his expedition to Damascus than he had dreamed possible. His caravan was loaded down with ivory from the lands to the east, not to mention other luxury items he had procured in the name of the King. Besides the King's bounty, he had done enough trading on his own to assure his family's future wealth.

Perhaps he would not need to go on another expedition for another year, and he could spend time with Keziah and his mother and sister. They had all been worried about him, he knew. He would take his time in getting his revenge on Talmon, and his family would never have to know about it.

Perhaps Keziah would be able to forgive him his behavior when he had found out about Talmon, and his lack of comfort to her when the baby died. He hoped the gift he had found her would win her over.

On his second morning in Damascus, Isaac had strolled through the long, colonnaded portico that lined the inside of the main gate of the city. Under the overhang of the guard's walkway, the space had all been filled with vendors, who took advantage of the protection it offered from the elements.

Because Damascus sat on the convergence of two major caravan routes, there was a tremendous amount of trading and selling to be done, and the protected space had long since been filled. Merchants had spilled out into the large quadrangle of space just inside the main gate. They set up their wares in baskets, on small tables, and on trays around them. The noise and confusion were greater even than the market in Jerusalem.

Isaac enjoyed it thoroughly. *Maybe this business of being a caravaner is going to work out after all,* he had thought as he made his way leisurely among the vendor's stalls. Having made all the arrangements for the disposition of his goods from the garrison command post the day before, he had time today to shop for personal items. He chose handsome rugs and a chair for his home, found a winter cloak of the softest wool, bordered with scarlet cord for Judith. He picked out a cover of blue and lavender for Adah's bed. But he could not decide on a gift for Keziah. What would she wish to have?

An hour passed, and he had still not made a choice for her. He decided to visit the gold merchants to make some purchases for the King's commission; gold cups and serving trays for the palace and the future temple, as well as gold ankle bracelets that were to be gifts for all the little royal princesses, ten in all.

While he was choosing the bracelets, he saw a stunning piece that was meant as either a necklace or a head ornament. It was a braided gold chain from which were suspended ten gold coins, each embossed with a palm leaf. Engraving of any kind was uncommon in Israel because of the commandment against graven images, but this botanical design was not forbidden, just rare.

It was the kind of necklace that might be given as a dowry to the pampered daughter of a wealthy man. At her marriage, such a girl would come to her husband wearing the golden coins, not as a necklace, but as a headpiece securing her bridal veil. All the guests would know by the value of the necklace how valued such a daughter was.

A mental image had come to Isaac of Keziah coming to him

with no dowry except a puny silver necklace with three small silver coins. He felt the insult her uncaring and selfish father had dealt her, not just at the wedding, but her whole life. Impulsively, Isaac picked up the expensive piece.

The necklace would certainly convey a message to his wife of his regard, were he to buy it for her. Of course, it was outrageously expensive. Even with the wealth he had acquired on his two caravan trips, it would mean he would have to postpone some phase of his building project to afford it.

Oh, well, what good was a huge house to a man if his wife felt unhappy and unappreciated? He bought the necklace for Keziah, smiling as he pictured her face when she first saw it, and imagining how the gold coins would look glinting against the rich color of her thick hair.

That sight would only be for his eyes, of course, and she would not be able to wear the necklace in public except on very special occasions—such as feast days and important weddings. But it would belong to her as a reminder that Isaac, her husband, valued and respected her.

Yes, this trip had accomplished more than he had ever dreamed possible. But his greatest triumph was not in the material wealth he had garnered. He had fulfilled a silent promise he had made to Ailea three years earlier, when she had lost her parents, her brother, and her home in the capture of Damascus by David's armies.

With her parents dead and her brother, Rezon escaping to the desert to form a band of raiders to harass the Israelites, Ailea was the only one of her family left at home in the occupied city. Jonathan had made the villa his headquarters, and Ailea had resisted vehemently his invasion of her home.

At that time, it had almost broken his heart to see the fiery beauty broken in spirit as she was taken away from all she ever knew. Of all the things from her former life, Isaac was aware that her two faithful servants, Shua and Malik, were missed more than anything else. He had spent much of his time in Damascus searching for Malik and Shua, who had been sold to other owners.

Regrettably, he found out that Shua had passed away more than a year ago, but Malik was still in good health and willing to make the trip to be with his former mistress in Ziph. Isaac could hardly wait to see the look on Ailea's face when she saw Malik. She would be so grateful to him. He envisioned how she would embrace him in her gratitude. It was the kind of fantasy he had often indulged in over the past three years. Now he felt a moment's guilt, reminding himself that he was married. But surely it was harmless to imagine Ailea praising him, admiring him as a friend.

He was eager to deliver the ivory and other goods to Jerusalem quickly so that he could hurry to Ziph. He would go straight there, then return home to Hebron. He nodded to himself in the dark as he lay on his pallet. It was a good plan.

The raiders came at dawn, before more than a handful of the caravan's numbers were awake. They rode right for the center of the camp. One of the bandits, heavily bearded and fierce, engaged Isaac.

He fought with a long-handled battle ax, while Isaac, with only a sword, was at a disadvantage in size and reach. Fortunately, after some moments, Malik sneaked up behind the enemy and felled him with a heavy bronze chest. As the man went down, the chest broke open, spilling out its treasure. Fine parchment and writing implements, along with various small decorative pots filled with caked ink, littered the ground. These were supplies for the King's scribe, Sheva, and possibly his historian, Jehoshaphat.

"I am sorry, my lord. I seem to have broken the chest," Malik remarked in all sincerity, causing Isaac to laugh in spite of the circumstances.

"Never mind that. Let's see what damage they have done," Isaac told him.

They had been robbed of all the ivory, as well as the precious gems; skins of fine wine had been spilled out, and delicate bolts of cloth had been trampled by the pack animals as they had been led away by the thieves. Isaac surveyed the ruin about him and seethed with rage. He had been attacked twice now. Was that a coincidence?

"My lord," said Malik, "I think I may know who has raided us. If not, he will have knowledge of who did. I think I shall go to Heshbon to test out my theory."

Isaac eyed the rotund servant keenly. "Do you think it is Rezon who led the raid?"

"My former master's son is known as the prince of the desert raiders, my lord. His fame grows year by year, as does his ill-gotten wealth. Some say that in the not-too-distant future, Rezon will wrest Damascus back from the Hebrews and rule there."

"You plan to confront him about this raid and persuade him to give back the booty? That is highly unlikely, Malik."

"The young master was always fond of me. And I will tell him you are taking me to the Cricket, umm—Ailea. In spite of Rezon's anger over her marriage to a Hebrew, Ailea is still his sister. They were very close as children."

Isaac shrugged. "I guess it's worth a try, but I will go with you, Malik. I'm not letting you out of my sight until I have safely delivered you to Ziph."

They sought out a certain widow in Heshbon by the name of Meshil, whom Malik knew to be Rezon's mistress. She contacted Rezon for them, and the next evening he appeared as they drank wine in Meshil's house. Meshil had gone out to meet him, and now he stood with one arm around her, leaning on the doorpost.

His smile showed a crescent of white in his swarthy face. His hair was clubbed back with a leather thong, revealing a large gold earring in his left ear. He had a scimitar tucked into his red girdle. Rezon looked fierce and wild and free, a man who did what he wished and feared no one, especially not the Hebrews who now occupied the lands that formerly belonged to the Arameans.

"Well, old man," he said to Malik, "I'm surprised you are still alive. You must be as ancient as Mt. Hermon." Rezon's voice was gruff as he greeted his father's former steward, but his eyes were dancing.

"I'm too stubborn to die, my lord. I see that you are as wild and headstrong as ever. Maybe even more headstrong than your sister."

The eyes that had been dancing flashed with anger. "I have no sister!"

Malik was not intimidated. He made a swiping motion with his hand as if he were batting away a pesky fly. "No matter how great your anger toward her, Ailea is still your sister, Rezon. Don't you remember how you saved her from drowning in the bathing pool that was in my master's courtyard? You were no more than four years old, and she had not reached her second year, yet you jumped in and saved her.

"And don't you remember the many days she played games with you when you had to be in bed with that cut on your leg that wouldn't heal? She devoted hours to you then. All these things are history between you and your sister, Rezon. Surely they account for more than just one act that caused you some displeasure. Besides, you know as well as I do that Ailea was taken captive and had no choice but to marry Jonathan of Ziph."

Rezon grunted. He was too proud to admit Malik was right, but it was an obvious softening in his attitude. "What do you want of me, old man?" he asked gruffly.

"My friend Isaac's caravan was raided last night. You would not, perchance, know anything about that?"

"If you are asking if my men and I did the raid, the answer is no."

Malik nodded. "Then would it be possible for you to find out who did the raid?"

"That would be a simple matter," Rezon answered.

"And could you recover what was lost?"

Rezon's mouth curved in just a hint of a smile. "That would not be so simple."

"But you could arrange it?"

"I could arrange it."

Isaac and Malik stayed as guests in the house of Meshil the widow. She told them the story of the time Jonathan had cast Ailea out, and she had come to stay with Meshil for several months. When Isaac related to her all the adventures that had happened to Ailea after she had left the widow's house three years ago, her trek in the wilderness and the birth of her son in a desert cave, she was not surprised. "The girl is much like her brother; very courageous, and too stubborn to die," she remarked.

The next morning, one of Rezon's men came to Meshil's house. He had with him not only most of the stolen goods but also a man who admitted to being the leader of the robbers. But the man told them he had been hired by a Hebrew who had promised him a large reward if he could bring proof of the death of the leader of the caravan.

"Who is the man who hired you?" Isaac asked impatiently.

"He never told me his name, but I know it. I will tell you if you will promise to let me go. I am just a man trying to earn my daily bread."

There was a sardonic lift to Isaac's brow when he answered the man. "You have my vow."

The robber nodded. "The man had paid us only half of what he promised because we did not succeed in killing you, and we were still arguing over that when another man arrived from Jericho with a message. He said he had a message for Talmon of Gibeah, and the man who had hired us claimed to be the same."

"I knew it! I knew he was behind these attacks. What did the message say?"

"I do not know, my lord, only that it appeared to be very important because he left in a great hurry. He left us with the shipment of ivory, and took only the gems for himself. I assumed it was because he didn't have time to transport the heavier load."

"Was there an older man with him? A man with two missing front teeth?"

The man shook his head. "No, only an Egyptian servant. This Talmon fellow mentioned that the servant had not been with him long. My master told me to go with you if you want to try to catch these thieves. But there are many places to hide among the rocks and caves of the desert. It is unlikely we will succeed."

Should he pursue Talmon and the gems or continue on with the part of the shipment they had recovered and deal with Talmon later?

When asked his opinion, Malik replied amiably, "Whatever you wish, my lord. An old man like me won't be of much use in catching the miscreants, but I stand ready to serve you."

Isaac chuckled. "You are too modest, Malik. You dealt with one of our thieves very effectively, as I remember."

Isaac finally decided to return to Judah; he could see how much control Talmon was having over him, and he decided to break the hold, just as Keziah and Judith had begged him to do. At least he would try.

They left Meshil and Rezon's servant and crossed the Jordan beyond Heshbon. No sooner had they made the crossing than they were intercepted by another messenger. This time it was Ailea who had sent the message. Isaac had the young runner repeat the message twice before he finally accepted what he was hearing.

As soon as the message had come to Ziph and Judith had rushed off for Hebron, Ailea had sent word that Adah had been kidnapped, and that Keziah had set off toward Jericho, followed by Judith a short time later. Adah was being held for a ransom of silver. Ailea had also sent a message to Jonathan, on the chance he might be able to get away from Rabbah to help.

Oh, yes, the messenger remembered, the women had taken with them for their protection Darkon whom Isaac had hired and the old army retiree named Simeon.

Isaac fumed for several minutes over the foolishness of his mother and his wife in undertaking such a mission on their own, with only two men to help them. He sent the caravan on to Jerusalem with the servants and turned toward Jericho.

Malik insisted on going with him. "I may be of help," he had reasoned. "You may not wish to be seen in some cases. I can investigate for you. I can also carry messages. Please, my lord, you have done so much for me in seeing that I am reunited with my Cricket."

"If you come with me, Malik, you may never see Ailea again. You could be killed. Not only are the kidnappers going to be dangerous, but also my worst enemy is in Jericho."

"Still, I would go with. . . . My lord, what is it? What is the matter?" Malik asked the question in great alarm. Isaac had halted his mule. His face was suddenly deathly pale, and his eyes widened in horror.

"Talmon! Talmon is in Jericho, Malik."

"Yes, my lord, as are the kidnappers of your sister."

"They are one and the same. It was Talmon's servant who sent him the message to come immediately to Jericho. Don't you see? The man—Ishobeam is his name—sent the urgent message to Talmon because he wanted him to know he had my sister in his power. And now my wife is headed to Jericho! Malik, we must get there before her. Keziah should never face Talmon alone. You have no idea the harm he has done her in the past."

Later, as they traveled toward Jericho as fast as their animals would take them, Isaac speculated grimly. "I wonder how Talmon found out that my wife was his victim a year ago and that she still lives. I can't believe he recognized her in Jerusalem, or he would have made some move against her by now. It must have given the beast a great deal of perverse satisfaction when he did learn the truth."

"We will retrieve her, my lord, and your sister as well," Malik tried to reassure him. "But we must remain calm. We mustn't let our passions rule us."

"You're right, Malik. But I'm afraid we need much more than rational thinking in this case. We need the intervention of the Lord of Hosts. We need to pray."

"Since the Hebrews took over rule in Damascus, I have begun praying to your invisible God. I would like to learn more about him," Malik said in all sincerity, though his intention was also to distract Isaac from his worry.

"You can't help but learn about him in Ziph. You will live in the household of Shageh the Rab. A Rab is a leader, a wise man in our country, and also a man who knows the Law of the Lord. He will teach you the ways of Adonai."

"But, has Ailea been accepted by your people? By your God? Does he look with favor on an Aramean?"

"The Lord looks with favor on the man who trusts in him and loves his Law. He is a merciful God. Our King has written songs about his tender mercies and his loyal love. No man can sink so low that the Lord cannot reach down and redeem him."

"This is truly astounding. Marduk and Sin and Ashtaroth, none of our gods have those characteristics. I will look forward to learning more of this."

Later, as Isaac was thinking about Keziah, it occurred to him that he had redeemed Keziah from death. He was thinking highly of himself for that, until it struck him that unlike God, who never changes, he had changed toward Keziah. As soon as he had found out the truth about her child, he had rejected her. His pride crumbled as he realized that he needed a few more lessons from the Rab himself.

Chapter Eighteen

Keziah and Judith had been in Jericho for two days and had still not been contacted by Ishobeam. "When I think of my daughter at the mercy of that horrible man, I feel like raging and screaming and tearing out my hair," Judith confided in her as they walked in the shade of the many palms at Jericho's spring, "but none of those things would do any good."

Simeon had allowed Keziah to come with him to Judith's camp to find out if she or Darkon had discovered anything. They were all disappointed that no one knew any more than they had when they had left Hebron. Keziah sought to encourage her mother-in-law.

"I know how you feel, Judith. I feel the same way, but the ransom note said we would be contacted at the end of a week, and that isn't until tomorrow."

But they didn't have to wait after all. As Keziah lay on her bed, trying not to think of what could be happening to Adah, repeating her prayer that the Lord would watch over her, she heard a slight sound at the open window. She looked up to see a dark figure standing over her. She opened her mouth, but before she could cry out, a hand covered her mouth and nose, shutting off air. She struggled until a disturbingly familiar voice hissed in her ear.

"Don't make a sound unless you want that old man who came

with you dead. I would put a knife in his gullet without blinking an eye, because I have absolutely no use for him. If you want to see the brat alive, bring the silver for the ransom and come quietly with me. Do you understand?"

When she nodded her agreement, he removed his hand. She gasped for air, then went to the small chest that held the silver. Her hand shook as she turned to face the man who now stood near enough to the window that his face was dimly illuminated. He was the one who had held her while she was attacked. Ishobeam. She would never forget the name.

"I am ready," she whispered. "Take me to Adah."

Simeon slept on through the deep hours of the night as Keziah followed Ishobeam out of the city to a cave in the surrounding hills. It was a steep climb halfway up a cliff to the mouth of the cave. Keziah noticed that Ishobeam, or more likely Talmon, had chosen a perfect defensive position. It would be virtually impossible to reach the cave either laterally or from above. The only feasible way was from below, where anyone approaching would be seen by the cave's occupants.

Keziah followed Ishobeam into the cave, and her fears were confirmed. Talmon's face was outlined by the light of a small torch set in the cave's wall. He was dressed in an immaculate tan tunic, belted with a dark leather sash. To a stranger she knew that he would appear impressively handsome, even regal. But Keziah was well acquainted with the malevolent intent that hid behind the pleasing facade. It took all her will power not to turn and attempt to flee from his presence.

Talmon's voice held a trace of amusement as he spoke to her. "When Ishobeam told me that you still lived, I found it hard to believe. That ravine was deep. What saved you?"

The bile rose in Keziah's throat. Talmon was speaking of his attempt to murder her as if it were of no more importance than swatting a fly. She would not give him the satisfaction of revealing that she was upset. She replied coolly. "There was a ledge a few feet down that you couldn't see. I landed on it."

As he chuckled diabolically Keziah cringed inwardly. Adah had been under the power of this madman. Frantically, she looked around. Where was the little girl? Her gaze lighted on what appeared to be a pile of rags at the back of the cave. Could Adah be under those rags? There was no movement. Keziah started to take a step in that direction when she was brought up short by a vicious yank on her long braid of hair.

"No, my lovely, you don't see the child until I hold the ransom in my hand. Did you bring it?"

Keziah reached into the pouch she had secured to her girdle. She brought out a handful of silver and thrust it toward Talmon. He looked at the silver for a moment, then his eyes narrowed. "This is not enough," he stated in a deadly voice.

Keziah again thrust her hand into the pouch and placed more silver in Talmon's outstretched hand. He tested its weight in his hand. Before he could comment, Keziah quickly explained. "I only brought half the amount you asked for. You don't think I would be so foolish as to bring it all when I have yet to see whether Adah is unharmed?"

Talmon looked for a moment as if he would strike her, then a look of grudging respect came into his eyes. He jerked his head toward the back of the cave. "Very well, then, see for yourself."

Keziah approached the back of the cave with some trepidation. She lifted a small burning torch from a niche in the cave wall and held it high over the pile of rags. She saw now that it was a tattered blanket. She carefully pulled the edge of the blanket back, and Adah's sleeping form was revealed. She could see the little girl's chest rise and fall rhythmically in sleep. She could also see that Adah's hands and feet had been bound tightly. There was blood on the ropes where her wrists and ankles had been rubbed raw.

"You have bound her too tightly!" she said to Talmon, her outrage causing her to forget caution. "She is bleeding. Untie her."

It was Ishobeam who responded to Keziah's demand. "The

brat caused the damage herself, trying to loosen the knots. She wouldn't listen when I told her that struggling would only cause the rope to tighten."

Talmon said nothing; he just stood there looking bored. Keziah had an insane urge to fly at him and claw that smug expression right off his face. She had to get control of her anger, or she and Adah would never get out of this. She said a quick prayer for wisdom. The answer seemed to be that she should be quiet and see what happened. She had been doing too much of the talking, revealing what was in her mind, while Talmon had said very little.

The moments stretched out as she and Talmon tried to wait each other out, or stare each other down. Keziah was alarmed by the fact that all the commotion hadn't wakened Adah, but she dared not show her concern, or Talmon would use it against her.

When Talmon spoke, she was so startled that she jumped. "Untie the child, Ishobeam." Ishobeam approached Adah with an ugly dagger, and Keziah clenched her hands at her sides to keep from stopping him. In a moment, the bonds had been cut.

The sudden release of her hands and feet woke Adah whereas the sound of voices had not. She whimpered and started to rub her wrists, then became very still as she woke fully and realized she was free. She looked up at Keziah, and a big smile broke over her face. *Dear God,* Keziah thought, *would that I could fulfill all the expectations she places on me.*

"So, you two young ladies are again our guests. You both behaved very badly the last time Ishobeam and I entertained you. Is that not right, Ishobeam?"

"Yes it is, master. And the little one there had scratched and kicked me every opportunity she got. I would like a chance to discipline her, I would."

Talmon shrugged, as if it mattered not to him what his servant did, and Ishobeam moved toward the child.

"No!" The anguished cry came from Keziah. "Leave Adah alone. Do whatever you will with me, but don't hurt her."

Talmon threw back his head and laughed. "You must have found our last encounter enjoyable then, since you sound so eager to repeat it." He walked over to Keziah, and she had to fight against her urge to shrink away from his touch. If she did, it would only give him a sense of satisfaction. So she stood perfectly still while he tilted her chin on one of his hands.

"We will get to know each other better this time, won't we, my dear? After all, I know your name now, Keziah, and I know that you belong to that whining fool who went crying to the King about me. As soon as he comes to rescue you and the child, we will see if he has the strength or the courage to take you from me. Yes, I think that will be very entertaining."

Keziah tried not to react to Talmon's taunting. She made her voice as cool and disdaining as she could. "Oh, Isaac has the strength, all right. In a fair fight, I have no doubt who the winner would be. But you don't intend to fight fairly, do you, Talmon?"

She didn't see the blow coming and was completely unprepared when Talmon struck her full across the face with his open palm. She was knocked back against the wall of the cave. Adah came up screeching her anger, and Talmon slapped her down as well. Keziah crawled over to the child and wrapped her arms around her. She was proud of Adah, who shook with fury and pain but did not cry.

Talmon observed them for a few minutes. A slow smile crossed his features. "How would you two like to be left alone, here in this cave? With no food or water, and no light? Is the little girl afraid of the dark, I wonder?

"Come, Ishobeam, let us leave the two ladies alone to talk privately. You and I will decide later what to do with them. Bring the torch with you."

Keziah stood bewildered as both men exited the cave. Then she heard Talmon's low voice giving instructions, followed by the sound of the two men straining as they rolled a huge stone across the entrance of the cave, leaving it in almost total darkness. Thankfully, a few faint rays came through at places where the stone did not perfectly fit the cave opening. Keziah put her arms around Adah, trying to fight off the feeling of entombment.

"They could have left us the torch," Adah remarked in a falsely brave voice.

"They have not a drop of human kindness in their blood," Keziah remarked. She stroked the child's back, feeling the tremors Adah was trying to hide. Keziah knew the little girl's control hung by a thread. So did her own.

"What will we do if they don't come back?" Adah asked, a tremor in her voice now.

"Oh, they'll come back. They want that ransom. I will demand that they take us both back to the city where they must let you go before I give them the remainder of the silver." Keziah tried to sound confident, but in truth, she wasn't sure if the men would ever come back. Perhaps they would intercept Isaac and kill him. Perhaps this was to be her grave—and Adah's.

Keziah kept Adah occupied by telling of their search for her. "Your mother followed close on my heels, Adah. She loves you very much. Even now she is close by, in Jericho. Soon you will have a chance to put her fears for you at rest."

"I can't believe Ahmi would strike out on her own like that. She is not a person to seek adventure, Keziah, or fight battles."

Keziah squeezed the little girl's shoulder. "For you she would do anything. Adah, there is nothing more dangerous than a mother seeking to protect her child, not even the bravest of the *Gibborim*. I feel sorry for Talmon and Ishobeam if Judith gets her hands on them." She was pleased to hear a small chuckle from Adah.

For two days they were left alone in the cave. The first night, with the setting of the sun, the cave was in darkness. Keziah and Adah talked unceasingly through the night. They talked until they once again could see the narrow band of light around the cave opening. They expected their captors to come back with the morning, but they did not, so the two captives fell into an uneasy sleep.

When they woke, they did not mention Talmon and Ishobeam, but each secretly hoped they would return. At least they would have some chance of distracting them, of trying to get away. But to die here alone was a horror they couldn't imagine. When the cave was once again in total darkness, Keziah tried to hide her own fear by singing songs, but when Adah began to cry quietly, she could not hold back her own tears. Both seemed to feel better after giving in to their true feelings, and finally fell asleep again.

"Keziah, I can feel air blowing up here on this ledge. Where do you think it's coming from?"

Keziah sat up abruptly, fighting back the familiar surge of panic at the pitch darkness. "Where are you, Adah? Why are you whispering?"

"I'm up here, on the ledge at the very back of the cave, and I am whispering because I don't want Ishobeam or Talmon to hear us if they are nearby."

Keziah had begun to doubt that the two men would ever come back, but she refused to share that opinion with Adah. Let her have hope for a little longer. Anyway, Keziah preferred death by starvation and thirst to the fate that would surely befall them if their captors returned. "Reach out your hand, Adah, so I can find you." Keziah's voice was raw because they had been left without any water. They wouldn't last much longer like this.

"Here I am. Here." Keziah felt the child's small hand grasp hers and choked back tears. If it weren't for her, none of this would have happened to Adah.

"Come here, Keziah, and put your hand near the roof of the cave. See, there is a breeze coming through. I mean, feel. I know you can't see."

"Yes, Adah. I feel the air. It has to be coming from the outside. Help me move some of these rocks."

In a matter of moments, they had unearthed a small fissure in the rocks that indeed opened to the outside. They could see the pale sky. Regrettably, it was a very small opening. They both clawed at the rocks and earth until the opening was a little larger.

"I think I can get through, Keziah."

"I don't know, Adah. What if you get stuck?"

"We might as well try. We can't be much worse off than we are now."

Amazing insight from one so young, Keziah thought, and she reluctantly agreed.

Adah did get stuck, but after a few minutes of struggling and Keziah's pushing, she popped out of the cave.

"Are you all right?"

"Yes, Keziah. Just a few scrapes. Now let me try to find something to make the opening larger so you can also get out." Adah was whispering very quietly, aware that Talmon and his servant could be nearby.

"Adah, I'm afraid our only hope is for you to leave me here and go to Jericho for help."

"No!" Adah cried, forgetting for a moment to whisper. Then she caught herself. "I won't leave you!" she whispered fiercely.

"Adah, the longer you stay the more likely it is that neither of us will get away. The men might come back at any minute. Go quickly and bring help. Find your mother. She is camped at the springs of Jericho. I will manage until you return."

~ ~ ~

Isaac tossed and turned on his pallet, which was composed of two blankets folded in half. He was covered with his cloak, more than adequate protection against the evening chill. Having been hardened by years of sleeping outdoors in all kinds of conditions, he should have been able to sleep. But from the moment he had realized that Adah and Keziah were very likely in Talmon's clutches, he hadn't been able to rest.

His pursuit of revenge against Talmon had brought danger to Keziah and Adah, and he knew he would never forgive himself if they were harmed. If only he could get his hands on Talmon, he would see to it that he never hurt anyone again. He had headed toward Jericho at a grueling speed.

Malik had kept up the pace, just as he had promised, not asking to stop for rest. But when the sun had set last night, and they were still miles from their destination, Isaac had called a halt, decreeing that they would need to be rested when they entered Jericho and that they could find out little at night anyway. Had he been alone, he would have pressed on, but he was concerned about the older man, though he would never let Malik know it. Now they were within four or five miles of Jericho, on the opposite side of the Jordan, and Isaac was anxious for dawn to come so that they could enter the city.

What they would do once they were in Jericho, Isaac did not know. He would have Malik trail behind to see what happened as he asked merchants and inhabitants what they had seen. The springs of Jericho were a good place to start, he supposed. He was almost certain that Talmon would be watching for him. He was only using Isaac's wife and sister as bait to lure him, Isaac was certain.

Isaac gave up the pretense of sleep and rose from his pallet. He couldn't bear to think about Keziah and Adah under Talmon's control. By the mercy of the Lord, perhaps Keziah and Judith had not arrived in the city yet.

Malik sat up with that vague look of one who has just awakened. "My lord, I am ready if you wish to go now. Will we be able to cross the river in the darkness?"

It really was too dark to travel, of course, and the two men stumbled along for a while, tripping over small bushes and rocks. It took them an hour to find the fording place. But it was gratifying to enter Jericho just as the sun showed itself on the horizon.

Chapter Nineteen

Slowly, the sleeping city awoke. Merchants were setting up their wares. Camel drovers were urging their camels toward the city's springs. Gradually the sound of human voices and animal noises increased as the sun rose in the sky.

Within an hour of entering Jericho, Isaac knew that his hopes were not entirely fulfilled. He found Judith almost immediately when he headed first for the oasis of palms around the springs where pilgrims and caravaners stopped. She was sitting on a flat rock near the spring with Simeon and Darkon. They did not see him approach because they were in such earnest conversation with very worried expressions on their faces. The look of relief on Judith's face when she saw Isaac brought a lump to his throat.

"I knew you would come, son," she said as she embraced him. "But I was afraid you might be too late."

"Mother, it was foolish for you to come here, but I am glad to see you. Where is Keziah?"

Judith's large brown eyes filled with tears. "I don't know. She disappeared two days ago. She was staying at the home of Simeon's brother, asleep in an upstairs chamber. Early the next morning—that would have been the day before yesterday—when the maid came to wake her, she was gone, along with the silver she brought to ransom Adah."

"And there has been no sign of Adah either?"

Judith shook her head. "No. I am sure Talmon has them both hidden somewhere. What does he want, Isaac? What can he possibly want with them?"

Isaac took the waterskin she offered him and drank deeply before answering his mother. "He wants me; he is using them to bring me to him. He won't be satisfied until I am dead. It is just as well, as I feel the same. But try not to worry, Mother. I will see that Keziah and Adah are returned safely to you before I kill him." Isaac handed the waterskin back to Judith and looked around the crowded spring.

Judith could not suppress a shiver as she studied her son's countenance. He was no longer a young man. His face was now etched in harder, leaner lines; his eyes glinted like polished stones. There was no warmth in them. This hatred, this obsession was destroying him, crowding out all that was gentle and loving. Even if Isaac managed to kill Talmon instead of Talmon murdering him, Talmon would still have won by causing Isaac to sink to his level. All Judith could do was pray that Isaac would wake up to that fact before it was too late.

Isaac and the other men agreed to fan out and search the city for any sign of Keziah, Adah, or their captors. Judith stayed at the spring, reluctantly agreeing to be there as a base for their endeavors. Isaac made a fruitless circuit of the city and returned, disheartened, to the spring to find Judith sitting on the only camp stool with Adah perched, legs dangling, on her lap. His sister jumped up as soon as she spotted him.

"Isaac! Isaac, you have to come! They've sealed her up in a horrid cave. I told her I'd hurry!" Adah was tugging at his hand, trying to lead him away from the tent.

"Wait a moment, little one. Slow down and explain exactly what has happened."

Tears started to gather in the little girl's eyes. "There's no time. You have to save Keziah. . . ." She resumed tugging.

"I will save Keziah, my sweet, but first I must know what happened, and exactly where she is." Isaac took Adah by the shoulders and gave a gentle shake. It seemed to get through to her, because she took a deep breath and quickly summarized events from the time Ishobeam had grabbed her from the lane in Hebron.

"Very good, little one," Isaac said when she finished. "Now take me to the cave." Tugging at his hand, the little girl led her brother away from the city of Jericho.

~ ~ ~

"I'm not sure, but I think it is that one over there." Adah was pointing to a place halfway up the cliff face—one of the steepest in the hills surrounding Jericho. "Yes, that's it, there—the one just below the boulder that looks like a man's nose." She tugged at Isaac. "See how it looks like a man's face with the nose and mouth? The round stone that looks like the mouth is the boulder that seals the cave where they put Keziah. Oh, hurry up and get her out, Isaac."

"I will, Adah, but are you very sure that is the cave?" Adah's head bobbed up and down vigorously. He had no choice but to act on her word. She was only a child, but a very bright one, and he had no other recourse.

After sending Simeon and Judith back with Adah, Isaac and Darkon split up. Darkon would approach the cave directly, and try to capture the attention of the kidnappers, while Isaac circled around and approached the hiding place from above. When he reached the foot of the hill below the cave, Darkon would veer off to the south, as if that were his destination. He would also circle around and try to arrive in time to be of help to Isaac if he were attacked.

Isaac had little hope that he would be able to spirit Keziah away unchallenged. Talmon would be prepared for him. *Well, let him come,* Isaac thought. *I am more than ready to kill him.*

His fists clenched as he thought of Keziah in Talmon's power. If he has touched her . . . O God, if he has touched her again he will die a slow death. Isaac had to make a conscious effort to push these disturbing thoughts to the back of his mind and concentrate on freeing Keziah.

The route around the other side of the hill and then down the steep cliff face was even more arduous than it had looked, but after two hours, Isaac was there. The small opening at the top of the cave was located just where Adah said it would be, bless her. It was just behind the bridge of the "nose" on the cliff face, hidden by a small, scraggly tree.

Isaac stared for a moment at the opening, amazed that even a child as small as Adah could have squeezed through it. He knelt down, placing his mouth near the aperture and called out in a loud whisper. He could not risk alerting Talmon if he were nearby. "Keziah, can you hear me? I have come to get you. Please answer. Keziah!"

He thought he heard a scrabbling sound then a shriek in a feminine register. "Isaac, is it truly you? Did Adah find you?"

"Shhh. . . . Keep your voice down, my love. We don't want to alert Talmon. Do you know where he is?"

"No. He shut us up in here two days ago and hasn't returned." He heard a gasp. "Isaac, you are in danger. He used us to get to you. Please be careful."

"Don't worry, Keziah, I'm well aware of Talmon's threat. Stand away from the opening, please. I'm going to try to enlarge it. If this doesn't work, I will try to move the boulder at the mouth of the cave." He began to dig and pry at the earth and stones, using the javelin he had brought along as a lever. It took almost an hour, but finally the hole was large enough to try to get Keziah out.

"Reach up, love, and grab my hands." When Keziah complied, Isaac began to lift her out. Her shoulders got stuck and painfully scraped, but finally, she was in the open air, in her husband's arms. "Are you hurt anywhere else?" he asked as he examined her bleeding scrapes.

"No, not really, but I need water. They didn't leave us any."

"I should have remembered. Mother said that Adah drank more than the camels when she first found her," Isaac told her as he opened his waterskin and let the cool liquid pour into Keziah's mouth. "Are you certain Talmon did you no harm?"

"No, she thought it would be more entertaining to wait until you could witness a repetition of our little encounter on the road to Adoraim. Did she tell you she was an unwilling participant? Women often use that excuse after the fact."

Both Keziah and Isaac turned toward the source of those mocking words. Isaac started to go after Talmon as he stood a little above them, a gloating smile on his face.

"I would suggest you stand very still. The Egyptian behind you keeps his lance sharper than a razor. It would take very little to persuade him to run you through."

Isaac froze as he felt the sharp point of the spear in his back and froze. If he were killed, Keziah would face these men alone. He couldn't risk it; he must rescue her at any cost. Ishobeam appeared in the next moment and came to stand beside Talmon. Where was Darkon? Isaac hoped he would keep himself hidden until the element of surprise could be used to advantage.

"Come here, girl." Isaac shook his head and reached for Keziah as soon as he heard Talmon's command, but a violent shove from behind sent him sprawling. He felt a trickle of blood as the Egyptian's lance was pressed into his neck.

"Come here now, girl, unless you want to see your husband die in the next moment. I had thought to let him live until I had finished with you, but it matters little, in the end. It's your choice."

Keziah moved closer to Talmon, trying not to show the terror she felt inside, hoping to distract him from harming Isaac.

"No, Keziah, run!" Isaac yelled as he reached behind his head, grabbed the shaft of the spear in his right hand, then rolled over, struggling with the Egyptian for possession of it.

Keziah knew it was hopeless to flee, but she pulled away

from Talmon and jumped down from the place where they stood to the wide ledge that formed the main opening of the cave. For a moment she lay stunned with all the wind knocked out of her. She had fallen a distance of some ten feet, and her tunic was torn at her right knee, which was deeply gashed and bleeding.

Looking up, she spotted Isaac still struggling with the Egyptian. *It is hopeless,* she thought. *How can he overcome two enemies; one as vicious as the devil himself, and the other twice his height and size?*

"Isaac, look out behind you," Keziah shouted as she attempted to scramble back up to help him. At that moment Isaac allowed the Egyptian to push him to his back on the ground. Using the leverage of the other man's weight, he flipped his adversary over his head with his feet, sending him flying into Talmon.

The two men fell into a tangled heap of arms and legs, and Isaac literally flew off the small ledge toward Keziah. "I told you to run," he chided breathlessly as he grasped her by the hand and led the two of them, half sliding, half running, down the rocky incline. Neither said another word as they ran for their lives.

The force of the heavy Egyptian landing on him had temporarily knocked the wind out of Talmon. "I'm all right, you fool, go after them," he managed to wheeze at the man, who had been helping him regain his feet. The Egyptian immediately obeyed, but Talmon knew that the man's ponderous weight would never let him catch up to his agile enemy.

He looked below him and broke into a self-satisfied smile when he saw Ishobeam. The servant had positioned himself on a large boulder, out of sight of Isaac and Keziah, but directly in the path where their frantic flight would take them. Ishobeam raised the dagger he carried in his girdle. By the time they reached the bottom of the slope, they would be just at the edge of the large boulder where he waited to strike.

As they navigated the final slope, before they reached level ground, Keziah looked up and spotted Ishobeam's dagger. With a gasp she pulled back on the arm that was leading her. Then she leaped in front of him, flinging her arm upward. At that moment Isaac saw the dagger that was sweeping down in an arc at him.

But instead of sinking into his heart, as it surely would have, it went through Keziah's outstretched hand and she gave a sharp cry. Ishobeam drew it back to try again, and Isaac saw the blood gush from Keziah's pierced hand as he leapt at Ishobeam and gave him a great shove. The servant went tumbling down the incline, his head hitting twice on protruding stones. He lay there, twitching and groaning, but unconscious. Ishobeam wouldn't be a threat any longer, but Talmon and the Egyptian were.

Isaac took his wife's uninjured hand and pulled her along until they were once more on flat ground. Still he did not stop. They were still vulnerable.

They continued on toward the city for several minutes when they saw dust rising between them and Jericho. Someone in a cart was driving straight toward them. Isaac stopped and squinted, but for a moment he couldn't make out who it was. Had Talmon hired some assassin to accost them in case they escaped? The cart, driven by a mule, was getting closer, and Isaac's face broke into a broad grin when he recognized the grizzled Simeon. He drew Keziah to his side and waved to get the older man's attention.

In moments, Simeon drew up beside them. "I thought you might need a conveyance," he said, dismounting from the cart. "I got this animal for his strength as well as his speed. As it happens, the man who sold him to me told me the truth about both. It is good to see you both safe and well. . . . My lady!"

Simeon's face turned nearly as gray as his beard as he took in Keziah's pierced hand and the crimson splotches on her tunic wherever the hand had touched it. His scrutiny seemed to bring both Isaac's and Keziah's attention to the wound for the first time. There had been no time to think about it during their run for their lives, and she hadn't made so much as a sound after that first small shriek.

Keziah lifted the injured hand and stared at it for a moment. Suddenly the pain that she had ignored for the sake of survival was there, pulling at her. "Oh . . ." was all she said before sinking into a faint.

Isaac caught her before she hit the ground. He lifted her into the cart, then removed the headband he wore and tied it tightly around the injury to stop the bleeding. "Ishobeam stabbed her," he informed Simeon. *She saved my life,* he wanted to say, started to say, but somehow the words clogged his throat. He climbed into the cart, took his wife into his arms, and said only, "Get us back to the city quickly so that I can see to the wound."

Seeing the look on Isaac's face, Simeon felt compelled to reassure him as he turned the mule and cart around. "It is not as serious as it looks, Isaac. Stopping the bleeding is the most important thing. She will be all right. But where is Darkon? Was he killed in the attack?"

Darkon! He had been so concerned for his wife that he hadn't spared a thought for his servant. "I'm sorry, Simeon, I forgot about him. We'll have to come back and search. We need to help Keziah first."

Again, Simeon heard the panic in Isaac's voice. "She will be all right. We won't have to come back for Darkon. That's him running toward us now."

Simeon drove the cart to meet the man. As they approached, they saw that he limped, and that he had his girdle pressed to his temple. He was bleeding.

"Forgive me, my lord," he said to Isaac as he climbed into the cart. "I was of no use to you at all. Someone hit me on the side of the head with something—a rock, I think. I lost consciousness for a while. When I came to, I rushed to find you and twisted my ankle."

Isaac nodded but made no reply.

A short time later, they drew up to the camp at the spring and were surrounded by Judith, Adah, and Simeon's brother and wife, who had come out to keep vigil and offer what help they could.

Everyone was jubilant until they noticed that Keziah was unconscious and Darkon was bleeding.

Darkon stepped from the cart, careful to put his weight on his uninjured foot. "I am not hurt badly. Please see to my lady," he said to Judith when she would have helped him.

"Help me see to her, Mother. She has lost a lot of blood," Isaac said as he started to lift her from the wagon.

Simeon's hand stayed him. "No, you can't care for her properly here. We will go immediately to my brother's house. He will be glad to be able to help; he felt so guilty about Keziah's being taken from there. Judith, you come with us in the cart. No, Adah, stay here and help Malik dismantle the camp. I will be back for you both as soon as I see Keziah settled."

Everyone obeyed Simeon's instructions as though he were the head of the family. Even Adah did not argue, although she stood staring after the cart as it rumbled away.

Simeon's niece-in-law led the way as Isaac carried his wife up the marble stairs of the house. He seemed to find it hard to relinquish his hold on her and stood for a long moment before depositing her on the bed. Judith's heart went out to her son at the fear in his voice and on his face. Keziah was still unconscious, and Judith was certain she must be very gravely injured for Isaac to be so clearly distraught. The bandage on Keziah's hand was bloody, as was her clothing. Had Talmon tortured Keziah?

Judith was surprised and relieved when she removed the bandage and looked at the wound. It was certainly ugly but not life-threatening. The bleeding had almost stopped. She quickly examined Keziah and saw no other injuries save a scraped knee and a few scratches.

"Ishobeam did this. He was going for my heart with his dagger. She stopped the blade with her hand. She saved my life, Mother. Keziah saved my life."

Judith heard the same fear that Simeon had heard earlier and placed her hand on her son's arm. "Truly, son, she will recover. There will always be a scar, but your wife will be fine. Look, even now she stirs. Probably the lack of food is as much responsible for her unconsciousness as the stab wound, though it certainly looks nasty."

"But I was supposed to save her. . . ." Judith turned to her son and frowned at the stunned look on his face as he stared at Keziah's hand. He was overreacting.

She decided to give him something to do. "Isaac, go and find clean linen cloths to wrap her hand. And ask the cook to make a broth. Go now dear. I will care for her."

When Isaac had reluctantly exited the room, a smile curved Judith's lips. Her son and his wife had certainly not had an auspicious beginning to their life together, but it was apparent that Isaac now cared for his wife, maybe more than he yet realized.

Isaac's obsessive concern lasted through the tending of the wound, through her first meal in four days, through the arrival of Adah. The child's reaction to their harrowing experiences and her worry over Keziah was the unloosing of her tongue, necessitating her removal from Keziah's side, Isaac insisted, lest she cause a setback in her recovery. His concern lasted throughout the night as he kept watch over Keziah, who slept a deep and healing sleep of exhaustion.

The next morning, Keziah opened her eyes to see her husband seated beside her bed, asleep with his head resting near hers.

He looked pale and haggard, and it frightened her. She could not remember clearly exactly what had happened in those last frantic moments of their escape, nor any of the events following it. Was he hurt? She reached out and touched his hand, just to reassure herself. Isaac immediately jerked up, wide awake. There was a distressed look on his face.

"Did they hurt you?" she asked, surprised that her voice sounded as cracked and uneven as that of an adolescent boy.

The question first seemed to confuse, then to anger him. "Did they hurt *me*? No, certainly not. My wife, fearing I am such a weak fellow that I cannot fight my own battles, protected me by throwing herself in the way of a dagger." He opened his arms wide. "You see? Not a mark on me." Abruptly, he stood and left the room. Why was he angry?

She did not have to wonder for long. In less than five minutes, Isaac stormed back into the room. "I am a man!" he shouted, pointing backward with this thumb to his chest. "You are a woman, and you are supposed to be delicate and pliant and depend on me to take care of you."

"But I am. . . . I did. All the time I was in the cave, I knew you would come, and you did. Why are you angry?"

"Why am I angry? Ha! There you are, lying half dead from throwing yourself between me and Ishobeam's dagger, and you wonder why I am angry. What did you think? That I needed you to protect me from Talmon? This is not unusual for you, is it? You did the same for Adah—let yourself be ravished in order to save my sister."

Keziah flushed with shame at that accusation. It sounded similar to her father's insinuations that the blame for Talmon's attack belonged to her. Her shoulders slumped in defeat. Isaac would never be able to forget her shame. Deep in his heart he would wonder if she could not have done something to prevent the assault. Isaac's exasperated voice interrupted her depressing thoughts.

"You are not attending to my words, wife. That is just another indication that you are stubborn and willful and determined to go your own way. But I am your husband, your protector, and I will no longer countenance your recklessness. I am sending you home, and there you will stay, if I have to lock you in your room. If you wish, you will go with me on my journeys, and I will see to your protection. If not, I will have Darkon and Simeon and my mother and Rachel vow to me that they will guard you well against your own foolishness."

Isaac stopped suddenly and took a deep breath when it struck him that he had been raving like a madman at his wife, who still had not recuperated from her ordeal. But he found it very difficult to admit to his wife when he had been foolish, so he blustered again. "Now, heed me well, wife. Go back to sleep. You are to rest all day. You still look awful." He made his escape quickly, lest his tongue betray him again.

He did not see his mother, who had been bringing Keziah warmed milk with poppy juice to help ease the pain of her bruises and injured hand. Judith was brought up short by the sound of her son's lecture, which was anything but quiet. For the second time since their return, Judith broke into a smile. She recognized her son's speech as concern. Her Ahiam had often sounded the same. Men, she had observed, often felt the need to bellow and flex their muscles when their emotions threatened to overwhelm them.

When she entered the room, she saw that her daughter-in-law did not view her meeting with Isaac in the same light. She was sitting up in bed, crying, the tears dripping onto her injured hand which she held clasped in the other.

Judith was tempted to tell Keziah that she had overheard everything, and to assure her that far from meaning he was disappointed in his wife, Isaac's blustering was a proof of his regard. But no, the younger woman would never believe her. Keziah's confidence, never strong, thanks to her father's undermining, had been so badly shaken by the terrible things that had happened to her that she would not be able to believe that Isaac loved her. She would simply be mortified that Judith had heard a listing of her failures.

So she said cheerfully, "Ah, I see that your hand is bothering you this morning. Don't worry, my dear. I have brought some goat's milk with poppy juice to ease you. By tomorrow the pain should almost have left you."

JERUSALEM

Isaac had left Jericho without speaking again to his wife. He pushed aside the guilt he felt for that by telling himself that none of them would be safe or live a normal life until the issue of Talmon had been settled once and for all. Keziah was still in a weakened state from her ordeal, and he assured himself that it was better that she not know where he was going or she would be worried sick.

He grinned to himself. She would also probably follow him and try to stand between him and his enemy.

His true reason for not seeing her was the inner turmoil he was experiencing over his feelings for his wife. Her actions had brought forth the conflicting emotions of irritation and pride in her. He found himself thinking of her day and night, crowding out even his desire for revenge.

Even now, his thoughts centered on the safety of Keziah and his mother and sister, rather than images of the different ways he might make Talmon suffer as he killed him. It no longer mattered as much to him. Nothing could bring his father back anyway. And his mother had been right. To bring up the issue of what Talmon had done to Keziah and force her to testify against him in a trial could possibly destroy her. So Isaac sought out Benaiah as soon as he reached the capital. Maybe the military veteran could advise him.

"Have you seen Talmon of Gibeah?" Isaac asked after a brief greeting.

"That viper? He knows to stay well out of my path. Besides, I just returned from Rabbah the day before yesterday. 'The Thirty' stayed for the ceremony of the surrender of the city. You knew that David came in person to take the city officially. A pity he did not come at the beginning. . . ."

Isaac nodded, realizing that Benaiah was thinking of the loss of Uriah and Ahiam and Benjamin, among others. Nothing the King or anyone else did now could bring those men back.

"I am looking for Talmon because he tried to take my life on more than one occasion and also threatened my family. This situation has to come to an end."

"Joab."

"What?"

"Talmon might well go to Joab for protection if he knows you are after him. You do intend to slay him, do you not?"

Isaac hesitated at the question. Just a few days ago his answer would have been immediate. But now he wasn't sure. If he killed Talmon, he would be breaking the King's command. David would have him punished if not put to death when he heard of it. Of course, David would probably relent if he was told the whole story, but that would require the truth about Keziah to come out. No, if there were any other way to resolve this, he would not slay Talmon; though at this point, he could think of no other solution.

"I don't know what will happen when I confront Talmon. I only know I must." He hedged in his answer to Benaiah's question.

The huge warrior quirked an eyebrow, then continued. "Talmon will likely seek Joab's help since his attempts to get rid of you have failed."

"But Joab did not speak up for him at the hearing when he was discharged from the army. Why should he now?"

"Oh, I think Talmon knows Joab well enough to realize he wouldn't act out of friendship. But Talmon was with Joab for three years, and he must know things Joab wishes to keep secret; for instance, the complete story about Rabbah. Talmon is the kind of man who would use blackmail to get what he wants." Benaiah gave a sardonic little chuckle. "I hope he is foolish enough to try it on Joab. If he does, your worries about Talmon might soon be over."

Isaac thought about what Benaiah had said as he made his way toward Joab's home. Joab owned land just outside the city walls and divided his time between his home there and his quarters in the palace. Isaac had never been in Joab's home but had admired the impressive estate from the road many times as he had passed it. Isaac followed the winding road that led down into the Kidron Valley from Jerusalem. He did not know what he would say to Joab, or what he would do if he did, after all, find Talmon.

For some reason, he recalled the lesson the Rab had taught his last time in Ziph. The text had been from the song of Moses: *So teach us to number our days, that we may gain a heart of wisdom. . . . Make us glad according to the days in which you have afflicted us, the years in which we have seen evil.* The Rab had talked about the evil all men must suffer, and how Adonai saw every wicked thought and deed. He had stressed the need to throw oneself on the Lord's mercy, and look for Him to work justice.

As he walked along, Isaac knew that he had not the wisdom to resolve his situation. "O Lord, how can I allow Talmon to escape the punishment he deserves? Am I wrong to hate him? Has my hatred truly turned me into a man who is more like Talmon than like my father?"

As Isaac walked along, he poured out his heart and cried out to Adonai to come to his aid. He stopped before the gate of Joab's house and was admitted by a porter who was fearsome in appearance. Joab took no chances lest an enemy accost him in his home.

He was taken, not into the mansion, but to a walled garden behind it. There Joab sat with Talmon and the ever-present Ishobeam.

"I have been expecting you, son of Ahiam," Joab commented in a falsely pleasant voice. "Talmon didn't think you would have the courage to come, but I pride myself in knowing the men who have served under me. You showed courage if not good sense when you insulted me and received your beating. I expected you to come, and you haven't disappointed me."

"I have come to finish it with Talmon, general. Will you interfere?"

"Why should I? Since you two have brought your grievances to my household, I intend to see that you resolve them honorably. I suggest a duel with swords."

Isaac's gaze moved from Joab to Talmon. "I suppose it had to come to this. I agree to a fight with swords. What say you, Talmon of Gibeah?"

Talmon grunted derisively. "You were running from me the last time I saw you. Have you perhaps drunk enough wine to give you courage?"

"I have never lacked the courage to face you, Talmon, and well you know it. The last time I saw you, I was not only outnumbered, I had my wife to protect. Now that I have seen to her safety, I have come to seek you out."

"You have likely been whining to the King; telling him I broke his command. It will be worth it to face his anger for the pleasure it will be to kill you. Give him your sword, Ishobeam."

The servant, looking none too happy to do so, handed over the weapon. Isaac tested its weight and feel by tossing it from one hand to the other several times. He was at a disadvantage by not having his own sword, but he had left it in his bundle of clothes still loaded on his donkey. He had thought it unlikely that Joab would let him enter his home armed.

He glanced at the general and saw that, quite the contrary, he had leaned back in his chair, his hands folded in his lap as if he were ready to be entertained. It struck Isaac that Joab would probably relish seeing the combatants kill each other

Without warning, Talmon lunged at him, and Isaac had but an instant to parry the blow. During the next few minutes the fight went first in Talmon's favor, then in Isaac's. The two men were fairly matched in skill. Then Isaac used his sword to block the downward sweep of Talmon's. The sword deflected the blow, but shattered, shaft from blade, and Isaac realized that he had been given a poorly tempered weapon, a fact Talmon was likely well aware of.

As he expected, Talmon did not halt his attack to allow Isaac to be given a good weapon, nor did Joab act as mediator and call for one. Talmon came forward to run Isaac through. Isaac jumped aside at the last minute. Talmon came again, this time with a strike intended to sever his head. Isaac turned it just in time and received no more than a gash down his cheek.

He ducked the next sweep of Talmon's sword, bringing up his arm to connect with Talmon's wrist as it went by. The sword was knocked out of Talmon's hand and went flying across the room. Both men went for it, but Isaac found himself caught by both arms from behind by Ishobeam. He was entering the fracas, and Joab was saying nothing to stop it.

Talmon picked up the sword and ran full-tilt at Isaac, aiming right for his heart. At the last second, Isaac used his greater strength to pull Ishobeam off balance and spin him around to a position between Isaac and the deadly weapon. Ishobeam screamed as the sword entered him. He dropped to the ground as Isaac let him go. Before Talmon could pull the sword from his dead servant's body and renew his attack, Isaac, enraged at the unfairness of the fight, pulled back his right arm, made a fist, and hit Talmon a stunning blow on the chin. His enemy dropped like a stone.

Isaac bent over, completely winded, and waited for his opponent to rise. Talmon stayed out. He nudged his enemy with his foot. He was still unconscious.

"Finish it."

Isaac looked up to see that Joab had not moved a fraction from his pose as he sat in his comfortable chair. "Pick up the sword and finish it, son of Ahiam."

Isaac again nudged Talmon with his foot. "Get up and fight."

But Talmon didn't move. His chest lifted in the same rhythm as a deep sleep. Isaac turned away in disgust. As he walked past Joab, the general snorted in disdain. "I'm glad you no longer serve under my command. You haven't the guts to be a decent warrior." Isaac knew it was the greatest insult Joab could give anyone, but somehow it seemed more of a compliment to Isaac at the moment.

Talmon was getting away with murder, rape, and kidnapping. The thought ate at Isaac all day as he made his way back to Jericho. How could he let his father's killer, his wife's attacker go unpunished? He thought about the King and all the pain and suffering he had unleashed by his unbridled desire for Bathsheba. He had also gone unpunished because he was king.

There then came to Isaac's mind the broken look on David's face at the death of his child. He remembered Bathsheba's inconsolable grief. He also thought about the jealous, bitter look on Maacah's face that night at the dinner as she watched her husband with his new wife, and the sullen rebellious attitude of his handsome young son.

Isaac had to admit that his mother had been right. Adonai still reigned from heaven. He observed the actions of men, and he meted out justice to the righteous and the unrighteous. Perhaps both David and Talmon would be best left to God's vengeance. He would go and fetch his family, and they would put the past behind them.

~ ~ ~

Talmon was furious when he awoke. His servant was dead and his enemy still lived. He had no one to turn his anger on but the general, and this he did, even though a part of his mind warned him that it was foolish to do so.

"I served you faithfully for years, and you let Isaac of Hebron escape. The man has offered you insult in the past. How could you let him get away?"

The general's mouth set in an angry line. "I don't answer to you," he said simply.

"I demand satisfaction! You let them force me out of the army, and you let my enemy get away. I have been your friend. I have never told anyone of the dispatch you received from the King. Nor have I mentioned the orders you conveyed through me that put Uriah and the others under the sword. For that silence, the least I expect is for you to help me get rid of Isaac."

Talmon was in the throes of his own fit of fury and failed to notice the deadly glint in Joab's eye. "What do you suggest I do?" Joab asked.

Talmon, believing the veiled threat had worked, paused to consider. "Isaac returns to Jericho. There are many bandits on the road between here and there. Perhaps he will meet his end at the hands of such outlaws."

"I will give your suggestion consideration."

Talmon, at last realizing he was in danger of pushing the general too far, thanked him and started to leave. He was stayed by Joab's strong hand. "Take that with you," he ordered, inclining his head toward the dead Ishobeam.

~ ~ ~

Talmon traveled the road between Jerusalem and Gibeah in the bright moonlight. He had made the trip so often that he knew every inch of the winding road, and his mind was so full of satisfying images of Isaac's demise at the hands of the "bandits" the general would send, that he had failed to notice the four men who followed him all the way from Jerusalem.

He paused to rest on a boulder beside the road, opening his wineskin and tilting it to his mouth. He had just taken a large swallow when he heard the thud of running footsteps. He did not even have time to drop the wineskin. He only had a split second to see in the moonlight a group of men surrounding him and the large club as it descended.

Chapter Twenty

"I am going on to Ziph with Malik. I would not miss the look on Ailea's face when she sees him. And I have other gifts to give them."

Isaac had stayed long enough after their arrival back in Hebron to partake of a large meal that Rachel had prepared in celebration of their return. Now he had risen from the low, round table around which his family still sat, and made his announcement.

"We would go with you, Isaac. Keziah and Ahmi and I don't want to be left behind." It was Adah who spoke. She had been watching Keziah as Isaac spoke and saw the hurt look that flashed in her eyes before she quickly masked it. Judith had also seen.

"Yes, Isaac, we all want to go. I need to visit Ailea. She is my best friend, after all, and now that I don't have your father anymore. . . ." Judith knew that a reminder of her recent bereavement would make it difficult to deny her request. She wasn't ordinarily a manipulative woman, but her son and daughter-in-law did not need to be separated any longer.

"But, Mother, I was depending on you to stay here with Keziah. . . . I suppose I could see if Simeon could stay while we are gone. And Adah should also stay to keep her company."

"I don't need anyone to look after me!" Keziah cut in. "I am not a child, and I am perfectly well now. You have made it clear, Isaac, that I am the one you don't wish to come, so you don't need to make anyone else stay here. I will be perfectly well." All eyes were on Keziah because she had actually raised her voice, which was a rare occurrence. She hurried from the room.

After she disappeared up the new staircase, Isaac turned to see both his mother and his sister staring balefully at him. "What?" he asked.

Judith shook her head. "You have hurt her feelings, son. She thinks you just do not want her present at Ziph. Go after her and beg her pardon."

"But I only thought she needed to rest here. . . ."

"I know, son, but Keziah is very strong, or she would not have survived thus far. She needs to be with you more than she needs rest." Isaac looked hard at his mother while her words sank in, then he slowly nodded and went to seek out his wife.

"Now you are ordering me to come with you, when only moments ago you were ordering me to stay here?" Keziah asked after he had informed her she was accompanying him after all.

Isaac let out an exasperated sigh. "Why must you always challenge me, Keziah? I only wanted you to stay because I thought you must be tired from traveling, but since you assured me you are completely recovered, then I want you to come with me. It is your duty as a wife."

As she flounced around the room, collecting her things and putting them into her woven bag, Isaac lamented his lack of skill in dealing with his wife. Why hadn't he just followed his mother's advice and apologized, he wondered.

Within the hour, they left for Ziph. They arrived an hour before sundown, taking Jonathan and his household completely by surprise. Jonathan had just returned from Rabbah. During the hiatus, Jonathan had made a quick trip home.

Ailea's reaction to the arrival of her old family servant was every bit as touching as Isaac had predicted. Ailea threw her arms around the old man and wept. Jonathan cleared his throat and looked away, trying not to show his emotions. Keziah looked at Isaac as he watched the scene. His eyes had misted. He was thrilled that he had been able to do this for the woman he loved so much. She did not know how she would be able to stand having to see the two of them together.

Tears stung her own eyes, but she brushed them away. She would not embarrass her husband or her hosts by showing jealousy. It was up to her to make Isaac love her. She would be gracious if it killed her.

Keziah slipped away early that evening to go to their room. Judith and Ailea were having a private conversation, and Jonathan had taken Isaac aside in order to get the whole story of what had happened with Talmon. Keziah decided she would get a start in proving herself a good wife by unpacking the belongings that had been deposited in their room. She untied the bundles that contained their clothing, the tunics and cloaks, and headdresses, laying them out flat in a corner. There were also several chests and bundles of goods that Keziah assumed were meant as gifts for Jonathan's family.

She had intended just to arrange them in an orderly fashion and place them in out of the way. But she could not resist a peek inside the largest item—a highly polished wooden chest. Inside she saw a miniature chariot with two carved horses—obviously a gift for little Micah.

Atop what appeared to be an expensive bolt of blue linen with silver threads running through it, she saw an ivory box, beautifully carved with pomegranates and palm branches. This must be the gift he had chosen for Ailea! It was certainly valuable, both the ivory and the rare carving made it so.

Keziah tried not to mind that her husband had chosen a beautiful gift for Ailea when, apparently, he had not remembered to get one for his wife. Of course, he had not given Judith and

Adah anything either, so perhaps there was something for all of them waiting at home in Hebron.

Keziah ran her finger across the smooth ivory of the box. She slipped the clasp loose and opened the lid. And gasped when she saw the beautiful necklace of golden coins. She lifted it in her hands.

It had to be for Ailea. This was certainly not meant for a man. What could Isaac have been thinking of? It would certainly be most inappropriate of him to give such a fabulous piece of jewelry to the wife of another man. Surely Jonathan would see immediately that Isaac loved Ailea very much to give her such a costly necklace. He would surely be furious, maybe challenge Isaac to fight to the death!

Keziah was afraid for her husband's life. Jonathan was a giant of a man, much larger than Isaac, and a seasoned veteran of countless battles. While Isaac was no novice, he still did not come close to having Jonathan's experience. But no one in Israel would fault Jonathan for killing a man who made such advances to his wife.

Keziah determined that she would think of something to lessen the insult when Isaac tried to present the gift. Or would he give it to Ailea in private? She trembled at the thought that Jonathan might come upon such a scene. She would just have to stay at Isaac's side while they were here. Tonight she would begin by making herself the kind of wife to whom a man would want to stay close.

~ ~ ~

A young servant girl escorted her to a three-sided latticed area in the rear courtyard that contained a small bathing pool. Keziah bathed, and the servant girl treated her skin with a cream made from the aloe plant and scented with cassia flowers. She put on a soft white tunic that tied at each shoulder. After her hair had been brushed, she went to await her husband.

Isaac entered the room quietly some time later, thinking his wife would have long since fallen asleep, but she stood illuminated by the light of a large oil lamp. And she took his breath away. She was beautiful, standing there with her hair flowing freely about her shoulder, her tunic fresh and white. And she smelled wonderful, even from halfway across the room. He could only stare at her.

Then she raised her arms to him. "Isaac, I have missed you. Come to me." She didn't have to ask twice. He took her into his arms, and never was a wife more loving, more giving, he thought as he held her. He tried to make up to her for the times he had wounded her tender feelings. He lingered over their lovemaking for a very long time, soothing her with long, gentle kisses and feather-light touches, concentrating on her pleasure, not his own.

And he made her happy, he knew, because she had a smile on her face, and she whispered "I love you" before her lids closed in sleep. She had not been aware of what she said, Isaac knew. She probably would not have risked confiding her love to him if she had been fully awake. And how could he blame her? He had yet to declare his love for her.

He smiled to himself as he thought of the gift he would give her tomorrow. He had considered doing it privately, but he thought it would please her for everyone to see the token of his deep regard. Surely it would make up for all the blunders he had made in the role of husband so far.

Keziah was almost euphoric the next day as she remembered her time in Isaac's arms. Surely he would not treat her with such care and consideration if he was not coming to love her at least a little. And she had seen his face when he had entered the room and found her waiting for him. The look on his face had been one of desire, certainly not one of repugnance or disappointment.

The morning passed with Jonathan and Isaac going to visit the thriving pottery works of Ziph, run by a man and his six sons. Adah had gone to the teaching rock with the Rab to receive a lesson in the Law of Moses. Ailea had gotten some grapevines from a friend's vineyard, and she and Judith and Keziah spent the morning planting them along a trellis that had been placed at a perpendicular angle to the front door. When the vines grew to cover it, the door would be protected from the hot afternoon sun. Even the inside of the house would be cooler.

On this day, Judith and Ailea included Keziah in their conversation, and she found herself feeling lighthearted as she dug and planted and talked. Ailea was really an interesting person, and very humorous. Keziah found herself laughing at the stories she told about herself and Micah and Jonathan. There was no doubt that Ailea's heart belonged entirely to her husband and her son.

Judith heard Keziah's frequent laughter, saw the glow on her face, and knew that her daughter-in-law was starting to blossom and enjoy life. Isaac must have made amends to her in some way for his surly behavior. *Oh, Ahiam, my love, I have missed you so, but I fear our son has needed you even more than I,* Judith spoke in her thoughts to her husband as she often did these days.

Keziah's happiness lasted until Isaac and Jonathan returned, and Isaac asked that everyone gather in the courtyard. "We must leave just after midday so that we can arrive in Hebron before dark. I think we have had too much excitement lately to risk being accosted by robbers." Everyone laughed. Keziah's heart sank when her husband continued. "I have brought back something from my travels for everyone." Adah jumped up and down in her pleasure and the others began to speculate what their gifts would be as they gathered around the rather substantial pile of gifts Isaac had placed on a bench.

He started by presenting Micah the tiny chariot and horses. The little boy ran off to play with his new treasure. The Rab received writing materials. Jonathan was presented with an intricately wrapped turban that would reflect his status as Ziph's most prosperous citizen.

Keziah's hands began to sweat, knowing that any moment

Isaac was going to present that gold necklace to Ailea. Desperately she reached down and lifted the ivory box off the dwindling pile of gifts. She stepped away from Isaac and opened the lid. "Jonathan, Ailea. Isaac . . . ah, we wanted you to know how much your friendship means to us." She lifted the heavy coins out of the box and almost laughed hysterically at the identical expressions of incredulity on Jonathan and Ailea's faces. Both of their jaws went slack and their eyes were bulging.

She felt a hand clamp down on her shoulder and rushed to get her explanation out. "It is for the whole family, of course. It can be passed down to your eldest daughter . . . uh, if you have one." She knew from their looks of confusion that her explanation had not made much sense, but it was the best she could do. Surely Jonathan wouldn't challenge Isaac if he believed the gift was from both of them to the entire family. Still, the gift was obviously meant for a woman. Maybe Jonathan would see through her ruse, because he was shaking his head vigorously.

"But we cannot accept a gift of such value."

"Of course you can't," Isaac replied, his hand squeezing her shoulder almost painfully now. He was warning her not to say anything more. He took the ivory box from her trembling hands. "My wife has made a mistake. You will have to forgive her. I suppose her captivity has taken a toll on her clarity of thinking."

Keziah could listen to no more. She wouldn't stay and hear the rest of Isaac's speech apologizing for her stupidity, or watch him present that wondrous necklace to Ailea. She ran in spite of her husband's calls to her to stop. She ran out of the courtyard, out of the village gate, past the teaching rock, and into the hills.

Finally, too exhausted to run anymore, she threw herself down under the shade of a large oak tree. She bent her knees, wrapping her arms around them and resting her head. She did not cry, she was too tired. She had made a fool of herself, and her husband would be very angry. Well, she had done it for him, surely she could make him understand that.

She heard a twig snap and knew Isaac had caught up with

her. She didn't lift her head because she knew that when she saw the anger and disgust on Isaac's face she would cry, and that would only make matters worse. He stood before her for a moment, then sat down beside her, leaning his back against the tree. She lifted her head but didn't look at her husband.

"Why did you run away?"

"Because I felt like a fool."

"I can see why you would feel that way. That was certainly a wild tale you told."

"It was a sinful lie, but I did it for you," she told him in a disgruntled voice.

"So you are blaming the transgression on me, wife? Don't you know that true repentance means accepting full responsibility for your own error?"

"All right, I accept full responsibility," Keziah grumbled, and was irritated when her husband laughed.

She felt a tug as he lifted a handful of her hair. "You left before you heard what I had to say."

"I didn't want to hear."

"Oh, I think you would have liked what I had to say." Again he chuckled. Keziah felt the urge to jerk away from him, but he still had hold of her hair.

"I would not have enjoyed hearing you present that necklace to Ailea," she said, despising the way her voice shook. Isaac was quiet for a long moment.

"No, I don't suppose any wife would want to see her husband give such a rare gift to another woman. You ran off without your veil." He smoothed the errant mass of her hair as he made the remark, and Keziah braced herself for a lecture on her impropriety. No wife left her home with her head uncovered. It was a brazen thing to do.

"I am sorry, Isaac. I forgot."

"Well, I am not sorry." He pulled her hair back from her face, then reached into his cloak. She felt something cool and heavy being place around her forehead. Isaac fumbled with the clasp for a moment, then stood, pulling her up with him. He took both her hands in his and stepped back.

"It looks just as I had imagined it would against that glorious mane of hair. You are beautiful, Keziah. You look just like a royal princess, ready to receive her subjects in the palace."

Keziah fingered the coins that encircled her head. "But you meant this for Ailea."

Isaac rolled his eyes. "You must have been knocked on the head during the kidnapping, wife, to believe I would do such a ridiculous thing, but I love you anyway. Now kiss me, wife."

Her mouth was open in surprise when he pulled her against him and kissed her. It was a very long, very thorough kiss. Isaac finally ended it and grinned at her, then kissed the tip of her nose. "I believe I have rendered you speechless, wife."

He was certainly right about that, Keziah thought as she lay her head on his shoulder. But in a moment, she did speak. "I thought you loved Ailea. You told me before we wed . . ."

"*Before* we wed, Keziah. I didn't know you then. I didn't know the difference then between infatuation and the love a man has for a wife. I do love Ailea, as I love Jonathan. I will always love them.

"But you have long since replaced her in my dreams and in my heart and in my life. You are the most courageous woman I know, and the most forgiving. I will tell our friends and neighbors the treasure I have in you. I will recount your virtues to our children. I will honor you until I cast aside the robe of my flesh and join Father Abraham."

Keziah wrapped her arms around Isaac and hugged him to her as hard as she could, to let him know how much she loved him. They stood that way for long moments before Keziah raised her eyes to his.

"I know why I didn't recognize your love, Isaac. I had never experienced love before."

Isaac swallowed against a lump in his throat as he thought about Aaron and his constant undermining of Keziah's self-respect and, added to that, Talmon's attack. His arms tightened reflexively as he promised himself he would spend the rest of his life making up for those things.

"I have just come to realize," she continued, "that everything that has happened is a gift from Adonai, just as the Rab told me. All that has happened has resulted in a great blessing in the end. Adonai used all those terrible things to ultimately bring me you. He has given me the desires of my heart."

"Yes, he has." Isaac agreed. "And he has given me mine." He kissed her tenderly, then smiled as he took her hand and led her back to the village.

And now, enjoy the first chapter from *The Heart of a Lion,* Kathy Hawkins' continuing story of the family of Jonathan and Ailea, book number three in the Heart of Zion Series.

Chapter One

The Rab was dying. Everyone in the small village of Ziph waited in hushed expectation, anticipating the loss of their most venerated citizen. A large number had gathered in the courtyard of the Rab Shageh's house. Periodically, Ailea of Damascus, the Rab's daughter-in-law, brought news of his condition, which had steadily worsened over the last several days. The rest of the time she spent trying to comfort the other family members, who kept a silent vigil in the corridor outside the dying man's chamber, waiting to be called to his deathbed.

Ailea felt bereft at the thought of losing the Rab, who had been her only friend when she had first been brought to Ziph as a captive bride. Her father-in-law had been a buffer between her and his son, Jonathan, during the first tumultuous months of their marriage. He had taught her about Adonai, the God of Israel, whom she had come to embrace as a result of the Rab's patient teaching of the Torah.

She felt an almost uncontrollable urge to go to the Rab's side. But Jonathan, his only son, deserved these private moments with his father. Ailea knew that Jonathan would call the remainder of the family to gather around the Rab when the end came. She waited patiently, fighting the urge to wail her grief as loudly as a child. Once in a while she would relate an amusing or touching story about her father-in-law. The others keeping watch seldom commented on her stories, but that wasn't important to Ailea. She just needed to talk about Shageh.

The Rab's daughter, Ruth, who was two years older than Jonathan, sat on a three-legged stool on Ailea's right, wiping an occasional tear from the corners of her eyes. When her father had taken ill, she had come from the nearby village where she lived in order to help. She was not a person of strong emotion or many words, but there was no doubt she was already grieving the loss of her father.

Jerusha, Jonathan and Ailea's young daughter, had certainly not taken after her aunt. She felt all her emotions strongly and was never hesitant to share them with others. Whether angry, happy, frightened, or sad, Jerusha never left any doubt as to how she felt. Now she sat on her brother's lap and sobbed brokenly.

"It isn't time for grandfather to leave us, Micah. He has hardly begun to teach me from the Torah. Oh, how I wish I had gone to the teaching rock with him last week instead of taking the sheep to feed in the hills. Now I may never have another chance to learn from him, and no one else would bother to teach it to a girl," she cried. Micah stroked her hair with his large hand and held her close, not denying her words, which he knew were true.

The Rab was truly a unique and irreplaceable teacher. Micah remembered his grandfather's response when one of the men of the village questioned him about his willingness to teach the girls of the village as well as the boys. "The Law of the Lord brings light into the life of the one who hears it. What man of reason would want his wife or his daughter to remain in darkness?" That had effectively silenced his critic.

No one would have guessed that Jerusha and Micah were siblings. She was delicate and her hair was black as pitch, while he was muscular, with brown hair streaked with golden highlights. Though he was a dozen years older than his sister, even a casual observer would have noticed their deep affection as Micah comforted Jerusha, and her complete trust in him as she poured out her grief.

~ ~ ~

Inside the room where the sick man lay propped up on a mountain of pillows to ease his breathing, Jonathan held his father's bony, parchment-like hand and spoke in low, soothing tones. The gentleness he showed the old man was incongruous with his fierce countenance and huge stature. As one of the *Gibborim,* or mighty men of King David, Jonathan ben Shageh had earned his status as one of the greatest warriors of Israel. Though he had recently turned fifty, few men in the kingdom could equal his strength, cunning, or strategic grasp of war.

But at this moment Jonathan was not the feared warrior of Israel's victorious armies. He was the son of the most beloved and respected man in the hill country of southern Judah, and he was remembering the times his father had held him, taught him, gently reproved him, and judiciously praised him. As he remembered, his eyes misted with tears. Soon, he must call the remainder of the family in. The time had come for the Rab, the wise man of Ziph, beloved father and grandfather, to utter his last words and give his final blessings to those he would leave behind. But it was hard, so hard, to let him go.

"I will call the others, Father," Jonathan said softly as he leaned over the old man.

"Just Micah. I must talk to Micah first."

"But Ruth will want to . . ."

"I will say my good-byes to my daughter afterward, but I would see Micah before I grow any weaker. There is . . . much I . . . need to tell him." The Rab's chest wheezed with difficulty, and Jonathan worried that he didn't have enough breath left to talk to his grandson, much less his other loved ones who waited in the hall. But he reluctantly went to fetch Micah. Few people failed to disregard the wishes of the Rab; certainly not his only son.

"I will be but a moment," Jonathan promised before slipping from the room. As soon as he opened the door his older sister came to him. She was in her late fifties, but her excellent health had always made her appear much younger than her actual age. Not today. Jonathan noticed the dark circles under her eyes. The lines in her face were prominent. Ruth looked old and haggard. Jonathan heaved a sigh. He supposed he looked old as well. Why were they all so stricken when they had expected this for months now? After all, Shageh was ninety years old!

"He still lives?" Ruth's eyes held a mixture of hope and anguish. When Jonathan nodded, Ruth started past him to the door of their father's room. He stayed her with a hand on her shoulder.

"Wait a bit, Ruth dear. He has asked to speak to Micah first."

"But I'm his daughter," she wailed in an almost childlike voice.

With a glance down the hallway at the other family members, Jonathan lowered his voice to a whisper. "And he is asking for you, but he has something to say to Micah first. This will be harder on the boy than on any of the rest of us," he reminded his sister, hoping her love for her nephew would allow her to put his interests first. She did not disappoint him.

"Yes. That is true. Of course, Micah must go in to him first. I will wait. But do you think he might die before . . ." She couldn't finish the sentence, and Jonathan hastened to reassure her.

"You know the Rab, sister. He has willed himself to live until he has bid us all good-bye. He won't disappoint us." He gave her a sad smile, and Ruth returned a wobbly one. Then Jonathan motioned to his son and Micah joined him at the doorway.

"He wants to speak privately with you, but don't take too long. He is very weak, and the others will be heartbroken if they don't get their chance to visit him once more." Micah nodded grimly and closed the door. Crossing the room to his grandfather's bed, he noticed that the Rab's eyes were closed. He leaned over and kissed each of the old man's wrinkled cheeks. "I am here, Grandfather."

Shageh opened his eyes slowly, as if they were very heavy, but managed a smile for his grandson. "Sit," the old man commanded, motioning weakly for Micah to sit on the bed beside him.

"I would give you my blessing, Micah, before I leave this earth. You must not grieve long at my death. I will always be with you, Micah. You will remember the things I have taught you when you are tested. There is much of me in you, as well as much of your father, and you will learn to reconcile the two natures as you grow older." The dying man's voice had grown stronger as he spoke his last words to his grandson, as if he knew how important they were to Micah.

The long fingers of the dying Rab clasped his grandson's with surprising pressure, and Micah grasped at this false hope. "You will get better, Grandfather. It is not time yet for you to leave us. We need you too much."

The old man gazed directly into his grandson's eyes, which were the same clear amber as his own. "No, Micah, you do not need me any longer. You are a man now. You have been a man for several years, and you will be greatly used of Adonai, for you have a heart for him. I want to talk to you about the vow you made to me when you were a lad. You know the one of which I am speaking."

Micah nodded and clasped the old man's hand more tightly. "I vowed I would never strike or harm another person as long as I live."

"It was a good vow you made, in many ways, Micah. But it is not one that is possible to keep for all time in all circumstances, so I release you from it."

Micah's frown revealed his confusion. "Grandfather, I'm not sure I want to be released from my promise. It has served me very well for all these years."

"Micah, you are about to enter a new season in your life, and for that you need to be free of all that would hold you back. I allowed you to make the vow to me, and not to Adonai, so I could release you from it when the time was right."

"I remember you stopping my words with your hand over my mouth and telling me that I must never make a vow to Adonai in the heat of the moment, or out of guilt, or pride, or anything else. You said that a man must make vows to the Lord most sparingly, but that you would allow me to vow it to you, and you would hold me accountable to keep it."

"That is right, Micah. A man should only vow to Adonai to serve only Him, to care for his wife and family, and very little else. Now you are at a crossroads, and need to decide the path your life will take. You must only follow the same path your father has chosen as a warrior if it is the right path for *you*. Speak honestly with Jonathan about your doubts. Never deny what you are, Micah."

"But that is the problem, Grandfather. I don't really know what I am—Hebrew or Aramean, warrior or teacher."

Shageh opened his mouth as if to respond, but his words subsided into a low, rasping wheeze, as though the very breath of life had begun its final journey across his lips. He closed his eyes and rested his head on the pillows.

Alarmed, Micah pleaded with Shageh not to die, but the old man only shook his head weakly and told him to call his Aunt Ruth. As Micah went to summon his aunt, he knew he had spent his last hour with the Rab.

A few minutes later, after her special time with her father, Ruth motioned the entire family into the room. "Come near, Little One," the old man rasped. His eyes were fastened not on Jerusha but on her mother. "Little One" had always been his pet name for Ailea.

As she leaned close to the dying man, Ailea could not keep the tears from flowing, and the Rab reached up with a shaking hand to brush them away. "Hush, Little One. I am tired, and it is time for me to join my fathers. You are strong and will continue to be. The God of Israel will be with you. Do you remember your first prayer to him, and how amazed you were when he answered it?"

Ailea smiled through her tears. "I asked him for a friend and he sent me Judith. I remember how anxious I was to tell you about it. I thought it such a wondrous thing. But you weren't surprised at all when I told you."

The Rab's lips curved into a smile. "I am never surprised at the power and lovingkindness of Adonai, Little One. That is why I am happy to go to him. Do not grieve too much. You have given me great joy because you give joy to my son. And you have given me my heritage in Israel, my precious grandchildren. They may struggle, or falter, but be assured. . . ." He gathered his remaining strength. "Their righteousness will shine as the stars. . . ." The Rab's voice trailed off and he became very still.

Jonathan laid his hand over his father's heart, expecting to find it had ceased beating. But though faint, its pulse remained steady. A few minutes later, the old man opened his eyes once more and whispered his granddaughter's name. In her typical, impetuous way, Jerusha climbed up on the bed, cupped her grandfather's face in her small hands, and planted several kisses. "Your heart is brave and your spirit is free, precious one," he told her in a surprisingly clear voice. "Guard you heart carefully and commit your spirit to Adonai. Do not let it turn to rebellion. If you do these things, the Lord will reward you."

As Jerusha enveloped her grandfather in a warm embrace, the Rab's eyelids fluttered and he fell into a deep sleep. Sensing the time was near, the family slowly moved back into the outer rooms.

Several hours later, Jonathan made his way to the courtyard where most of the villagers were keeping a vigil, though darkness had fallen, necessitating the lighting of torches. His announcement that their beloved leader was dead started the process of mourning that would last for many days.

EIGHT MONTHS LATER

Micah awoke early. He had to make the journey to Jerusalem today. He didn't want to go back, but his father couldn't make the trip himself—or so he had claimed. He had insisted that Micah must go in his place.

It had come as somewhat of a surprise to Micah that Jonathan would choose him as his representative. After all, just a few weeks ago Micah had been sent back home to Ziph in disgrace—dismissed by Joab, the general of Israel's army, accused of cowardice and under suspicion of treason. It must have been a blow to Jonathan's pride as a military man that his son had failed as an army recruit.

Despite his grandfather's dying words instructing him to tell his father that his heart was not in it, Micah had enlisted in the army at twenty, the age the Law specified a young man to be eligible for the draft. In David's kingdom, however, there was no need for a draft; the volunteer army had won victory after victory during his reign, and now all the surrounding kingdoms had been brought under the domination of Israel.

Jonathan had pointed out to Micah that during peacetime it would not be unpatriotic to choose to stay home, gradually taking over the spiritual leadership of Ziph and the other small villages in the southern hill country, teaching young boys the Torah as Shageh the Rab had done.

But Micah was convinced that his father was wrong. He felt he had to prove himself first as a warrior before the people would accept him as leader. Despite Jonathan's stature among the most loyal and powerful warriors in the kingdom, Micah had never been completely trusted or accepted. After all, he was not a full-blooded Israelite. His mother was an Aramean from Damascus, and though the villagers had eventually accepted her, they still treated her and her children with the polite restraint that marked them as outsiders.

Micah felt he had something to prove, not only to the village, but also to his father, whom he admired above all men. He wanted to prove himself as a warrior to make his father proud, even though his father assured him he would not be disappointed if Micah did not choose a military career. Besides, life in the village was not the same without the Rab, and Micah had felt that maybe a change would help him deal better with the grief of losing his grandfather.

Micah had gone to Jerusalem to train directly under Joab himself. His father had been uneasy about that. There was no love lost between the general and Jonathan. Never had been. Jonathan had warned Micah that the general would likely be more demanding, more critical of him because he was Jonathan's son. But in truth, the general had been scrupulously fair.

The accusation of cowardice had come from the ranks of Micah's unit, where he had been challenged from the first day. Certain other recruits had mocked and goaded him from the very beginning. Because of his size—he was taller and heavier than any man in his unit, perhaps in Israel's entire army of nearly one hundred thousand—he had been taunted almost daily to fight some fellow who wanted to prove himself. Because of his sanguine nature and tendency to negotiate rather than fight, some had branded him a coward, mistaking his peaceful nature for weakness. They secretly feared him, but covered their fear with animosity. When they saw that Micah had chosen to live a chaste life, they taunted him constantly about women.

A warrior in the standing army was guaranteed to be sought after by women, and most of the young men took full advantage, with little concern about impurity. They would chide Micah as they left the barracks for a night of debauchery. "When will you be old enough to go with us, son of Jonathan? Are you yet a lad?"

"Aye, he's a lad. Not full grown yet," someone else would respond. They would all laugh mockingly, but Micah laughed right along with them until they gave up goading him and went their way. Even when they made veiled hints that Micah was somehow unnatural because he wasn't licentious, he didn't retaliate.

Their fear and guilt remained a barrier to his acceptance. Still, his ability with weapons of war, in which Jonathan had tutored him well, and his sheer size made Micah a candidate for leadership, and Joab had appointed him a squadron. The men followed his orders well enough until one day when their assignment was to chase a group of desert bandits during a training mission in the Transjordan.

Many of the men were anticipating their first taste of victory in battle, ready to spill the blood of the outlaws. Instead, when the robbers were surrounded, Micah did not allow his squadron to use their swords. He ordered his men to simply confiscate the stolen goods and let the bandits go.

Micah's show of mercy angered his men, and some complained directly to Joab. Micah was called before the commander and asked pointedly whether he had let the outlaws escape because they were Aramean, and thus had greater claim on his loyalty than the king. Micah flushed at the insult and clenched his fists in anger. He knew why the general had asked the question.

His parents had told him many times how Joab had opposed Jonathan's marriage to Ailea when he had brought her back to Israel as a captive. Joab had suspected her of spying for her brother, Rezon, who had become a raider and a guerrilla fighter against Israel after the defeat of the Aramean alliance more than twenty years ago. The general had never trusted Micah's father after his marriage to Ailea, and now he thought the worst of the son.

Micah patiently explained the incident to Joab. "Those raiders were not Aramean, though if they had been, I still would have let them go. They posed no threat to Israel. They were from a poor village near the Jordan and were only raiding to feed their families. I confiscated their booty and sent them home."

"Is it true that you sent your own unit's food rations with them as well?" Micah admitted he had sent enough bread to feed the tiny village for a week. Joab shook his head in disgust and mumbled something about it being a pity that a giant as big as Goliath should have a heart as soft as a woman's. He gruffly ordered Micah to return home while he contemplated whether he was worthy to be trained as a soldier.

Micah groaned at the memory and rose from his bed. He stretched, able to flatten his hands on the ceiling of the room, so great was his height. Micah ben Jonathan certainly did not look like a man who was either soft or cowardly. The truth was, Micah did not fear anyone, but not everyone knew that—including, apparently, Joab.

Micah shook off his unpleasant thoughts as he walked to the window, opened the shutters, and gazed out on the prosperous village of Ziph. "Oh, Grandfather, I wish you were still here." Micah's grief over the loss of the Rab had hardly abated over the past months. In order to escape it, he had joined the army only one week after his grandfather's funeral. But his homesickness in Jerusalem only made him sadder. His grief had been particularly acute when he had come home in disgrace and had to confess to Jonathan that he had been at least temporarily suspended from the army.

Though Jonathan had been angry on his son's behalf, he showed no sign of being ashamed of him. Still, Micah couldn't help but feel he had disappointed his father sorely. Grandfather would have understood how he felt.

Micah turned from the window to a small table nearby. He picked up a scroll tied with a scarlet cord. It was a copy of the Torah, a gift to the Rab from King David years ago. Upon Shageh's death, it had passed to Micah, who had not once failed to follow his grandfather's instruction to read it daily. After reading a passage, he prostrated himself in front of the window and began to praise and thank Adonai for life, for material blessings, for his family and health. He prayed for forgiveness of his sins, and finally, for wisdom. His devotions finished, he felt up to facing the unpleasant journey before him, and went to break his fast. It took a lot of food to fuel the massive frame he had inherited from Jonathan. But his other characteristics were the legacy of his grandfather, especially his height and his clear, amber eyes. Shageh had towered six inches above his son's six-foot height. So did Micah.

Not only did Micah resemble his grandfather physically, but everyone said his personality was uncannily like the Rab's. Both of them had a great reverence for Adonai, and for all creatures that he had made. Each had a calm, contemplative nature, and a disconcerting way of assessing people that saw beyond their facades. They had been as one in spirit, and although he loved his parents dearly, he was convinced that no one would ever understand him like Shageh had.

As he left his room, Micah heard someone moving about in the courtyard. He knew it would be his mother, drawing water from the cistern for the day's needs. She had already fired up the oven, and he smelled the enticing aroma of baking bread. Micah smiled as he remembered all the times his father had insisted that his wife had no business tending to such mundane chores.

Jonathan was a wealthy man, after all, and had provided his wife with several household servants to see to such things. But Ailea always rose before anyone, even the servants, and had much of the household work underway before anyone else could help. Micah always suspected that Ailea did this to irritate his father. The tiny woman seemed to revel in any opportunity to stand up to the mighty warrior she had married. It was possible also that his mother wanted to prove to the other women of Ziph that though she had been raised in the privileged home of Eliada, a powerful general in the city of Damascus, she did not think herself above them. The respect they accorded her had been hard won.

Ailea smiled at her son as he entered the courtyard, craning her neck to look up at him. People often remarked how amazing it was that tiny Ailea had borne this giant of a son. After greeting him and motioning for him to sit, she brought him crusty bread and goat's milk and commanded him to eat. When he sat, she still wasn't quite at eye level with him.

"I baked early so you would have fresh bread to take on your journey."

His response was interrupted when his scrap of a sister appeared. The girl was the exact image of her mother and the apple of her father's eye. She was also a handful, as stubborn as a goat, shunning the attributes of a proper young lady for the freedom of the hills as a shepherd girl. This seemed to scandalize their provincial little village, but Habaz, the chief shepherd, could hardly protest. Jonathan had provided him with most of the stock for his herds.

She was barefoot, as usual, and in the process of wrapping her hair up in a haphazard turban. Somehow her green eyes looked twice as large without her hair framing her face. "Is that bread almost done, Ahmi? It smells wonderful! Do you mind if I take some for Reuben? And the cheese as well?"

Micah knew the answer before his mother spoke. She had a soft spot in her heart for old Habaz, raising his grandson alone. The boy's mother had died giving birth to him, and his father had died of a fever not long ago.

Micah brought his thoughts back to the moment at hand. "Thank you, Mother. You take good care of me—of all of us."

"You are the joy of my life," she answered simply.

He watched her bustling about, and thought with pride that she was as beautiful as a young girl, with her long black hair that had hardly a sprinkling of gray. Her form and energy were that of a much younger woman. She often drove her husband to distraction. Jonathan's father had warned him teasingly never to marry a woman a decade younger than himself, else she would run him ragged. Micah knew that his father's plaints were made affectionately. Jonathan loved his wife more than anything.

"Good morning," a voice boomed, and Micah looked up to see his father descending the steps that led to his parents' rooftop apartment. Over the years, Jonathan had improved and added to the compound until it was now twice the size of any other home in the village. "I see you are ready to travel," Jonathan commented as he accepted food and a kiss on the cheek from his wife.

"Are you certain you want me to go?" Micah asked again, as he had over the past several days.

"You know I do. I want to send you to the feast in my stead so everyone will know I am proud of you and count you worthy to receive this honor on my behalf. You have done nothing to be ashamed of, and the sooner you go back to Jerusalem to face these groundless accusations, the quicker everyone will know that."

"Some of your friends in the army wouldn't agree," Micah commented as he bit into another piece of the fragrant, rich bread. He remembered the mumbled comments and sly remarks that had circulated in the barracks in Jerusalem, both from officers and recruits.

"Those who are my friends would agree. Those who don't are no friends of mine. When you return, I will demand to know the names of any who would dare slight you."

Jonathan's eyes took on a hard, cold look, and his brows beetled together as he spoke. "Father, you can't come to my rescue. It would only make matters worse. We've spoken of this before."

Jonathan growled his reluctant agreement. "Just don't forget that the king is our friend. Appeal to him directly."

Micah shook his head. "I will appeal first to Joab. I know you don't trust him, but he is giving me the benefit of the doubt, even though he thinks I acted foolishly. But I will compromise and ask that I present my case to Joab in the king's presence. I am partially guilty of the accusations. I did allow the bandits to go free, but certainly not because I believed them to be Rezon's men. Joab really had no recourse but to send me home after several men asked not to serve in my unit because they didn't trust me."

"But you know you are neither a traitor nor a coward, Son, and so do I."

"No, but my reasons were just as bad in the eyes of some warriors. I'm afraid I don't have the stomach for slaughter. I can fight to defend myself, and I will gladly attack in battle for my king, and for Adonai, but even then the killing haunts me."

"You are much like your grandfather, Micah, and that's nothing to be ashamed of. Do not think that because I am one of the *Gibborim* you must follow in my steps. In truth, there are nights when the eyes of those I have slain haunt my dreams, and on some days, when your mother puts her soft hand in mine, I feel unworthy because these hands have shed blood. No, I would be just as happy if you decide that the military life is not for you."

"But *look* at me, Father. Has not Adonai expressed his will in how he made me? You know that one such as I will never be accepted as anything but a warrior. Both my size and my Aramean blood proclaim that I must be a warrior to prove my worth. You don't know how many times I have wished I were as short as Perez next door. He has more friends than he can count because no one either fears or envies him."

"You will come to peace within yourself, Son. Do not worry. I am proud of you, no matter what you do. Go to Jerusalem and offer your services to the king. As peaceable as the kingdom has been in recent years, it is possible that David may send you as his emissary on a diplomatic mission."

Jonathan often forgot to speak of the king in formal terms. After all, he had joined David's band when Israel's sweet singer had been a fugitive from King Saul, hiding in the caves of Adullam. Jonathan had earned the position of Mighty One when barely into manhood. Now, decades later, he still served on active duty as one of David's war counselors, making trips to Jerusalem several times a year to train new recruits and lead forays to the border between Israel and the Philistines, to make sure they stayed close to their coastal cities of Ashdod and Ashkelon.

"Father, I wish you would at least come with me. You and Mother haven't been to Jerusalem for some time, and you deserve the honor the king will bestow on you. I have done nothing to deserve recognition. Are you not afraid that your name as a great warrior will be sullied by bringing attention to a son deemed unworthy?"

Jonathan's eyes flashed in anger. "You are not unworthy. I

have instructed you to go in my stead so that all may know that I believe in you. I will not go with you. I will not embarrass you by intervening in these ridiculous accusations that have been made against you. I know I would not restrain myself if someone slighted you, and it would wound your pride if I came to your defense.

"And your mother! Well, you have not had as many occasions to have her fury unleashed on you, but believe me, if someone were to offer insult to her only son, she would attack immediately, whether in the streets of Jerusalem or inside the palace itself. Unless you wish to witness such a scene, I suggest you leave the two of us here and head to Jerusalem alone. Of course, you are welcome to take Jerusha with you."

The look of horror that crossed Micah's face caused Jonathan to double up in laughter. Micah soon joined in. Ailea, who had overheard the conversation, complained, "You two may think it's amusing, but you both have to help me do something about that child! She is running completely wild."

"I will help, Mother, I promise, as soon as I return from Jerusalem."

"It might not be such a bad idea to take her, Micah. She needs to see that there is more to life than these hills and the animals she loves so dearly."

Jonathan chuckled again at the look of dismay Micah gave his mother, and took pity on him. He patted Ailea's cheek. "Her love of animals she got from you. I remember sleeping with a smelly goat a few times when you thought the weather was too wet for your pet to stay outdoors. We will take Jerusha to the city for Passover, but Micah has too many distractions to look after her this time."

Ailea gave her husband a disgruntled look. "Amal wasn't just another goat, Jonathan, and you know it. I haven't had another pet since he died."

Jonathan laughed. "Well, I know he wasn't just another goat. He was trouble. That's why I named him 'Trouble.' And even though you haven't had a pet of your own since he died, you have seen to it that Micah and Jerusha have always had one. Let me see if I can remember them all. There was the badger, the ferret, the owl, not to mention a handful of sheep and goats that avoided the oven by currying favor with either you or the children."

"The sheep and goats provided us with milk and wool! And as for the other creatures, what was I to do when the children brought home abandoned or wounded animals—break their hearts by telling them the creatures had to die?"

"Father is only jesting, Mother. He was as fond of those pets as we were. He only feared it would make him appear less fierce if he showed it, and thus weaken his position as a warrior." Micah took the last bite of bread, drained his cup of milk, and stood. "I had better start my journey, or else I'll arrive in Jerusalem too late to find lodging."

If you missed *The Heart of a Stranger,* Kathy Hawkins' first novel, please enjoy this excerpt from the story that began the Heart of Zion Series.

Chapter One

At noontime the Damascus sun smoldered in a white-hot sky, scorching everything in its path. Not even an insect's hum disturbed the heavy stillness.

Ailea climbed up onto the rooftop and looked about cautiously. No one was in sight. Good. She could expect to be alone for at least another hour or so. At this time of day her family and the servants would be seeking whatever relief they could find around the courtyard pool.

Only when the sun sank lower in the sky would the giant cedars and date palms that encircled the spacious stone house provide enough shade to dispel the blistering heat. Then the entire household would gravitate to the roof to relax on the couches and catch any breath of breeze that might be stirring. Reclining in the cool shade of the ancient trees, they would enjoy the evening meal as the last light of evening danced on the edges of the palm fronds. But right now one of those trees would serve a more useful function.

Ailea untied her sandals and removed her outer robe. Clad only in a knee-length linen undertunic, she ran nimbly across the roof, the hot tiles burning underfoot. She shimmied up the ancient date palm that grew on the north side of the house and towered over sixty feet into the air. She hoped no one below would look up to see her doing such an unheard-of thing. For a female of any age to climb a tree was scandalous—but doubly so for one nearly nineteen years old and already a grown woman. But she and her brother, Rezon, had spent many hours as children playing in the leafy fronds of the huge tree, and now her climbing ability was being put to good use.

From her vantage point Ailea could see over the city wall to the confluence of the Abanah and Pharpar Rivers, which made this large city an oasis on the high desert plateau south of the Euphrates. With several trade routes converging on Damascus, caravans entered the main gate in a steady stream. Ailea was proud to be a citizen of this strategic city just as she was proud to be the daughter of Eliada, one of King Hadadezer's generals.

Even now the king's army was gathering out in the desert to the northeast. Her father, commander of the city's troops and mercenaries, would be in charge of thousands in this campaign designed to extend the boundaries of Aram-Zobah, an alliance of city-states that made up Hadadezer's kingdom. Damascus was a vital part of the alliance.

Rezon was accompanying her father into battle. Not quite two years her senior, Rezon had been Ailea's constant companion until three years ago when he joined his father in the military. Ailea missed her brother very much now that he was frequently away fighting. Her brother, who had taught her so many things that most girls didn't know—the game of chess, climbing trees, and the use of bow and arrow and sling—hardly had any time to spare for her anymore. His mind was always on military matters.

Rezon was furious that Hadadezer had drawn troops from Damascus, leaving the city vulnerable. Ailea had listened to the two men discussing the danger of this strategy, but unlike his son, Eliada was the consummate military man. If his superior—in this case it was Shobach, commander-in-chief of Zobah's armies—issued an order, Eliada would obey without question.

Rezon had warned his father that taking troops out of Damascus was a tactical error and made no attempt to hide his disdain for the plan or for Shobach himself. Rezon also believed that Eliada, not Shobach, should have been given the leadership of Hadadezer's army and claimed that Shobach was too arrogant by far. Ailea could barely suppress a smile at these words. In her opinion, it was her older brother who had more than his own share of arrogance.

For the moment Ailea left off her musing and turned her attention to the northeast. Scanning the horizon, she caught a glint of sunlight reflecting off something in the distance. There it was again. Could it be spears? Shields? Maybe the shiny gold helmets worn by Eliada and other officers in Hadadezer's army? She thought the troops were to have been deployed farther north—if it wasn't Zobah's army out there, then whose could it be?

The reflections were coming from the desert—nowhere near the trade routes. Perhaps Toi, the king of Hamath, a minor kingdom northwest of Damascus, had decided to challenge Hadadezer. It was no secret that the two leaders hated each other. But despite his animosity, Toi was no fool. He could not field an army even a quarter of the size of Zobah's.

Could they be troops from Israel? Surely not. King David must know that he, too, was vastly outnumbered by a superior force.

Ailea descended carefully from her vantage point in the palm tree and ran to the other corner of the rooftop where she climbed another tall date palm, but she could make out nothing to the north. In the streets below, however, she saw a number of soldiers who had been left to guard the city, and she felt a renewed sense of security. No one could take Damascus—especially not that low-born king of the Hebrews!

She climbed back down to the roof and donned her robe and sandals, wishing for the thousandth time that she had been born a male. She felt no lack of familial love, and she knew that her mother and father took pride in her beauty, hoping to marry her to a man who would add to their wealth and prestige. But other than a commodity for barter, what good was a daughter? It was Rezon who would inherit the beautiful home she loved; it was her brother who would carry the honor of the family into battle and later into the marketplace.

Men had all the power, she fumed inwardly. They could go wherever they pleased, do whatever they pleased, while women were hidden away at home to cook, bear children, and wait for the return of their men!

Ailea loved her mother dearly. Nariah was kind and beautiful, but she was weak, capable of being reduced to tears by nothing more than a stern look from her husband. And she was a lonely woman, for Eliada's responsibilities with the army kept him away from home for long periods of time.

For that reason Ailea had determined never to marry a military man. No, she would marry an older man who adored her, one whom she could wrap around her smallest finger. If the gods smiled on her, perhaps she could even cajole him into giving her more freedom than most wives even dreamed of. Or better still—and her conscience winced a little at the cold calculation of her thought—perhaps he would leave her a wealthy widow. Only such women had any power at all.

Shrugging aside her dismal mood, Ailea descended the stairs that led to the inner courtyard. Perhaps she could talk Malik into taking her out to the bazaar where she could learn for herself what was happening on the field of battle and whose troops she had sighted from the rooftop.

She found Nariah napping on one of the couches by the pool, her personal servant, Shua, on another couch nearby. Her mother often rested here in the heat of the day for the gurgling of the fountain lulled her to sleep.

Moving quietly to the opposite side of the pool, Ailea removed her sandals once again and dangled her feet in the cool water. She would have enjoyed a refreshing bath, but her splashing would be sure to awaken Nariah.

Restless, Ailea determined to go in search of Malik at once. He would grumble, no doubt. But after twenty years of service to the family, the head steward could be depended upon to do her bidding. She had only to charm him a little before he would consent to take her into the streets of Damascus—a ploy she had used on countless occasions in the past.

Malik believed her to be spoiled, she smiled to herself, but what did it matter? Or that the old servant considered her to be lacking in the feminine graces, that she should be more like her mother? Never! Ailea hoped never to be like her mother whose whole life had been lived in the shadow of her husband, who made herself ill with worry when he was away on a military mission. Ailea would rather be dead than submit herself to such a fate!

Her thoughts shifted again to the army. She could not dismiss the sense of growing uneasiness she felt whenever she thought of her father and brother. Nothing she could do would influence the outcome of this campaign, but—there! She was acting just like her mother, and she gave her head a quick, defiant toss that shook the loose wisps of hair back from her face. Just then she saw Malik enter the courtyard, and she motioned him over with a quick gesture.

"What are you scheming, Cricket?" he asked in a low tone, one brow lifted in a blend of caution and curiosity.

Ailea gave him a wounded look. "I'm not scheming anything, Malik. I merely need to buy some thread in the market, and I want you to take me."

He chuckled softly. "You don't need any thread, Cricket. You wish only to go running about, getting into mischief and asking irritating questions. I call you 'Cricket' not only because of your size, you know. You hop around just as endlessly and make just as much noise."

Ailea knew that Malik was jesting with her for the most part. The loyal retainer still had trouble accepting the fact that she was grown up, even though he knew very well that she had been responsible for the running of the household since her mother's melancholy so frequently incapacitated her. But one thing Eliada had absolutely insisted on was that Malik always accompany her to the marketplace. The last time she had ignored this rule, Eliada had found out and had confined her to her room for a week. Although usually too busy to bother disciplining her, he had a few unbreakable rules, and this was one of them. So Malik knew that Ailea was at his mercy when it came to trips outside the house, and he often used this last bit of authority to get the best of her. But she knew that down deep, Malik was devoted to her as he was to the rest of the family, so she persisted with a little pout. "Please!"

"Come now, you just want to learn news of the battle. Thread, indeed!"

"Well, yes, I just might overhear some news from a trader," she answered, looking off in no particular direction. "You know that Mother and I are worried so about Rezon and Father—just as you are, Malik, aren't you?" Tilting her head upwards and lowering her voice to a conspiratorial whisper, she took a more direct tactic. "Let's do go and talk to some of the soldiers and find out what they've heard."

Malik repressed a laugh at the predictable ploy of his little Cricket and signaled his surrender with a practiced shrug of his rather stooped shoulders. "I suppose I could take you, Cricket—but later, when the sun is not so high." He raised a hand in admonishment. "But you must let me ask the questions. And you must not ask me to take you into the more dangerous sections of the city." He eyed her with a respectful appraisal. "You don't realize the—uh—attention you draw to yourself."

"But I don't try to draw attention to myself!" she argued with a sudden flush of color in her face.

He stroked his graying beard and studied the exceptional features of his master's daughter. "I know, child. I know. But you have grown into a beautiful young woman. You must accept the restrictions that such blessings from the gods bring. Now go and get ready. I will take you in another hour. And, Cricket—don't forget to wear a veil."

Ailea rose and gave the burly servant a hug. "I won't forget, Malik. I promise."

Malik watched the mistress of the house as she left the enclosed courtyard, her hip-length ebony braid swinging behind her. She was small, almost boyish in stature but perfectly formed. And that face—especially the unusual green eyes—he would have to guard her very closely. Malik wished her father would hurry and find a suitable husband for her so that he could be free of the burden of protecting her. But that wasn't likely to happen soon although it was long past time for Ailea to be wed. Eliada had always pleaded that he was much too busy with military affairs to attend to matters of marriage, but Malik suspected that the general was more than a little reluctant to relinquish the beautiful desert flower that had bloomed in his home. With the current skirmish in the desert, he had one more excuse for postponing negotiations. The suitors would have to be patient, Malik thought. As would he.

Besides, her mother did not have the strength to insist on a marriage. If the truth be known, the woman needed to keep her daughter with her, what with Rezon and the master away most of the time. Ailea had taken over most of the responsibility for running the household some time ago, and Malik had to admit that she did it very effectively. She had no concept of her limitations as a woman, however, and Malik felt increasingly ill-suited in his role as head steward and handmaid to the young mistress. Maybe it was time to secure a female servant for Ailea.

Most of the girl's friends were wed by now, some already mothers, Malik fretted. Well, he could only do his best to keep his Cricket out of trouble. "I'm getting too old for this," he muttered to himself. "Just too old."

~ ~ ~

A light westerly breeze had begun to stir in the late afternoon as the old man and his young charge made their way through the crowded bazaar. Here the stench of overheated human bodies, goats, camels, and the aroma of various foods cooked over the braziers of street vendors assailed their nostrils. The bleating of sheep, the haggling of shopkeepers, and the rumbling of wagon wheels combined to make thinking, much less conversation, difficult.

Malik had questioned several of the king's soldiers already with little success. The soldiers guarding the city were not privy to any information about maneuvers against the Hebrews. Furthermore, they were surly, resenting the fact that they had been given the boring duty of patrolling the city instead of the excitement of battle. None of them expected the fighting to reach Damascus, and Ailea had taken this as a good sign.

When they reached the city gate, however, Malik craned his neck, narrowing his gaze to scan the crowd. With an abrupt movement he began shouldering his way through the throng, dragging Ailea by the arm behind him. He came to an abrupt halt, and Ailea stood on tiptoe to peer around his bulk.

A small caravan of three camels and two donkeys had just entered the gate, and the leader was speaking in a loud voice to the sentinels. "I tell you, they are out there! Just five or six miles to the southeast! Their rear guard gave chase to us, but we were already too near the city when they sighted us!"

"Probably a troop from Helam," the tall sentinel told the agitated man.

"No, not soldiers of Aram-Zobah but the army of Israel! I'm telling you, their whole army is out there!"

The wild look of fear in the man's eyes made Ailea pull back against Malik's firm grip. The army of Israel—could that have been the reflections she had seen off in the distance?

"If you did indeed see Hebrew soldiers, it was probably just a scouting party. Now put a bridle on your tongue before you sow panic in the city," the captain of the guard ordered. With that, the soldiers pushed the trembling man toward his camels and mounted the steps that led to the lookout atop the city wall.